THE LOVELIEST
chocolate shop
IN PARIS
A NOVEL IN RECIPES

JENNY COLGAN

sourcebooks
landmark

Published by Sourcebooks Landmark, an imprint of Sourcebooks
P.O. Box 4410, Naperville, Illinois 60567-4410
(630) 961-3900
sourcebooks.com

Originally published in 2013 in the UK by Sphere, an imprint of Little, Brown Book Group. This edition issued based on the paperback edition published in 2014 by Sourcebooks Landmark, an imprint of Sourcebooks.

Library of Congress Cataloging-in-Publication Data

Colgan, Jenny.
  The loveliest chocolate shop in Paris / Jenny Colgan.
     pages cm.
  (pbk. : alk. paper) 1. Chocolate industry--France--Fiction. 2. Bakers--Fiction. 3. Paris (France)--Fiction. I. Title.
  PR6053.O4225L68 2014
  823'.914--dc23

2013031055

Printed and bound in Canada.
MBP 10 9 8 7 6 5 4 3 2 1

a word from jenny

There are lots of marvelous artisan chocolate shops in Paris. My favorite is called Paul Rogers on the rue du Faubourg. I would strongly recommend a visit there and a taste of their hot chocolate, whichever season you go. They're run by the eponymous Paul, who is, indeed, a curly-haired, twinkly-eyed, roguish-looking chap.

This book is not based on any of those shops in a single detail, but instead on the principle that when people dedicate their lives to one thing that they really, really love and learn a lot about, amazing things can happen.

Somebody once said the reason we love chocolate so much is that it melts at the same temperature as the inside of our mouths. Scientists also talk about releasing endorphins and so on, which may be the chemical reason for it, but whatever the explanations, it is a wonderful thing.

It's not just a woman thing—if you don't believe me, try a random sample of six-year-olds. I can't even smuggle a packet of chocolate cookies into my house without my husband sniffing them out and guzzling them. So I've put some really lovely recipes in here too. I like to think as I get older that I can actually cook with chocolate instead of just, you know, accidentally eating it as soon as it gets in the house or sometimes in the car.

When we moved to France a while back (for my husband's work), I was surprised to find they took chocolate as seriously as they take any kind of food. La Maison du Chocolat is a really high-end chain and you'll find one in most towns, where you can chat with the chocolatier about what you want and what else you're going to be eating, like a wine waiter. But I personally am just as happy with a great big slab of Dairy Milk or Toblerone or my absolute fave, Fry's Chocolate Cream (plain). Not everything has to be luxury to be enjoyed. Alas, my children have now reached the age where it's becoming obvious who keeps stealing the Kinder bars out of their party bags. Kids, hum, look, I hate to have to tell you this. It was definitely your dad.

Before we start, I wanted to say a word about language. In my experience, learning another language is really bloody difficult, unless you're one of those people who pick things up in two seconds flat, in which case I would say *bleurgh* (that's me poking my tongue out) to you because I am extremely jealous.

Traditionally, too, when people in books are speaking a foreign language, it's indicated in *italics*. So you should know that anyone Anna speaks to in Paris is speaking French back to her unless I've mentioned otherwise. To which you and I would think, cor, that's AMAZING she learned such fantastic French so fast. Obviously she has lots of lessons with Claire, but if you've ever learned another language, you'll know that you can be totally confident in a classroom then turn up in the country and everybody goes "wabbawabbawabbawabbaWAH?" to you at, like, a million miles an hour, and you panic because you can't understand a single bloody word of it. That's certainly what happened to me.

So, anyway, you need to take it on trust that it's exactly the same for Anna, but for purposes of not repeating myself endlessly and slowing down the story, I've taken out the millions and millions of times she says "What?" or "Can you say that again please?" or needs to check her dictionary.

I do hope you enjoy it, and let me know how you get on with the recipes. And bon appétit!

Jenny x

1

The really weird thing about it was that although I knew instantly that something was wrong—very, very wrong, something sharp, something very serious, an insult to my entire body—I couldn't stop laughing. Laughing hysterically.

I was lying there, covered—drenched—in spilled melted chocolate and I couldn't stop giggling. There were other faces now, looking down on me; some I was sure I even recognized. They weren't laughing. They all looked very serious in fact. This somehow struck me as even funnier and set me off again.

From the periphery, I heard someone say "Pick them up!" and someone else say "No way! You pick them up! Gross!" And then I heard someone else, who I thought was Flynn, the new stock boy, say "I'll dial 911" and someone else say "Flynn, don't be stupid; it's 999. You're not American" and someone else say "I think you can dial 911 now because there were so many idiots who kept dialing it." And someone else taking out their phone and saying something about needing an ambulance, which I thought was hilarious as well, and then someone, who was definitely Del, our old grumpy janitor, saying, "Well, they're probably going to want to throw this batch away then." And the idea that they might not throw away the enormous vat of chocolate but try to sell it instead when it had landed all over me actually was funny.

After that, thank God, I don't remember anything, although later, in the hospital, an ambulance man came over and said I was a total bloody nutter in the ambulance and that he'd always been told that shock affected people in different ways, but mine was just about the differentest he'd ever seen. Then he saw my face and said, "Cheer up, love; you'll laugh again." But at that point I wasn't exactly sure I ever would.

• • • •

"Oh, come off it, Debs, love. It's only her foot. It could have been a lot worse. What if it had been her nose?"

That was my dad, talking to my mum. He liked to look on the bright side.

"Well, they could have given her a new nose. She hates her nose anyway."

That was definitely my mum. She's not quite as good as my dad at looking on the bright side. In fact, I could hear her sobbing. But somehow, my body shied away from the light; I couldn't open my eyes. I didn't think it was a light; it felt like the sun or something. Maybe I was on holiday. I couldn't be at home—the sun never bloody shines in Kidinsborough, my hometown, voted worst town in England three years in a row before local political pressure got the show taken off the air.

My parents zoned out of earshot, just drifted off like someone tuning a radio. I had no idea if they were there or if they ever had been. I knew I wasn't moving, but inside I felt as though I was squirming and wriggling and trapped inside a body-shaped prison someone had buried me in. I could shout, but no one could hear me. I tried to move, but it wasn't working. The dazzle would turn to black and back again to the sun, and none of it made the faintest bit of sense to me as I dreamt—or lived—great big nightmares about toes and feet and parents who spontaneously disappear and whether this was going crazy and whether I'd actually dreamt my whole other life, the bit about being me, Anna Trent, thirty years old, taster in a chocolate factory.

Yes, actually. While we're at it, here are my top ten "Taster in a Chocolate Factory" jokes that I get at Faces, our local nightclub. It's not a very nice nightclub, but the rest are really much, much worse:

1. Yes, I will give you some free samples.
2. No, I'm not as fat as you clearly expected me to be.
3. Yes, it is exactly like *Charlie and the Chocolate Factory*.
4. No, no one has ever done a poo in the chocolate vat. (Though I wouldn't necessarily have put it past Flynn.)
5. No, it actually doesn't make me more popular than a normal person, as I am thirty, not seven.
6. No, I don't feel sick when confronted with chocolate; I absolutely adore it. But if it makes you feel better about your job to think that I am, feel free.
7. Oh, that is so interesting that you have something even tastier than chocolate in your underpants, yawn. (N.B.: I would like to be brave enough to say that, but I'm not that brave really. I normally just grimace and look at something else for a while. My best mate, Cath, soon takes care of them anyway. Or, occasionally, dates them.)
8. Yes, I will suggest your peanut/beer/vodka/jam-flavored chocolate idea, but I doubt we'll be as rich as you think.
9. Yes, I can make actual real chocolate, although at Braders Family Chocolates, they're all processed automatically in a huge vat and I'm more of a supervisor really. I wish I did more complex work, but according to the bosses, nobody wants their chocolates messed about with; they want them tasting exactly the same and lasting a long time. So it's quite a synthetic process.
10. No, it's not the best job in the world. But it's mine and I like it. Or at least I did, until I ended up in here.

Then I normally say, "Rum and coke, thanks for asking."

"Anna."

A man was sitting on the end of my bed. I couldn't focus on him. He knew my name but I didn't know his. That seemed unfair.

I tried to open my mouth. It was full of sand. Someone had put sand in my mouth. Why would anyone do that?

"Anna."

The voice came again. It was definitely real, and it was definitely connected to the shadow at the end of my bed.

"Can you hear me?"

Well, of course I can hear you. You're sitting on the end of my bed shouting at me was what I wanted to say, but all that came out was a kind of dry croak.

"That's great, that's great, very good. Would you like a drink of water?"

I nodded. It seemed easiest.

"Good, good. Don't nod too much; you'll dislodge the wires. NURSE!"

I don't know whether the nurse came or not, because I was suddenly gone again. My last conscious thought was that I hoped she or he didn't mind being yelled at by people who sat on other people's beds. And I couldn't remember: Had my parents said something was wrong with my nose?

● ● ● ●

"Here she is."

It was the same voice, but how much later I couldn't tell. The light seemed different. A sudden shock of pain traveled through me like a lightning bolt and I gasped.

"There you go; she's going to be great."

Dad.

"Oh, I don't like the look of this."

Mum.

"Um…can I have that water?" I asked, but it came out like "Ca ha wa?"

Thankfully someone spoke desert sand, because instantly a plastic cup was put to my lips. That small cup of tepid chalky tap water was the single best thing I had ever put in my mouth in my entire life, and that includes the first time I tasted a crème egg.

I slurped it down and asked for another, but someone said no, and that was that. Maybe I was in prison.

"Can you open your eyes for us?" came the commanding voice.

"Course she can."

"Oh, Pete, I don't know. I just don't know."

Oddly, it was slightly to spite my mother's lack of ambition for me in the eye-opening department that really made me try. I flickered and suddenly hazing into view was the shape sitting on the end of my bed I'd been aware of before—I wished he'd stop that—and two shapes as familiar as my own hands.

I could make out my mother's reddish hair that she colored at home, even though my best mate, Cath, had offered to do it down at the salon for a price that she thought was next to nothing, but my mother thought that was extravagant and that Cath was loose (that last bit was true, though that had nothing to do with how good she was at hair, which admittedly also wasn't very), so about one week a month my mum had this kind of odd, henna-like fringe around the top of her forehead where she hadn't wiped it off properly. And my dad was in his best shirt, which really made me worry. He didn't dress like that for anything but weddings and funerals, and I was pretty much 100 percent sure I wasn't getting married, unless Darr had suddenly regenerated into a completely different physical and personality type, and I figured that unlikely.

"Hello?" I said, feeling a rush that somewhere, the desert sands were retreating, that the division between what was real and what was a writhing sandy ball of confusion and pain was retreating, that Anna was back, that the skin I was wearing was mine after all.

"Darling!"

My mum burst into tears. My dad, not prone to huge outbursts of affection, gently squeezed my hand—the hand, I noticed, that didn't have a big tube going into it, right under the skin. My other hand did. It was the grossest thing I'd ever seen in my life.

"Ugh, gah," I said. "What's this? It's disgusting."

The figure at the end of my bed smiled in a rather patronizing way.

"I think you'd find things a lot more disgusting if it wasn't there," he said. "It's giving you painkillers and medication."

"Well, can I have some more?" I said. The lightning-sharp pain flashed through me again, from the toes of my left foot upward right through my body.

I suddenly became aware of other tubes on me, some going in and out of places I didn't really want to discuss in front of my dad. I went quiet. I felt really, really weird.

"Is your head spinning?" said the bed-sitter. "That's quite normal."

My mum was still sniffing.

"It's all right, mum."

What she said next chilled me to the bone.

"It's not all right, love. It's not all right at all."

● ● ● ●

Over the next few days, I seemed to fall asleep on and off and at completely random moments. Dr. Ed—yes, really, that's how he referred to himself—was my named specialist. Yeah, all right, I know he was a doctor and everything, tra la la, but you can be Ed or you can be, like, Dr. Smith or something. Anything else is just showing off, like you're a doctor on TV or something.

I think Dr. Ed would have LOVED to have been a doctor on TV, looking at people who've got two bumholes and things. He was always very smartly turned out and did things like sit on the end of the bed, which other doctors didn't do, and look at you in the eye, like he was making a huge effort to be with you as a person. I think I preferred the snotty consultant who came around once a week, barely looked at me, and asked his medical students embarrassing questions.

Anyway, Dr. Ed shouldn't have been so chummy because it was kind of his fault that I was even there. I had slipped at the factory— everyone had gotten very excited wondering if there was some health and safety rule that hadn't been followed and we were all about to become millionaires, but actually as it turned out it was completely my fault. It was an unusually warm spring day and I'd decided to try out my new shoes, which turned out to be hilariously inappropriate for the factory floor, and I'd skidded and, in a total freak, hit a vat ladder and upended the entire thing. Then I'd come into the hospital and gotten sick.

"A bug tried to eat me?" I asked Dr. Ed.

"Well, yes, that's about right," he said, smiling to show overtly white teeth that he must have gotten whitened somewhere. Maybe he just liked to practice for going on television. "Not a big bug, Anna, like a spider."

"Spiders aren't bugs," I said crossly.

"Ha! No." He flicked his hair. "Well, these things are very, very tiny, so small you couldn't see a thousand of them even if they were sitting right here on my finger!"

Perhaps there was something misprinted on my medical notes that said instead of being nearly thirty-one, I was in fact eight.

"I don't care what size they are," I said. "They make me feel like total crap."

"And that's why we're fighting them with every weapon we have!" said Dr. Ed, like he was Spider-Man or something. I didn't mention that if everyone had cleaned up with every mop they had, I probably wouldn't have caught it in the first place.

And anyway, oh Lord, I just felt so rough. I didn't feel like eating or drinking anything but water. (Dad brought me some marshmallows and Mum practically whacked him because she was 100 percent certain they'd get trapped in my throat and I'd totally die right there in front of him.) I slept a lot, and when I wasn't sleeping, I didn't feel well enough to watch TV or read or speak to people on the phone or anything. I had a lot of messages on Facebook, according to my phone, which someone—Cath, I was guessing—had plugged in beside my bed, but I wasn't really fussed to read any of them.

I felt different, as if I'd woken up foreign, or in a strange land where nobody spoke my language—not Mum, not Dad, not my friends. They didn't speak the language of strange hazy days where nothing made much sense, or constant aching, or the idea of moving being too difficult to contemplate, even moving an arm across a bed. The country of the sick seemed a very different place, where you were fed and moved and everyone spoke to you like a child and you were always, always hot.

● ● ● ●

I dozed off again and heard a noise. Something familiar, I was sure of it, but I couldn't tell from when. I was at school. School figured a lot in my fever dreams. I had hated it. Mum had always said she wasn't academic so I wouldn't be either, and that had pretty much sealed the deal, which in retrospect seems absolutely stupid. So for ages when I hallucinated my old teachers' faces in front of me, I didn't take it too seriously. Then one day I woke up very early, when the hospital was still cool and as quiet as it ever got, which wasn't very, and I turned my head carefully to the side, and there, just in the next bed, not a dream or a hallucination, was Mrs. Shawcourt, my old French teacher, gazing at me calmly.

I blinked in case she would go away. She didn't.

It was a small four-bed side ward I'd been put on, a few days or a couple of weeks earlier—it was hard to tell precisely—which seemed a bit strange; either I was infectious or I wasn't, surely. The other two beds were empty and over the days to come had a fairly speedy turnover of extremely old ladies who didn't seem to do much but cry.

"Hello," she said. "I know you, don't I?"

I suddenly felt a flush, like I hadn't done my homework.

I had never done my homework. Me and Cath used to bunk off— French, it was totally useless, who could possibly need that?—and go sit around the back field where the teachers couldn't see you and speak with fake Mancunian accents about how crap Kidinsborough was and how we were going to leave the first chance we got.

"Anna Trent."

I nodded.

"I had you for two years."

I peered at her more closely. She'd always stood out in the school; she was by far the best dressed teacher, since most of them were a right bunch of slobs. She used to wear these really nicely fitted dresses that made her look a bit different. You could tell she hadn't gotten them down at Matalan. She'd had blond hair then...

I realized with a bit of a shock that now she didn't have any hair at all. She was very thin, but then she always had been thin, but now she was really, really thin.

I said the stupidest thing I could think of—in my defense, I really wasn't well.

"Are you sick then?"

"No," said Mrs. Shawcourt. "I'm on holiday."

There was a pause, then I grinned. I remembered that, actually, she was a really good teacher.

"I'm sorry to hear about your toes," she said briskly.

I glanced down at the bandage covering my right foot.

"Ah, they'll be all right, just had a bit of a fall," I said. Then I saw her face. And I realized that all the time people had been talking about my fever and my illness and my accident, nobody had actually thought to tell me the whole truth.

• • • •

It couldn't be though. I could feel them.

I stared at her, and she unblinkingly held my gaze.

"I can feel them," I said.

"I can't believe nobody told you," she said. "Bloody hospitals. My darling, I heard them discuss it."

I stared at the bandage again. I wanted to be sick. Then I was sick, in a big cardboard bedpan they left a supply of by the side of my bed, for every time I wanted to be sick.

• • • •

Dr. Ed came by later and sat on my bed. I scowled at him.

"Now"—he checked his notes—"Anna, I'm sorry you weren't aware of the full gravity of the situation."

"Because you kept talking about 'accidents' and 'regrettable incidents,'" I said crossly. "I didn't realize they'd gone altogether. AND I can feel them. They really hurt."

He nodded.

"That's quite common, I'm afraid."

"Why didn't anyone tell me? Everyone kept banging on about fever and bugs and things."

"Well, that's what we were worried about. Losing a couple of toes was a lot less likely to kill you."

"Well, that's good to know. And it's not 'a couple of toes.' It's MY TOES."

As we spoke, a nurse was gently unwrapping the bandages from my foot. I gulped, worried I was going to throw up again.

Did you ever play that game at school where you lie on your front with your eyes closed and someone pulls your arms taut above your head, then very slowly lowers them so it feels like your arms are going down a hole?

That was what this was like. My brain couldn't compute what it was seeing, what it could feel and knew to be true. My toes were there. They were there. But in front of my eyes was a curious diagonal slicing; two tiny stumps taken off in a descending line, very sharp, like it had been done on purpose with a razor.

"Now," Dr. Ed was saying, "you know you are actually very lucky, because if you'd lost your big toe or your little one, you'd have had real problems with balance…".

I looked at him like he had horns growing out of his head.

"I absolutely and definitely do not feel lucky," I said.

"Try being me," came a voice from behind the next curtain, where Mrs. Shawcourt was awaiting her next round of chemotherapy.

Suddenly, without warning, we both started to laugh.

•   •   •   •

I was in the hospital for another three weeks. Loads of my mates came by and said I'd been in the paper and could they have a look (no, even when I got my dressing changed, I couldn't bear to look at them), and keeping me up to date on social events that, suddenly, I really found I'd lost interest in. In fact, the only person I could talk to was Mrs. Shawcourt, except of course she told me to call her Claire, which took a bit of getting used to and made me feel a bit too grown-up. She had two sons who came to visit, who always looked a bit pushed for time, and her daughters-in-law, who were dead nice and used to give me their gossip mags because Claire couldn't be bothered with them.

Once they brought some little girls in, both of whom got completely freaked out by the wires and the smell and the beeping. It was the only time I saw Claire really, truly sad.

The rest of the time, we talked. Well, I talked. Mostly about how bored I was and how was I ever going to learn to walk properly again. (Physio was rubbish. For two things I had NEVER, ever thought about, except when I was getting a pedicure and not really even then, my toes were annoyingly useful when it came to getting about. Even more embarrassing, I had to use the same physio lab as people who had really horrible traumatic injuries and were in wheelchairs and stuff, and I felt the most horrendous fraud marching up and down parallel bars with an injury most people thought was quite amusing, if anything. So I could hardly complain. I did though.)

Claire understood. She was such easy company, and sometimes, when she was very ill, I'd read to her. Most of her books, though, were in French.

"I can't read this," I said.

"You ought to be able to," she said. "You had me."

"Yeah, kind of," I muttered.

"You were a good student," said Claire. "You showed a real aptitude, I remember."

Suddenly I flashed back on my first-year report card. In amid the *doesn't apply herself*s and *could do better*s, I suddenly remembered my French mark had been good. Why hadn't I applied myself?

"I don't know," I said. "I thought school was stupid."

Claire shook her head. "But I've met your parents; they're lovely. You're from such a nice family."

"You don't have to live with them," I said, then felt guilty that I'd been mean about them. They'd been in every single day even if, as Dad complained almost constantly, the parking charges were appalling.

"You still live at home?" she asked, surprised, and I felt a bit defensive.

"Neh. I lived with my boyfriend for a bit, but he turned out to be a pillock, so I moved back in, that's all."

"I see," said Claire. She looked at her watch. It was only 9:30 in the morning. We'd already been up for three hours and lunch wasn't until 12:00.

"If you like," she said, "I'm bored too. If I taught you some French, you could read to me. And I would feel less like a big, sick, bored bald plum who does nothing but dwell on the past and feel old and stupid and useless. Would you like that?"

I looked down at the magazine I was holding, which had an enormous picture of Kim Kardashian's arse on it. And she had ten toes.

"Yeah, all right," I said.

•　•　•　•

1972

"It's nothing," the man was saying, speaking to be heard over the stiff sea breeze and the honking of the ferries and the rattle of the trains. "It is a tiny…look, la manche. You can swim it. We won't."

This did nothing to stem the tide of tears rolling down the girl's cheeks.

"I would," she said. "I will swim it for you."

"You," he said, "will go back and finish school and do wonderful things and be happy."

"I don't want to," she groaned. "I want to stay here with you."

The man grimaced and attempted to stop her tears with kisses. They were dripping on his new, oddly shiny uniform.

"Well, they will make me march up and down like an ape, you see. And I will be an idiot with nothing else to do and nothing else to think about except for you. Shh, bout'chou. Shh. We will be together again, you see."

"I love you," said the girl. "I will never love anyone so much my entire life."

"I love you too," said the man. "I care for you and I love you and I shall see you again and I shall write you letters and you shall finish school and you shall see, all will be well."

The girl's sobs started to quiet.

"I can't...I can't bear it," she said.

"Ah, love," said the man, his accent strong. "That is what it is, the need to bear things."

He buried his face in her hair.

"Alors. My love. Come back. Soon."

"I will," said the girl. "Of course I will come back soon."

2

My two brothers stopped coming to visit me the instant it was clear I wasn't actually going to snuff it—I loved them, but at twenty-two and twenty, you have a lot of other things to do that aren't talking to your weird big sister about her weird accident in the hospital. Cath, bless her, of course, she was brilliant—I couldn't do without her, but she worked really long hours at the hair salon. It was a forty-five-minute bus ride from the hospital, so she couldn't come that often, though I so appreciated it when she did. She liked to tell me who won hideous hairstyle of the week and all the times she tried to convince them to make it less hideous but they fought on regardless, desperate to emulate a Kardashian, even though they had short, greasy brown wisps that wouldn't take an extension. They'd be back in a week shouting and screaming and threatening to sue because what was left of their hair was falling out.

"I tell 'em," said Cath. "They don't listen. Nobody listens to me."

She'd made me look in the bathroom mirror and told me I'd be all right. I looked absolutely hellish. My blue eyes were bloodshot all the time from the antibiotics and looked a bit yellow; my curly pale hair—normally blond with the help of Cath, now all growing out—was frizzy and all over the place, like a crazy person; and my pale skin was the same color and texture as hospital porridge. Cath tried to say encouraging things, mostly because she's like that and also because she has to say encouraging things in the salon to sixty-year-old women who are two hundred pounds overweight and come in asking to look like Jennifer Lawrence, but we both knew it was a vain effort.

A lot of the time, though, it was just me and Claire. It was a weird situation, in that we got to know each other a lot faster than I supposed we would have otherwise. But I also realized, with a bit of a shock, that I was kind of glad, really, that I wasn't with Darr anymore. He was a nice bloke and everything, but not one for conversation. If he'd had to come and see me every day, it would have been a disaster—we'd have been talking about nothing but fries and his favorite football team by day three. I don't know how we'd have carried on exactly, without the possibility of a snog. (I still had a tube in my arm and a tube up my pee hole—sorry—and even if I didn't, there was something about the idea of only having eight toes that made the idea of ever feeling sexy again rather unlikely.) Being sick gave me a lot of perspective; I'd been gutted when we broke up—he kept trying to be unfaithful, and in a town the size of Kidinsborough, that didn't stay secret for long. His defense—that he'd been serially unsuccessful—didn't help him, although I had liked the little flat we'd rented together. That was my one regret, even now. I missed that flat.

But he gave my brother Joe a box of chocolates to pass on to me (which Joe promptly ate, being twenty) and texted me to see if I was okay. I think he might even have taken me back, toes or no toes. I had heard his dating had been about as successful single as it had been with me, though that might just have been Cath trying to make me feel better.

But, oh, I was glad to have Claire. I'd bought a cheap smartphone six months before and now cursed my luck for not having something to play with that had anything better than, basically, Snake on it. I grumbled aloud at hospitals not having Wi-Fi connections, even when they told me they would interfere with the machines. (I'm not a scientist, right, but I bet that is totally, like, not even true.) I read lots of books, but there's a difference between reading a book when you're tired after working all day (desperate to get into the bath and enjoy a few pages with a cup of tea, even when Joe is banging on the door shouting about hair gel) and having nothing else to do.

Plus, I was on lots of medication and it was a bit tricky to concentrate. There was a TV in the far corner blaring away, but it was set to the same channel all day and I got really tired of watching loud, fat people shouting at each other, so I kept my headphones on. It was kind of great to see people, except I had nothing to say to them except how much fluid my wound was draining and other fricking disgusting things, so I didn't really like chatting.

The nurses were a great laugh, but they were always in a rush, and the doctors were always knackered-looking and not really interested— they were all interested in my foot, but it might as well have been connected to a cat for all the interest they showed in me above the ankle. And everyone else on the ward was old. Really, really old. Really "Where am I? Is this the war?" old. I felt sorry for them and their anxious, exhausted-looking families coming in every day to hear "no change," but I couldn't really communicate with them. I didn't realize young people—youngish—don't often get that sick. Or if they did, they were over in surgery, having glamorous bits chopped off, or in accident and emergency recovering from a fabulous night out that got a bit out of hand, not over here in medicine, which was aging patients with a million things wrong with them and nowhere else to go.

So it was an absolute relief to sit calmly with Claire and repeat, steadily, rote memorizing *avoir* and *être* and the difference between the recent past and the ongoing past and learning how to roll my *r*'s properly. ("You must," she said, over and over again, "work so hard on your accent. Be French. Be the Frenchiest French accent of anyone. Do a massive Inspector Clouseau and wave your arms about." "I feel like an idiot," I said. "You will," agreed Claire, "until you speak some French and a French person understands you.")

We puzzled our way through children's books and flashcards and test extracts. It was good for me to realize that Claire was enjoying it too, much more than her short, slightly awkward conversations with her sons—she had been divorced for a long time, I found out.

Finally, eventually, like a musician tentatively picking up an instrument, we started to speak a little—haltingly, painfully—in French. I found it easier to listen than to speak, but Claire was endlessly patient—we had so little else to do—and so gentle when she corrected me that I couldn't believe what an idiot I had been not to have paid closer attention to this wonderful teacher when I'd had the chance.

"Did you live in France—*est-ce que tu habitas en France?*" I asked slowly one dank spring morning, when the green buds on the trees outside seemed to be enjoying the rain, but nobody else did. It was always the same temperature inside the hospital anyway, a hermetically sealed ship disconnected from the outside world.

"A long time ago," she replied, not quite meeting my eyes. "And not for very long."

• • • •

1972

It was, Claire knew, the daftest form of rebellion. Hardly rebellion at all, really. Still. She sat, fixed at the breakfast table, staring at her cereal. She was too old, at seventeen, for children's cereal, she knew. She'd rather have coffee, but it wasn't a fight she was prepared to take on. On this other matter, however...

"You're not wearing those things to my chapel."

Those things referred to a new pair of flares Claire had saved up for. She'd had a Christmas holiday job in Chelsea Girl. Her father had had a very difficult time reconciling himself to the fact that she was willing to take on the mantle of hard work (which he did believe in, very much) against the fact that it was very clearly taking place in a den of iniquity that sold harlot's clothing. Her mother, as so often, must have had a word behind the scenes; she had never, and would never, dare contradict the Reverend Marcus Forest in public. Few would.

Claire glanced down at her denim-clad legs. She had spent her entire life being relentlessly unfashionable. Her father thought fashion was a fast track to eternal torment. Her mother instead had made her pinafores and long school skirts and dirndls for Sundays.

But working had opened her eyes, made her feel more grown-up. The other girls in the shop were twenty, older even, worldly wise. They discussed nightclubs and boys and makeup (strictly banned at Claire's house) and found Claire's life (everyone knew the Reverend) hilarious. The older, sophisticated girls took her under their wings, made her dress up in the latest clothes, cooing over her slender figure and undyed pale blond hair that always made her look, as far as she was concerned, washed out (although there weren't many mirrors in the house). The boys hadn't asked her out at school. She had told herself that it was because of her father but feared, inside, that it was something else, that she was so quiet, and uninteresting, and her pale hair and eyebrows meant she sometimes felt she was barely there at all.

As the three weeks passed, every day she grew a little bolder. It finished nastily one weekend, when her father was trying to write his Christmas sermon and she arrived back in from the shop with her eyes heavily made up, dramatically kohled in a shimmering emerald green with brown shading all the way around the socket and—most shocking of all—her eyebrows, colored in dark brown with a pencil one of the girls had produced. She had stared and stared at her reflection in the mirror of the strange, mysterious creature she had become, no longer pale and colorless. She did not look skinny and gaunt; instead, she looked slender and glamorous. Cassie had pulled her pale hair off her face and pinned back her childish fringe, and it added years to her. All the girls had laughed and insisted she come out with them that Saturday.

Claire didn't think so.

19

Her father stood up, furious.

"Get it off," he said quietly. "Take it off. Not under my roof."

He didn't get angry or shout. He never did; that wasn't his way. He just told her exactly how it would be. In Claire's mind, the voice of her father and the voice of God, in whom she believed completely, were very much the same. There was no doubt.

Her mother followed her to the avocado-colored bathroom and gave her a consoling cuddle.

"You do look lovely," she said, as Claire furiously wiped her face with a brown washcloth. "You know," she said, "in a year or two, you can go off to secretarial school or teacher training, and you can do whatever you like. It's not long to wait, my darling."

But to Claire, it felt like a million years away. All the other girls got to dress up and go out and have boyfriends with tinny old cars or terrifying motorbikes.

"That job… I thought it was a good idea but…" Her mother shook her head. "You know what he's like. It's driving him crazy. I just thought you needed a bit of independence…"

Then she disappeared and Claire heard, late into the night, a conversation, whispered, that she wasn't meant to overhear, but could tell, always, by the tone that it was about her. It was difficult being an only child sometimes. Her father seemed to treat her as someone who wanted nothing more than to get into terrible trouble at five seconds' notice, which drove her mad. Her mother did what she could, but when the Reverend went into one of his glowering sulks, they could last for days, and it made the atmosphere in the house very, very unpleasant. He was used to the two women in his life doing his bidding without question. But Claire yearned, more than anything else, for a bit of freedom.

The job was over, even after the shop offered to keep her on as a Saturday girl. She was desperate to do it, but it wasn't worth the grief. So she remained in her role of working hard at school—they had mentioned university, but the Reverend wasn't a huge fan of education for women and wanted to keep her closer to home than York or Liverpool. Claire didn't really think it could happen. Sometimes, late at night after her parents had gone to bed, she'd stay up late watching the movie on BBC2 and feeling a tiny clutch of panic around her heart that she would stay in Kidinsborough forever, watching her parents get older and older.

Two months later, in early March, her mother came to breakfast with a sly expression on her face and an envelope with a stripe of red and blue airmail around the corner of the pale blue paper and looping, exotic-looking handwriting.

"Well, it's all decided," she said, as the Reverend looked up from his grapefruit half.

"What?" he growled.

"For the summer. Claire has been invited to go and au pair."

Claire had never even heard the expression.

"You're going to nanny. For my pen pal."

"That French woman?" said the Reverend, folding his Daily Telegraph. "I thought you'd never met."

"We haven't," said Claire's mother proudly.

Claire looked from one to the other. She didn't know anything about this. "Who is it?"

"Well, I have a pen pal," said her mother, and Claire suddenly remembered the Christmas cards that arrived with Meilleurs Voeux written on them. "From school. When I was eleven, we all got pen pals. Like you, remember?"

Claire remembered, guiltily, that she had stopped writing to Jerome in Rouen before she had turned fifteen.

"Oh, yes," she said.

"Well, Marie-Noelle and I have kept it up…here and there of course, not very often. But I know she has two children now, and I wrote to her and asked if she would like to take you for the summer. And she said yes! You will look after the children; she has a cleaner she says here…goodness."

Her mother's face went a little strained.

21

"*I hope they're not terribly posh,*" she said, looking around at the very nice but plainly furnished vicarage. A churchman's stipend didn't go terribly far, and Claire had always known better than to expect new things. It wasn't until much later in her life that Claire reflected as to whether her bright, spirited mother had ever regretted falling in love with the committed, passionate young reverend, and the life that followed it. But Claire lost her beloved mum far too young, a victim of the cancer that had already set itself ticking in her own DNA.

"*I don't care if they're posh. Are they decent people?*" asked the Reverend.

"*Oh yes,*" said her mother cheerfully. "*There's a little boy and a little girl, Arnaud and Claudette. Aren't those the loveliest names?*"

Claire's heart was starting to race.

"*Where…whereabouts in France?*"

"*Oh, sorry, where's my head?*" said her mother. "*Paris, of course.*"

3

The settlement from the chocolate factory was not at all life-changing. It was barely anything-changing once I'd paid off my credit card. I wondered if maybe we should have gotten more, seeing as I now walked with a pronounced limp and had nearly died and everything, but they said that bit was the hospital's fault. The hospital said I was getting better now and getting me better was technically all they had to do really, and I did mention to Dr. Ed that actually if the hospital hadn't let me get so sick, they would have been able to reattach my toes. He had smiled and patted my hand in the manner of doctors he'd seen on television and told me if I ever had any questions, just to go right ahead, which completely bamboozled me as I thought I'd just asked one, and then he gave me a smile and a wink—I have no idea what the wink was, maybe it was his "style"—and floated on to sit on Claire's bed.

It was time to go home. After dreaming of being set free for so long, I suddenly realized I didn't actually want to go. Or rather, that it would be weird to lose the institutionalized days of drugs and meals and physio and not having to focus on anything else but getting better.

Now I had to face the world again and find a new job. It was a feature of the settlement that I didn't go back to Braders, presumably in case I had another one-in-a-million freak accident. If anything, I would have thought I'd have been a safer bet than other people, statistically speaking.

And I was going to miss Claire. We'd chatted more and more in French, to the annoyance of almost everyone, and it was truly the one good thing in my life, demonstrating that I could learn something, that I had a new skill. Everything else was just dread. There weren't any jobs, I knew that much. Cath said I could come and sweep up in the hairdressing salon, but that paid about absolutely nothing, and I wasn't that good at bending down without falling over yet. On the upside, I'd lost about fifteen pounds. That was the only upside. But I wouldn't recommend my method of losing the weight.

I told Claire about my worries, and she looked pensive.

"I've been thinking," she said.

"What?"

"Well," she said, "I knew...I knew someone in Paris who worked in chocolate. It was a long time ago though. I don't know what he's doing now."

"Ooh," I said. "A young flirtation?"

Her thin face took on a little color.

"I don't think that's any of your business."

"Where you madly in looove?"

We'd gotten to know each other well enough that I could tease her, but she could still get a teacherly glint in her eye. She did so now.

"He is not very good at writing letters," she mused, glancing out the window. "But I will try. I shall ask Ricky to use that email thingy when he comes. You can find anyone these days, can't you?"

"You can," I said. "But if he's a friend of yours, why haven't you gone back to Paris for so long?"

Claire's lips pursed.

"Well, I was busy raising a family. I had a job. I couldn't just jump on a plane whenever I felt like it."

"Hmm," I said, suspicious. She was very touchy all of a sudden.

"You could though," said Claire. "You can do whatever you like."

I laughed. "I don't think so. Hopalong Cassidy, that's me."

• • • •

I realized later that the impact—the emotional impact—of the accident didn't really hit until I went back home to Mum and Dad's. In the hospital I'd been, well, special, I suppose. I'd gotten flowers and gifts and was the center of everyone's attention, and people brought me drugs and asked after me, and even though it was kind of horrible, I was being taken care of.

Home, though—it was just home. The boys clattering in late at night, grumbling because they had to share a room again; Mum fussing around, steadily predicting doom for my chances of finding another job and how they would cut disability living allowance, to which I said, "Don't be stupid, I'm not disabled," and we both looked at my crutches, and then she would sigh again. My face in the mirror: my pale blue eyes looked so tired, and my fairish hair, without its usual highlights by Cath, just looked colorless. I had lost weight, but because I hadn't moved around at all, I just looked slack and saggy sometimes. I used to love putting makeup on to get ready for a night out, but it had been so long I'd kind of forgotten how, and the drugs had made my skin so dry.

That's when I really got sad. I cried in my little childhood bed, I slept later and later in the morning, and I got less and less interested in doing my exercises and listening to my friends' stories about new boyfriends and fall-outs and all sorts of things that sounded completely inconsequential to me now. I knew my parents were worried about me, but I just couldn't find in myself what to do; I just didn't know. My foot was slowly healing, apparently—but I could feel my toes, feel them all the time. They itched, they twitched, they hurt, and I lay awake at night staring at the ceiling and listening to the boiler make the same noises it had since my childhood and thinking, "What now? What now?"

• • • •

1972

Her mother had wanted to accompany her, have a "girls' day out" in London, but the Reverend had looked very suspicious indeed and hemmed and hawed about it. Seemingly the fleshpots of Paris wouldn't be quite as fearsome as the den of iniquity that was London—he hadn't, she thought, quite gotten the hang of 1968—and he had numerous and repeated instructions, both from her mother and from Mme. LeGuarde on the telephone, that the house was extremely traditional and strict and that it would be nothing but childcare and learning another language, a refinement in young ladies the Reverend did approve of. So after several lists and imprecations about how she was expected to behave—Claire was already absolutely terrified of Mme. LeGuarde; her mother made her sound posh, rich, and demanding, and Claire didn't know how she was going to cope with small children she could barely talk to—he had driven her to the railway station one spring morning, the sky already threatening large amounts of rain.

Already excited, she opened her Tupperware sandwich box as the train pulled out of Crewe, nervous and jittery and filled with the sense that she was leaving, going on a journey, by herself, and that it was going to be vastly important.

Rainie Callendar, the school bully, had cornered her before school broke up.

"Off to get even more stuck up?" she sniffed.

Claire did what she always did. She kept her head down as all Rainie's cronies burst out laughing and moved away as quickly as possible to try to escape their gaze. It rarely succeeded. She decided in herself, she couldn't wait for the holidays. However much she was going to get locked in a cupboard looking after French brats, it was still going to be better than bouncing between here and the Reverend.

Inside the box was a little note from her mother.

"Have a wonderful time," it said. Not "Behave yourself" or "Don't forget to clean up after yourself" or "Don't go out alone." Just "Have a wonderful time."

Claire was quite a young seventeen. She'd never really thought about her mother's life in any terms, apart from the fact that she was just there, providing meals, cleaning their clothes, agreeing with the Reverend whenever he had something new to say about the long-haired youths with hippie values that had reached even Kidinsborough. It didn't cross her mind that her mother might have been jealous.

• • • •

Claire was nervous getting on the ferry, terrified she wouldn't know what to do. It was absolutely huge. The only boat she'd ever been on was a paddle boat at Scarborough. The great white ship seemed to her romantic—the smell of the diesel, the great honk of the horn as it came alongside the huge terminal at Dover, lined with adventurous-looking people with station wagons piled high with tents and pegs and, even more exotically, Citroën 2CVs with real French people opening their picnics (a lot more exotic than Claire's meat paste sandwiches) with actual bottles of wine and glasses and long sticks of bread. She gazed around at everyone, drinking it in, then went up to the very front of the boat—it was a blowy day, white clouds flicking across the sky. She felt the breeze in her face and looked hungrily back toward England (her very first time leaving it) and forward toward France and thought she had rarely felt more alive.

• • • •

"Come and have a coffee," the message from Claire said on my phone. She'd been discharged, temporarily, and she sounded a little breathy, a little tentative, and I called her back—this was one thing I could manage—to arrange for us to meet up in the cozy bookshop coffee shop, where I thought she'd be more comfortable.

Her nice daughter-in-law Patsy dropped her off and made her promise not to buy too many books. Claire had rolled her eyes when she left and said she loved Patsy, but everyone seemed to equate being sick with being four, and then she remembered she didn't have to tell me that, and we cheered ourselves up by doing imitations of Dr. Ed sitting on the bed doing his empathizing.

Then there was a pause during which, in a normal conversation, someone would have said "Hey, you look well" or "You've cut your hair" or "You look healthy" (code for "Cor, you've gotten fat," as everybody knows), but neither of us could say anything. In the hospital, with its crisp white sheets and Claire's neat, spotless cream pajamas, she didn't look well, but she seemed to belong there. Out here in public, she looked terrifying. So thin that she might break, a scarf tied artfully around her head that served only to announce "I've had cancer for so long I've gotten really good at tying scarves," a smart dress that would have looked rather nice if it had fitted her but clearly didn't as she was far too thin, and drawn-in cheekbones. She looked… Wow, she looked sick.

I got up to go fetch us some coffee and some chocolate brownie cake, even though she had said she didn't want any, and I said she would when she tasted the homemade stuff they did in here. She smiled thinly and said "Of course, that would be great" in a way that wouldn't have fooled a horse. I was conscious of her eyes on me as I limped across the floor. I still wasn't at all confident with my stick and had basically decided to get rid of it. Cath kept trying to get me to come out, saying that everyone was dying to hear all about it, but that thought filled me with total horror. I did though desperately need to get my hair done. And some new clothes. I was in my daggiest old jeans and a striped top that had been absolutely no effort whatsoever, and it showed.

"So," she said when I was back. The lady had agreed to bring over the tray, thank goodness. We shared a look.

"We're like the old nag's corner," I said, and Claire smiled. The lady didn't. I think she was very concerned that we were about to throw up or fall over in her lovely café. The chocolate brownie cake was exceptionally good, though, and worth all the weird looks we were getting.

"So..." Claire suddenly flushed a little and looked excited. "I got a letter."

"An actual letter?" I said, impressed. I never got letters, just instant messages from Cath telling me some bloke was either totally fit or a right turd or both.

She nodded.

"Well, more of a postcard... Regardless. He said he does need a new factory worker, yes. And I know of an apartment where you could stay."

I looked at her, totally taken aback.

"What?"

"Well, I didn't...I didn't think you'd actually do it," I said, stunned and touched. "I mean, go to all that trouble."

"It was two letters," said Claire. "I hope that's not your idea of hard work. I've talked you up quite dramatically."

"Uh-oh," I said.

She smiled. "It was...it was nice to hear back after all this time."

"This was definitely a romance," I said.

"It was definitely a long time ago," she said crisply in her teacher's voice again.

"Don't you want to go?" I said.

"Oh, no," she said quickly. "That time of my life is well over with, quite done and dusted. And I have quite enough on my plate. But you're still young..."

"I'm thirty," I said, moaning.

"That's young," she said very sharply. "That's very young."

"So, what's it like, this factory?" I said, changing the subject. Her own kids weren't much older than me and all married and settled with good jobs, and I didn't think I could handle the comparison.

"Oh, it's probably changed a bit," she said, looking a bit dreamy. Then she came back to herself. "Anyway, it's not a factory, more an *atelier*—a workshop. *Le Chapeau Chocolat.*"

"The Chocolate Hat?" I said. "That sounds... I mean, do they actually make hats out of chocolate?"

Claire ignored me.

"They'll take you on as a general factotum, normal hours, and they normally use a room nearby, apparently, that you can stay in. It's extremely expensive in that area of Paris, incredibly, so it's very helpful. He says they're busy until about October, so you could stay that long then come back. By then, the UK shops will be gearing up for Christmas, so I'm sure you'll get a job then."

"Don't they have Christmas in France?"

Claire smiled at me. "Yes, but it isn't the crazy obsession it is here. A few oysters and some time with your family; that's about the size of it."

"That sounds rubbish," I said, suddenly a bit cross at how much this had been sorted out. I still felt as if I were being railroaded a bit, rather than being worried about and cosseted. Everyone was saying things like how I should stand on my own two feet, which I found particularly annoying as I didn't really have two feet anymore.

"It's lovely," said Claire, her thin face going a bit dreamy. "The rain hits the pavement and the lights go all misty over the bridges, and you huddle up in front of the fire..."

"And eat oysters," I said. "Bleurgh."

Claire took her glasses off and rubbed her sore-looking eyes. "Well," she said hopefully. "I think it's a very generous offer, considering he's never met you."

"What about speaking French?" I said, sounding slightly panicky. "I won't be able to speak all the French."

"Don't be silly, you're coming along brilliantly."

"Yes, but that's talking to you. Real French people will talk like this…zubba zubba zubba zubba zuBBAH, at, like, one hundred miles an hour. One hundred kilometers an hour," I said gloomily.

Claire laughed. "The trick is not to panic. Trust your brain to know what people are saying. Also, people talk just as much rubbish in French as they do in English. They repeat themselves all the time, just like real people do. Don't worry about it."

I blinked.

"Does he speak English?"

Claire smiled shyly.

"Not a word, as far as I remember."

• • • •

1972

His mustache had been the first thing she'd noticed about him—not because it was a mustache, because lots of men had them at that time, along with long unruly sideburns, which he also had, but because it had chocolate on the ends. She had blinked at it.

"What?" he had said instantly, waggling his eyebrows at her. "What? Tell me—you cannot believe such a devastatingly handsome man has just walked through the door?"

She had smiled involuntarily—with his thick mop of dark brown curly hair, mischievous brown eyes, and burly, large body, he was undeniably attractive, but handsome, no. Especially not in the traditional French style, where the men were neat and well-groomed, slim and rather refined. There was nothing refined about this man; he looked a bit like a lost bear.

"You are laughing? It's funny that I am not handsome? Hmm? How is that funny?"

He then mimed a position of extreme woundedness.

Claire had been wallflowering near the elaborately corniced door, waiting for Mme. LeGuarde to want to go, for nearly an hour.

Her hosts were terribly polite and not the terrible tyrants she had been dreading and her father had been hoping for, but they also thought it was quite the privilege to be allowed to take part in their social lives.

Claire, though, found it incomprehensibly sophisticated and suffered from terrible nerves, not knowing what to say. There were young men in berets arguing furiously about communism, stunning slender women smoking and occasionally raising an eyebrow at the men or mentioning how boring such and such an exhibition was. She wasn't a party person, even among people she knew. Paris itself was knocking her out daily with its astonishing beauty. But the people absolutely terrified her.

She treated it as an extension of her language classes and tried to listen in as much as she could, but in her mind these people were undoubtedly grown-ups. And she, equally undoubtedly, was not. She felt neither one thing nor the other, and the fun and glamour made her feel more and more like an uneducated country hick. She found it hard enough to follow what people were saying, they spoke so fast. She was constantly dazzled by how beautifully everybody dressed, so different from her mother's homely style, and on top of that, everyone talked about exhibitions they'd seen and writers they'd met, and everyone talked about food absolutely without stopping. It was exhausting. People took an interest in the LeGuardes' English girl—she was pretty and endearing-looking—but she found herself clamming up, like the worst kind of wallflower. She could see Mme. LeGuarde, who was extremely beautiful and well-groomed, wasn't particularly impressed by this, but after Kidinsborough and the rectory, Paris was completely overwhelming.

This chap, on the other hand, was different. He had a spark of mischief in his eyes that he couldn't hide.

"I didn't mean it," she said, hiding her mouth with her hand so he wouldn't see her smirking.

"OH! An English woman!" he said immediately, standing back as if in

amazement. "Enchanté, mademoiselle! Thank you so much for bestowing a visit on our little backwater town here."

"You are teasing me," said Claire, trying to match his humorous tone.

"That is not possible, mademoiselle! *I am French and therefore of course have no sense of humor."*

"What have you got on your mustache?" she said, noticing a smudge.

He made a comical face trying to see it.

"I don't know. Is it a sense of humor?"

"It's brown."

"Ah, well, of course…that is my job."

This made no sense to Claire, just as the host of the party turned around and noticed him standing there. Delighted, he marched up and bustled him away, introducing him to everyone, who were, it seemed, far more delighted to make his acquaintance than they had been when introduced to the LeGuardes' new *au pair.*

"Who is that?" she asked Mme. LeGuarde in a whisper.

"Oh, the talk of the town, *Thierry Girard,*" said Mme. LeGuarde, eyeing him affectionately. "They say he is the most gifted chocolatier since Persion."

Claire was amazed that this was news of any kind or that that was so important. On the other hand, it explained what was on his mustache, which was a good thing at least.

"Is he going to be a big success?" she asked casually.

Mme. LeGuarde watched him talk to a top food critic, charming him effortlessly by insisting on drawing out his latest recipe.

"Oh, I think so," she said. "He studied in Switzerland and Bruges. I think he's going to be really terribly good."

After touring the room and accepting a second glass of the delicious, icy champagne, Claire, back in observational mode, realized he was the focus of attention and laughter in the room. People just seemed to flock to him. As someone who people tended to simply not notice—the curse of being quiet—Claire was transfixed. His big, shaggy bear face was not at all *handsome, but it was so cheerful and animated, it was hard not to enjoy looking at it or wish that its sunshiny beam of attention might come near you. She spotted several of the beautiful women, who had been so sulky and superior before, suddenly start laughing and fluttering about in front of him. Claire bit her lip. She would have liked another glass of the amazing, freezing cold champagne—she'd never had it before—but suspected, rightly, that Mme. LeGuarde would disapprove. In fact, even now they looked like they were getting ready to leave. She glanced around for her coat before remembering that it had been taken by a maid at the door.*

"You are not leaving," came a growly voice. She turned around, her heart suddenly jumping. Thierry was standing there, his face crestfallen. "Where are you going?"

"I have to work tomorrow," she stuttered. "And Mme. LeGuarde…she is taking me home. I have to go with her."

He waggled his eyebrows. "Ah, mam'zelle, I did not realize you were a child."

"I'm not a child," she said emphatically, realizing immediately as she did so what a child she sounded.

"Alors, then I will take you home."

"You shall not," said Mme. LeGuarde, who had suddenly materialized out of nowhere and was giving him a freezing stare.

"Enchanté," said Thierry, not in the least perturbed. He bent and kissed her hand.

"This is your sister?"

Mme. LeGuarde rolled her eyes.

"This is my au pair, and while she is here, my ward," she said crisply. "Claire, it is time to go."

"Claire," said Thierry, rolling the name around his mouth as if he were savoring it. "Of course, you will visit my new shop?"

Claire realized immediately that was difficult for Madame. Obviously all of Paris would have to try the new shop, otherwise how to admit it at the next soirée? She cut a sideways glimpse at Claire. Claire thought, and

34

always would, that she was trying to think of ways to keep her apart from this fascinating person.

In fact, she couldn't have been further from the truth.

Marie-Noelle LeGuarde was a woman of the world and thought Claire had been ridiculously protected and cosseted at home, completely stifled in the English bourgeois fashion. If she didn't open her eyes soon, she'd end up buried in some ghastly English tomb like her mother and never have a day's proper fun and experience in her life. She had just rather hoped it would be one of the charming, well-educated sons of her friends who would take her in hand, let her live a little, and send her home with wonderful memories of Paris and a horizon broader than her local church flower-arranging society. Not this hoofing peasant from Lot-et-Garonne. She sensed a hidden spirit in the young girl and felt it her responsibility, as a woman of the world, to give it wings, both for her and for her wonderful spirited mother, who had married the charismatic up-and-coming young churchman and lived to rue the day. But with someone suitable, and careful. She didn't want to send her back knocked up by a fat cook.

"Bien sûr, of course," she said swiftly to Thierry, simultaneously signaling to the maid to bring their coats. Extinguishing a cigarette, they left into the still-crisp spring evening. Claire, looking behind from the back window of the taxi cab, glimpsed the huge French windows of the apartment, flung open to the night, exuding a glow and the noise of music and chatter and cigar smoke drifting upward into the hazy night.

4

Dad never came up to my room, not since I was about twelve or so. It was my sanctum, my escape from the boys. Also, he just isn't the kind of dad that goes in for long chats. He's the kind of dad that makes really awful jokes to your friends and makes sure your bike chain is oiled up and gets a bit pink in the face at Christmas and doesn't remove his party hat all day. I doubt he's said "I love you" in his entire life, not even to Mum. I know he does, though, so it totally doesn't matter. He also spends his life calling the boys buggers, but I knew he was proud of me when I got promoted at Braders.

Anyway, my mum had been rabbiting on about what I was going to do and what I was up to and what my future was going to be, and even hearing it was so exhausting—I'd lost two toes. I wasn't paralyzed or in a wheelchair; I didn't even qualify for a blue parking badge for my dad's car (much to Mum's evident disappointment, seriously).

Then Mum read something in one of her magazines and decided I was "depressed" and started muttering about seeing someone and that was annoying too, because depression is a horrid illness that people get and not a way to describe feeling a bit sad when you've lost a bit of you off the end, which, in my opinion, is a totally natural way of thinking and doesn't need to be talked through: "I'm sad because I've had my toes chopped off." "Oh yes, quite right, that'll be sixty pounds please." Or, heaven forbid, put me on drugs or something. But then again, I couldn't deny that I didn't really feel myself. Have you ever had a really bad hangover that's gone into a second day? Well, it was like that second day. I just couldn't summon up the energy to do the million and one things I knew I needed to do. There were just so many things.

Dad knocked quietly, which was interesting, as Mum never knocks and the boys never drop by, just holler from the bottom of the stairs.

"Hello, love," he said, proffering me a cup of tea. I wouldn't say we were a really old-fashioned family, but one thing was for sure: Dad never made the tea.

"Did you make this?" I said, eyeing it suspiciously.

"Yes," said my dad quickly. "Two sugars?"

He must have asked Mum.

"Can I come in?"

"It's your house," I said, surprised. He looked nervous. Worse than that, before he sat down, he carefully removed two wrapped chocolate cookies from his pocket. I looked up at him.

"What's wrong?"

"Nothing's wrong."

"Something's wrong, if it needs a chocolate cookie. Tell me, quickly."

My dad shook his head. "I just thought you'd like a chocolate cookie."

I just stared at him, unconvinced.

"Listen," he said. "I got a call from your teacher friend…"

"She's not my teacher anymore," I said.

"Sounds like she's been teaching you a few things," he said, sitting at my white vanity unit. He looked strange there. The back of his head reflected in the mirror; he was getting really bald back there.

I shrugged.

"Just something to do, you know."

He glanced on my bed, where there were several French books Claire had lent me that I'd been puzzling through with the help of a massive dictionary. It was a slow, boring business, but light was beginning to dawn.

"Well," he said, "she says she's offered you a job."

I shook my head. "She hasn't really. She just knows someone…or she used to know him. It was ages ago. She reckons I might be able to help out in the summer."

"She says it's in your line of work."

"Yes—in another country. Sweeping up floors probably."

Dad shrugged. "What's wrong with working in another country?"

"What, you want me out of the house now?"

"No," he said carefully. "All I mean is, you're thirty, you've got no ties, you're still young… Don't you want to travel a bit? See the world?"

I shrugged. I hadn't really thought of it like that. In fact, I'd only really thought about what a gigantic pain in the arse this was for me and how people should be feeling more sorry for me, not what I was going to do next. I'd lost two bits of myself. That was enough for one year, surely.

When Dad was saying it, though, I did think, for a second, that it would be quite nice to go somewhere where nobody knew what had happened to me and didn't eye me up with looks of concern and slightly prurient interest. The kids on the estate definitely talked about me when I went by. The one time I'd gone out with Cath so far, Mark Farmer had cornered me, drunk, at about 1:00 a.m. and begged to take a look at it. I hadn't much fancied going out again after that. I didn't want to be the local freak show. And I knew what it was like here in Kidinsborough. Sandy Verden had pooed her pants once in year four, and no one had let her forget it yet.

Dad looked at me kindly.

"Love, you know, I don't like to give advice."

"I know," I said. "And I appreciate it. Mum gives me LOTS."

He smiled, a little sadly.

"Honestly, love. At your age. The chance to go see somewhere new, live somewhere different, even if it's just for a little while…I'd jump at it. I think you'd be mad not to."

I'd never seen my dad so passionate about anything, not even when the Kidinsborough Wanderers won the league in 1994 and everyone went demented for about a month and a half. (The next season they got demoted, so it was a short run good thing.)

"Please," he said, then he sighed. "The boys, you know, good for nothing, half of them... They'd have been down a pit in the old days or doing something useful, but now there's nothing for them but to hang around, wait on building work... It's a damn shame is what it is. But you..."

He looked at me, his tired, kind face full of something so emotional I found it quite difficult to look at. "You were so good at school, Anna, we couldn't believe it when you left so early. Mrs. Shawcourt rang us then too, you know?"

I did know. She had told my parents I should stay on, go to college, but I really didn't see the point of it. I already knew I wanted to work in food and I wanted a wage. I didn't really understand that I could have gone to college to specialize, to spend a couple of years really learning stuff rather than picking it up here and there in industrial kitchens...well. After that, my pride wouldn't let me go. My dad kept saying it wasn't too late, but I was used to a wage by then and didn't want to go back to being a student. Students were supposed to be spotty losers anyway; that's what people said around the factory. I always thought it looked like fun, watching them heading up to the big agricultural college we had nearby, laughing and looking carefree with their folders and laptop bags, while we slouched into work every morning. Anyway.

Mrs. Shawcourt had said I had a real gift for languages and I should stay and do more exams. I'd snorted and wondered what the point of doing that was. Wasted on teenagers, education. Well, teenagers like I had been.

Dad was still talking.

"You know," he said mildly, "I really believe you could. I totally believe you could do it."

I half-smiled at him. "But you also told me that I could grow up to become Spider-Man."

"I believe that too," he said, getting up, more slowly than he used to I noticed (I always noticed people's walks these days), and kissing me gently on the head.

5

Two Months Later

If one more person told me how lucky I was, I was going to scream. I didn't feel lucky at all. At the huge, mobbed railway station in Paris where the Eurostar stopped, everyone had charged off in every direction as if holding a "look how well I know Paris" competition and left me standing there feeling totally exposed, so then of course I figured I would look like someone totally exposed and then become a massive target for pickpockets. This is why my mum and my dad have been to Scarborough every single year for a hundred and seventy years, I swear to God. At least in Scarborough, you know which end of the pier to avoid and you can tell if someone's wearing a real police uniform or a novelty hat for fun, and here I couldn't read the signs or know what to think and I didn't dare take a cab. I limped down an escalator pulling my wheelie bag and thinking of all the people who'd swooned and said I was so lucky to be in Paris and how amazing it was going to be and all I could think was, well, yes, I'll probably sit by myself in a room for six weeks watching it all go on around me and not notice a thing. That was entirely within the realm of possibility. And I wouldn't like the food.

I looked up at the Metro map. It made totally no sense to me, none of it. I gazed at it, hand clutching tightly to my wallet and passport. It could have been on upside down as far as I could tell.

None of the lines had names, just numbers, but the notice boards had names.

I finally figured out that they were giving the names of the stations at the end of the lines. Or so I thought. I boldly strode forward and got a ticket from the man behind the counter, who I then asked in my best French for the way to my stop. He gave me a gigantically long stream of hugely complicated directions. I didn't understand any of them, but said thank you and went to walk away. He shouted at me loudly and I turned around, panicked, as he indicated that I had already started heading off in the wrong direction. I thanked him, tears pricking my eyes with embarrassment.

The tunnel platform was mobbed with every conceivable type of person, most of them speaking French loudly at a billion miles an hour as if showing off and a few of them looking like horribly lost tourists, just like me. We avoided each other like plague victims, too scared to reveal our vulnerability and ignorance. If I could have turned around and gotten back on the nice cozy Eurostar, I would have in a heartbeat. I glanced at my watch. I'd changed the time, so it was four o'clock here, which meant three o'clock in Kidinsborough. Tea break time. At Braders I'd have been sitting down with a cuppa and a packet of salt 'n' vinegar chips. Even thinking of that stupid factory, which I hated and detested and where I slagged off almost continuously, was making me homesick now. Around about now in the hospital, they served custard creams.

I stared nervously through the dirty graffitied window of the loud silver train. It rattled past stops including, I thought, the one I should have gotten off at. Within another few minutes, we were practically out in open fields. Wherever it was I was meant to be going, it wasn't out in open fields. My heart racing, I jumped out at the first station when the train, after a hundred years, finally started to slow down. Several people in the carriage watched me with amused eyes, which made me hot and cross and anxious. I took the first train going the other way, which thank goodness, did turn out to be a slow stopping train with two levels, halfway up and halfway down. I took a tiny orange plastic seat near the door and strained my eyes at the passing signs, trying to stop the train by willpower alone.

When I finally reached Châtelet-Les Halles, I got my suitcase shut in the revolving door but was helpfully freed by a very well-dressed man who was rushing past. I turned to thank him, but instead he shot me a look that gave me a very strict telling off for getting in his well-shod way. I stood up above ground again finally, dirty, hot, and grumpy, and tried to orient myself with my tiny map. Thank God she'd said island; a bridge, a bridge I could see. Stupid bloody Paris and its stupid bloody hard-to-get-about Metro and its grumpy people and its shouting railway staff and stupid well-dressed men… I was very close to tears. My toes were killing me.

Next to the Metro station was a little café with tables and chairs pushed out onto the pavement, despite cars running close by and exhaust fumes in the air and a florist whose blooms spilled over onto and under the chairs. I felt for my wallet for the 198th time that afternoon, then collapsed into a chair. A little man in trousers and a white shirt came running out importantly.

"Madame?" he said fussily. I didn't know what I wanted, really. Just to sit down. And given the perilous state of my finances, I really would have liked just a glass of water, but that wasn't going to go well, I could tell already. I glanced at the next table. An old man with an equally old dog dozing under his chair raised an eyebrow at me. In front of him was a tall, large glass filled with brimming, icy cold-looking lager. The waiter followed my eyes.

"*Comme ça?*"—like that one?—he barked. I nodded my head gratefully. Yes. Fine. Bit naughty at four o'clock in the afternoon, but then I'd been up since five because Mum was utterly convinced I was going to miss all my connections. And I was hot and tired and cross and it was nice, for two seconds, to stop panicking about everything

I had to do and whether I was going to lose my ticket on the train or drop my passport or leave my bag unattended and have it blown up.

I sat back in the chair and turned my face to the sun. Having left England in a cold fog, I hadn't expected spring sunshine, but out of the wind, it was warm and gentle on my face. Blinking and wondering where I'd packed my sunglasses, I took a deep breath as my beer arrived fast as lightning, took a sip—it was freezing and delicious—and glanced around me.

I couldn't help but smile. Forget the dirty Metro or the rattling suburbs or the hard-to-maneuver ticket barriers. Instead, here, I found myself on a corner of a crossroads of cobbled streets, leading toward, on my right, a great hump-backed bridge over the Seine from which I could just make out the back of a huge church. My heart leaped. It was Notre Dame; it had to be. On my other side were long rows of huge white buildings, seven or eight stories high, one leading down the embankment of the river, one backward filled with shops, the road several lanes wide, shops and restaurants with striped awnings poking out onto the pavements as far as the eye could see.

Slowly, my shoulders began to lower themselves, and my heart rose a little as I took another sip of beer, despite my tiredness and worry and anxiety. (I know, I know, there are people who travel without ever worrying about it, who turn up and bounce on trains and planes and enjoy it and wake up in a new city without even batting an eyelid—I wonder what their lives are like, I really do, because I am not like that; I worry all the time.) Next door, at the flower shop, a handsome young man with slicked-back hair came out looking slightly furtive and carrying a large bunch of white lilies. I wondered who they were for. As I wondered, he caught my eye, boldly staring at me, and winked as he walked off. Heh. I grinned at that too.

The people started to leave work—early by my standards for rush hour, but they were leaving nonetheless. The women all looked like they'd just been in the hairdressers. Their makeup was subtle; their hair was dark and lovely and didn't even look dyed—I thought regretfully of the highlights Cath put in, which cost me a fortune once every six weeks and was basically like being on a payment plan even at mate's rates—and they mostly wore really subtle clothes of black or navy or gray; not many trousers, I noticed. The female managers at Braders wore trouser suits mostly, too tight trousers over fat bottoms with little short jackets perched on the top. It was not a look, I felt, that suited them. Here, if the women did wear trousers, they were over tiny, nonexistent bottoms and were flowingly cut and looked rather chic and boyish, not a containment exercise. Of course, I thought. This was how Mrs. Shawcourt—Claire—dressed. This was obviously where she had learned. I wondered how she had done it.

The old man at the next table leaned over.

"*Anglaise?*" he asked. Well, yes. Although I wished it wasn't QUITE so obvious. I nodded, smiling.

"You 'ave been to Paris before?" he said.

I shook my head.

"Oh," he said, his face completely creased with wrinkles. "Oh, you will adore it. To be young, and in Paris for the first time… *Mademoiselle*, I envy you."

I tried to smile back as if I wasn't desperate for a bath and feeling positively ancient compared to the beautiful young French girls rushing back and forth. I tried for a second to let myself believe that he was right, that a whole new world of adventure and excitement could open up for me, Anna Trent, from Kidinsborough, here in Paris. The idea was ridiculous and absurd. The most exciting thing that happened to me was finding those boots I loved 70 percent off in the Debenhams sale. But as I drained the rest of my golden beer and looked around at the warm-tinged early Parisian evening, I let myself, just for a moment, wonder if it might be true.

6

I knocked on the door carefully. The Île de la Cité was an island—there were two—right in the middle of Paris, connected by a series of bridges. It was mostly large buildings—a huge hospital and the law courts and police stations in proud, imposing stone, with Notre Dame Cathedral marking the west side—but around the back of the smart edifices were little streets too, cobbled and twisted, marking out an older city, and it was down one of these I finally found myself, on a road called the rue des Ursins, which was down some steps from the pavement, near a bridge, and across from some cobbles surrounding a tiny triangle of garden.

The street numbers didn't seem to make any sense; they jumped hither and thither, and areas called arrondissements just seemed to pop out of nowhere. There's something about the first time you go to a place—it takes far, far too long and you notice little details that you then notice forever, like the wrought iron lamps that lit the way as night started to fall. But finally I tracked it down. It was on the sixth floor of an old building made of golden stone that had wrought iron balconies with flowerpots full of pansies and large, floor-length windows.

When I first saw it, my heart leapt. As I drew closer, I noticed that the stone was a little shabby, that the pansies were dead or plastic, that the beautiful windows had old rattling frames and were single-glazed. It was not a set of smart apartments, but rather a subdivided old house, rather neglected. I sighed. Our house was small and smelled of boy and lynx aftershave and fish fingers and sometimes our farty old dog, but my little room was warm and cozy. Mum liked to whack the heating up, and Dad would chide her for it getting too expensive, and it was double-glazed and nice and modern. I'd never lived in an old building before. It was almost impossible to work out what the color of the huge old door had once been; a sort of sandy red seemed to cover it, just about. There was a jumble of old bells with writing all over them, and the steps were worn smooth. I couldn't see the name—Sami—that I was meant to push, so I tentatively pushed at the door. It creaked ominously straight in front of me, and I stepped in.

"*Bonjour?*" I cried out. There was no response. "*Bonjour?*"

Nothing. There was a glassed door at the end of the broken parquet hallway that let in just enough light to let me see the dusty piles of old mail over the floor and a tired looking pot plant by the stairwell. The stairs led up into the dark. I fumbled a bit and found a light switch, turned it on, and moved upward—there was nothing on this floor—but before I was halfway up, the light went out. I cursed crossly under my breath and trailed my hand until I found another switch. This wasn't, it turned out, a light switch, but instead a loud doorbell that went off like a gun.

"ALLO?" shouted an old lady's voice. I knew I was meant to be on the top floor, so I cried out a quick "*Pardon*, Madame" and continued on my way.

What was with these accursed lights that couldn't stay on? One had to dart between them. The staircase was incredibly twisted and narrow, so it was difficult to get up without scrabbling a bit on my toes, and I was beginning to feel terribly nervous when I finally made it to the top. Down below, the lady whose bell I had rung by accident was shouting her head off now, saying things I couldn't make out, but I think one of them was police. I cursed again under my breath, some proper Anglo-Saxon words, hauling my now incredibly heavy bag up the steps.

Finally I emerged onto a tiny little landing with—thank goodness—its own light coming through a dirty skylight above me. It was a tiny space, like being inside a turret. Someone had put a little white book-shelf crammed full of books at the top of the steps, so I couldn't get my bag past it. On the other levels, there had been two apartments, but here there was only one, as if the building had run out. I stepped forward. Beside the low white door was a little brass plaque that had "Sami" written in very tiny letters. I blew out a breath of relief. I didn't fancy reliving the stairway of death. It then occurred to me that, if I was going to live here, I was going to have to negotiate the stairway of death on eight toes every day, but I put that thought out of my mind for once.

I knocked sharply on the door. "Hello?"

Inside, I heard the sound of someone moving about. Thank good-ness; I didn't know what I would do if I had to turn around again. *Probably just get back on the train*, I thought to myself. No. No, I wouldn't do that. Definitely not.

"*J'arrive!*" a voice called, sounding slightly panicked. There was a clattering noise inside. I wondered what was going on.

Finally, the door was flung open. A gigantically tall man stood there. His skin was a dark olive color, his eyebrows black and bushy, his jaw bristly and jutting. He was wearing a patterned robe which didn't appear to have much underneath it. He glanced at me without the slightest flicker of recognition or awareness whatsoever.

"*Bonjour?*" I said. "Anna Trent? From England?"

I worried suddenly that Claire hadn't done it right, hadn't managed to set it up, or there'd been some misunderstanding, or he'd changed his mind, or…

He squinted. "*Attends*," he commanded. "Wait."

He returned two seconds later with a huge pair of black-rimmed glasses. I sniffed. He smelled of sandalwood.

With the glasses on, he squinted once more.

"*La petite anglaise!*" he said, a sudden smile splitting his face. He switched to English. "Welcome! Welcome! Come in! Come in! I will say, I did forget. You will say, 'ow could you forget, and I will say...I will say...welcome à Paris!"

The second I stepped into the room, I could see there was absolutely no doubt that he had indeed forgotten. There was almost no hallway, just room for a hat stand with a collection of esoteric hats on it—I counted a fez, a trilby, and the head of a gorilla costume—then it opened out into a room. It wasn't a large room, but it was incredibly stuffed. There were capes and material, feathers, scissors, fur stoles, pillowcases, ashtrays, empty champagne bottles, and an enormous red sofa with huge cushions strewn about it and over the floor. In the corner was a kitchenette that had blatantly never been used. The peculiar man straightened up, even though the ceilings were much lower than I'd expected and he could hardly stand up; he must have been six foot five.

"*Non,*" he said sadly, looking around at the mess. "I did forget."

He turned to face me happily.

"But what if I said, yes, welcome, Anna Trent..."

He pronounced it "a-NA Tron."

"...thees is always my house prepared at its best for visitor? You would not like that."

I shook my head to indicate that I wouldn't.

"You are cross with me," he said. "You are sad."

I shook my head. I was neither of those things; I was just a bit overwhelmed and tearful and exhausted with traveling and as far away from home as I'd been in my whole life really, and I kind of just wanted a table and a chair and a cup of tea, not some crazy bohemian workshop super mess, if that was all right with everyone. I had no idea who this guy was, except I knew I had to share with someone who didn't work in the shop.

"What is all this stuff?" I said, gesticulating.

"Oh, I bring my work home," he said. "I work too hard, this is my problem."

This, I was to discover, was nothing like Sami's worst problem, but I took him at his word.

It turned out Sami worked at the Paris Opera in their costume department, earning next to nothing at all, with dozens of tiny seamstresses, making clothes for the opera productions. He'd really come to work in one of the big couture houses but had had no luck and was practicing his trade letting out stays for singers and complaining about fat tenors and sullen sopranos who insisted they needed space in their costumes to sing but were, he confided, just too greedy.

But that all came later. Now it just all seemed a big mess.

"I have a room for you!" he said. "It is nothing like this."

His face looked briefly panicked.

"Wait here," he said and vanished through a door at the back. From a quick count of the doors, I ascertained, with some relief, that there must be another bedroom and a bathroom. For a hideous second, I'd thought that might be it and that I would be stuck in one hideously messy room with a distracted giant.

Within a few moments, and looking rather as if he were concealing something about his person, Sami returned rather sheepishly.

"It is *prêt*, ready for you," he said, bowing from the waist. Sami would have, quite frankly, gotten killed at our school. Probably literally. It would have been on the news.

I followed with my clumpy bag, feeling very nondescript and plain, where he was pointing.

My old bedroom in Kidinsborough was very small, so it wasn't like I wasn't expecting it. But there's something about being thirty and walking into something tinier than a prison cell… It was absolutely minuscule. Tiny. The size of the single bed they'd squeezed in there—who knows how—and a tiny chest of drawers crammed up against it and nothing else at all; there just wasn't the space. I blinked once, twice. I wasn't going to start crying. For starters, there was nowhere private to do it. I must admit, I'd fantasized, maybe a tiny bit. About a little bitty en suite, maybe, or some grand space; I'd seen them in magazines. Paris had all those grand apartments with the posh rooms and marble fireplaces and high ceilings and…this was basically a coffin. Probably where the maids used to sleep or something. It was painted totally white, with dark brown scuffed parquet on the floor.

"What do you think?" said Sami. "Isn't it AMAZING?"

I put my head back out of the doorway.

Amazing? I wondered. What on earth must his be like?

"AMAZING!" he said. I blinked at him.

"Oh, AnNA Tron, she is very sad and cross with me," he said, making his face go sad. "Can I get you something?"

"Tea?" I ventured.

"I 'ave no tea."

"Coffee?"

"*Mais bien sûr!*"

He clattered happily over to the tiny kitchenette, while I advanced inside my little monk cell with my large purple bag. I put it on the bed—there was literally nowhere else it could possibly go—and clambered past the chest of drawers over to the window. And that's when I saw it. I gasped.

The window opened sideways and was full-length. I thought briefly of how many children must have fallen out of it. But I didn't think it for long before seeing past the net curtain and opening the catch, to find outside two extraordinary things: the tiniest balcony, only just big enough to fit a tiny wrought iron table and two wrought iron chairs, but directly in the path of the sun and, from six floors up on the Île de la Cité—Paris. Paris all around. The rooftops of the other buildings across the water, with tables out on their south-facing side. The road down, and the bridges all the way down the Seine. To my left, to the northwest, I could just make out the ominous looking black tip of La Défense, the great center of the financial district, which looks like a sinister black bridge. And everywhere, the teeming, pulsating life of the city, the noise insulated from six stories up—the little fruit van chugging its way furiously down the street; a collection of stunningly attractive people emerging from a sleek black car to a chic bar; two little lines of schoolchildren walking politely down the next street hand in hand. And if I craned my neck really, really far to the left, to the west, I could see it. The one and only unmistakable fretted iron of the Eiffel Tower.

I gazed and gazed and gazed at the pinkening skyline, as if I were thirsty and this was water. I could no longer feel the pain in my foot, or my longing for a shower, or my general exhaustion.

"Your café," said Sami, coming in my room without bothering to knock. "You really not like?"

I smiled.

"I didn't see the balcony. It's amazing. Amazing."

He had given me a tiny cup of black stuff with a sugar lump sitting next to it. I normally just like lattes or Nescafé. I looked at him.

"Have you got any milk for the coffee?" I asked apologetically.

"Milk? No. Milk is a feelthy thing. You suck the teets of a cow. No. Milk. No."

"Okay," I said.

"Brandy? I have a leetle brandy."

And as it was such a gorgeous evening, I said yes, why not, and we sat out on my little *balcon* (he had one too, on the opposite side of the sitting room; we could wave to each other in the morning) and drank coffee with brandy in it and looked out over Paris. I don't think if anyone could have looked up and seen me (which they couldn't, because we were up in the eaves, where pigeons flew by and the sky turned pink and yellow and lavender, and there was no one else there but the birds) that they would have thought for a second that I was anything other than as much a part of Paris as anybody else, and I looked out on the strange and extraordinary foreign landscape and I wondered. I wondered.

• • • •

1972

Claire was totally charmed by Arnaud and Claudette, her charges. They were incredibly polite, thought her accent was hilarious, and tested her endlessly on words she did and didn't know, marveling at the way she said "Mickey Mouse."

In return, she let them dictate the pace of the lazy spring days; normally a stroll around the play park of the Tuileries, in the shadow of the Eiffel Tower; a goûter, or snack, of warm croissants, torn apart and guzzled on a bench, followed by home for lunch. The two children still took naps in the afternoon, leaving Claire free to read or do her French grammar (Madame was very strict on the matter), and on Fridays, Madame liked to take the children to their swimming lessons, so she had the afternoon off.

At first, unsure what to do with herself, she took herself off to the exhibitions and museums she felt she ought to see, as if ticking things off in a guidebook. Madame would ask her questions about them when she returned and occasionally ask her to take the children. But it was hard for Claire to enjoy them; she felt lonely, among large families and young lovers and lines of schoolchildren nattering away without a care in the language she found so difficult to master. She didn't know a soul here, and Kidinsborough felt a long way away.

But as she grew more confident, she began to stride farther afield, and she found, gradually, her fear falling away as she saw and visited more— Montmartre, with its winding streets, odd, highly perched church, and candy-colored steps stole her heart almost immediately. She spent many days there, looking at the young women with their scooters, helmetless, scarves tied around their thick hair, chatting and laughing with the young men on the steps, their cigarettes drooping from their mouths. She spent warm afternoons with books in the Luxembourg Gardens, seeing her legs go brown. Everywhere, it seemed, were couples kissing, chatting, gesticulating in the air, sharing a picnic with wine in unmarked bottles. To feel alone at seventeen is to feel very lonely indeed, and even as she looked forward all week to her free time, she found the Friday afternoons sometimes very long. It was a relief, as her French improved, to be able to slip into a cinema on the boulevard du Montparnasse, where it didn't matter that she was by herself, or at least not so much. There were, she had heard, places for young English people to meet, but Mme. LeGuarde had made it clear she didn't think they were a good idea if she was to have a proper French experience, and Claire always wanted to please.

So after meeting Thierry, she couldn't deny it. She wanted to see him again—partly because she had liked him, she thought, but mostly because he had shown some interest in her, and at the moment, nobody was showing the least bit of interest in her; they were too busy being in Paris and being glamorous and busy and having stuff to do that she simply didn't have. Two Fridays after the party, she found herself straying closer and closer to the part of the Île de la Cité where she'd heard, from fervent eavesdropping at one of Madame's lunches, that the new shop was to open, the first of its kind in Paris. (Lunch with Claire's mum when her friends came around was a large tray of homemade ham sandwiches on white bread with margarine and a packet of chocolate cookies for after, dished up with pints of dark brown tea. Lunch for Madame's friends involved much planning, four courses, an ice bucket full of champagne, and lots of running back and forth to the fishmongers early in the morning.) There was Persion's, which had been in situ since 1794 and was respected for that, but there was a rumor that its products had grown as dusty as its upper stories, and its offerings hadn't changed in centuries.

Friday afternoon in early July on the Île de la Cité was hot and sticky and bustling with tourists. Away from the formal "placement" of the organized streets and wide boulevards, the far corner betrayed its twisty, hugger-mugger medieval origins: little alleyways springing hither and thither, roads narrowing to nearly nothing or ending abruptly at the wall of one of the great churches. It was hot; Claire had taken out a summer dress that she'd brought from home the weekend before, when she was to accompany the children as the family went to a wedding. Mme. LeGuarde had immediately shaken her head, pointed out to Claire that it didn't actually fit very well, and disappeared. When she returned, it was with a soft brown and green silk dress, very loose and almost weightless.

"This was mine," she said. "After the children, pfft. I cannot wear."

Claire pointed out that she was very slim still, which Mme. LeGuarde knew but waved away.

"It does not matter, my shape," she said. "It is my age, my outlook that cannot wear it."

For a moment, she looked sad.

"Oh, these days come and go," she said. Claire had barely met her husband, Bernard; he traveled almost constantly for work and seemed tired and distracted when he did appear. But the LeGuardes were, to her, so grown-up; far more so than her own warm family. They were sophisticated, worldly socialites who dressed for dinner and drank cocktails. Claire simply assumed that anything they did was correct.

The dress was totally out of style—fashionable women in Paris were wearing soft flared denims on their long skinny legs, big hair, huge sunglasses, and large, soft felt hats tied around with Hermès scarves. But the soft leaf pattern and pulled-in waist suited Claire's shape and made a virtue out of her slenderness; by making her look petite and delicate, the dress turned her short stature into a positive attribute. In her jeans, she was often overshadowed.

"There," said Madame. "Much better."

Claire walked out with a basket to pick up some bits and bobs and with soft sandals on her feet. Several men were actively appreciative as she walked past, often with an approving smile or a murmured, "Très jolie, mam'zelle," *which made a difference to the shouts and wolf whistles girls were subjected to at home and added a bounce to her steps, and her nerves added a pinkness to her face and a sparkle to her eyes.*

Of course, she told herself, he was hardly likely to remember someone he'd met for two seconds at a party. And he would doubtless be far too busy; the shop would be a huge success, and he wouldn't have two seconds to spend on her. Still, what would she even say to him if he did? Maybe he wouldn't even be there, too busy off being creative somewhere else?

She decided to pretend to herself that anyway, she was only going to find some lovely chocolate, nothing more, and try to stay concentrating on how excited Arnaud and Claudette would be when she brought some home. Yes. That was all.

There was a bustle of people outside the shop as she arrived; already the buzz around town was growing. Claire couldn't help smiling; she was so pleased. It seemed such a bold thing to do, to announce to the world that you had made something wonderful, and everyone was welcome to come and pay you money to have it. She couldn't imagine anything she could do possibly being worth that amount of attention. There was as yet no name painted above the door.

She advanced a little closer, drawn by the window. A crowd stood, just looking at it, and Claire realized why as she came closer—it was an entire, beautiful scene in the window, a fairy-tale castle with a carriage arriving at the door and a princess emerging. In the sky above was a hot air balloon, Montgolfier *in French. Every single bit was sculpted from chocolate. There was white piping on the princess's lacy gown, and the castle windows were of dark chocolate, cut into shapes. A tree had chocolate leaves and the balloon white chocolate designs inlaid on it. In the middle of the courtyard of the castle stood a fountain, chocolate bubbling through it merrily.*

It was so childlike and adorable and witty, Claire couldn't help it—she burst into a huge smile and clapped her hands together. As she did so, she suddenly felt someone's eyes upon her and glanced up. Frozen on the other side of the glass, clearly in the middle of talking to somebody else, was Thierry, suddenly stock still and gazing at her like he couldn't tear his face away. Claire felt her smile fade from her face and her cheeks go pink. She bit her lip anxiously. Without even realizing it, it was as if all the crowds, the customers, the noise and bustle of the summer in the city had completely vanished. Tentatively, she raised her hand in a gesture of hello and pressed it against the vitrine, *the shop window. Thierry put down his scoop—his customer started talking to him, but he completely ignored her—and raised his great bearlike paw. Claire noticed what she hadn't seen before; his thick black eyelashes were ridiculously long—they protruded over the dark brown, lively eyes and hooded lids. She felt, even through the window, as if she could see every last one, trace every hair, every cell.*

Suddenly someone, trying to get a better look, jostled her out of the way. Instantly it was as if the spell was broken. She staggered slightly to the side, and in an instant, Thierry was out of the door, pushing his way through the crowd.

"Are you all right? Are you hurt? Who did that?" he barked.

The crowd sidled away from one slightly awkward-looking small man.

"You!" said Thierry, waggling his finger directly in the man's face. "You are banned from this shop forever. Go!"

The man blushed violently, muttered some words of apology in Claire's direction, then disappeared.

"Bon!" said Thierry. "Everyone else, come in. Well, only if you wish to experience the best chocolate in the world. Otherwise, it is unimportant to me what you would like to do."

People started flooding into the shop, but Thierry led from the front, a huge arm around Claire's shoulders. Next to him, she thought, all the other men looked puny.

He led her straight through the selling area, with its original '30s golden lettering and polished glass cases. The walls were lined, Claire saw, with great old jars for different kinds of sugar—vanilla, demerara, violet, lemon, icing. He led her through to the back of the shop, where a grumpy old man with a unibrow was tending, and nodded him through to the front. The man went, looking sullen.

Claire hardly noticed. She had just seen the room for the first time. To her, the far back wall was a flower garden. Many of the herbs and plants she didn't even recognize; her family's meals at home were plain affairs. Her mother had attempted spaghetti Bolognese once and everyone had felt it dangerously daring. Mme. LeGuarde believed in eating lightly and cleanly, so there was much plain steamed fish and vast amounts of salad and vegetables. But this was something else; all the greenery sent its competing perfumes into the air, set against the warm, comforting, utterly solid scent of chocolate everywhere; warm and thick and comforting, the scent, Claire realized later, of Thierry himself.

"You like it?" he said.

She beamed, her face and heart full. "I…I love it!" she said, completely sincerely. She saw how much this pleased him; he couldn't hide anything he felt in his face.

"Here, here," he said, beckoning her to the large copper vat. He dropped in the long ladle spoon, then drew it up to her. Then he stopped. "Non," he said. "Close your eyes."

Claire looked at him quizzically. Inside her chest, she could feel her heart beat. "Why?" she said.

"Oh! Coquette!" he said smiling. "So I can kidnap you and sell you to white traders. Then, so I can chop up your body and disguise it in the chocolate."

He took a handkerchief from his pocket—"clean, I most solemnly vow"—and tied it around her eyes.

"It is so," he said, his voice suddenly disturbingly close to her ear, "you can truly taste it. So you shut out distractions."

Claire, her eyes tight shut against the handkerchief which smelled exactly as he did—of chocolate and tobacco—felt as distracted as she had ever been in her entire life.

"Only then can you truly appreciate it."

She felt his breath briefly on her neck, then he left. Then, the next second, she felt something at her lips prodding and pushing them aside— the spoon of the ladle.

"Take it," said Thierry, and she opened her mouth a little wider as he tipped in a large mouthful of just melted chocolate, warmed to creaminess, the same temperature as her body, filling her mouth. It was absolutely extraordinarily sensual and good. She was conscious, even as she tasted it, that he was, for once, silent, his eyes on her, watching her.

At last it was gone, and she felt her tongue round her lips, looking for more. Now his voice was lower, all mischief gone.

"You like?"

"Yes," she said.

7

Sami had come over from Algeria, I learned, at the age of six on a scholarship from a kindly great-uncle who had done well in France. He was considered the most promising and the only boy in his family and had been sent to good schools—he had seen his parents only once a year from that time forward and expected to go on to a good university. Instead, he had spent all his time pouring over fashion magazines and choosing clothes. It had been, he said, with commendable understatement for someone so flamboyant, a difficult time for everyone.

But he had finally worked his own way through fashion college and had made it alone ever since, poorer, he said, than Job, renting this tiny eyrie so he didn't have to commute too far and taking all his exercise, he explained, getting up and down the seven flights of stairs, something I was to learn myself only too quickly. He worked late in the evenings, but I was not to worry, as he was very difficult to wake in the mornings, a fact I discovered to be true as he snored loud enough to shake the entire flat.

That first morning was freezing. My alarm woke me in my little white cell, and I was completely disoriented at first. Although I was exhausted—I'd fallen asleep as soon as my head hit the pillow—I felt a sudden jolt of excitement. I was here! In Paris! Alone! From the other side of the sitting room came a deep and resonant snoring that wouldn't have allowed me to fall asleep again even if I'd wanted to. I jumped up, had a bath (there wasn't much hot water in the tiny half-tub; I hoped it would heat up again before Sami woke up), then looked at my map of Paris—I should be right around the corner and had been ordered to present myself there at 5:30 a.m., which was clearly ridiculous and possibly just a first-day test, I told myself. It was still dark outside. I didn't know how to work the odd stove-top coffee pot Sami had left on top of the cooker and didn't want to start making noise before I'd been there five minutes, so I cleaned my teeth quickly, added an extra sweater, and made my way down the pitch-black stairwell, trying to make it from light switch to light switch. To my utter horror, I accidentally pressed the first floor bell again, and ran out like a wet cat before the voice started up.

• • • •

63 rue Chanoinesse, the address of the shop, was a large white building, similar to the one I was staying in, though not quite so scruffy. Within two streets, the boulevards had widened slightly. There was a beautiful square leading to a church and smart shops and cafés under striped awnings. The sun was just starting to creep over the horizon, and people were up and about; little trucks going to markets and restaurants full of leeks and flower bulbs and lobsters; bundled-up quiet people making their way to cleaning jobs; bus drivers, yawning and stretching in their warmly lit cabs. Silent bicycles squeaked past me. On every corner was a bakery, casting a pool of light forward; the smell of warm bread was intoxicating, but alas, even they weren't open yet. I felt like a child with my nose pressed against the window, my stomach completely hollow. I hadn't had the energy to sort out dinner the night before and had ended up foraging old sandwiches in my luggage.

After a couple of wrong turns, suddenly there it was in front of me. I saw it right away, then smelled it a moment later. *Le Chapeau Chocolat de Thierry Girard* was written on the brown-painted walls in pale rose-colored script; it wasn't blaring, shouting out about the shop. It was a gentle note that they were there, almost easy to overlook and more impressive for that in its confidence. Outside stood a young man smoking a cigarette. As I watched, another, larger man came up to him and gesticulated at him, and as if in response, the younger man threw his cigarette into the gutter. I wasn't fluent enough to divine whether the older man was telling him off about his smoking or he just moved his arms a lot. They turned to go when I stepped onto the cobbles tentatively and caught their attention.

"Uh, *bonjour*?" I said. I wondered which of them was the famous Thierry Girard. It couldn't be the young one, surely.

The two men stared at me. Then they looked at each other, and the younger one clasped his hand to his forehead. I didn't need much French to know what that meant. That meant "I have completely forgotten that you were coming today" in every language in the world.

"*J'arrive…d'Angleterre*"—I've come from England, I stuttered.

"*Oui oui oui oui*," said the little one, looking furious with himself. The larger one let loose a stream of invective at the younger one, which the younger one totally ignored. He had wild, romping, curly, black gypsy hair, a huge nose, and an intense expression and was looking longingly at his discarded cigarette.

Finally, his expressive face seemed to decide something.

"WELCOME," he said loudly in English. "*Benoît, voici…*"

He pointed his arm toward me, clearly without a clue as to what I was called. This was beginning to feel like something of a theme.

"I'm Anna…Anna Trent," I said.

The larger man looked mutinous. He had the build of a rugby player, solid and wide.

"AnNA Tron," he said crossly. "*Bonjour*, madame."

And he turned and stomped into the shop. The younger one didn't seem to see anything strange or rude about this at all. In fact, he smiled cheerfully.

"He doesn't say much," he said. He glanced back toward the shop. "I believe that may be it for today."

"*Vous êtes…*Thierry?" Are you Thierry? I asked tentatively. At this he laughed, revealing very white teeth.

"*Non non non. Je ne suis pas* Thierry. I am Frédéric. MUCH more handsome." He looked at the pavement. "So, AnNA Tron, shall we see if we have some things for you to do?"

"Did you forget I was coming?"

"*Non non non.* Yes. Yes, I did do that."

He looked up at me with a charming smile. "You understand…many things happen…many nights… I cannot remember all lovely girls."

Even though it wasn't even 6:00 a.m. and I knew for a fact I looked like death, and he looked a little peaky himself and had no clue what I was doing there, I was absolutely impressed by the fact that he still felt a bit duty-bound to chat me up. Not seriously or intently, just as if he was passing by. I wasn't tempted but I was quite impressed.

From the outside, the shop looked like nothing at all, a tiny, discreet storefront leading to a selling space the size of somebody's front room. At the moment, it was empty, just glass display cases polished clear, standing to attention. The streetlights outside cast an orange glow from their wrought iron posts through the front windows, and I could make out an old polished wooden floor and shelving filled with boxes behind the cabinets. Over everything lay a layer of scent, a heavy deep smell of dark, dense chocolate, thick as tobacco smoke. It was as if it were rubbed into the wood, used as varnish on the floor, as if the whole building were steeped in it. I wondered how long I would notice it for; it was almost intoxicating, even in the empty room.

Frédéric had already threaded past to a small door set in the back wall. It had a swing door and a half round window, like an old-fashioned restaurant kitchen. I tried not to let the door hit me on the rebound.

"'Ere we are!" said Frédéric. "Willy Wonka *existe!*"

I smiled at him, but it was true. I had never seen such an odd room in my entire life. It wasn't a room at all, in fact. Back at Braders, everything was done in large industrial stainless steel vats, something that never failed to disappoint every child I had ever met. (Well, either that or they refused to believe me.) But here, the tiny front room of the shop widened out considerably to form a large glassed-in back warehouse, not unlike a huge greenhouse. It was peeling and very old and must have been built in what at one time would have been a garden for the *bâtiment*, the building. It was wood-framed and rickety, but I could feel a humming in the air of an ionizer; the space was perfectly controlled for temperature and humidity. Frédéric nodded toward a large industrial sink by the door and I quickly washed my hands with antibacterial gel.

The room was lit warmly with lamps, not fluorescent lights. At the back, window boxes of fresh herbs lined the sill: rosemary, lavender, mint, and a small chili pepper tree. It made the room feel even more like a greenhouse. Beans were ground in the large brass machines that looked like coffee grinders. Three large copper pots—dark, milk, and white, I assumed—stood in the middle of the room, but there were a whole load of burners, test tubes, ovens, pipes, and utensils that I had simply never seen before in my life. It smelled like heaven but looked like a mad gardener's shed.

There was no chocolate to be seen. Not a drop anywhere. The copper pots were empty, the arms not turning. The smell hung heavy in the air, but apart from that, the place could have been a museum. Frédéric approached, holding a tiny cup filled with sticky black coffee which I accepted gratefully, choking it down.

"The elves come," he said, smiling at my obvious shock. "Oh yes. For Thierry Girard, we start anew every day."

An unpleasant thought struck me suddenly.

"You scrub everything out? Every day?"

Frédéric nodded solemnly.

"...and now I'm here."

Frédéric's impish face turned solemn all of a sudden. He nodded. I realized then that I hadn't thought too much about the actual "work" part, just the "getting away" part. In my old job, I'd advised on flavorings, worked on quality control, carried a clipboard. And I supposed I had allowed myself a little fantasy—of aiding and perhaps even inspiring the greatest chocolatier of his generation, of fluently swapping tips and ideas with his customers, of perhaps even coming up with my own brilliant new recipes, capturing the heart of the famous store...

I wondered gloomily what the French was for "rubber gloves."

"Eet is a great experience and privilege," said Frédéric gravely.

"Is that what they told you when you started?" I said.

"*Oui*," said Frédéric, clearly not in the least sorry. He looked like a freed sprite. He looked at my hands. "I would not spend too much money on *le mani, non?*"

It was true; I had gotten my hands done specially for coming. In a French polish, on purpose. Seeing it now made me want to bite them off.

"But that is just one of many, many interesting things you will be doing through the day," said Frédéric, raising his eyebrows. "Come, I will show you."

And I couldn't deny it; it was interesting. It had never even occurred to me that chocolate was something that needed to be eaten fresh. Indeed, one of its great benefits was that it could be stored, could travel. It wasn't like milk or eggs.

"Thierry would describe it to you," said Frédéric, "but he does not like to talk to us leetle people so much. He likes everybody to think he is a genius inventor like the Wizard of Oz who does not need us leetle ants who scurry in his house. So I, Frédéric, shall tell you."

He took me to the back of the workshop and started grinding the first of the large green cocoa beans.

"Fresh chocolate is of the utmost importance," he said, as if reciting from a script. "For with the freshness, you get lightness, and churn, and a delicacy that does not come from a huge slab that sits on the shelf for three months, getting heavier and heavier and sinking into itself. *NON!* This is not good. Chocolate should be treated as a delicacy, something to be plucked fresh from the trees."

Benoît had laid down a large box of raw cocoa beans and fired up a huge industrial oven.

"From first principles," said Frédéric. The cocoa beans smelled dark and wonderful. Benoît poured them into a huge rotating drum that looked like the inside of a washing machine. The noise was phenomenal.

"Okay now," said Frédéric after about fifteen minutes, after I had wandered around smelling the delicious herbs, lined up on rows along the back of the greenhouse. Then he said something I didn't understand and motioned me to copy him as he, ferociously quick, started cracking the tiny beans with a hammer and unleashing their warm chocolaty insides. Every fourth one, he threw away.

"I thought you made chocolate," he said, puzzled as I stared at him in disbelief.

"A machine made chocolate," I said. "I kind of switched it on and off."

He made a very Gallic pouting face at me. Benoît barely glanced up before continuing on with his hammer. This seemed extraordinary, like we were making chocolate in the Middle Ages.

"Handmade is how we do things," Frédéric said patiently. He'd lost his flirtatious edge, I noticed. Perhaps he only liked girls who knew how to hand-make chocolate. That must cut his prospective pool down quite substantially.

Frédéric nodded toward a spare hammer. I took it and tentatively hit a bean. Nothing. I hit it harder. *Splat.* It went flat on the ground. Benoît wordlessly took it and threw it in the bin. I gulped. I wasn't entirely sure how much help I was going to be here.

"Perhaps you just watch for now," said Frédéric. And I did and noticed a quick little flick of the wrists they made as they assaulted the beans. It was a bit like a very, very good game of Whack-a-Mole.

Then Frédéric took out a surprisingly dainty mini vac and blew away all the husks. I finished up my scalding little coffee, which tasted less like coffee and more like a very strong cleaning solution. There was absolutely no way I could drink the filthy stuff. I would never get used to it.

"Now, we feed the beans," he said, indicating a large industrial grinder.

"So you do use a machine," I said, as if I'd scored a point. I got a look.

Benoît came back in, lugging in huge crates of milk, butter, and cream from outside. It was all in rough, reused glass. I hadn't seen milk delivered in a glass bottle for a long time. Benoît was calling a farewell to someone out of the back door. It still wasn't light, but the sky wasn't as pitch-black as it had been.

"We use only one dairy," said Frédéric. "The Oise. It delivers every morning. Swiss would be better, alas, but time is of the urgency to us."

He started up the grinding machine. The noise was incredible. Then, little by little, he fed in the precious beans, gently and care-fully. Gradually, at the bottom, a thick, dark liquid started to gather, strained through a net in the collection bottle. Frédéric stared at it happily. When it finally stopped, I straightened up carefully.

"Now what?" I said.

We just started with the liquid and hurled stuff at it at Braders, but I didn't want to admit that.

"You conch," said Frédéric.

The word was the same in English. To conch was to mix up the dif-ferent ingredients, the levels, to make the chocolate dark, light, milk, flavored. A tiny mistake one way or the other would make it disgust-ing, too sweet, grainy, or crystalline. Our machines were calibrated to make everything the same every time; they used cheap milk powder and life prolongers and additives.

"Of course, that is for Thierry," said Frédéric, lowering his head. "It is the most important, the most sacred part."

To conch by hand was very difficult. And then it would need refining and tempering so it held together. I raised an eyebrow.

"This is for tomorrow," explained Frédéric, and indeed, Benoît had now moved on to pouring a thick gooey mass from a pot and working it back and forth with a spatula while he stirred another pot on the stove gently. Normally people would use a thermometer for this, but Benoît had been practically raised in the shop, I learned later. He knew it as instinctively as a top musician knows when his instrument is out of tune. If he was happy, he would hum tunelessly. If he was not, he would dump everything back in the huge pot and start all over again until it was perfect.

Finally, he was ready.

"*Rien plus*," shouted Frédéric, only just audible above the din of the grinder. "No more. Nothing but the finest of dark beans from Costa Rica, the finest of fresh cream milk from the best fed cows this side of Normandy, the finest cane sugar from Jamaica, all churned to perfection in the traditional way, not by huge machines full of fat and preservative and old bits of *truc* and the Band-Aids of the *paisants, non*?"

The colors blending together and being poured into molds looked absolutely beautiful; in fact, looking at them, you'd be hard pressed to disagree with Thierry's philosophy, that chocolate was something meant to be made fresh and consumed fresh, no less than coffee or a croissant. And the smell was warmer, richer, purer than anything back in the UK, where we'd used a hefty dose of vegetable fats to bolster up the mix (which was why so many people who loved British chocolate found the posh stuff so hard to take to—it was the comforting fats they really liked).

"Do not dip the fingers," ordered Frédéric, but I would never, ever touch food being prepared; I'd had enough tedious health and safety courses to have gotten that one through my head. I wasn't an idiot. Frédéric was, however, passing me up a long ladle, which looked to be one solid piece of curved metal with a tiny tasting spoon at the end. Benoît stood out of my way.

"Attention," he warned. "Be careful."

Frédéric shook his head but declined to say any more, simply watching my face curiously and intently. He was staring very closely at my lips. I found it oddly off-putting, but in a nice way. I carefully let down the ladle and scooped up a mouthful of the pale brown liquid.

Blowing on it to let it cool, Frédéric staring at me all the while, I raised it to my lips.

Heroin addicts often say that all they are ever doing is chasing that first hit, the first time they felt wrapped in cotton wool, all the worries of the world behind them. I wouldn't say I was quite as dramatic as that. Nonetheless, the moment the still-warm, gently thickening substance hit my tongue, I really did think, for an instant, that I was going to fall onto the table—no, worse, that I was going to DIVE in, to shovel every morsel of that sweet (but not too sweet), creamy, (but not sickly), dense, deeply flavored, rich, smooth, all-enveloping, chocolatey goodness. It felt like someone giving you a warm hug. As soon as I had swallowed it, I wanted the taste back in my mouth again, wanted to cram myself full of it. I found myself embarrassed suddenly, blushing, as I noticed Frédéric's eyes still on my lips, intently watching me. My hand went automatically to dip the spoon again, then at the last minute, I realized this would look desperate, unprofessional, greedy, hungry, or risky. Instead, I lifted it out, empty. Frédéric raised an eyebrow.

"It's…" What could I say? That it pissed on almost anything else I'd ever eaten anywhere? That it was so good I felt like I wanted to almost cry? That I would never eat anything else as long as I lived? And it was still not even set.

"It's very good," I said finally. Frédéric glanced at Benoît, who shrugged. Just as the roaster in the corner was heating up the room uncomfortably, the air conditioner clicked on and a cooling hum began. Everything here was rickety, antiquated, and held together with tape. But there was absolutely no doubt that it worked. It worked beyond the wildest dreams of Braders, beyond the wildest dreams of every chocolate I'd ever eaten in my entire life.

"Eet ees better than very good, *non?*" Frédéric asked. He seemed insulted.

"I'm sorry," I said. "It's...*le style anglais.*"

He seemed happier about this. Typical British stiff upper lip couldn't be passionate about anything, I suspected, as far as he was concerned. In truth, I didn't want to tell him how impressed I was. It would make me sound like a rube, like I knew nothing about chocolate when in fact I'd been sent there to help. The gap between what I'd been making and what they were doing here was like the difference between a liquid dish soap bottle rocket and the NASA Mars mission. So I decided it was best to keep my mouth shut. At least, until I could fill it with more of that unbelievable chocolate. In secret.

So I stayed quiet as Frédéric, with some relish, showed me where the cleaning equipment was kept and what my duties were, got me to hammer pounds of cocoa beans until I stopped ruining their stock, showed me how to winnow for husks, and took me through the schedule of the shop. By the time we were finished, it was nearly 10:00 a.m. and the sun was shining strongly through the long planters of herbs, making it look more like a greenhouse than ever. I wondered if we were about to open, as Frédéric and Benoît glanced nervously at their watches, but as it turned out five minutes later, they were not. The door was unlocked, then thrown open with a spectacular clang. Benoît suddenly made himself completely invisible. The jolly puckish look on Frédéric's features was replaced with a kind of servile watchfulness. I looked around behind me as the swing doors into the little factory swung heavily.

"*ALLONS-Y!*" LET'S GO! came a huge, booming voice.

Of all the surprises Claire had vouchsafed me, of all the confusions, this was by far the weirdest.

The way she had spoken, the way she had gone pink when she spoke of him, it was clear to me that this had been someone serious in her life, whereas whenever she mentioned her ex-husband, Richard, it was with pained courtesy.

You could still see in her the traces of the younger woman she had been; she'd been beautiful. She still was, in a certain light, when the years of pain weren't so strongly etched on her brow.

I had fantasized, perhaps, of a suave, gray-haired type, perhaps with jet black eyebrows, wearing chef's whites or maybe a very well-cut suit. Smart and stylish, just like her—chic and a little bit distant. Perhaps we would smile wryly when Claire's name came up, or, perhaps sadly, he would barely remember her at all, just a girl from very long ago who had had a wild crush on him, a summer of his youth, but nothing to do with his real life at all. Romantic and handsome, obviously, perhaps a little sad…

None of these described Thierry Girard.

I don't know if Thierry spoke any English. I couldn't imagine how he made his trips to Australia and America, where he was feted and famous, if he couldn't. But I never heard him speak a single word. He was huge; he never spent any time in the shop without making it look as if there wasn't any room for anybody else. His belly, normally enswathed in a huge white apron, seemed to be a separate entity from himself, as it entered rooms before he did.

"Who is this?" he boomed as he entered the kitchen. "Frédéric, have you been bringing night girls home with you again?"

At this stage, my French was a beat behind what was actually being said, so it was too late to realize I was being horribly insulted until a moment or so later. Which was a relief because if I'd have shot my mouth off, I'd have been out of a job about two milliseconds later.

"This is AnNA Tron," said Frédéric. "The new kitchen assistant."

Thierry lowered his enormous face toward mine. He had a little beard, which was lucky as his face was so sunk in fat that without it, it would have been borderline featureless. His little black eyes were like raisins stuck in a huge muffin. His skin was doughy, and hair came out of his flat nostrils. He gazed at me.

"Women in among my chocolate," he said. "I'm not sure."

I was taken aback. You would never hear this type of thing in the UK. Just as I was about to get annoyed about it, his enormous meaty shoulders shook with a huge belly laugh.

"I am joking! I joke! I joke!"

He looked at me, then suddenly snapped his fingers.

"I know who you are!"

I wasn't at all sure he would.

"You are Claire's friend."

I nodded.

"Ha! She spoke French like a dog eats salad."

I bristled. "She was a wonderful teacher."

His eyes blinked rapidly, twice. "Ah yes. I'm sure she was. I can imagine she was. Mind you, she was a terrible nanny... Although, *alors*, perhaps that was my fault..."

He drifted off then and I shifted uncomfortably. I wasn't at all sure how much he knew about Claire's illness, nor how serious it was.

"And you were ill?"

"I'm fine," I said stoutly. I wasn't really in the mood for volunteering exactly what was wrong with me unless somebody absolutely had to ask.

"You are fine for working hard, yes?"

"Without a doubt," I said, smiling as hard as I could.

"*Bon. Bon.*"

His face looked far away again.

"And Claire...she is also ill."

I nodded, not quite trusting myself to speak. He looked as if he were about to ask more, then stopped himself.

"*Alors*. Welcome, welcome. Do you know your chocolate?"

I looked into his big friendly giant's face sincerely. This I could answer.

"I do, sir. I've worked in chocolate for ten years."

He looked at me expectantly.

"Yours is the best," I said simply, not sure I could trust my French to elaborate. He paused, then the huge laugh was back.

"Listen to her!" he yelled. "Alice! ALICE! Come, you must hear this. A countryman of yours."

A languid, incredibly scrawny woman who must have been about fifty—but a really, really well-preserved fifty, her lipstick red on her wide mouth, her hair a perfect black helmet with an elegant swoop of pure white at the front—emerged into the back room. She was wearing cigarette pant trousers and a man's jacket and looked—there was no two ways about it—absolutely amazing. She was originally English but, I would discover, kept insisting that she had lived in Paris for so long, she had forgotten it all, when what she actually meant was she didn't want to waste time speaking to a guttersnipe like me or any of the English press–reading expat clusters who gathered together by the Shakespeare bookshop or the Frog or the Smiths on the rue de Rivoli. The best way to annoy Alice was to guess she was British before she opened her mouth, something I often prompted people to do. Which was childish, but she really was very rude to me.

She raised an eyebrow at Thierry.

"*Chéri*?"

"We have an English girl!"

Alice looked at me and I was suddenly very conscious of my plain skirt, my flat shoes, my Gap bag, my morning hair.

"Evidently," she said. I couldn't believe this snotty cow was English. Well, I could, but she couldn't have looked more French had she been wearing a beret, a small twirled mustache, and a Breton shirt and been carrying a chain of onions around her neck while riding a bicycle and surrendering a war.

"Hello," I said in English.

"*Bonjour*," she replied, then immediately glanced elsewhere in the room as if bored to death. I don't know exactly what had made Thierry go from lovely Claire to this, but no wonder he ate all the time.

Thierry beckoned me over. First, he turned his attention to the fresh cocoa. Frédéric added it to a large vat, and Thierry, with a deftness unexpected in such a large man, flicked the tap so the vat filled up with warm, gently steaming, thick chocolate liquid, followed by the milk, and he added a fresh powder snowfall of sugar, stopping, tasting, stopping, tasting, so quickly he looked like a blur. "Yes, no, yes, no, more, quick!" he yelled as the men rushed to follow his bidding. Finally he declared himself satisfied.

"Now we really start," he pronounced.

"*Lavendre!*" he barked, and Frédéric rushed to chop some off the box at the end of the room. Thierry chopped it incredibly fine with a knife so quickly I thought he would lose a finger, then popped it, along with a tiny crystal bottle of lavender essence so potent that, as soon as he opened the little flacon, the entire room was overcome with the scent, like a spring meadow. Delicately, his little finger tilted upward, he let two…three drops into the basin, whisking all the time with his other hand. The tiny purple flecks of the plant were almost completely hidden, and he paced across the room one, two, three times, his left hand working furiously, his right holding the basin close. Occasionally he would stop, dip in a finger, lick, and resume, possibly adding a tiny drop more cream or a little of the dark chocolate from the other vat. Finally he announced himself satisfied and stepped away from the vat. Benoît carried it over to the side of the oven, where it would be shaped and melted and tempered, ready for tomorrow.

Then Thierry hollered "molds," and immediately, Frédéric was there with the fresh batch. He poured the chocolate expertly into the molds without spilling a drop, then inserted the tray into the large industrial fridge. Without pausing, he turned around; Benoît had already silently placed a large box of small jellies in front of him. Thierry chopped them into the tiniest of diamond shapes, each exactly alike and perfect. By the time he had finished, the chocolate had hardened and he removed them briskly from the fridge, turning the mold upside down so thirty-two perfect chocolates popped out onto the workshop top. He pressed the diamonds of jellied fruit into the tops of the whirls, then, with a mere glance, sent one down to me.

"Tell me what you think," he said.

I bit into it. The soft sweet edge of citrus—it must have been cut from the lime plant—mellowed the perfectly balanced chocolate; the entire thing tasted so light it could have been good for you. The chocolate flavor didn't fade away in the mouth; its richness intensified, grew stronger. The tiny tart jelly on the top perfectly stopped the sweetness from overpowering the rest of the bonbon. It was perfect, exquisite. I smiled in pure happiness.

"That is what I like to see, heh?" Thierry indicated to the rest of the room. "That is the face I like. Always the face I like. Today we will make lavender four hundred piece, rosemary and *confiture*, mint…"

He turned to Alice. "You want to try?"

She gave him a stony look.

"I joke," he said to me. "She does not eat. Like a robot."

"I do eat," said Alice frostily. "I just eat food, not poison."

The wonderful aftertaste of the chocolate suddenly turned ashy in my mouth and I wanted to cough. Thierry looked at me mischievously and winked broadly, and I smiled back, but I wasn't sure I liked that either, being lumped in with the massive fatties.

"It passes?" said Thierry.

"It is sublime," I said honestly. Frédéric smiled at me, which gave me the impression that I wasn't doing so badly so far. Thierry snapped his fingers and Benoît gave him an espresso into which he poured copious amounts of sugar, then necked it. There was a silence in the room for one hanging half-second, then he announced, "Finish!"

He and Alice swept òut of the workroom, and the men immediately started to move. Frédéric gave me my mop and instructed me to basically wash and polish anything that wasn't tied down. Once they'd gotten going, they moved with awesome speed, turning out Thierry's creation exactly over and over again with huge molds; the lime, then the rosemary and jam, which sounded very peculiar to me until they let me taste it. As soon as I had tried it, I couldn't imagine why anyone would ever eat anything else.

At 11:00 a.m., Frédéric took off his dirty apron, swapped it for a smarter, more formal clean one with the name of the shop and his own name embroidered on the pocket, and went to open up. The shutters made a loud rattling noise, echoing throughout the street as the other shops, cafés, and emporiums started opening up for business. Even though I'd seen the sun was up through the hazy workroom windows, seeing it beam in through the front of the shop made me blink.

It was a ravishing day. Even though my back was already sore from stooping to clean so many nooks and crannies in the workshop, and Benoît had indicated he wanted me to start on the copper vats, which had a complicated-looking box of harsh-smelling cleaning products attached to it. Claire hadn't been wrong about the hard work.

But Frédéric beckoned me out for a cigarette break at the front. I didn't smoke, but I kept him company as he waved and bantered with the other shop holders setting out their stalls; the little bookshop was putting racks of paperbacks outside, some of them, I noticed, looking a bit dog-eared; there was a little print shop with maps of vintage Paris in careful plastic pockets, framed in card, and some larger touristy work—Monets, Klimts—on the walls for sale. One shop seemed to sell nothing but hundreds of different types of tea, all in little metal boxes, brightly colored, lining the walls in a hundred flavors: mint, cardamom, grapefruit, caramel. That shop smelled dry and refined, of leaves, not the earthy deep flavors of Thierry's. But from the friendly way Frédéric hailed the proprietor, a tall, thin older man who looked as desiccated as the leaves he sold, as if a stiff breeze would blow him away, I imagined they must get on all right, the two things complementing each other. Next door to us directly was a shop selling bits and bobs, new brooms and dustpans and mop heads and nails.

Above street level, windows were being opened; the little roads were so narrow here, you could see everybody living cheek by jowl. Coffee was being drunk, papers unfurled—*Le Matin, France Soir*—and everywhere the smooth rattle and chatter of French, background chatter reduced to a mélange, to a pleasant background on the radio. I couldn't quite believe it; here I was, hanging out with a true French person, in a road full of professional French people, working in a French place, drinking sticky coffee, and watching the world go by. I was slightly delirious with the lack of sleep and on a bit of a sugar rush if I was being perfectly honest, but I couldn't help the huge bubble of excitement boiling up inside me, even though I was, when you got down to it, about to spend the rest of the day scrubbing a gigantic metal vat. (Only two flavors of chocolate were made each day, so one vat could rotate its cleaning. You had to be, I was assured, very, very careful not to infect the vat with cleaning products, nor disturb its patina, which gave the mixing depth. Frédéric had gone on about it until I was cross-eyed.) Well, I would deal with that problem in a moment. For now, I was happy just standing outside, smelling Frédéric's heavy Gauloises smoke, watching a perky-looking dog with a newspaper in its mouth prance up the street, seeing a trio of pigeons spiral up among the high roofs, and hearing the chime of different bells from across the river and down the whole wind of the Seine. I liked the sound.

"He likes you," said Frédéric. "Be careful. Alice will not like you."

"I can handle Alice," I said, which was sheer bravado and actually a bare-faced lie. People confident enough to be rude always rather impressed me.

"Anyway, isn't she just his girlfriend?"

Frédéric snorted.

"Without Alice, Thierry would stay in bed all day every day, eating his own work. She is the one who pushes him, who made him famous. She is always worried that someone will steal him."

But he looks like a gigantic pig, I didn't say. And also surely unbelievably glamorous and worldly Alice was hardly going to bother with me.

The first tourists of the day were already heading down the cobbled street, cooing and remarking on the quaintness of everything. One or two were following guides, and when they saw our sign, their faces lit up.

"The hordes descend," said Frédéric, flicking his cigarette quickly into the gutter and returning quickly to the shop with a large smile pasted on his face. "*Bonjour, messieurs, dames!*"

From inside the workshop where I was scrubbing, very slowly, the gigantic pan with a toothbrush, like some kind of sadistic punishment, I could see the heads of people in the shop bobbing around through the window in the swinging doors; sometimes Frédéric would put his head through and bellow at Benoît, who continued, utterly methodically, setting out tray after tray of the fresh chocolates, which sold as quickly, it appeared, as he could set them in the fridge, even though the prices were absolutely startling. I couldn't believe how much they cost. Frédéric explained to me later that yes, it was expensive to make chocolate the way Thierry did it, with the utter best of everything, but even the very best of herbs didn't cost that much money. Alice had decided that unless customers found things unwaveringly costly, they didn't appreciate it so much, and they'd also found that every time they increased prices, the shop got busier and they got profiled in more up-market magazines. And so it went on, until people came from across the world to visit the famous, the one and only fresh chocolate shop on the rue Chanoinesse, and Thierry kept on doing what he did, and they were paid, Frédéric remarked crossly, very little, while Alice salted it away and bought Chanel handbags. I wondered how much of this was true and how much just anti-Alice speculation.

At midday promptly, Frédéric shut the door and brought the shutters down. Benoît turned off all the machines and vanished on a wobbly bicycle that looked too small for his big frame.

"Where's he gone?" I asked.

"For a siesta, of course," said Frédéric. "And lunch."

"How long do we get for lunch?" I asked. In the factory, we got forty-five minutes—it had been brought down from an hour in a concession round to let us leave a bit earlier—but that was annoying as it wasn't long enough to go into town or shop or meet anyone or anything like that. Frédéric shrugged. "We shall open again at three o'clock."

I looked at him, not sure if he was joking or not. Surely he was.

"Three hours?"

Frédéric didn't seem to see this as the least bit surprising.

"Well, yes, you have lunch to do and perhaps a little nap…"

Now he mentioned it, a nap didn't seem like a bad idea. I'd been up since the crack of dawn. He smiled gaily and sauntered off, leaving me standing alone. Alice marched off without a good-bye into a van laden with fresh boxes. Thierry turned around after waving them off and fixed me with a surprisingly humorous eye.

"Lunch?" he said.

8

A part from the chocolates, I'd had nothing to eat all morning and I'd been up for such a long time. Thierry offered me his arm—he wasn't a very fast walker—and we crossed the Pont Louis-Philippe and vanished through a maze of streets, mostly filled with tourists, with the occasional local who recognized and nodded a head to Thierry. We passed wide roads with long chains of cafés and restaurants with picture menus outside and optimistic tables set in the street. He ignored these completely, and when we got to the far end of the Marais, he twisted quickly into a tiny alleyway between two large blocks of apartments with white shutters and washing hanging from the top windows. It was cobbled, and you wouldn't have noticed it was there if you didn't know exactly where you were headed. At the end of the tiny lane was a little wooden sign swaying in the breeze with a large pot on it. It looked like something out of Diagon Alley, and I looked at Thierry questioningly. He said nothing but winked at me.

It was, in fact, a restaurant, and when we opened the old brown door, a gust of noise and smells and warm air flooded out. Inside everything was brown and wooden; there were coppers on the wall and it was ferociously hot. Tiny brown wooden tables and benches, built for earlier, thinner generations I would have said, were crammed together higgledy-piggledy on different levels. Everyone appeared to be shouting, and I couldn't see a vacant table anywhere. A large woman in a dirty white apron and glasses appeared and kissed Thierry rapidly on both cheeks, gabbling something I couldn't recognize, then led us both to the back of the room, from where I could see, behind the bar, a huge brick oven roaring away.

We were jammed into two seats cheek by jowl with two men who appeared to be having a furious argument about something but who would abruptly stop every so often and burst out laughing. I had just squeezed in when the old lady returned, cocking an eyebrow. Thierry leaned over to me. "I will order you the duck," he said, and then, when I agreed, simply nodded to the woman, who vanished and sent over a very small whippet-thin boy with water, bread, napkins, utensils, and a small carafe of deep, fruity-looking wine and two very small glasses, all of which he unfolded onto the table at lightning speed. Thierry poured a tiny glass of wine for me—I thought it was to taste it—and a rather larger one for himself. Then he dipped a piece of bread into a bowl of olive oil, started chewing it contemplatively, and sat back, happy. He seemed fairly content not to ask me too much about my life or even what I was doing there. I felt very nervous suddenly.

"So," I said, "you've always had the shop?"

He shook his head. "Not always. I was a soldier too."

"Really?" I couldn't imagine Thierry as a lean, mean fighting machine.

"Well, I was an army cook. Yes."

"What was that like?"

He shrugged. "Horrible. But then I came back to my shop. Then I was much happier."

"Why is it called Le Chapeau Chocolat?"

He smiled at that, but before he could answer, our food appeared.

I had never eaten duck before, I hadn't wanted to say, except with pancakes at the Chinese when Cath and I were flush. But I had thought duck was a small thing. This was a huge breast, like a monster Christmas turkey. On the top was a thick crispy skin, like crackling. There was a green salad and small roast potatoes on the side and a yellow sauce. I watched Thierry as he chopped into his duck right across the middle and dunked it in the sauce. I immediately did the same thing.

The juicy, crunchy skin of the duck exploded in my mouth. The taste was just incredible, hot and salty and tender all at once. I looked up at Thierry. "This is amazing," I said.

He raised an eyebrow. "Oh yes, it is good."

I looked around at the other tables. Almost everyone else was also eating duck. This was what the place sold: oven-roasted duck. Amazing. I smiled, then wiped away some grease that wanted to run down my chin. The potatoes were hot and salty, and the salad was peppery arugula. Everything complemented everything else. It was one of the best meals I had ever had. Everyone else was taking it completely in their stride, chatting, carrying on, pretending this was normal. Perhaps if you lived in Paris, I supposed, this was normal.

Thierry launched excitedly into explaining to me how they made sure the oven was exactly the right temperature and how they balanced out the flavors. He was fascinating on where they sourced the animals (who had to live happy lives—a stressed duck was a bad duck apparently). He was genuinely interesting and animated, completely and utterly obsessed with his food, and I stopped noticing his bulk and breathlessness and caught only his hearty laugh and obsession. Maybe I could see what Claire had seen, just a glimpse.

Finally, after waving his knife in the air claiming he thought he could smell his neighbor's wine was corked, he caught himself and laughed.

"Ah, always I talk too much," he said. "I get carried away, you know."

"It's good, I like it," I said. He raised his eyebrows ruefully.

"No, no, I don't pay enough attention... So tell me, you leave your boyfriend in England?"

"I don't have a boyfriend," I said shortly.

Thierry raised his eyes. "But a woman like you..."

I couldn't work out what he meant, whether "a woman as nice as you" or "a woman as old as you."

"Uh-huh?" I said.

"You look like you should have a boyfriend," he said.

"Well," I said. Maybe he meant dumpy, as if I'd settled down and given up. "Well, I don't."

Thierry returned to his plate and, on finding it empty, looked sad.

"Well. Do not fall in love with Frédéric. He has nine girlfriends."

Given that I could probably squash Frédéric in a strong breeze, I felt this to be unlikely. I finished off my meal and did as Thierry did, running bread around the plate to mop up the juices. Oh, it was so good.

"And what about our friend Claire?"

I realized I hadn't been able to check my email since I'd gotten here and let her know how we were getting on. Surely Sami would know, although he seemed a bit too exotic for email, as if he would actually get everything delivered by carrier pigeons wearing bow ties.

I shrugged. "Was it glamorous, Paris in the '70s?"

"Paris is always glamorous, no?"

I nodded.

He looked distracted for a moment. "We were good friends, her and I," he said, then stared at my bread and grinned broadly.

"It is very sexy, a woman who eats," said Thierry. "You will find a boyfriend in less than five minutes, I am sure. Stay away from the Bourse; they are all bad, bad men."

The Bourse, it turned out, was the stock exchange, and he launched into a very funny attack railing against privileged bankers, and then lunch was over.

Thierry sat back in contentment after his meal, ordering us both another coffee, which came accompanied by a tiny flute of clear spirit.

"*Eau de vie*," said Thierry. "Essential."

He swigged it down and I did likewise, only to find out it was a ludicrously hard spirit that made my eyes water, and I started to cough. Thierry laughed.

"Nice to make acquaintance," he said in stilted English, then reverted back to French.

"Likewise," I said.

"And now, a nap!"

I had a tiny moment of wondering if this wasn't some kind of ridiculous seduction technique—surely not—but no. Thierry headed back to the shop, and I clambered up the many steps to the tiny apartment (half crawling the last flight), tumbled into bed, and fell fast asleep as soon as my head touched the pillow.

Thank goodness for Sami. At about three o'clock, he emerged from his bedroom where he'd only just gotten up, loudly singing an operatic song that was far too high for him (he rather bounced about) and making coffee hiss on the stove. When I came around, still a little drunk on food and *eau de vie*, I hadn't the faintest idea where I was.

"*Chérie!*" said Sami as I emerged, blinking, into the warm afternoon light in the apartment. He glanced at his watch. "I thought you had a job."

My heart leapt in my mouth.

"I do!" I said, panicking. "I did. Shit."

"*Arrête!*" Stop, said Sami. He came over and deliberately smoothed down my hair and wiped under my eyes where, presumably, I was all streaked with mascara. "Do not worry about it, *chérie*. You may be a little late."

"It's my first day!" I moaned. In the factory, you had to clock in and clock out; otherwise, you got your money docked. Not to mention the fact that it was ridiculously rude, and I was an idiot not to set my alarm.

Sami eyed me up carefully. "It is a siesta," he declared. "Not an invitation to become completely unconscious."

A slender slip of a person hurried out of Sami's room to the little bathroom. I smiled at Sami, who completely ignored me.

"*Allons*, go," he said. "Rush. And do not say you are sorry. British people say they are sorry one thousand times a day. Why? You do not mean it. You are not really sorry. You should save it for when you are actually sorry. Otherwise, it is meaningless."

"Sorry," I said without thinking.

He gave me a stern look. "Now. Go. Do not get drunk."

"I'm not drunk," I said, offended.

"No, but you're English. So it can happen at any time without warning. Come home later. I might have some friends here."

I catapulted down the stairs, deciding to save time by not switching on the lights, which turned out to be a terrible plan as I jarred my ankles on the bottom steps, then hared out of the block. I heard the first floor door open and close quickly. Ugh, nosey old woman.

As I turned into the rue Chanoinesse, my heart sank. The shop was opened up once again, its striped awning rolled out, its subtle gray frontage glinting in the afternoon sun, a line of happy punters queuing up outside. But worse—Thierry, I saw, was already there, with Alice. Her lip curled when she saw me. Why was she being so snooty?

"Ah, it's you," she said, not even bothering to search for my name. "We thought you'd found the work too hard and gone home."

"I fell asleep," I said, feeling my cheeks flare up bright red. With the others, I might have managed to laugh it off, but this woman was like a scary headmistress. She looked disapproving.

"Well, I don't think the most successful artisan business in Paris runs particularly well on people being asleep," she said icily. "I'm not sure this is going to work out."

I bit my lip. She couldn't mean to fire me, could she? Not when I'd just started. "I'm really sorry," I said. "It won't happen again."

Thierry turned around with a huge grin as I scampered in under Alice's gimlet gaze.

"We thought you had escaped! And taken all my secrets to Patrick Roger, huh? He would love to get his eyes on my workshop."

I shook my head vigorously, tears stinging behind the lids.

Thierry turned to Alice. "I took her to Le Brulot," he said, looking mock-sad, like a little boy. "So you see, it is all my fault."

"Who paid?" asked Alice immediately and neither of us answered— I'd never even seen the bill.

"She is a new girl in Paris," said Thierry. "She should understand lunch, yes?"

Alice still looked mutinous. His voice softened. "You were a new girl in Paris once, *non*?"

"I don't eat lunch," said Alice. But the aggression had gone out of her and she tutted and shook her head at Thierry, not me, who shot me a glance of secret triumph. I couldn't help but smile.

● ● ● ●

The afternoon showed the other side of Thierry, away from his quick perfectionist bent in the workshop at the back. As I tidied, fetched, and scrubbed, I watched him with the customers, flirting, cajoling, letting them taste a little bit, giving tiny sips of the hot chocolate to children. He was as much a master out here as he was through the back of the shop, and when the enormous bills arrived, he would stare them out manfully so they handed over their credit cards without a murmur. It was a class act, I decided. He believed in his product so thoroughly he couldn't help but transmit his enthusiasm, and the queues outside onto the cobbles were there to see him as much as anything.

At seven promptly, the shutters were pulled down and I looked around. The shop was almost entirely empty, like a baker's at the end of the day. Anything not sold was immediately thrown out, and I cleaned like a demon. Eventually Thierry came into the back of the shop, smiling to see me polishing the brass.

"*Ça va*?" he said. "All right?"

I nodded frantically, desperate to make it up to him. He glanced behind him. For the first time, I didn't see Alice there.

"How is…" He went quiet, his natural exuberance suddenly seeming a little stifled. "How is Claire?"

I carried on polishing so he didn't have to see my face. I knew it would betray the worst. When I had been at home, the recipient of the best physio and rehab the National Health Service had to offer, Claire had had an argument with her oncologist. She had told him she wanted an end point for chemo, after which she didn't want to do it anymore. He had gotten very cross with her and reminded her she wasn't that old. She had been very sharp with him, then so crotchety when I saw her that I had suggested immediately I shouldn't go to Paris, and it's the only time I saw her get even a little cross with me. She had said what was the point of anything if I couldn't even do that, and she was going to be absolutely fine, if only to spite her bloody oncologist.

I shrugged.

"She's…she's been better," I said.

"And she is, what…your aunt?"

"No, no. She was my teacher."

"Your teacher?" He beamed suddenly, surprise on his face. "What did she teach?"

"Well, French, of course," I said.

He snorted. "Ha. Well, you can tell her from me you have the accent. Terrible, terrible accent."

He laughed at my expression. "I'm teasing you. It's a joke. Your French is very good."

I sniffed. I'd thought I had done very well actually, considering I'd never visited the bloody country before.

"Very well," he said again, obviously sorry he'd hurt my feelings. "Tell me more about Claire. All I got was her letter."

"Well, we were in the hospital together," I said. "So we kind of became friends. She's the one who told me to get away. Well, forced me actually," I said, remembering. "She made me do it."

"Good for her," said Thierry. "And is she… She has a husband, a family?"

I shook my head. "No. She's divorced."

Instantly I saw in his eyes a sadness—and something else too, perhaps.

"Truly? Oh, but she was a beautiful girl. A beautiful, beautiful girl."

I agreed; in our little town, before she got ill, she had shined like a star.

Thierry shook his head. "But she will recover, *non*? She is not old. Oh, well, we are all old," he grumbled to himself. "But she…she was so beautiful."

"Who was so beautiful?" came Alice's perfect vowels, her accent retaining a tiny hint of the aristocratic English it must have been once.

"No one, no one, darling," said Thierry, turning around and pasting his beaming jolly grin back on his face. "Let us leave. Do we have a quiet evening?"

Alice looked at me with her eyes narrowed. Then said, "Yes, darling. We must drop in to the François's cocktail party; they are expecting you. And the ambassador's. It is all business."

"It is all ridiculously tedious," said Thierry, grumbling. "People are no fun anymore. In the old days, it was all wonderful and we could dance and smoke, and now it is just everyone standing and looking worried and muttering about money, money, money."

"Well, if you didn't eat and drink so much, you might enjoy it more."

"*Non*, I have to eat and drink to enjoy it at all."

They headed off into the evening twilight. Frédéric had zoomed off on his scooter; Benoît was waiting for me to finish, tapping his heavy keys in his hand but not saying a word. I smiled at him in a jolly fashion as I left, but he did not return it.

"Bye then!" I said cheerily in English, but he didn't turn around.

I was still weary—and a bit shell-shocked. Practicing with Claire was one thing; doing nothing but speak French all day long was a bit horrific and exhausting and had done nothing but prove to me how terrible my French was. I clambered up the stairs. My missing toes were tugging painfully at me. This drove me crazy. Honestly, when I had all my toes, I swear I couldn't tell them apart. Now I'd lost a couple, it was all I could think about. My missing toes acted as a bellwether, telling me when I was a bit tired or run down or doing too much—all of which I could have predicted would happen today— then suddenly I would feel them there. Darr said, the first time I displayed my hideous foot, *Oh, you hardly notice*, but I did. All the time.

No more sandals in the summer; no more lovely pedicures for when you go on holiday and get your feet all lovely and brown and the pink reflects off the tan, and you feel lovely and summery for long after the end of the trip. Now I was stuck in great, big, clumpy, ugly shoes all the time—high heels were kind of difficult too, because anything pointed at the toe twisted my other toes very painfully, and my podiatrist had told me to steer well clear. She'd also told me not to worry about it, hardly anybody walked up and down a beach counting other people's toes, and plenty of people had six to a foot and no one ever noticed and other things like that, and I had smiled and pretended to agree with her and nod, all the while vowing never to show off my foot ever again.

How I would manage if I ever met someone, I put to the back of my mind. I was too busy focusing on convalescence and trying to figure out how to survive for the rest of my life with the only half-decent employer in the district no longer in need of my services and my settlement money running down. Anyway. No one would get to see my deformity, and that was the end of it. Which meant I couldn't mention it, at risk of turning into a freak show right away. My brothers had been fascinated with what exactly had happened to them—had they been thrown into a bin? Could I keep them in a jar? Had they been set on fire? (They had been set on fire, thrown in the incinerator when I was too poorly for them to risk reattachment. I had lied and told them they were keeping them to clone another one of me.)

I limped up the stairs, then perked up as Sami stood there, waving a green bottle at me. He was wearing a multicolored silk bathrobe that was far too short for him. I tried not to look upward as I ascended the stairs.

"*Alors!*" he shouted. "The evening is beginning."

"Not for me," I said quickly. "I'm exhausted."

Sami looked hurt.

"You don't want to meet my friends?"

I really, really didn't. For one, my French had finished. The end. *Finis.* The idea of going out with Sami's doubtless colorful friends to somewhere noisy and coming over as a total dud was depressing. Really, what I wanted to do was slump in front of the television, but I saw the TV was already on and remembered—which was stupid, of course, why wouldn't it be—that the TV was in French and seemed to consist of four blokes around a table shouting at one another. I sighed. I'd give anything for a dog doing cartwheels on *Britain's Got Talent*, possibly accompanied by pizza. I'd thought at lunchtime I'd eaten enough for the entire day, but my stomach seemed to think otherwise. I should have gotten some shopping, but I wasn't sure where to go. And there wasn't a thing in the apartment, I could tell. It smelled of exotic shower gel and cigarette smoke and a large sandalwood candle.

Also, apart from meeting Claire, I had changed. The accident had changed me, it really had. I'd kind of felt up for anything before that, and the realization that I wasn't, in fact, invulnerable was actually really hurtful. I'd called it getting better, but actually, it was more like hiding.

9

There was, as I was to discover over the course of many, many evenings, no point whatsoever in trying to avoid a night out with Sami. And also, a night out with Sami wasn't like a night out for many people. When me and Cath went out, for example, we'd tell some other people where we were going, then there'd be lots of texts and messages from people about which bar we'd be in, then we'd always end up at Faces because it had a dance floor and we'd do some dancing, then we'd end the night with a kebab at Pontin Ali's. That's what everybody did. All the nights were roughly the same, some more fun than others. Normally we saw a fight, and occasionally Cath got into one.

Sami, however, had the skill, just as he did with his costumes at the opera house—he could take the everyday, the bland, the tawdry, and with hardly any money but a bit of imagination, he could turn it into magic.

He could always find out where an art exhibit or a flash mob was going to happen. One evening, he led us all to the great Monaco circus, which had just arrived in town, and we sat on the tiny roof terrace of a cheap restaurant that served the best bouillabaisse in Paris, at mismatched tables festooned with tiny fairy lights, and watched the elephant and the tigers march out of their smart transporters. One night, he insisted everyone wear the color blue, then talked us into a private showing of a hot young artist as the entertainment, where we drank their wine and talked loudly and pretentiously about the sculptures until asked to leave. He had an ever-shifting coterie of nighttime friends: bar workers, box office staff, butchers, bakers, actresses, and guitar players, anyone who worked antisocial hours, who finished when the restaurants and bars were closing up and needed to know someone who knew how to have a good time in the twilight world. He was the *demimonde* to me.

I didn't know any of that that first evening though. All I knew was that, although I was tired, I was eager too; for company, to watch people who didn't know all about me, who wouldn't make tired old jokes week after week about Long John Silver (I had only just stopped using the cane; I kept leaving it everywhere anyway). My long sleep at lunchtime and the adrenalin of all the new experiences had left me energized and overexcited; it was the first time I had worked in so long. I felt I needed to do something; there was, I realized, no way I was going to sleep if I just went to bed. None at all.

"Go on then."

I dressed in a very plain black dress that Claire had seen on an online shop and sent me over to suggest I buy it. To me it looked like absolutely nothing; I preferred things a bit more stand out-y, but she'd said this was more how to dress in Paris, so I had huffed, then agreed when it went on sale. It was weighted down in the hem, so it actually did lie very nicely—and the only, the ONLY benefit of being so stupidly ill was that I currently weighed less than I had done my entire adult life, so it fitted me smoothly without any of my normal lumps and bumps (usually I had two handfuls of stuff around the bottom of my back I could just kind of lift). Well, I supposed a couple of months of working in a chocolatier's would sort that out for me.

Sami came and watched me getting ready.

"Aren't you going to wear any makeup?" he said. I shrugged, then glanced over at him. He was wearing peacock-blue eye shadow that kind of glittered. Oddly, it didn't make him look less masculine;

it simply highlighted his luscious dark eyes and gave him a very dangerous look.

"Are you a transvestite?" I asked. One thing about having to get by in another language: I never was able to make space for niceties or anything other than being very up front.

Sami laughed. "No," he said, "I just like to be beautiful." He gazed in the mirror, obviously reassuring himself that he was. He certainly was, but I'd never heard a man speak like that before. He was wearing a tight-fitting black suit that looked incredibly expensive, with a new white shirt, a turquoise tie, and a bright turquoise handkerchief in the top pocket that exactly matched his eye shadow.

"You are," I said approvingly. To me he was like some exotic bird of paradise. He turned me by the shoulders and put me in front of the mirror.

"You look half-gypsy," he said approvingly of my pale curly hair that never would settle down. "*Arrête!*"

He vanished and came back with an enormous professional makeup case laden with potions and ointments.

"Stand still."

I submitted myself to his bidding and closed my eyes. When I opened them again, I was amazed at what I saw.

Sami had drawn a thick line of kohl right across the top of my lashes, fanning it out way past my eyes. It gave them huge, smoky definition, and he'd smudged powder on top of that and added mascara. LOTS of mascara. Suddenly my eyes looked enormous in my face.

"No lipstick," he said. "Better like this. You may look mysterious and like you are wearing black on purpose and not because you are lazy about your clothes."

"I'm not lazy about my clothes!" I protested, but I knew it was true. There wasn't much point in buying nice things when (a) I couldn't afford them, and (b) I had to wear a uniform at the chocolate factory, so I just tended to sling on jeans and a top underneath. It was quicker and easier and I didn't really have to think about it. Then Cath and I liked to dress up for going out at the weekends, but that meant I always needed new outfits, so I had to buy the cheapest I could find, really, so I didn't wear the same things all the time.

Anyway, so it wasn't a case of being lazy. It was a case of being practical.

In the slim-fitting black dress though (I always chose clothes to disguise the bits I didn't like, especially at the back), with the huge eyes…suddenly I looked like someone completely different. Not the young, who cares, back of the class Anna. And not the more recent Anna, with the slightly shell-shocked expression, the definite lines of weariness and wariness around the eyes. No, I looked like someone totally strange and new. I attempted a smile, but it didn't go with my new look, which was more mysterious, less friendly.

Sami laughed at me.

"Are you pouting?"

"No!" I said, jumping up and blushing.

"You are! You are loving looking at yourself!"

"NO!"

"That is good!" he said. "That is exactly right. Now. Come. Martini."

I followed him out into the darkening city night. The tourists with their colorful backpacks and upside-down maps had retreated now to their hotels and the large restaurants with pictures on the menus that thronged the Place de la Concorde. Instead, the night felt like ours. We jumped on a bus that took us over the bridges and up the steady hill to the north, to Montmartre again.

Claire had often spoken about Montmartre; it was her favorite place in the city. She said on hot days it was often the only place you could get a breath of wind, climbing up the steps and sitting at the top. She said they used to park their little car up there—good luck, I thought, seeing the parking restrictions there now—and picnic at the top of the steps.

Sami hopped off the bus and led me down a side alley and through another. I had not the faintest idea where I was. Occasionally I would hear snatches of clinking glasses and happy conversation, or smell the scent of garlic and onions and oil simmering in a kitchen, or the bakeries that ran all night, releasing their bright warm scent of bread. Finally he came to a stop and indicated a large building that was completely silent. There was a tiny side passage and it was up here he led me; in the side was a tiny door, behind which shone a bright yellow light.

Sami knocked brightly three times, and the door was opened by a young girl dressed like a '50s cigarette girl. As she opened it, a huge blast of heat and light and noise blew out at us, and I stepped backward. She accepted some cash from Sami and ushered us inside.

Down a long flight of stairs, we found ourselves underneath the street in a huge crypt. It must have been a cellar of some sort, or some kind of storage.

At any rate, now it had been transformed into a club. At one end was a makeshift stage, and on it was a group of musicians playing fast and furiously for all they were worth: a trumpeter, a tall man wearing a fedora playing the double bass, a drummer who reminded me of Animal from the Muppets, and a tall woman in a fuchsia dress scatting into the microphone. Around people were dancing or sitting at cheap foldaway wooden tables. Condensation dripped off the walls. Many of the people were wearing '40s clothes. I noticed to my horror that most people were smoking; I knew there was a smoking ban in France too, but nobody seemed to observe it, and down here in this place with one rickety stairwell and no fire exits as far as I could see, it felt dangerous.

Over in one corner was a hatch serving great pitchers of wine and nothing else; there was also corner seating further away from the band, and Sami immediately saw some people he knew and bounced up to introduce us. A waitress stopped by and asked if we wanted wine, but Sami immediately demanded she go make us a proper martini, and after rolling her eyes, she agreed.

I'd never had a martini before. Not a proper one, at any rate, clearly. It tasted like someone had nicked it out of someone's gas tank. I spluttered and coughed until I attracted attention, then had to pretend that nothing had happened.

The music was very loud, and as soon as we sat down, people started to circle our table and come up to Sami, who obviously knew everyone there. Obviously this wasn't that surprising; of course he did. People who are very friendly, I have found, tend to be friendly to everyone. I felt a little foolish, in fact, thinking that Sami's eagerness to take me out was to do with something intrinsically interesting about me, rather than a typical benevolence toward everyone in the world. In fact, as I sipped my martini, I saw he greeted everyone with the same excitement, launching into high-volume complaints about how shitty his job or his love life was. Sami, I concluded, was simply one of those people who likes everyone, requires an audience, and wasn't terribly fussy who it was.

Well, that was all right, I told myself, as everyone else barely looked at me. I wasn't truly surprised; the girls were all so glamorous, with heavy dark eye shadow that had gone out of fashion in the UK years ago, set against pale skin—no fake tan—and they were all fashionably skinny. The boys were even more so, and they dressed better. They wore heavy rimmed glasses and nobody smiled or laughed except for Sami; they just waved their hands in the air. Eventually one of the skinny boys grabbed one of the skinny girls to take her dancing. She pouted even more than she had been doing previously, which clearly meant yes. I watched them disappear into the sweaty moving crowd, looking sinuous and elegant and somehow strangely out of time.

I took another sip of my cocktail—in fact, a second cocktail; I appeared to have finished the first—and felt strangely dislocated and dreamy. The odd thing is, although I knew on one level that where I was glamorous and interesting and different—everything I was meant to be here to discover—it wasn't me, I could see, looking around. I didn't fit in. I wasn't Parisian and sophisticated and skinny and beautifully dressed. I was too old, too parochial. It was an interesting world to see, to visit, I thought, looking at Sami with his head back, taking part in four conversations at once, downing his martini, and smoking a cigarette through a holder. But these easy bohemians…I didn't think there was much point in me trying to ingratiate myself, even if I did manage to understand a word anyone said. Sami had briefly introduced me to everyone, but no one had given me a second glance. And I looked at my watch. It was late. I stood up.

"I have to go," I said to Sami.

He looked up at me, surprised. I didn't think it was just tobacco in his cigarette; the pupils of his eyes were huge.

"Go? But we've just arrived! And there's a sky-top party we all simply must go to later…in a bit…"

"Thanks," I said, "but I have work tomorrow."

"How will you get home?"

"I'll find a cab," I said boldly. I had no idea how I'd get home.

Sami waved a lazy hand. "All right, my *petite anglaise* who works so hard. Everyone say good night to Anna."

A man was standing there who had just arrived, to whom I hadn't been introduced. He turned to Sami and said something in a low voice.

"Of course she will," said Sami crossly. "Darling. More martinis please." Then he blinked.

"Of course. You two have to meet." He grabbed the man, who was tall and slightly thicker-set than most of the good-looking young *beau monde* around, by the arm. The man had been draped around one of the very skinny model-looking types and looked rather annoyed at being disturbed.

"Laurent! It's Anna."

Laurent, whoever he was, looked completely nonplussed by this information. Rather than kiss me on both cheeks or say "*enchanté*" like most of the other people I'd met, he thrust out a hand rather brusquely without looking me in the eye.

"Well, hello," I said, taken aback.

He was still talking, crossly, to Sami.

"She'll never find a taxi," he was saying.

"Of course she will," said Sami. "Or a bus, or a friend."

Laurent rolled his eyes.

"I'll be fine," I said. I was tired and a bit drunk and cross from the martinis and I suddenly wanted very much to be in my bed. I didn't like these strangers discussing me like a piece of furniture. The subways were probably still running anyway. I stood up and smiled shortly.

"Good night."

• • • •

As it turned out, the rather grumpy young man had turned out to be right. It was far later than I had thought, and the streets were completely deserted. So much, I thought, for this being a big all-night party town. I'd been to London twice, and as far as I could tell, Soho and Trafalgar Square kept going all night every night. Here, though, it was practically silent.

All the taxis cruising the streets seemed to have lights on but didn't stop. My heart started to jump a bit. Maybe the system was different here. Maybe if you had a light on that meant you weren't free. So I tried hailing a few cars without lights, but that didn't do me any good either, until one car with one man in it started slowing down a bit close to me and I turned tail and scampered up some steps. Then I turned around, worrying a bit about the sound of my shoes on the steps and wondering exactly how safe Paris was, after all. About ten people had warned me already about pickpockets. What about muggers?

I heard a footfall somewhere behind me. The streetlights, utterly charming though they were, wrought iron in the old-fashioned style, gave out picturesque circles of light. At the moment, though, I would have liked full-beam motorway service station blindingness. I could barely see my way ahead and hadn't a clue where I was going. I started walking up the church steps a little faster. The footsteps behind me sped up.

Oh crap, I thought to myself. Oh god. I was stupid, after all, coming out by myself. I was stupid coming out at all, full stop, with a new flatmate I barely knew. I should have stayed inside and eaten packet noodles and, I don't know, had a good cry or something. I moved faster, trying to see a street that led somewhere more wide open with more chance of company, but all the roads ahead seemed equally tiny and mysterious. Oh bugger.

Straight ahead was the outline of the huge church, the Sacré-Coeur. I decided to head for that, from some old-fashioned idea about sanctuary, but truly from the expectation that it would have some kind of big courtyard, somewhere with lights—you could see the floodlighting right across the city. I ran up more steps, and behind me, the feet were faster too, closing and closing, my heart pounding in my mouth, my hand searching in my bag for something I could use as a weapon. I closed on the great big old-fashioned iron key that opened the building door and told myself to aim for his eye.

"*HÉ!*"

The voice was deep and throaty, and I could tell by the tread that it was someone heavy. Shit. Right. This was it. The steps were closing in. I was in a small cobbled courtyard nowhere near the church, surrounded by boarded-up shops and tightly shuttered flats. Would they open up their shutters for me? I doubted it. Never mind, there were plenty of quiet-looking alleyways nearby.

"AAARRRGH!!!!!"

I screamed with all my might and leapt on the dark shadowy figure, the keys outstretched in my hand, trying to stab them into his face. I caught him off guard, and he toppled over hard on the cobblestones, me coming down on top of him, still trying to get at him with the keys and screaming the worst obscenities I could think of.

I didn't realize at first that there was an equally terrified screaming coming from underneath me. A pair of extremely strong arms was trying to keep me away from his face. I had reverted to English—extremely Anglo-Saxon—and was trying to whack him; he suddenly spoke in English too.

"Pleeze, pleeze stop…pleeze…I don't mean harm. Any harm. Pleeze."

The meaning didn't filter through straightaway, and I was so crazy with adrenalin, I'm not sure when exactly I would have stopped, if a shutter at the top of the apartment block we were underneath hadn't suddenly opened, and, without warning, a bucket of water poured down on our heads.

That stopped us. Panting, I realized I was sitting on top of the grumpy man from the bar. He was holding my hand in a vice grip at arm's length, but I had already managed, I saw, to make a good bloody cut in his forehead. Seeing the blood, now being washed by the water, suddenly made me wobble.

"Oh," I said, shock and faintness washing over me. I wobbled and nearly collapsed on top of him. He quickly moved his hands to my waist, holding me up.

"What the…what the HELL did you think you were doing?" I finally managed to gasp as I clambered up. I was soaking.

"I was shouting at you. Didn't you hear me? I didn't catch your name the first time."

"You don't follow a woman like that!"

"Well, you don't march out into a foreign city if you don't know your way home. Sami is fun, but he's always going to choose the party over you."

I brushed down my hair as he lumbered to his feet. His English was extremely good, only the merest hint of a French accent.

"So you were…"

"I'd come to find you. I was only meant to meet you anyway, and I'm heading back your way. Actually, I'm knackered. Sami is never where he says he's going to be…"

"I can imagine," I said, which was as close as I could get right then to an apology, with my heart still racing at a million miles an hour. "Oh God, I've hurt you."

As if he hadn't realized before, he put a large hand to his face, only to feel the blood trickling down. He pulled his hand away and looked at it.

"Gross," I said, appalled. I felt in my bag in case I had a tissue, but I didn't have one on me.

"That is awful," he said, suddenly looking very wobbly himself. "Have you stabbed me?"

"Of course I haven't stabbed you," I said defiantly. "I've keyed you."

He didn't understand the word until I showed him the keys, then recognition dawned. My already anxious body suddenly pounded with fear that he was going to be furious. Instead, to my enormous, shattering relief, he shook his head, opened his mouth, revealing a white-toothed smile, and started to laugh.

"Come, come with me," he said, then directed me up a tiny alley-way that looked forbiddingly dark. I had one more second of panic, at which he said, "Please. I certainly wouldn't attack you again."

"I have my keys," I said, nervously giggling as the adrenalin finally started to leave my body.

To my total surprise, the narrow alleyway opened out onto a wide, brightly lit thoroughfare that still had cars thundering down it and, here and there, a café still open. The man led me through to a tiny coffee shop, tucked away, inhabited by several Turkish men using a hookah and a dark-eyed proprietress with bags under her eyes who raised an eyebrow but nodded brusquely as the man asked her for two coffees and a bathroom.

I sat there quietly until he came back, his wound cleaned up some-what, holding tissue paper to his head.

"I'm sorry," I said again quietly. The coffee arrived. It was hot, black, and about 50 percent sugar. It was just what I wanted.

He shook his head, then glanced at his watch.

"Argh," he said.

"Don't show me," I said. "I have to be up in a few hours."

"I know," he said.

I looked at him. "Who are you?"

He grinned and I caught something then…saw something in his face.

"I'm Laurent," he said. "You're Anna, I remember now. You work for my dad."

• • • •

1972

Thierry worked from first thing in the morning, but at noon he made a stated decision to close the shop for three hours rather than the traditional two. When Benoît Sr. suggested this was commercial suicide, he pointed out that Italian shops closed for four hours and would he rather that, and that people would wait.

They would.

Then Claire would put the children down for their naps, under the cheerful guidance of Inez, the housemaid, and slip out, Mme. LeGuarde and Inez swapping meaningful looks.

They would wander across Paris's bridges, each more beautiful than the last—on one foggy day, which turned the city into black and white, like a Doisneau photograph, they strolled the Pont Neuf, every cobble, it felt to Claire, smoothed away by lovers meandering across it for hundreds of years.

Thierry would talk and talk—of flavors and schemes and what he had learned, in Innsbruck and Geneva and Bruges, and occasionally would remember to ask Claire what she thought of things too, but it didn't really matter to Claire; she was happy to listen to him, to rejoice in her understanding, which improved day by day, to revel in the warmth of his full attention, because when he got back to the shop, or went out, he would instantly be surrounded by people who wanted a piece of him— some business, or a word, or an idea, or to congratulate him on his taste or ask him about something in the newspaper. When they were in public, he was everybody's. Tracing out their own, circuitous routes of Paris, he was all hers, and she found herself unable to ask any more.

Usually by the time he thought to ask her what she thought, it was nearing time for him to get back—never again in Claire's life would time speed away from her as quickly as it did during those walks, those lunches. Three hours felt like the blinking of an eye, and she would float through the afternoon, so light-humored and good-natured that Arnaud and Claudette would cling to her, happily repeating the English songs she taught them, lisping along to "Hun-eee oh! Sugar, sugar."

Mme. LeGuarde kept a close eye on her and, when she judged the time to be right, casually came in to Claire's room one night and sat down on the bed.

"Now, chérie," she said kindly, "please tell me you know about contraception."

Of all the shocking and strange things that had happened to Claire on her trip, none was as strange and bizarre as this elegant lady of the world referring to…well…matters. Of course she had a rough idea, picked up from her time at Chelsea Girl; she knew what a rubber was, kind of, and the girls spoke casually about being on the pill, although the thought of going to nice old Doctor Black, who'd known her since she was a baby, and asking him for pills to have sex, even if she had met anyone she'd have liked to have sex with apart from Davy Jones, was completely beyond her comprehension levels. The idea of these matters being discussed under the Reverend's roof was simply impossible.

It being in another language helped, of course. But Mme. LeGuarde's cool, confident manner in discussing sexual hygiene, as if it were nothing more nor less important than regular hygiene (which, indeed, in Mme.

LeGuarde's eyes, it wasn't), was an eye-opener to Claire in more ways than one. Firstly, she declined the offer of prophylactics but promised to ensure they were used. Secondly, she took Mme. LeGuarde's matter-of-fact tone and unflustered manner and stored it away somewhere. Years later, she was to end up taking all the sexual education classes in the school, as most of the other teachers couldn't bear it. Statisticians in later years always marked down the lower rate of STDs and teen pregnancies in the Standish ward of Kidinsborough, an otherwise very deprived area, as a blip. It was nothing of the sort.

● ● ● ●

Of course, as soon as he said it, I realized immediately. Of course he was. The build, the dark brown eyes; he was far more handsome than Thierry could ever have been, but fundamentally they were very similar, down to the long black eyelashes and the spark of mischief in the eyes, now the panicking was over.

"You look…"

"Please don't say I am like a thin version of my father." Laurent looked down and patted his small stomach with a weary look. "Aha, not so thin."

Actually he wasn't fat at all—just big, with a barrel chest and broad shoulders.

"Well, you can't look that much like him," I said. "Otherwise I wouldn't have stabbed you with those keys."

"Well, unless he's really difficult to work for," said Laurent, downing his coffee. "Ah. That's better. Am I dry?"

His curly hair stuck up in all directions and he had a lot of dark stubble on his chin.

"Do you have any big meetings tomorrow?" I said.

"That bad, huh?" he said. "Hmm."

"So why did Sami want to introduce us?" I said.

"Oh, Sami likes to think he knows everyone." Laurent thought about this and qualified the statement. "Okay, he does know everyone. He thought it was funny, you turning up."

"Why?"

"Well…because."

"What?"

"Because he knows my dad and I…we don't get on that well."

It was hard to imagine anyone not getting on with the avuncular Thierry.

"Oh no! Why not?"

Laurent held up his hands. "Just father-son stuff… Nothing, really."

"He seems pretty happy to me," I said.

Laurent looked quite fiery. "Really? That is why he weighs six hundred pounds maybe? This is what a happy man looks like?"

I looked nervous. "Well, your mother seems to keep him in line."

"That's not my mother."

I figured I'd probably said enough for one night, as Laurent finished his coffee up. He looked up at me, his smile back, his shortness forgotten.

"Sorry," he said. "I don't think I make a very good first impression."

"Apart from the attempted mugging and the terrible parent issues," I said, "you're doing totally fine. Do you want me to pay for the coffee too?"

He looked a little shocked until he saw I was joking.

"No," he said. "Are you any good? At chocolate, I mean. Not violence."

I shrugged. "My old boss said I had a nose, whatever that is. But your father does things very differently. I'm going to try my best."

"Hmm," he said. "Maybe I should poach you."

"Good luck with that," I said, smiling. Suddenly I felt exhausted. "I…I owe someone a favor," I said. "To stay. And do what I'm doing."

I looked around onto the street, still thronged with night people.

"Even if coming to Paris is a bit…"

"*Un peu trop?*" said Laurent quietly, in French. A little too much?

"It's been a long day."

"Come on then," he said. "I came to take you home. I will."

I followed him out onto the street, wondering where his car was. But it wasn't a car. Tucked up just under a railway bridge, about three hundred feet away, was a beautiful shiny little powder blue Vespa.

"Only way in town," he said, when he saw me look at it.

"It's cool," I said.

"It's essential," he said, even though he looked too big for it. He unlocked the seat and handed me a pale blue helmet that matched the bike, putting on a vintage black one with large old-fashioned goggles of his own.

"What is this, the girl's helmet?" I joked, before realizing it smelled partly of hair spray. Well, of course, he must have a girlfriend. Probably tons. I felt a little odd putting it on.

"You've been on a scooter before?" he asked.

"Oh no, I haven't," I said, the helmet halfway up my head. "Is it just like a bike?"

"No," he said, scratching his head. "No, it really isn't. Um. Just. Okay, move when I move, okay? Like, if I lean over…"

"Lean the other way, for balance," I said promptly.

"Uh-oh," said Laurent.

"No?"

"The opposite. When I lean, you lean."

"Won't we fall over?"

"Probably," said Laurent. "How bouncy are you?"

●　●　●　●

Riding through the Parisian dark, clutching a large man on a tiny bike (with a man bag over his shoulder—all French men had them, I noticed; they seemed to make perfect sense), I tried to follow his lead as to when to lean (it got easier after the first few times). It was hard to predict though, as he never signaled and often didn't wait for lights to change, simply plowing straight ahead. The first few times, I buried my face in his soft leather jacket. After that, finding myself still alive, I attempted to trust him and began to take some notice of my surroundings.

We roared down the Champs-Élysées, its broad pavements and tall white buildings glowing in the moonlight, and the buildings, tall and stately, glowing in the lights. The cars honked, and every time we turned slightly toward the left, I would see it there, following us like the moon: the great, unmistakable form of the zigzagging Eiffel Tower, lit up with spotlights like a VIP, which of course, she is. I couldn't take my eyes off her, standing there so brazenly, nothing tall around her that could lessen her impact.

"What are you doing?" growled the voice on the front of the bike as I twisted my body to get a better look.

"Sightseeing," I said back, half my answer lost in the wind rushing past us.

"Well, stop it. Follow me."

And he grabbed my right knee quite forcibly and tugged it more tightly around his waist. I clung on tighter and let the sights of Paris come to me as they would; a church here, its square belfry askew; the great shop windows of the stores glinting in the streetlights; the occasional snatches of west African rap from passing cars; once, on a street corner, a couple slow dancing to music only they could hear. A crescent moon, a gentle scent of perfume and flowers as we passed the Place des Vosges, the air fresh but not cold against my skin, Laurent in front still traveling at what seemed to me terrifying speeds, the old street lamps flashing past us.

Suddenly, even though I didn't know where I was or what I was doing, not really, and quite possibly with the help of two martinis, I felt amazing. Nobody, nobody in the world, apart from Laurent, who didn't count as I didn't know him—nobody knew where I was, or what I was doing, or what I was up to. I didn't know what lay ahead, I didn't know what I was going to do with the rest of my life, whether I was going to succeed or fail, meet someone or stay single, travel or go home.

It sounds so stupid seeing as I was thirty, had no money, eight toes, a garret rental with a socialite giant, and a temporary job. But suddenly, I felt so free.

10

1972

Spaghetti Bolognese."

"*No.*"

"*That is not possible.*"

"*I tried spaghetti hoops,*" said Claire, lying back on the grass.

"*I do not know what that is.*"

"*They're all right.*"

"*All right. All right. Why would you put something in your mouth that is only all right?*"

Claire giggled. They were having a picnic in the Jardin du Luxembourg. It felt almost magical to Claire that only weeks before she had been looking at the young lovers, so smug and contented with their wicker baskets, their casually discarded bicycles, and empty wine bottles. They made it look so simple; she had been so envious.

And now, here she was too, lying half on a rug, half on the grass under a blazing blue sky. M. and Mme. LeGuarde had taken the children to Provence for a week. Originally Claire had been supposed to go with them. When Mme. LeGuarde had said she wouldn't be necessary, Claire had immediately panicked and worried she'd done something wrong. Being sent back to the Reverend in disgrace would be more than she could bear.

Mme. LeGuarde laughed at her worried face. In fact, she wanted Claire to give her love life more of a chance without them around, have *a little adventure of her own. It hadn't passed her notice that Claire had come more out of her shell; she was loving and carefree with the children, more willing to speak up. She had roses in her cheeks and a light golden tan from hours walking outside and playing with Arnaud and Claudette in parks; her appetite was good, her eyes were sparkling, her French coming on in leaps and bounds. She was already a long way from the worryingly pale, hopelessly introverted schoolgirl who had arrived on their doorstep two months before. Now, Mme. LeGuarde thought, Claire should have a holiday too.*

First, she took her shopping.

"As a thank-you," she murmured, brushing off Claire's stammering that they had already done so, so much for her.

She took her to her own atelier, situated just off the Marais. It was a tiny shop front, with a sole sewing machine in the window and no signage. A woman in an immaculate black knit dress cut starkly to the knee with a starched white collar and perfect cheekbones appeared in front of them.

"Marie-France," said Mme. LeGuarde. The ladies kissed, but with no noticeable warmth. Then she turned her pale blue eyes to Claire, who felt herself quailing under the weight of such scrutiny.

"Her legs are short," she barked.

"I know," said Mme. LeGuarde, uncharacteristically humble. "What can you do?"

"But the lower part of the leg should equal the length of the thigh."

"I shall have them rebroken immediately."

Marie-France harrumphed and indicated to Claire, without saying anything, that she should follow her up the perilously narrow twisted staircase.

The first floor, in complete contrast to the pokey shop front, was a large, airy room, lit by enormous windows on both sides. At one end, two seamstresses, both tiny bent ladies, hunched over sewing machines without looking up. Another tiny woman was pinning the most beautiful material—a huge, heavy swath of pale gray taffeta that shimmered and reflected the light like running water—onto a dressmaker's dummy, ruching it at the bust, then pulling it in toward the waist, making tiny, invisible darts with a clutch of pins from her mouth so quickly it was almost impossible to make out what she was doing. Claire stared at her, utterly fascinated.

"Disrobe," said Marie-France without emotion. If Mme. LeGuarde found this in the slightest odd, she didn't let on to Claire with even a twitch of the lips, as Claire took off her cheap cotton summer dress and stripped down to her petticoat and bra. With a tcch, Marie-France made it clear that the petticoat also had to come off. Claire felt cross and a bit shaky. Did she really have to be so rude? She'd never taken her clothes off in front of a stranger before. Even thinking this made her think of Thierry and then blush.

Marie-France watched her impatiently, then whipped a long tape measure that had been hanging around her neck like a pale white snake and, at the speed of light, started measuring her up, shouting out measurements—in centimeters, of course, Claire realized, two seconds after she wondered if she'd put on lots of weight without noticing—to the woman who had been pinning taffeta and was now jotting down details in a large, heavy-bound navy blue book.

"Nice flat bosom," she said to Mme. LeGuarde. Claire had certainly never heard it described like that before. "And the waist is small. Good."

She glanced up at Claire and addressed her in perfect English, even though Claire had given every indication that she understood her in French.

"That is what your waist should measure now for the rest of your life. It is in the book."

Mme. LeGuarde smiled. Claire glanced at her.

"That's good," whispered Mme. LeGuarde. "If it goes in the book, that means she approves of it."

Marie-France snorted again.

"I've yet to meet an English girl that could hold on to it."

She looked up.

"The babies come, they think, aha, now I shall lie in a field like a large cow and wait to be fed."

Claire thought of her own mother, with her lovely rounded bosom and strong capable arms. She had always thought of her mother as beautiful. But you couldn't get away from the fact that it was difficult to believe that she and Mme. LeGuarde had been schoolgirls at the same time, were the same age. Mme. LeGuarde looked closer to her own age.

"Raise your arms."

After rapidly jotting everything down, Marie-France made a nod to her assistant, who had led them up another flight of stairs. This room was dark and cramped, lined ceiling to floor and wall to wall with every kind of material possible. It was like an Aladdin's cave; there was gold ribbon, and silks in the deepest of hues: turquoise, pink, scarlet. There were many different tones of black, in every possible material, from the finest, softest mohair wool, to the lightest, most delicate chiffon; navy too. Florals large and small, some so loud you couldn't imagine who could wear them, to daisies etched on a heavy sunken cotton so tiny you could barely make them out. There was cut-out voile and large rolls of calico for pattern cutting; stripes in every conceivable colorway, and, over in the far corner, protected by a dust sheet, was the lace, the satin, in white and oyster and cream, for the brides. Claire couldn't help it—she gasped. Marie-France almost let a twitch cross her lips.

"I see you're thinking ahead," she muttered.

Claire colored again and turned back.

"Now," said Mme. LeGuarde, all business. "Nothing too somber. She's not a French girl; she'll just look like a clumpy English girl on her way to a funeral."

Claire was barely listening; she was still following the form and feel of the fabrics lining the extraordinary treasure cave of a room. The street noise and traffic of Paris outside had disappeared; she felt as if she were in another world.

Marie-France did a sniff. "She cannot be chic."

"I don't want her to be chic," fired back Mme. LeGuarde. "Chic is for spoiled bobo girls who never work a day in their lives. I want her to be what she is; young and pretty and unspoiled."

"For how long?" said Marie-France, and Claire wondered how such a rude woman could even get up in the morning without everyone she knew wanting to kill her, but she didn't have much time to think about that as Mme. LeGuarde, with a practiced eye, picked out a light cream poplin lined with a navy stripe, and a soft, green fine cotton, with a border of gentle yellow wildflowers.

Seconds later, to her regret, she was back in the main atelier, where the tiny woman, who didn't say a word through her mouthful of pins, started pinning her at the speed of light, as Marie-France and Mme. LeGuarde bickered and disputed and lengthened and shortened. There was no mirror ahead of her, so Claire let her thoughts wander…to what Thierry would say when he saw her in her new finery, and beyond, what she would do…what she could do…in a week where she would have the entire house to herself. It made her heart beat terribly fast. Of course Thierry had asked her back to his apartment, and of course she had refused. It didn't seem right.

It wouldn't seem right under her host's roof either, but Mme. LeGuarde had been so matter-of-fact, so open about what she thought was a healthy stage of development that…well, she didn't think she would mind. Claire bit her lip nervously. But would it seem terribly forward? Terribly rude?

But then, the way Thierry made her feel every time he touched her hand, every time he maneuvered her by the elbow down the street… it made her feel hot and cold and completely overwhelmed, unable to concentrate on anything. And now it was mid-July, and in just a few short weeks, she would be headed back, back to Kidinsborough, and the Reverend, and sixth form college, and then on to secretarial, or the grim teacher-training college they had up the road, not the university her teachers had been so keen to encourage her to. Who would pay for it? Not Mme. LeGuarde.

But did she dare?

"Bon," said Marie-France, finally, without smiling. "You can stop. You stood well."

"She liked you," said Mme. LeGuarde, as they stepped out on the hot pavement. They shared a look, then, an instant later, both of them dissolved in giggles, for one instant, more like friends than employee and friend of the parents. Claire didn't think she'd ever seen Mme. LeGuarde laugh like that before. It made her look even younger.

• • • •

A mere week later, the dresses were ready. Claire went nervously into the shop, where the wordless seamstress was making final adjustments. Marie-France raised an eyebrow and barked a quick Bonjour in greeting, then marched her upstairs. This time Claire was grudgingly accepting of the fact that she would be stripping down in public and had worn her whitest set of underwear. The first dress shimmied over her head like a light silken waterfall. As the silent seamstress zipped up the side zip, Claire could already feel it fitted her absolutely perfectly. For a tiny second, Marie-France and Mme. LeGuarde regarded her, totally silently, until Claire worried if there was something terribly wrong with it or it didn't suit her. Until Marie-France sighed, just a touch, and said, very quietly, "Oh, to be young again," and with a move of her hand, indicated to the seamstress to roll out a long mirror that had been hidden behind the wall. The sun streaming through the back windows, Claire suddenly caught a glimpse of herself—not, as she was used to in the bathroom mirror, the pinched, pale-faced English girl with the scrubbed-looking nose and slightly doleful expression, the hair colorless, the shoulders thin.

The summer Parisian sun had added a very light, golden tan to her skin and brought out tiny, cute freckles all over her nose. The green of the silk dress pulled out the color of her eyes and gave them an intensity they'd never had before. Her hair had light streaks in it and had grown down *past her shoulders, and suddenly her thinness, which had always caused her to be described as peaky-looking, was flattered and emphasized by the dress; her tiny waist was cinched in, then curves had been added to her hips by the full skirt—not at all in fashion, but what did it matter when it suited her so well. The line of yellow flowers along the bottom emphasized the pretty leanness of her calves, without drawing attention to the fact that she was still shorter than average.*

It was beautiful. And even though Claire Forest, little, scrawny, shy only child of the fearsome Reverend Forest, had never been praised for her looks in her life—her father thought it vain and rather wicked to be proud of the way you looked—Claire too felt beautiful.

●   ●   ●   ●

The next few weeks, I started to settle in. The work was extremely hard and unrelenting, but I liked it and was even starting to get the hang of the husking and the conch. Frédéric was funny and flirtatious. (A different girl every week would turn up for him at the shop, all of them pouty and disdainful, which was exactly how he liked them—he liked, he explained, to prostrate himself fully in front of a strong woman who would control everything. It was no surprise our flirtation hadn't exactly progressed.) He was voluble and fiercely purist about every stage of the chocolate-making process. Benoît continued to treat his job like a monastic calling. Alice never quite got over the look of distaste she put on every day to see me turn up, but Thierry was taken with me and liked to chat—and I liked to listen, thankfully—as he pontificated on life, and chocolate, with chocolate being by far the most important, obviously. He would often take me for lunch while Alice toiled away, showing me the best *croque-madame* or how to eat shellfish properly. I would set my alarm for naps, then often go out with Sami too, after work, who turned out to be the most fun omnisexual Algerian flatmate I'd ever had, when he wasn't complaining about opera singers who got too fat and budgets that got too small. I didn't see Laurent about much after he'd dropped me off. Sami said he was quite the *boulevardier*, always with a different model on his arm. I imagined Thierry had been similar when he'd been younger. Poor Claire.

After two months of this, I found I loved getting up at the crack of dawn, patting Nelson Eddy the dog, who fetched the newspaper for his mistress who lived on our street every morning, pit-patting past our door as we opened up; seeing the freshly cleaned cobbles come to life, water dribbling down the drains; the tiny funny-looking vans delivering drinks and fresh food; the smells of bread baking everywhere; the running hither and thither of kitchen staff. The sheer number of restaurants in Paris was dizzying, and Thierry seemed intent on visiting all of them; then the glancing up through the roofs and pigeons to the tiny floating clouds miles above to see if it was going to be another glorious day. That summer, it seemed, every day was a good day. I liked most of all getting dressed and going out on my little terrace first thing. The whole of Paris, laid out in front of me like a huge tray of macaroons, glowed rose pink, and I would think of the boarded-up high street of Kidinsborough with the pound shop and Kash4Gold, and how when it rained, the canal would spit old bikes out on the tow path, and feel as far away from home as if I'd landed on the moon. I did no food shopping (during my lunch hour, everything else was shut too, which drove me absolutely crazy), and mixed and scrubbed with all my might. I thought—I thought—one morning that I might even have actually had a dream in French. Sami and I often crossed paths at 4:00 a.m., he coming in, me arising for work, and we would often stop and take a coffee (with brandy for him, nothing for me, as every time I ran out of milk, I had to go down seven dark flights to find some, and it never seemed worth it, so I just learned to drink it black). Sometimes he was with chaps, sometimes with girls, sometimes alone, sometimes with an entire party. It was very fortunate I didn't work normal hours; it could

have been a disaster. The eyrie remained absolutely tiny, with no working kitchen beyond coffee, no shower, and a bath you had to sit in with
your knees pulled up to your chin.

I loved it.

I tried to keep in contact with home, but it seemed so far away sometimes.

I knew I was getting into it when Cath and I swapped email. I
think I was just a bit overexcited and needed to tell someone. In retrospect, Cath probably wasn't the right person.

Hi C! I just got back from the most amazing party on a boat in the
middle of the Seine. There were fire jugglers (my flatmate took me,
everyone he knows does something stupid like that) and they kept
setting drinks on fire and people kept trying to leap over them.
Then these two chefs came on. One of them is my boss's son, but
they've fallen out with each other. Anyway, they were trying to hurl
crepes over the flames in little pans, but they kept falling out and it
was hysterical and brilliant. Hope you're good. Anna.

Dear Anna,

On Tuesday I put four hours' worth of extensions in "Ermine" (she
used to be called Sal, do you remember? daft bint) McGuire's
head for her *X-Factor* audition. She smoked through the entire
thing. I think I've gone blind. She wanted red, white, and blue and
kept on talking about how she was going to pull Simon Cowell.
It took all afternoon and I had to have the door blowing open on
account of her wanting to smoke. I think I've got bronchitis. And
I lost one of my new snakeskin nails in it. I said what was she
doing, being the new Michelle McManus? And she told me to
shut it, but I'd been standing all bloody day. Then she came in
yesterday, her eyes red with crying, and said nobody had even
seen her and she'd waited nine hours in the hosing rain and the

colors had all run and it was my fault and she wanted her money back. I said she could go whistle and she said she could go punch me in the head. I got out the big scissors.

The police have said they won't press charges, but I have to give her the hair back in a box. I said I wouldn't be touching it, it probably had crabs already. PC Johnson smiled and said he got off at 9. So I'm off.

Come back soon,
  Cath

I hadn't meant to gush to Cath, but it was really a proper fun night. Well, it had started in the morning. Thierry had marched in huffing something about refrigeration. He was furious about it; even if we were running horribly late, you could never, ever put his work in the fridge, because it took away the highly polished shine. Anyway, we'd had an electricity bill and Alice was spitting feathers about it and basically implying why couldn't we work in the dark or something, and Frédéric had mentioned the fridges and Thierry had started huffing and puffing and getting red in the face, until eventually he'd signaled something to Benoît, who had immediately run up the street and returned with two dozen eggs.

"Anna! Come with me!" Thierry hollered. He had kind of taken me under his wing a bit. I was happy about this, obviously, in that I wasn't going to get sent home to annoy Claire, but I could always feel Alice's gimlet eyes boring into me.

"Chocolate pots," said Thierry. "Seeing as we are paying for all this electricity…" He glared balefully at the large fridges, which were full of milk and butter actually. He grabbed the eggs and started separating them into a bowl, so quickly and deftly it was fascinating to watch. Then he took the whites, passed me over a bowl, and started to whisk them up at the speed of light.

"Can't we do that in the mixer?" I asked tentatively, my wrist getting tired.

"We can buy them from the supermarket," he barked back. "Would you like that? Would that suit you?"

Next, he started to melt some of the day's fresh plain in a huge double boiler style device over boiling water, very carefully, stirring all the time. He added milk powder and cocoa powder, even though I raised my eyebrows at him. "You make it stick together if you want," he said. "Don't question my methods."

But he was smiling though, so I knew it was all right. He made the whole lot into a kind of paste, then he studied the line at the back of the greenhouse for a long time, humming and hawing. After changing his mind several times and picking up and putting down a large bag of almonds, eventually he settled on half ginger and half lime, sprinkling them and tasting liberally in the two different vats. Then, once again with that dainty step of his, indicating to me to do the other ones, he poured one of the double boilers into two dozen little ramekin pots. Not taking any chances, I put mine in with a big soup ladle. Then we lined them up on trays.

Thierry flung open the doors of the fridge, saying, "Ta-da!!! Now I shall make use of you, you money-guzzling goddess!" But of course the fridge was actually full. Benoît dashed to clear some shelf space for us to put in *les petits pots*.

Thierry took himself off for a midmorning *digestif*, and by the time he returned, the little pots had set and darkened to a glossy sheen. He frowned, then announced to the fridge that this was all they were good for, this and eating his money. He took out a tiny silver spoon and let me taste a side of the lime one. It was extraordinary. Lighter than air, whisked into a melting nothingness that left a dark rich sensation on the tongue and an extraordinary desire to eat more of it; it was hardly like eating at all, more like a dream of flavor.

He priced them at something extortionate. We sold out in fifteen minutes. I made him promise to stand over me one more time while I made them, and he said he didn't have the necessary forty years to teach me where I was going wrong, but I was pleased nonetheless.

When I got back that evening, Sami was cross. He was making costumes for a production called *La Bohème*. (He said it in a way that assumed I had heard of it. I had never heard of it, but nodded my head importantly. I guess to him it was like someone saying they'd never heard of Michael Jackson.) Anyway, he said his bohemians had all gone too far bohemian and he couldn't get them to come to any fittings, so he was going to have to track them down at their house, except they were living on a barge and setting it loose.

It was a gorgeous evening; the light in Paris felt like dripping gold.

"I don't suppose you're going to come," said Sami with some sarcasm, because he kept asking me to come out in the evenings and I hardly ever said yes, partly because I was shy, and a lot because I was constantly knackered, embarrassed about my French, and smelled of greenhouse.

But I was buoyed by Thierry's careful lesson of the day and how accepted it was making me feel, and for once not too exhausted, so I said yes, to his total surprise.

The singers were living on a houseboat on the Seine. It was full of people enjoying the evening, drinking and juggling and hanging out. I pasted on my best grin as Sami got swallowed up by a hundred of his closest acquaintances and got myself a glass of champagne (I was quite impressed that they didn't have enough money to rent an apartment but wouldn't dream of stinting on the fizz), and by the time I came back up deck from the tiny galley, someone had started up the engines and we were putting out into the Seine itself. I wasn't entirely sure this was legal and looked around dubiously as the barge narrowly avoided the pleasure boats—the *bateaux mouches*—that patrolled the waters. The boat went upstream under the bridges and passed the crowded stone banks. The towers of Notre Dame and the Eiffel Tower bobbed in and out of sight as we moved. The party grew wilder as we moored just off the Île de la Cité, and suddenly two men, to huge roars of encouragement, took out huge brands that were their fire-eating torches. At first I was horrified—they were going to set the boat on fire and kill us all. But then I sort of thought, well, I am away, in a foreign country, having an *extremely* foreign experience, and anyway I can't get off the boat, so I may as well just go with it. But I made sure I was as far back as possible.

The boys, stripped to the waist, lit the torches and then, to my excited horror, started juggling with them. The boat was bobbing up and down but they kept their balance perfectly, and it was both funny and frightening at once. People on the banks of the river were hailing each other to watch. Sami was ring-mastering, shouting and gesticulating with his arms.

Suddenly I saw a familiar face, bent low in conversation with a girl, but, it seemed, not really paying attention to what she was saying. His eyes searched the boat. Then they saw me and smiled, briefly, in recognition, and he raised his hand. Before I realized what I'd done, I'd smiled too and waved back. It was Laurent, Thierry's son. Instantly I felt rather guilty, as if I were double-crossing the lovely day I'd had at work with his dad. I bit my lip, and he grinned and got back into conversation with the girl, but not before Sami grabbed his arm and started yelling at him. At first he shook his head no, no, definitely not, but before I knew it, someone had stuck a frying pan in his hand and a white chef's hat on his head, and the music had been turned up and everyone was clapping. He lifted his hands in a gesture of surrender and, in the oddest coincidence, started cracking eggs into a bowl. His deft strong fingers behaved exactly like his father's. I was hypnotized. Someone brought up flour too, and milk, and he whisked it up—again in the same way—and the fire-eaters brought their torches down and started throwing them more gently, as, to my utter astonishment, Laurent melted some butter in the little pan, then started to cook pancakes over the flames of the fire-jugglers' torches. This must have been a party trick; each new one was flung in the air in near-perfect timing with the torches themselves and greeted with rounds of applause, particularly the one that flew right off the boat, to be immediately snapped up by an enormous seagull.

It was true; everyone Sami knows is basically in show business. I am completely the most normal person Sami has ever met. He thinks I'm really exotic as a consequence. He keeps asking me if it's true that we eat things out of paper and what toast is.

It was stunning to watch. At one point, Laurent had to reach for a pancake he'd flipped right up out of the pan and stretched a long arm over me, lost his footing, and landed nearly in my lap.

"Oof," he said. "*Bonsoir, mam'zelle.*"

"Hello, Laurent," I said. He'd straightened up really quickly.

"The spy!" he said, but his eyes were twinkling in a way I'd seen before.

"I'm not a spy! How could I be a spy? What, I'm going to steal a pancake recipe?"

"You shall tell my father I am a partying good-for-nothing," he said, his big black eyes sparkling at me.

"That very much depends," I said, "on whether or not I get the next pancake."

He looked at it, all perfectly cooked, then grabbed a bottle from the side of the boat and poured Grand Marnier, the orange liqueur, all over the top. It sizzled, and as the alcohol burned off, a delicious smell filled the air. Then he picked up a napkin and, in a move that seemed almost like magic, flicked the pancake onto it, and in a trice, folded it up into an envelope so I could eat it.

"I shall tell him you're a very good boy," I said. The crepe was painfully hot, but totally delicious.

Something crossed his face at that moment, something that wasn't just about him being a party boy. Some remembered pain.

"No," he said quietly. "No. Don't tell him anything at all."

I looked straight at him, wondering what these two larger-than-life personalities could possibly have fallen out about that was this bad.

"Come in and see me," I said, a bit tipsy, not quite realizing what I was saying. Then I stopped horrified.

"I don't mean like that," I said. "I mean, come by to see me and you can see your dad. But not like that."

He smiled, put out a calloused hand, and suddenly, out of the blue, touched my cheek. I flushed a fiery red.

"Ah, not like that, huh?"

I reminded myself about Frédéric and that this was what French men were like. Incorrigible flirts. Ridiculously flirtatious. Cor, they were good at it though. I resisted a sudden strong temptation to reach out and touch his stubbled chin, his thick curly hair.

"Laurent! Laurent! More crepes! Encore!"

The girls were calling for him from the other side of the boat, the torches still burning high. I checked my watch. It was late; I was up early. Someone moored the boat to give me time to get off, and a party of people dressed as Harlequins to get on.

He smiled, as if he knew exactly what was going through my mind, gave me a quick kiss on either cheek—perfectly normal here, I knew, absolutely standard French behavior, brothers did it to one another, so there was no reason for it to set my cheeks flaming so, or for me to catch the slightly burned sugar smell that came off his warm skin—and vanished back into the crowd, as I, with a mix of relief and regret, found my own way across the gangplank and back to the safe ground of the Île de la Cité—no long walk home for me, lost in the big city. I knew the way. The lights and the fire and the laughter and music from the barge lit up the river all the way home.

11

I didn't mention the previous evening when Thierry marched in the next day. It was barely eight o'clock and I was sweeping up the husks when I heard the *ting* of the front doorbell. Frédéric and Benoît looked at me, confused. They had been playing the radio loudly. French pop music was, I discovered, very much an acquired taste. Frédéric immediately turned it down and called out, "*Bonjour.*"

But standing in the doorway, without Alice or any bluster from yesterday or any of the constant motion I'm used to, was Thierry, his large bulk outlined in the still hazy light from the front door, his normal broad grin completely absent.

"Anna," he said. "Come, walk with me."

• • • •

I did as he said. It was going to be a beautiful day, but there was still a hint of dawn chilliness in the air. There were many fewer tourists about this time in the morning; it was mostly just shop keepers, the rattling of grates, the sluicing of dirty water in the mop buckets going down the drains, everywhere the scent of coffee and fresh baking.

"Let us walk," he repeated, without saying anything else. I glanced at him quickly, wondering if his knees were up to it. He didn't look like he took any exercise at all. He saw me glancing and smiled, though less ebulliently than usual.

"I used to love to walk," he said. "I used to walk everywhere. It was my favorite thing to do. Look!"

He took me down the cobbled lane that led to Île Saint-Louis and then across the beautiful Pont de Sully, which is lined with the padlocks of lovers. People just leave them there, to signify their love, and the authorities let them stay. They're beautiful. A *bateau mouche* wended lazily down the river, and a large flock of seagulls took off just in front of us. Ahead was the somber, riveting wall of the old Bastille.

"Paris changes too much," he said, even though I was thinking absolutely the opposite, pointing out a huge field of banners over on the Left Bank. "Look, they are having a festival," he said. "Food from all around the world."

"Why don't we take a stall," I said, not thinking about it.

He looked at me. "Because we do not need to! We are far too good," he said.

"All right," I said. "It was just an idea."

"Does Chanel take a stall at a market? Does Christian Dior?"

I didn't point out that you could find these brands all over the world, but decided to change the subject.

"Why don't you walk so much anymore?"

"Because I am busy, because Alice does not like to walk; she thinks it is vulgar."

"How is walking vulgar?" I couldn't stop myself from asking.

"Well, because you cannot wear beautiful shoes, and you look like you cannot afford a car."

I thought that was possibly the stupidest thing I had ever heard in my life, but I'd already insulted him once this morning, so I decided to keep it to myself.

"I like it," I ventured instead. "It's a good way to see a place."

"It is!" agreed Thierry fervently. We'd reached the other side of the bridge; the morning rush-hour traffic was inelegantly struggling for places on the roundabout, but we ignored them all. He turned and gestured back at what I'd already come to think of as my home; the Île de la Cité, the square familiar towers of Notre Dame Cathedral visible through the gaps.

"Look at it! A perfect tiny city-state in miniature. Everything you could possibly want is there."

Except a supermarket that opens at lunchtime, I thought but didn't say.

"You could live on that island forever and never leave. People did. It was the first inhabited area of Paris. Right in the heart of the world."

I smiled at his absolute certainty that where he was was the heart of the world. He moved surprisingly swiftly for such a large man.

He looked at me.

"I got another letter from Claire."

There wasn't any point in prevaricating.

"She is very unwell," he said.

"She is," I said. I felt immediately guilty. Sami had the oldest laptop in the world and sometimes we could hook on to our neighbor's Wi-Fi, but I hadn't kept in touch anything like as much as I should have. She didn't have a lot to occupy her days; a bit of gossip would have come in very handy. Later she told me she was thrilled I was too busy and happy to write, just as her own mum had been, so convincingly I almost believed her. I called Mum and Dad every Sunday and told them about new things I'd tried and new food and they tried to sound interested, but I don't think they were really. They told me about the dog (barbed wire in paw) and Joe (new building apprenticeship, fat girlfriend). And Cath texted from time to time. But my new life felt so immersive. I vowed at the very least to be better at talking to Claire.

"What was wrong with you?" he said.

"I lost two toes," I said.

Thierry scrunched up his face in pained sympathy. "Ah, look." He showed me his littlest finger. It was slightly blunted. He'd obviously

126

sliced the top off. "This is how I knew I was bound for sweets, *non*? No more butchering for me. No more cooking for big hungry soldiers in the desert. Ugh."

I nodded in sympathy.

"So," he said. "And she…she has all her toes?"

"She has cancer," I said.

"Yes."

We were walking above the embankment by the river, which was running fast today, a kind of dark blue color. There were a lot of boats up and down; goods and coal were coming in.

Thierry stared at the water as if he didn't see it.

"Ah, the cancer," he said simply. "It is the sniper at the party. Everyone, we are happy, then…boom."

We kept staring.

"They can do many, many good things for cancer now," he said.

I shook my head. "Maybe. She has it in three places. It is hard to have it in three places. And she is stubborn."

Thierry glanced at me then looked away very quickly. "So it is as bad as that."

"Maybe," I shrugged. I didn't want to think about it.

"And her family is kind."

"Her sons are very good."

"She has sons?"

"Two."

"Ah, sons," he said, and I supposed he was thinking of Laurent. "They are kind? They look after her?"

"They're wonderful," I said.

He harrumphed.

"Mine would not call the *pompiers* if I were on fire."

Thierry bit his lip at this.

"Oh, my little Claire," he said suddenly, as if I wasn't there. "My little English bird. My little Claire."

• • • •

1972

"You look…you look beautiful."

Claire giggled. She had never seen Thierry lost for words; she didn't think it was possible. He was as greedy for words, for ideas and new information and jokes, as he was for food, for wine, for chocolate, for Paris, for her.

But here, out in the garden of the LeGuarde house, all closed down as the family decamped to Provence, leaving her alone in Paris, it felt like everyone had left, en masse. The entire city had emptied out, leaving the heat for the soft breezes and mimosas of the South. Businesses had closed down, restaurants were no longer serving. The city was like a ghost town. Or a playground.

In a feat of devastating boldness, Claire had left a note. A little note, at the shop, in the morning before he would be in. She had thought about it many times. She had gone to Papeterie Saint-Sabin, the great stationers, and spent an enormous amount of her earned cash on the most exquisite stationery. She had been almost unable to choose from how beautiful it all was. Finally she had gone for a pale green and yellow flower, very similar to her new dress. The heavy cream envelope was lined with pale green and gold stripes. It was absolutely beautiful. Her heart in her mouth, she had slipped into M. LeGuarde's private office, all leather chairs and heavy furniture, and borrowed one of his fountain pens, trying to make sure not to blot the ink. And she had written, simply, a time and the address, her hand shaking with excitement.

Of course he had come; had found her, as she planned, around the back door. He took off his hat, his face a little pink in the heat, mopping his brow. The garden was built high, with fruit trees bordering the edge to give the area privacy. On the perfectly straight lawn, Claire had put out a picnic: the finest Morbier cheese, which she knew he adored; some pâté and heavy sourdough bread from the tiny southern bakery on the corner; grapes, big, shiny, and pitted with seeds—he liked to chop them with a tiny knife, nipping out the seeds with extraordinary dexterity in his huge bearlike paws; carved Serrano ham from the terrifying butcher that she had had to pluck up a lot of courage to enter; and, chilling in a bucket of ice, a bottle of Laurent Perrier '68. Mme. LeGuarde had told her to help herself to whatever she wanted. This was clearly pushing it, Claire realized. She would make it up to them, she told herself.

The sun fell heavy and huge, rippling through the great old oak trees as she sought out some shade. The light felt thick and golden, almost like syrup, as Claire sat, waiting, unable to concentrate, fiddling with her hair, her new dress, the food, the delicate china she had carefully removed from the tall armoire in the dining room, the small jar of fresh flowers she'd picked from the beds, behind other plants so hopefully nobody would notice. She had showered as late as possible and sat, anxiously. He made his way around to the door which led onto the little back alleyway between their grand imposing street and the next, knocked quickly, then entered, taking off his hat and wondering where his handkerchief was.

Then she stood up. The sun lit up her pale hair, made it shine as if it were gold. The gentle green silk of her dress ran off her like a river; she looked like something conjured from the water, or a dryad from the trees.

"Claire. You look…you look beautiful," he breathed quietly, for once moved to silence. She moved toward him, and he pulled her close, then sat her on his lap in the shade of the great green tree. Nothing was eaten. Words were no longer necessary. Some little time later, the birds started into the bright blue sky.

●　●　●　●

Thierry led me down to the corner of the street, where there was a tiny, packed boulangerie with a few tables and chairs very close. You could no longer see the river, nor the Île de la Cité, which sat in the middle like a great ship. Thierry barked a quick order to the waiter, who came charging back right through the middle of everyone with two tiny coffees, each with four sugar lumps placed on the side, and two enormous *religieuse* buns—two profiteroles, one smaller than the other, covered in chocolate and held together by cream, so they look like little nuns or priests. He ate his without thinking about it, then held up his hand for another, like a cowboy downing whisky shots at a bar.

Then he paused while I waited for him. The bun was totally delicious.

"It was difficult," he said. "Her father…well. We were very young. It was the summer. She had to return, then I got called up…"

He looked up at me, and suddenly through his jolly, tubby demeanor, I saw a lot of sadness in his eyes.

"When you are young," he said, "you think you will get lots of chances at love. You are careless, you spend your youth and your freedom and your love because you think you will be rich with all these things forever. But they do not last. You spend it all, then you see if you have spent wisely."

He took a more reflective bite of his second cake.

"I thought…I thought we would have time, always. That the summer would never end, that things would never have to change… I am an old fool, Anna. Don't be like me."

"Things aren't so bad for you," I said instantly.

He smiled. "Ha. Thank you. You are kind." He leaned forward. "Do you think…do you think I could talk to Claire?"

I tutted. "Have you never heard of the telephone? You can talk to her whenever you like."

"I feel uncomfortable on the telephone," said Thierry. "And also I did not know; what if she didn't want to talk to me?"

"You two are worse than teenagers," I said, meaning it. When my brother Joe had a crush on Selma Torrington, he sat in his bedroom for a week. James found a poem he'd written and we were so taken with the horrible seriousness of it all, we didn't even tease him about it.

"You're grown-ups," I said. "Just phone her. Or write back to her."

His face looked unhappy again. "I don't... I am not so good with the letters."

"Well, you have to do something."

"Then I shall do that," he said. "You think she would be pleased to hear from me?" he asked again, beckoning over the bill.

"Of *course*!" I said, exasperated, and he smiled.

He positively bounced back along the riverbank with me, sweating slightly and seemingly full of newly inspired energy, pointing out various landmarks and asking did I think Claire would be able to travel and would she like to come and see them again, and pondering how much they might have changed in forty years and how she had been in the interim without him, and asking questions I couldn't answer, like what her husband was like.

"Oh," I said. I had been wondering when would be a good time to bring this up, but hadn't seen an opening in the conversation so far. "I met your son."

He stopped short and looked at me.

"Why?" he said. "How did you meet my son?"

I didn't say I had thought he was going to try to attack me and steal my mobile phone.

"Um, just about town," I said. Thierry narrowed his eyes at this.

"I thought this was your first time in Paris," he said.

"It is," I stammered. "I just have a very sociable flatmate."

Thierry looked displeased. "Well. He is a do-nothing."

"Doesn't he have a job?" I said, a bit shocked. I'd just assumed he did. Maybe that was why he had such a tiny scooter.

"Well, if you call making ridiculous confections for a great big company that is not your father's company and is in fact in direct competition..."

His face went brick red.

"Sorry," I said. "I really am. I didn't realize things were quite as bad as that."

He shook his head. "He says I was not a good father. He makes Alice smoke too much."

I wondered if Thierry's self-obsession and gadfly enthusiasms, while fun, might not be ideally suited to fatherhood.

"Maybe you are very alike," I ventured.

"We are not at all alike," he said, and as soon as he said it, I got the family resemblance in the brown eyes with their thick fringe of lashes. "He doesn't listen."

"Shall we get back?" I said. I didn't particularly want Benoît to take against me any more than he had already, and they'd be shutting for lunch soon and I still had pots to clean.

"He never listens to me, his father," said Thierry, not listening to me. He stepped out into the road suddenly. A car screeched and swerved to avoid him, and we both jumped back, frightened.

"Idiot!" shouted Thierry, his face purple, shaking his fist in a rage at the disappearing little gray Peugeot. "Bloody monster! You cannot drive! You should not be allowed to drive!"

The lights had changed, and I ushered him across the cobbled road, as he continued to shout threats and gesticulate behind him.

"You bloody son of a pig! You do not look where you are going!"

We were one step onto the Pont Neuf when it happened. The pavement was busy, thronged with people going to work in the huge Ministry of Justice building, and ready to visit the cathedral, and several people found their way blocked as the huge man suddenly stopped short in the middle of the pavement, clutching his chest and left arm.

12

1972

*T*here we are," thought Mme. LeGuarde, *as they returned from Provence, the children tanned and happy to do little more each day than paddle in the stream at the end of the garden, try to catch snakes in pillowcases, and fall asleep in restaurants in the evening, little Claudette often under the table, as they met up with friends—the same friends, Mme. LeGuarde noticed with more amusement every passing year, that they saw all the time in Paris, dressed a little more casually and discussing the local dishes with some passion. Ah, well, that was the life of the bon chic, bon genre. More than once, her thoughts strayed to Claire and whether she had done the right thing leaving her alone with that bear of a man. She had, she decided. The girl was nearly eighteen years old and had never been allowed an inch of freedom her entire life. She was a sensible child, and he was a kind man. This would be good for her.*

Nonetheless, her eyes swept the house on her return, everything so anxiously placed perfectly and Claire standing there with wide, nervous eyes—she'd obviously been up all night making sure everything was just right. There was a (watery, poor) shepherd's pie in the fridge she'd made for them, and to Mme. LeGuarde's practiced eye, Claire looked rosy, happy, anxious, overtired, and well and truly in love.

Claire herself felt delirious. She was happy, excited, transported. She was terribly nervous and had no idea how she was going to look after the children. Somehow she'd thought that when she and Thierry got together—if they ever did; she hadn't quite been able to believe it would ever happen until the very second it actually did—it would somehow calm her down, quell the craziness in her breast, the fact that she spent every moment of the day thinking about him. In fact, if anything it had gotten worse. The softness of his curly hair, the fire and tenderness in his eyes, the bulk of him...they spent every moment together they could: eating, talking, making love, all of them done with Thierry's huge appetite for life. She felt as if he had brought her to life, that she had been leading a black-and-white existence, and with the arrival of this affable Frenchman, everything had burst into color. The Reverend's house was Kansas, and Paris, to her, was Oz.

Mme. LeGuarde caught up with her after they'd been home a couple of days. Claire had been beyond conscientious with the children, listening patiently to all their stories of sticklebacks and wading and hammocks and bees, playing and painting with them, and taking them to the new exhibitions. But her soul lived only until five, when she would run to the shop, and he would be there, dragging her into the back room, hiding behind the huge copper vats, kissing her passionately as if he hadn't seen her for months, insisting she try this or that, a new taste, a new flavor, then a restaurant where he would inveigle her into snails, or foie gras, or linguine with tiny clams she had to pry from their shells, or lobster Thermidor to a backdrop of wildly kicking girls. Then he would take her back to his little set of rooms at the top of Place des Arts, the noises of the street and the streetlamps still bright beneath them, the chatter of French at high speed and cars occasionally whooshing past, and they would make love, over and over again, then he would dress and courteously take her home, dropping her before midnight with a kiss and the certain knowledge that they could do it all again tomorrow.

"My dear," Mme. LeGuarde said quietly as Claire was preparing to go out, this time in the pale cream stripe. Claire's back stiffened, as it always did. There was something inside her, deep down, that didn't feel as if she deserved this, that she was doing something wrong. In her father's eyes of course, she was. Her polite, stiff weekly letters to her parents, full of the doings of the children and the sights of Paris, gave so little away her mother worried that she was actually terribly miserable and lonely, but surely if she'd been so unhappy she'd have found out a way to make an international phone call. Her mother made sure she answered the phone all the time, just in case it was the operator asking them to accept a reverse charge call and the Reverend said no, he didn't believe in them.

"It's all right," said Mme. LeGuarde to Claire's back. She was fastening in some tiny emerald earrings Thierry had bought her. She had laughed and said he didn't have to buy her anything at all and he had said he knew that, really he would like to buy her diamonds like Elizabeth Taylor, but he was just starting out and this was all he could do. They were very small, like tiny green chips, but they matched her eyes and were beautifully set in an antique twist of silver. She would have loved them anyway, because he had chosen them for her. The fact that they were tasteful too made her hug herself gleefully inside. They had made love wearing nothing else but the earrings, and she had giggled and called herself a kept woman.

"You're not in trouble," said Mme. LeGuarde. Claire felt relieved. It was ridiculous, to keep panicking like this. Thierry thought she was being hilarious. She was a grown woman. Who could begrudge her her happiness? Claire wasn't so sure. God was always watching. And so much happiness, so much pleasure. It didn't feel right, somehow. She didn't feel like she deserved it. Somewhere in the back of her head, a tiny voice kept telling her she was wicked.

Claire turned around.

"Good," she said. "You know, the children really are wonderful, Mme. LeGuarde. You've done such a great job with them."

Mme. LeGuarde waved her hand. In her opinion, like that of many French women, children flourished the less their parents interfered.

"I just wanted to say, my dear. We have grown very fond of you during your stay here."

Claire felt herself blushing and felt awkward. How could they like her, when she had been…when she had been out every night like an alley cat, her inner voice—that sounded a lot like her father—said. "We will be very sad when you have to leave us…in two weeks."

Mme. LeGuarde was doing her best to be gentle.

"You are going back to school, non? I think that will be right for you. You should continue your studies; you have plenty of brains. University life would suit you."

"I don't think so," said Claire, shaking her head miserably. Most of her energy went on not thinking about leaving. Two weeks was forever. It was a long time. She could worry about it later.

"My father thinks it's a waste of time. He thinks secretarial school. Or teacher training."

Mme. LeGuarde frowned. "Well, you are good with children…but don't you think there are other things you could do? Or other people you might meet?"

Mme. LeGuarde was nothing if not practical.

Claire swallowed, all her happiness gone. She stared fixedly at the parquet floor, not trusting herself to speak. Mme. LeGuarde gently lifted up her head and looked her in the eye.

"I hope you have been happy here," she said, very clearly and distinctly. "And that when you go home, you will have many happy memories."

Claire understood, of course she did. She was only a girl. Thierry was barely twenty-two, at the very beginning of his career. What did she think was going to happen, that she was going to stay in Paris and get married?

Of course, on one level, deep down, that was exactly what she thought. Not to go back to school, not to go home at all. She had a silly girlish vision of Thierry and her, her in something from the special, lace-heavy corner of Marie-France's shop, in a beautiful park on the Île de la Cité…not that they could get married in a park of course; that was ridiculous. And not that she could afford a wedding dress. And they had only known each other a few weeks. The whole thing was ridiculous, impossible. She was too much of a Northern girl not to know that, even if Thierry had even mentioned anything beyond August at all. He had not.

She couldn't imagine Thierry in Kidinsborough, catching the number 19 bus, walking to the Asian shop on the corner to pick up some super-noodles for supper like the boys liked. She couldn't see him propping up the corner of the Crown, her dad's pub, drinking a pint and talking seriously about who was going to score on Saturday. He didn't even speak English. How would he choke down her mother's Yorkshires, which shattered like glass or resembled mush? The first time she had eaten glazed carrots at Mortons, she genuinely refused to believe it was the same vegetable they ate at home. He couldn't come over. The idea was ridiculous.

But Arnaud and Claudette were starting school; she wasn't needed around here. She had to go back to school herself. And Thierry could afford to neglect his business in August, when there were no galas, no parties, no social set to cater for. That would change for him too, in September; he would have to work harder than ever just to keep afloat. There would be no room for her in all of this. She knew this.

She thought of all this in the split second it took to lift her head.

"I will," she said, returning Mme. LeGuarde's steady gaze. "I will have good memories."

■ ■ ■ ■

Thierry staggered back and many of the passersby stopped and cleared a space; I grabbed his arm, and thankfully a strong-looking man with a beard helped me lower him to the ground, as he made horrible sounds. I pulled out my phone and stabbed 999 over and over again, but it didn't go through, and I felt as if I were in a horrible nightmare. The bearded man took my phone and showed me how to dial 112 instead. It hadn't even occurred to me that the emergency number might be different, but when the operator answered in French, I suddenly found myself struck completely dumb and unable to talk.

Thankfully the man took the phone back from me and barked our location into the mouthpiece.

Behind me, a woman who introduced herself as a nurse had put a scarf under Thierry's head; he now appeared to have lost consciousness. I crouched down and held his hand, whispering in English that everything was going to be all right, even though I didn't know whether it would be at all. Someone came along and shouted "Thierry Girard"—it wasn't until much later I thought that only in Paris would someone recognize a chocolate maker in the street—and many other people stopped after that and looked concerned and murmured to each other. Somebody took out a phone, and the man with the beard growled and called them a filthy name until they sidled away, head down. The nurse, thank God, climbed onto him and started doing chest compressions. I swore with everything I had in me that I was going to attend a St. John's Ambulance course, just like they'd suggested every year in the factory. The idea of having to give fake mouth to mouth to Mr. Asten, the first aider, was so repulsive we had just laughed and scoffed every time it had come up. I vowed now that I would take it and make everyone else do it too, just as long as…as long as he was all right. He had to be all right.

Seconds or minutes later, thank God, I heard the ambulance. The nurse had told us to hang on, that he was breathing and that the guys who were coming would know a lot better than us, and sure enough they jumped out. Then they looked at Thierry and looked at the stretcher and shook their heads and there was some conversation. I still felt trapped in a nightmare, shouting at them to get him in, as they made increasingly clear that they couldn't get him onto it.

Finally, one of the paramedics, taking over for the nurse, and the man with the beard called six strong-looking men out of the crowd. They wheeled the stretcher back into the ambulance and secured it there, then the men altogether carefully lifted Thierry's enormous bulk inside, as I sobbed with relief and felt cross that Alice and Laurent between them hadn't done something, hadn't insisted on him curbing his appetites and his greed. Then I remembered that I myself that morning had watched him eat four cream buns and most of a loaf of bread and a glass of cider and smoke three cigarettes. I could no more have told him not to than fly to the moon.

The paramedic motioned me inside, and I was torn. I needed to get back to the shop to tell everyone what had happened and—oh God—contact Laurent. I didn't even have his telephone number; he'd zoomed off into the night without warning. But of course I had to go with him. Someone had to.

• • • •

The smell of hospitals doesn't seem to change so much from country to country. The paramedics called ahead, and when we got there, they had a much larger stretcher brought down from somewhere already. I trailed along uselessly behind, then got sidelined by an administrator who needed all his insurance details, none of which, of course, I had. I didn't even realize the medical system was different here, that you couldn't just turn up. And there was nothing in my phone, not even the number of the shop. The administrator made it entirely plain and clear that I was a someone simply trying her luck who had no business snarling up her morning with my boss's inconvenient heart attacks and I was fervently thankful that, despite its faults, the National Health Service would just fix you without shouting at you for paperwork first. Suddenly I became terrified they were going to ask for a credit card, until finally one of the nurses brought in his wallet, which she went through with practiced ease until she found a green card that was obviously what she was looking for. She then gave me the glad eye, as if I'd known all this and had been keeping it from her.

And after that, there wasn't much to do but go in search of an internet connection or a phone book or anything that could get me in touch with the shop. Except I didn't want to travel too far from Thierry's side in case something happened or he simply needed a hand to hold. From time to time, I would dart into a corridor in search of a phone box, as every so often a young doctor would come out and in polite and slow English ask me if I knew his blood type or whether he was diabetic or whether I could sign a consent form. It was horrible; I had no idea of the number for directory inquiries, and after a few stabs at it, I sighed and nearly threw the phone down, as it dropped another bar and came close to running out of charge.

Eventually, there was only one thing I could think of. I called.

•　　•　　•　　•

Claire sounded half asleep and groggy when she picked up her home phone. It was a relief though, firstly that she was there, and secondly that she was obviously getting some sleep. At times in the treatment, she couldn't sleep at all.

"Anna!" she said, clearly delighted to hear from me. "How are things? I've been thinking about you! How are you getting on? How are you settling in?"

I made a mental note to write her a long—very long—email as soon as I had the time, but right at that moment, I had no time.

"I'll tell you everything," I said quickly, "but right now I'm in a bit of a tight spot and first of all I need to ask you something really quickly and then I'll call you back, okay?"

"Well, yes, all right," she said, sounding a bit taken aback. "Is everything all right?"

"I'll call you later," I said. "But please, can I ask you—do you know the shop telephone number? Um, I've come out without it. Do you have any way you could track it down?"

There wasn't even a moment's pause. Not a second.

"54-67-89-12-15," she rattled off.

I couldn't hang up straightaway.

"You know it by heart?" I said.

"Oh yes," she said, suddenly sounding far away. Then she pulled herself together. "Well, no mobiles in those days. You had to learn all your phone numbers by heart."

"And you still remember *all* your phone numbers?"

There was a little pause.

"Not all of them, no."

I swallowed.

"I really do have to go," I said. "I'll call you back, I promise."

And I hung up before she could ask any more or get any more worried.

●　●　●　●

The phone in the shop rang for so long that I thought they'd closed up for the morning. I prayed they hadn't. And that Frédéric would answer, not Benoît.

Thankfully, for once, my prayers were answered. I could hear Frédéric's shock as I explained as well as I could—my French was all over the place suddenly; it was like something had shaken loose in my brain and I had completely forgotten how to talk. I realized when he asked me which hospital I was in that I didn't even know and had to ask the grumpy administrator again, who looked at me like I was the biggest idiot ever to walk the face of the earth.

"Hôtel-Dieu," I said.

"Fine," said Frédéric. "It's close by. I'll shut the shop and let people know…"

He paused and his voice cracked a little.

"Is he… I mean, he's going to be all right, isn't he? They're fixing him?"

"I don't know," I said honestly. "I really don't know."

The doctors invited me in to see him as he was prepped for surgery.

It felt absurd, somehow, to care so much for someone I'd known for only a few weeks, but to see him there, unconscious, the great life force of him flat on the bed like a huge walrus, his mustache flopping sadly, covered by a tube inserted in his nose—I immediately burst into tears.

"We give him bypass," said the young doctor in English. "We hope…we hope it will work. He is a difficult patient."

"You mean he is too big?" I said.

The doctor nodded. "He is… It is difficult for us to do what we need to do."

I nodded. It must be. I didn't envy her, having to get down through all those layers.

"But," I found myself saying, "he has…he has a big heart, you know? It is worth it."

She nodded without smiling and snapped briskly, "It's always worth it."

● ● ● ●

After that and squeezing his hand once more, watching him go in the specially big bed, I sat in the foyer, idly leafing through a magazine I wasn't even slightly interested in, trying to leave my phone alone, because it really would run completely out of charge if I even touched it once more. When everyone else came, I would go and call Claire and tell her. Although I worried slightly. Thierry had obviously been a friend of hers for a long time. Would it upset her more to know? I could just tell her I'd been lost or something, make some excuse. But then, would that be fair? And also, a little voice said to me again, it was still so very odd that she hadn't seen him in such a long time. They couldn't really be such good friends, could they?

I scanned the entrance, waiting for someone, anyone, to show up. I didn't think I'd ever felt so lonely in my whole life.

• • • •

1972

To Thierry, it seemed perfectly simple.

"You are my girl," he said. "You come back, huh? At Christmas? We shall have a wonderful time; Paris is sensational then. They light up the boulevards with a hundred tiny candles and the Tour Eiffel glows red and green. Perhaps it will snow, and I will keep you warm in my little garret, non? And I will make my hot chocolate for you. It is stirred one thousand times and filled with cream so that it melts down your neck like being embraced by a man who loves you, huh, chérie?"

She tried to smile, as she did so, kicking the first of the falling autumn leaves from the pathway. In four days' time, she would be putting on a school uniform she had undoubtedly grown out of since last year. She had filled out, she knew. There was color in her cheeks. She had come to Paris a girl and now she felt, indubitably, a woman.

"I don't know," she said. Christmas in Kidinsborough involved a lot of helping the Reverend with his Christmas load: visiting the sick in the hospital, giving Bibles as gifts to poor families who might, perhaps, have preferred food or toys. And homework, of course. She groaned. She'd brought a whole pile of textbooks with her, thinking she might get some revision done while the children were asleep. Of course, that had not happened. In terms of cause and effect, she did sometimes wonder if her choices might have been different for that very reason. But then of course if she had, she wouldn't have met Thierry... It was a circular argument with no clear solution, and of course pointless to dwell on.

She clutched his big paw tightly as the first chilling winds of autumn breezed through her thin coat, making her shiver. As much as they were trying to pretend the summer wasn't over, they both knew it was.

Thierry looked at her.

"Look at you, freezing, my little bird," he said. "I have a new recipe for hot chocolate, and you are going to be my first customer. Come with me."

Sitting where Thierry had lifted her onto the low wooden bar that shut off the counter into one single bar, he fussed around her, constantly stirring the huge mixing jug, adding more cream or taking some away, popping in the tiniest bit of rum, letting it smoke off then adding more. He was in a whirl that day, even though it wasn't even that cold; he wouldn't let her taste it until he had added tiny pinches of this and that, tasted it, thought about it, bounced in and out the back of the shop, shouted at Benoît, considered melting another batch of chocolate altogether, finally dribbling in a pinch of salt, and at last considering himself satisfied.

As soon as she took one sip, she knew he was right. It spread right through her body, warming every vein. It made her curl up her toes in delight. It tasted like something the White Witch of Narnia might have given Edmund to betray his family, and it tasted like it would have worked.

"Thierry," she said, aghast.

"I know, I know," he said distractedly. He was jotting notes on a piece of paper—he never wrote anything down normally, and he had found a small jar with a screw top, into which he was decanting some of the liquid.

"BENOÎT!" he growled through the back, as the burly man came running out. "Make this until it tastes like this. Then lock up the recipe in the safe."

Benoît nodded, quickly, then took a sip. He stopped short then gazed at Thierry.

"Chef," he said, in a tone of wonderment.

"I know," said Thierry, a brief look of satisfaction crossing his face. "I know. I've done it."

Claire smiled at him. He turned to her.

"And you!" he said. "You are my muse!" He kissed her, licking away the thick stain from her lips. "Oh, mixed with you, it is only more delicious," he said, kissing her again.

"You see? You must stay. I need you. You have inspired possibly my greatest creation."

One of the other customers in the shop turned around.

"May I try it?"

Thierry looked at him sternly. "I don't know. Are you a good man? So far, this has only been tried by good people."

"I don't know if I'm a good man," said the gentleman, who was wearing a Homburg hat and a yellow scarf against the encroaching colder weather. "But I am a journalist at Le Monde.*"*

Thierry filled him a huge cup to the brim. "My friend! Drink and be happy."

The man did so. And then he took out his notebook.

Thierry gave Claire a happy glance. "You see? You have made me a genius."

Laughing with delight, Claire had never been closer to ripping up her return ticket, packing up her bag, living in sin. She threw back her head and tossed down more of the astonishing hot chocolate. She was almost purely happy.

Except she remembered her mother's last letter, which had details of her new uniform, asking if she'd grown much, passing on good wishes from friends and relatives, talking excitedly about the new youth club that had opened adjacent to the church, about having a little party for her eighteenth birthday, and she knew—a tiny little corner of her knew—that she would have to go back, of course she would.

● ● ● ●

The door to the waiting room flew open with a crash. I raised my head; I realized I'd been nodding off. It seemed an odd reaction to the stress, but I'd been here for over two hours, the battery on my phone was completely gone, and I seemed to have run out of other options.

I'd seen Laurent around from time to time, usually with quite a fast set of loud young chefs and models. Sami preferred artists and musicians, so he could be a bit snotty about them. Laurent often had a scrawny pouty-looking girl on his arm—not the same one, as far as I could tell, and would nod at me, but little more; I was clearly siding with the enemy, and I dismissed him as irritating and obviously shallow. He didn't look shallow now though; he looked demented with worry.

His face struck me as being like his father's more than ever, but without the heavy weight of the fatness. His skin was a darker olive, huge, expressive Bambi eyes now looking alarmed and worried, the mouth, wide and sensual. He still seemed very tall compared to other French men I'd seen, and with a solid bulk that wasn't fat, just a kind of comforting size to him. I jumped up, wiping my mouth and wishing I had a stick of gum.

"What's happening? What's going on? Where is he?" shouted Laurent, sounding furious, as if it were my fault.

"He's in surgery," I said, trying to sound gentle and consolatory. "They said it might take a while."

"Why? Why is it taking a while?"

I shrugged. "I think it's difficult when…when the patient is a bit heavier than normal…"

"Is it because he's so fat? Stupid bastard. He's such a stupid bastard." He glared around. "Where's Alice?"

"Didn't Frédéric ring her?"

"He probably wouldn't; he hates her," said Laurent.

"Not that much, surely."

He ignored that. "What was he doing? What were you doing with him?"

"I wasn't doing anything with him," I said indignantly. I wasn't the one who'd let him eat himself to death for over forty years. "He asked me to go for a walk, that's all."

"That's all? Did he stop for brandy?"

"If it was my job to stop him drinking brandy, I think somebody should have made it a bit clearer to me!" I said, almost shouting.

He stopped short. "Sorry," he said muttering. "Sorry, that's not fair. I'm just…I'm just upset."

"I know," I said. "Of course you are. Hopefully they'll let us know soon."

He looked around. "He can't…he can't die…"

"Anna," I added helpfully.

"I knew that," he said, putting his hands distractedly through his thick brown hair.

"You know, we haven't spoken for months," he muttered. "He can't… It can't…"

I shook my head. "He spoke about you this morning," I said.

"What, to say what an ignoramus I am?"

"Yes," I said. "But in a loving way."

Laurent's face looked gray. "Christ," he said, looking at his watch. "Where are those doctors?"

I swallowed.

"What else?" he asked suddenly. "Why was he confiding in you? You've just gotten here…some English girl…" Then his eyes widened. "You're not…you're not connected to…"

I nodded slowly. "Claire sent me."

He looked so feverishly furious I thought he was going to spit. "That woman!" he cursed.

"I don't think she did anything wrong," I said quickly.

"Tell that to my mother," he said. "When he walked out on her for some scrawny English witch that reminded him of the first one."

"Alice is nothing like Claire," I said stoutly.

"Well, he found that out a bit late, didn't he?" said Laurent. "He'd already wrecked our family. Too scared to mess it up again. Thank God they didn't have any children." He snorted. Then he looked sad.

He stared again at the door, as if gazing at it might make something happen, then sighed.

"Oh God."

Finally the door swung open. Laurent was halfway to his feet before he realized it was Alice.

She looked absolutely white, the black scarf she was wearing a slash against her pale neck, her lips devoid of lipstick and looking naked and thin, stretched in her face. A vein stood out in her throat. For the first time, I thought, she looked old.

"*What have you done?*" was the first thing she said, almost hissed. It wasn't clear if this was directed at either or both of us.

"What have *you* done?" said Laurent, standing up completely this time. "You're the one who punted him around so many boring dinners and lunches with your *beau monde* chums to show him off, where he had nothing to do but get bored and eat and drink too much. You couldn't just leave him alone, could you, doing what he did best—creating and enjoying himself."

"How would you know?" said Alice, sneering. "We never see you. You're off too busy 'making it on your own,' except of course, oh how convenient, you appear to have a very useful last name."

Laurent looked utterly furious for a second and a half, then turned away.

"Oh yes, we're all so concerned about his welfare now," spat Alice, two circles of pink appearing high on her cheekbones. "Bit too late, don't you think?"

I stepped up. "Um, maybe we should all calm down?" I ventured. "I don't think Thierry would want us to be squabbling... Bad karma?"

They both turned on me, and for a second I thought I was going to get it in the neck. Then Laurent held up his hands in resignation.

"Yes, yes, you're right," he said. He fixed Alice with a hard stare. "I think we should put aside our differences for Thierry, do you agree?"

Alice gave a shrug so Gallic it was impossible to believe she wasn't French born and bred, and whipped out her mobile phone.

Moments later, the atmosphere was lifted somewhat by Benoît and Frédéric arriving, both of their heads down. They were so obviously miserable, it gave me something to do, to comfort them. They had closed the shop for the afternoon for the first time outside of August in forty years. Already, worried customers had come around asking if it were true, and the newspapers had been on the phone. By the sound of her, Alice was dealing with that side of things. Now all five of us stood or sat, Laurent not looking at any of us, Alice walking up and down talking on her mobile, as if making herself busy would in itself make a difference. I focused hard on the linoleum. Every minute that ticked by made me feel less optimistic.

Suddenly the doctor was standing at the door, removing her mask. Her face was completely unreadable.

•   •   •   •

Claire clutched the handle of the chair very carefully. She had tried to call Anna back—she knew there was something wrong, there had to be, she could hear it in her voice—but she couldn't get anyone to pick up the phone. She bit her lip. Monserrat, her caregiver, was fussing about cheerfully in the background, clearing up, lining up her medicine bottles for later when the community nurse would come around. Monserrat was great, but she didn't want to get into a big conversation about how she felt and what was up.

It had been her decision, when first diagnosed, not to tell people. She couldn't have explained why. She didn't want to draw lots of attention to herself to begin with; she couldn't bear to see pity in people's eyes. She never could. Not when her marriage broke up, not when she had flunked her A-levels. It felt more painful than chemo ever could. She knew on some level that it was pride; stupid pride, inherited from her father more likely than not, but it didn't make it any different.

Also, what was her ex-husband Richard going to do anyway? Drop everything and rush back and undo their entire lives? And the boys were busy. When it finally got so much and she had to tell them, they had been wonderful, and those nice girls they married, but she had always attempted to minimize any pain or discomfort so they wouldn't worry so much. She much more enjoyed the stories of what the children were doing and, sometimes, their hand-drawn cards. Anything that took her out of herself, that helped her stop thinking "cancer cancer cancer" was all for the best.

Project Anna had been the best thing she'd found to date. She had told herself it was purely about extending the girl's life experience; showing her a different way of doing things, the same way, once, Mme. LeGuarde had shown her, for Anna to enjoy her own youth. She only had the memories of the lovely girl she had been once. (And she could look back now without embarrassment; she had indeed been lovely.) These days her body was all pale folds, swollen by steroids and strong drugs, softened by childbearing and age. She felt herself starting to hang loose from her bones, her teeth softening in her head.

But then, seventeen and fair-haired and fresh—she could understand now why Thierry had been so attracted to her, even if then it had seemed completely out of the blue. Anyway, she didn't want to ruin those memories. When she'd first gotten the internet (quite late; she'd had the prickling sensation that, even though he'd been dead many long years, the Reverend would not have approved of the internet one bit), she had of course looked him up. And she'd found him too, still often in the pages of the French press, or in many, many cookery books and guides to Paris. His heft had surprised her, although she remembered with pleasure his gargantuan appetites for everything—for food, for chocolate, for sex and wine and cigars, and for her. It wasn't entirely surprising, she supposed, that it had caught up with him. On the other hand, she had led a blameless life of teaching and cooking healthy meals for her family and keeping her weight down and not smoking and not drinking to excess and look where she had ended up, on a ward with tubes sticking out of her, feeling like she was 190 years old, so did it matter, really, in the end?

She had idly wondered, many times, what would happen if she wrote him a quick letter—she knew where to find him, after all. But she had always stopped herself. It was ludicrous, a crush from so long ago, a two-month wonder. He must never think of her at all. She couldn't imagine anything more embarrassing than someone turning up in your life you completely forgotten ever existed. She imagined him searching his memory, trying to be polite, the awful dawning realization of how much thought she'd given him throughout her entire life, how much time. It was a ghastly idea. Until Anna had given her the perfect excuse.

● ● ● ●

1972

"There, there," her mother had said, as she lay back in her old bedroom, with its ridiculous posters of Davy Jones and ponies. It was the room of a child, utterly stupid to her eyes now, and seeing it had only seemed to confirm how much she no longer fitted in in this place.

She had cried all the way back on the train, on the ferry, and on the train again, even as she remembered Thierry's fervent words—do not forget me, do not leave, come back, come back. And she had promised, she really had, but she had no money and no hope and no idea of what to do, and she was trapped in a pale blue bedroom with ducks on the mantelpiece and a valance on the bed, and a school uniform hanging up in the cupboard.

Mme. LeGuarde had held her hands on the last evening, genuinely sad to see her go; Arnaud and Claudette had held on to her legs.

"I hope you have gotten a lot out of your stay," she said, and Claire had gotten tears in her eyes and sworn that she had, that she could never be grateful enough.

"I don't want to be patronizing," said Mme. LeGuarde, *"but it is nice to have love affairs when you are young. But there will be many, you understand? 'One swallow does not make a summer' is the English phrase, I know. You are confident now and you have learned many things on your way toward being a grown-up woman, so take these memories. But do not cling on to Paris, no? You have your own life, your own way to make. You are far too clever to hang around, waiting for crumbs, relying on other people, you understand me?"*

And Claire, struck dumb with misery, had nodded and remembered the words and she knew deep down it was wise advice. But oh, how much she didn't want to hear it. She wanted Mme. LeGuarde to say, *"We cannot do without you. Forget school, come stay with us until you marry Thierry."* Even thinking something so ridiculous brought a blush to Claire.

Back home, her mother had been so pleased to see her, but Claire felt like a stranger in her mother's arms; how could it only have been two and a half months? She was a new person. A woman of independence, who worked, then spent her evenings as she chose. How could she be expected to concentrate on algebra and verb declensions?

Her father had looked her up and down. He had never particularly enjoyed Claire growing up, even though she had been as respectful and obedient an adolescent as one could find. It was evident even to his unpracticed eye that she was growing further away from him than ever. He grunted.

"I hope you haven't picked up any fancy ways in Paree," he said. *"They're loose over there."*

"She's a good girl," assured her mother, stroking her all over. *"You look wonderful, dear. So kind of Marie-Noelle to take such good care of you. She wrote to me."*

"*Did she?*" said Claire, looking startled.

Her mother smiled a secret smile. It had obviously been everything she'd hoped for her gorgeous but too staid daughter.

"*Don't worry, nothing bad. Apparently she was a credit to the family, Marcus.*"

"*Well, I would hope so,*" said the Reverend, looking slightly mollified. "*You would hate to be neither use nor ornament, hmm, Claire?*"

Claire nodded. It had rained all the way on the train home. After the golden heavy light of Paris unfolding onto ancient cobblestones, of verdant parks and iron railings and great churches, the bland red brick and corrugated iron of Kidinsborough, the already dripping cement of the new NCP car park and the shopping center, with its overturned trolleys outside, felt worse than ever. She couldn't believe what she was doing back there. She wished she had a best friend to confide in, for once.

Her mother had made mince and potatoes for her homecoming, once her favorite. "*I'm really not hungry,*" she said to her mother apologetically. "*I might just go to bed. I'm so tired.*"

"*Your mother has made good food,*" said the Reverend. "*It would be a sin to waste it.*"

So she had had to sit, in the old dowdy traveling clothes she had last worn at the beginning of the summer—now too short in the leg and too tight in the bust, and try to choke down the overboiled carrots and mushy potato, try not to think about melting Camembert that came in its own little wooden basket, baked in the oven with herbs and served on a crisp green salad (the only salad that had hit Kidinsborough in the early seventies was a couple of leaves of damp iceberg lettuce served with tasteless quartered tomatoes and salad dressing). Or the golden roasted chickens they bought from a man who sold them on a spit that tasted so hot and salty that they had let the grease run down their chins, and Thierry had licked it off, and she had laughed and laughed, and they had mopped up the rest of the juices with the most incredible fresh bread, still warm from the oven. Thierry had shown her how to know when bread was at *its freshest by the crackling noise it made when you broke into it, adding smugly, "But Pierre would never give me second bread."*

She could barely remember that girl. And as the days grew shorter, and school started again, she felt like she was trapped, trapped in the body of a child who needed to do what she was told.

Every day, she woke up early, terrified she might miss the postman. Her father wouldn't understand Thierry's letters but her mother could, and her father would get the gist, surely, or just disapprove in general. She watched him like a hawk; she couldn't trust the Reverend not to block any incoming post, but he seemed his normal irascible self, grumbling over his newspaper about the terrible state of everything and how Britain was going to the dogs and how the union men were "wicked, wicked."

He started preaching this, too, from his pulpit, which did not go down at all well with the local population of Kidinsborough, who were hanging on to their steelworks by the skin of their teeth. His congregation dwindled, and men came from the bishopric in the evening, talking to him in low voices.

Every day, Claire got up early to make sure her father didn't make it to the post before her, but he never did. So as the days went by, it became stranger and stranger that she had received no letters. She had returned to school, gazing at the stranger she had become in the mirror—not the carefree girl striding happily down the Bois de Boulogne, but a sullen teenager in a short gray skirt and a too-tight tie, looking just like anyone else.

In class she barely paid attention, except in French, instead writing endless letters to Thierry, circular in tone, about how much she missed him and how much she hated Kidinsborough and how next summer she would find another position and come back to Paris and this time they couldn't make her go back, nobody could, sending it to the shop, although who knew where he was now, where he was posted.

There was no response.

In November, they moved.

Claire cried. She begged. She pleaded. She ran the whole gamut of teenage rebellion, slamming doors, staying out late, sulking, but nothing worked. Complaints against her father were growing; his old-school, fire-and-brimstone sermons had fallen out of fashion. "Hippies," the Reverend complained. "Nothing but g-damned hippies getting into everything. They're going to ruin everything."

As a result of this, Claire went out and bought incense, which turned him practically apoplectic with rage.

Claire sent one last letter, not to the garret but to the shop, where she knew for an absolute fact he would receive it.

Chéri,

Mes parents horribles insistent que nous déménageons. Je les déteste. Alors, si tu penses de moi du tout, s'il te plaît sauve-moi! Sauve-moi! Je suis à 'the Pines, 14 Orchard Grove, Tillensley.'

Si tu ne réponds pas, je comprendrai que tu ne m'aimes pas et je ne te contacterai encore.

Mon coeur, mon amour, viens avec vitesse,

                                                    Claire

Nothing.

13

I do think there is something about the French psyche that can be incredibly useful. That solid practicality—it is very unusual for a French person to be over the top with excitement or laid low with misery—is useful. They do not feel it necessary to be cheery or even terribly polite if the occasion doesn't warrant it. Which means you can get a lot of necessary information in an unemotional way.

Laurent started up.

"How is he?"

Alice whipped around and, without saying a word, shut off her phone. The doctor's face was still completely impassive, and I could feel my heart beating a mile a minute, pounding my chest. I suddenly found I wished I could take Laurent's hand, squeeze it. Just to have someone there while we faced the worst. I looked at his large, hairy hand, hanging down by his jacket pocket. It was shaking.

"It's far from clear," said the doctor, her voice impeccable, ringing out in the small dingy room. "We have operated, inserted stents. But his general condition…" The tone of her voice made it very clear that this was a reproach. "His general condition makes it very difficult to see what the outcome will be."

"But he's still alive now," said Laurent, his face an animated mixture of hope and terror.

She nodded curtly. "*Bah oui*," she said. "He will be unconscious for some time."

"I want to see him," said Laurent. She nodded and turned around.

We all followed the clacking of her heels up the shiny linoleum floor, until she turned around.

"Not too many," she instructed. Frédéric and Benoît immediately backed off, and I did too. But Laurent, almost without realizing what he was doing, tugged at my sleeve.

"You come," he said quietly. I realized later, of course, that he just didn't want to be alone with her, with Alice, and all the unsaid things that passed between them, and that I was a witness; I'd been there. But at the time, it felt more than that; I felt like I'd been chosen. Although in the same way, I still felt that if he died, it would be my fault.

"Of course," I said, trying not to betray the nerves in my voice.

"Why is she coming?" asked Alice loudly, but Laurent ignored her. I just stayed out of her way.

* * * *

The recovery room was gloomy, the lights low. Machines bleeped and whirred to themselves; I looked around to make sure I wouldn't stumble over any essential tubes or wires. In the center, dimly lit by above, Thierry made a huge mound in the bed, like a gigantic Easter egg. They had, to my terrible sadness, shaved his mustache to insert the tubes up his nose. Without it, he looked odd, insulted somehow.

His skin was gray, absolutely gray. It was a horrible muddy color you couldn't look at for any length of time at all. Alice coughed and glanced down. Laurent though was just staring at Thierry's great barrel chest, still moving up and down.

"Papa," he cried, stepping over to the bed, his arms open wide. He sounded like a child. The doctor gave a disapproving clicking noise and he stepped back, not wanting to disrupt anything, but there were tears in his eyes. Then he turned back to the doctor.

"Thank you," he said.

The doctor shrugged. "Don't thank me yet," she said.

She left after warning us for the fiftieth time not to touch anything, and we three, an odd company, were alone in the room, with Thierry, like a great beached walrus, spread out between us. There was a silence broken only by the bleeping and the great hiss of the respirator, which moved up and down like a broken accordion.

"So," said Alice at last. Laurent wasn't listening; he was sitting forward hard in his chair, staring at his father. "This is what it takes to get you to visit your dad."

I really wanted to knock her block off then. It was like she'd searched the world for the most unpleasant thing she could possibly say and then gone ahead and said it anyway.

Laurent must have noticed my horrified face, because he patted me on the arm.

"It's all right. She's always like this," he said in English, which was clever, because Alice pretended all the time she didn't know any English or that she'd forgotten it all.

"Actually it wasn't my dad I was avoiding, it was you," he said pleasantly. "Now would you like to smoke in here and make him worse? Or maybe you'd just like to lever him up and wheel him out to one of your soirées."

Alice went very white again. "Actually, I'll have to go and organize the business you want no part of," she said. "With two half-wits and whatever she is. By myself. Thanks though."

I was struck with a hand of fear. It had never occurred to me I was going to have to work for Alice now, but of course she was right. Oh goodness. I hardly knew what I was doing yet, and now I was going to have to do it under the disapproving eye of this person who thought I'd try to kill myself.

"Of course, you'd ask if you needed help," said Laurent.

There was a standoff then, neither of them prepared to move at all.

• • • •

It became increasingly clear that neither of them wanted to be the first to leave, in case Thierry woke up. It was warm in the room, and with horror I realized I was becoming very drowsy. There must be loads of people they needed to contact, but both were sticking by the signs that there were no mobile phones allowed near the equipment. It was like a power struggle between the two of them, and it made me very cross. Eventually I snapped.

"I'm going to get coffee," I said. "Does anyone want anything?"

Alice jumped up, obviously cross she hadn't thought of it.

"No, I'll go," she said brusquely, her fingers already fumbling in her Hermès bag for her lighter and phone. "I'll be back in two minutes."

After she had left the room and vanished down the long corridor, Laurent collapsed back onto the chair and let out a long sigh. He let his curly head continue on downward, until it was level with the bottom of the bed. Then he let it collapse into the soft sheets. After several moments of witnessing his shoulders shaking, I realized he was crying.

I stood up.

"There, there," I said, rubbing his back. "There, there. He's going to be all right, isn't he? There, there. Look at him, all alive on the bed and everything."

I was speaking absolute nonsense, I knew, just crooning reassuring nothings, but it seemed to do the trick. After another moment, without lifting his head, Laurent took my arm and held it.

"Thank you," he said, his face muffled in the pillow.

I patted him. "It's all right," I said again. "It's going to be all right."

"It's never all right," came the voice.

I knelt down beside him. "Well," I said, "maybe this is a really good time to make it up with your dad."

"What, before he passes his gun to his left?" said Laurent, turning his face toward me and half-smiling. "Yeah, right. Thanks."

"Well, lots of people never get a chance to say good-bye," I said. "You're going to be lucky. Be sure of it."

"Are you my lucky charm?"

I smiled. I was the unluckiest person in the world, didn't he know?

"If you like."

Laurent sat up and wiped his eyes, then ran his fingers through his hair. "Do I look red?" he asked. "I don't want the wicked witch to know I've been crying."

"Maybe it'll soften her up," I said. "She can see how much you really care."

"You couldn't soften her up with a marshmallow massage," said Laurent crossly. "I really do think she's made out of old leather."

"She's panicking," I said. "People say strange things when they're worried."

"Then she's permanently worried," he said.

"I rather think she is," I said, patting him again. "Look, I haven't seen much, but I'm a fast learner, and I bet Frédéric and Benoît can do just about anything. Let's carry on with the shop for a bit until Thierry's better. It will cheer him up, I think, to know we've gone on in his absence."

"Or completely ruin him by the fact that he's replaceable," said Laurent with a twisted smile on his face. I noticed he was holding his father's empty-looking hand in his living one. Apart from the fact that Thierry's hand was more bloated and a paler color, they were the same hands.

"Well, we'll tell him it is obviously much, much worse," I suggested.

"Oh, you won't have to do that," said Laurent wryly. "He thinks everything is much, much worse without him in it."

"Maybe he's right," I said. Just then, Alice came back, with three tiny plastic cups of black liquid on a little tray. I squeezed Laurent's shoulder once more. "I'll get back to the shop," I said. "I'm not much use here."

Laurent nodded. "I know," he said reluctantly. "Yes. Do. And answer the phone, do you mind?"

"Not at all," I said. "I'll say he's… I'll say he's…"

"Say he is going to be *fine*," said Alice in a voice that brooked no argument. "Say that he is going to be completely back to normal and that the shop will go on and everything will stay just as it is."

Laurent would have probably said that this was just Alice seeking to preserve her investment. I didn't see it like that though. I saw Alice keeping Thierry alive just by saying she was going to. And even though I didn't want to be, I was slightly impressed.

● ● ● ●

It felt amazing to me that I stepped back out of the hospital on that same, beautiful June day. The sky had tiny ribbons of cloud floating across it, and the afternoon sun fell warmly on the backs and necks of shoppers and sightseers, every one of them, I speculated, happy and carefree without a problem in the world.

I realized I had no idea where I was, walked a long way, then figured out I could see the Eiffel Tower over my left shoulder and that therefore I was on the Left Bank, had gone the wrong way, and needed to cross the river again. Yes, I'd been on the Île de la Cité the whole time. If I craned my neck, I could just make out the familiar shape of Notre Dame, far away to my right. It would have been a lot quicker to take a cab or the Metro—everything in Paris is farther away than it looks—but I decided I needed the walk to clear my head. Incredibly careful when looking for traffic, I stepped out, my toes hurting again because they had responded badly to the smell of hospitals, I thought. Or bad weather was coming, but as far as I was concerned, all the bad things were already here. So I walked, slowing myself down to a tourist's pace instead of the bustling Parisian march, as the locals threaded themselves in and out of the visitors, occasionally huffing their displeasure. I zigged and zagged the roads. But as long as I could keep Notre Dame in my sights, I kept heading doggedly onward.

There was something about it—I knew; forever it had stood for sanctuary, back when the city was really no more than the island and its church. It was impossible not to think about the Hunchback, and Esmeralda, or to look at the gargoyles and shudder to think of a world where people believed in them absolutely, believed that hell was only a blink or a misstep away, that it was pain for all eternity and the monsters carved on the wall were literal and real and there to tear you apart.

At secondary school, there was a bit of religious education and it was quite fashionable for a while—don't ask me why—to go to church and pray and stuff. I don't know why except it was seen as quite a clever thing to do, or to match with the Muslim kids who prayed properly and were seen as much cooler, and church kind of turned into this big social event, and I toyed with it until I asked Mrs. Shawcourt about it and her face went a bit stiff and she just said, "Ooh, I have had a *lot* of church, believe me. Quite enough to be getting on with for this lifetime," and I was a lot less committed after that.

Around Notre Dame though, I felt something else. Seeing the queues of people waiting to get in—most of them bored-looking Italian school kids larking about, or rich-looking young American students talking really loudly, or elderly couples dressed almost exactly alike, ticking things off in their books. But among them were different people—nuns and people on their own who didn't have a holiday look about them at all, but rather something very serious and grave. The distinctive twin towers at the front made it seem different, somehow special.

As I drew nearer, I realized you only had to queue if you wanted a tour or to go up and see the bells and things. If you just wanted to peek in, you could wander up. Even though my feet were killing me and I hadn't eaten a thing for hours and I just wanted to lie down and rest, I found myself mounting the steps.

Inside it was huge. It smelled faintly of flowers and floor polish and something else that I supposed was that incense-y stuff my gran says Catholics use. They were playing organ music gently through speakers, which was a bit confusing. The scale of it was massive. If I thought it was massive now, living in the days of skyscrapers and jumbo jets and cruise ships, I can't imagine what it must have felt like hundreds of years ago. The huge friezes of the Stations of the Cross covered the walls in intricate details, like the huge rose stained-glass window. It must have been like watching television.

Dotted on the pews, looking tiny as ants, were people, mostly singly, just sitting, contemplating. I couldn't join them without paying the entrance fee, and I didn't have a God I could talk to, and even if I did I couldn't imagine any kind of God taking time off from massacres and famines to help out an aging, very, very fat man I barely knew. But even so. My heart formed a silent plea—*please*—said over and over again. *Please. Just, please.*

I felt better.

• • • •

The shop had a sign on it—*fermé cause de maladie*—and some concerned people milling around outside, who'd obviously made the trip specially and everything. I knocked heavily on the roll door. The workshop around the back technically had a fire exit, but I had no idea where it went out, so I kept banging until I heard Frédéric.

"We're shut! Go away!" he shouted.

"It's me!" I yelled.

Immediately the shutters were raised.

"Why didn't you call? Where have you been?" he shouted at me.

"Because my phone is dead," I explained. "And you can't use the phones in the hospital."

"Well, that's not very helpful," he grumbled. "We've been waiting. Any change?"

"No," I said. "I don't think so. But no change is good at this point."

Frédéric snorted. "I don't know about that."

I noticed something. There was no noise in the shop.

"Why are the churns switched off?" I asked.

Frédéric shrugged. "Oh, of course we cannot continue without the chef, *chérie*. It's not possible."

"What do you mean, it's not possible? Are you going on strike?"

"No. But without him…"

"You're telling me you've worked here all these years and you don't know what he's doing?"

Frédéric's little face grew cross.

"Of course we see what he is doing. But what he is doing and what an artisan would do…for the conch, it is not precisely the same, madame. It is the difference between daubs on a wall and an artist's canvas. It could not be."

I was used to working in a factory, where our industrial processes basically meant that a monkey could turn out the same chocolate day after day as long as he could remember what sequence of buttons to push. It might mean a lot of banana flavor though.

"Of course you can," I prodded. "Benoît has been here man and boy. Surely we can honor Thierry and continue making chocolate."

"It is impossible," he said, looking at me as if he was explaining something very simple to a particularly stupid child. "It cannot be the same."

"Well, I hope it can," I said. "Because I think Alice wants us all to stay open. If you want to say no to her, though, go ahead, be my guest."

Frédéric visibly paled.

"She cannot say that," he said.

"She did," I said. "I heard her at the hospital."

He shook his head. "She does not understand."

I was kind of on Alice's side over this. Wages had to be paid, I assumed, hopefully including mine. People would still come.

Thierry was mostly all about the sizzle and the salesmanship at the front of the shop, I was sure of it; Frédéric and Benoît could carry out all the workshop duties. And I could help, I thought to myself. I'd watched them all over the weeks, hadn't I? I had a good nose for this kind of thing.

Frédéric called on Benoît, and in a low, deep-seated, 100 mile per hour growl that reminded me once again how much people were modifying the way they spoke when they spoke to me so I could understand it, started to explain how crazy everyone was being. Benoît as usual did little more than grunt in response, but in a way that seemed to indicate more displeasure than usual.

"*Les anglais*" was the only remark he made eventually, which made me indignant, as he'd obviously lumped me in with Alice's side of everything.

"It's nothing to do with me," I said eventually, backing away. "Speak to Alice, okay? Do we need cleaning up?"

Benoît shook his head.

"It's done," he said ominously. And then in English: "It's over."

14

I could hardly climb the stairs. All I wanted was to get back in, to be home, to get some sleep. Oh God, and I would have to phone Claire, of course I would. I hadn't even thought about that. Well, I would need to charge the phone first, then I could think about it. Maybe after a bath.

Of course, Sami was there. Today he was wearing a peacock-blue fringed shawl over his tanned torso, and bright blue eyeliner. He was obviously waiting for me.

"*Darling!*" he exclaimed. "I heard the horrible, horrible news. Look, I have cognac. It's good for shock."

At that point in time, cognac didn't seem like a bad idea, even though I had only the haziest idea what it actually was. Sami just liked to be in on the good gossip.

"It is the talk of Paris! Where will we get our hot chocolate now? You know, the tenor, Istoban Emerenovitz, will only sing here if he has a constant supply! Now we shall lose him to the New York Met and the world will mourn."

I wasn't exactly sure that the world would mourn something like that, but I gave a half-smile and said not to worry, everything was going to be all right. It was odd how, in the space of a few hours, suddenly I had become the center of information.

"And you were there?" said Sami, kindness fighting with his curiosity for gossip. "Poor little bird. Was it awful?"

For the first time since the nightmarish dash to the hospital and all its memories, I just let myself go and burst into floods of tears.

"Oh, my little bird," said Sami, giving me a rather oddly scented hug. "Would you like your uncle Sami to take you to a party? Yes? We shall go to a party and you can tell everyone all about it and feel much better."

At that precise moment, there was nothing I would rather do less. I explained this to Sami, who got exactly the same confused dog look about my not wanting to go to a party as Frédéric had gotten at the idea of imitating Thierry's recipes, but he eventually left me in peace.

I had little doubt that Alice would get her way—she was just that kind of person—so I was going to spend the next few weeks very busy indeed. I just hoped I was going to be up to it.

● ● ● ●

1972

Although completely wrapped up in herself when she got back to school, it finally penetrated Claire's haze that something was up with another girl. At first she couldn't put her finger on what was different about Lorraine Hennessy. Then everyone started gossiping and whispering, and poor Lorraine could no longer do her skirt up and that was that; she had gotten herself pregnant, some people said by a boy who'd come around that summer on the carny and whizzed her too hard on the Tilt-a-Whirl.

It wasn't quite still the days of sending women off to special homes for fallen ladies then in Kidinsborough, but they weren't that far away. And for Lorraine to have made it all the way to senior year...as the wives gossiped in the covered market, you think you get that far, then everything is plain sailing after that. Poor Lorraine had fallen at the last hurdle, for a twinkling-eyed boy with a missing tooth, dirty fingernails, and wild, long, curly hair. She left school at the autumn half-term and most people carried on regardless.

Claire, though, was obsessed. Even when the Reverend brought it up at supper, with much tutting and judgment and disapproval, she couldn't help thinking about it. She was simply too careful. She imagined herself carrying Thierry's baby, a round, chubby, pink-cheeked laughing little cherub. She looked carefully every day at her stomach, just in case. Yes, they used precautions, but as the Reverend had said in one of his more risqué sermons, contraception was next to useless; the only true protection was chastity and the love of Jesus Christ.

She wished they'd been less careful. When she ran into Lorraine in the high street—her mother, conscious that her father's spies might be around, wanted to hurry her back—Claire stopped and said hello. She couldn't help it; she drank in every feature of Lorraine's full vase-shape; her newly rounded, pale breasts; the tight, high bump, so unfathomable that inside was another being; the trembling, defiant look in her eye.

"Good luck," she said to Lorraine. In the two minutes they'd been standing there, they'd both already ignored whispers from passersby.

"Aye," said Lorraine, whose mother, next to her, seemed to have aged ten years. Lorraine didn't look proud, but her glowing, fruitful body did. Claire was the only girl at Kidinsborough Modern who envied her, who didn't join in the nasty chatter disguised as concern. She would have taken her bump in her arms and gone straight to the ferry and taken the train and turned up late at night in Thierry's garret, and he would have been delighted to see her. She ignored, once more, the lack of letters, the possibility that in fact his face would fall as she arrived, confused, that there might even be some other girl in his bed; she was under no illusion that he was short of offers. No, she would be there and he would jump up, that wonderful broad smile on his face, his mustache tickling her belly as he kissed it and kissed it again and they sat up all night making plans for their little one and how he would be the bonniest, best fed baby in all of Paris, until the dawning sun hit the rooftops of the rue de Rivoli and bright pink morning turned Paris's white streets into a sea of roses with the promise of a fresh golden day beyond...

"You seem distracted." It was Mrs. Carr, the French teacher. She had been unflatteringly surprised at the improvement of Claire's French during

the holidays and was pushing her hard to take it to a higher level—Claire was smart; she could go to university, be a translator, travel the world… Claire's distraction and lack of interest drove her crazy. Years later, Claire tried harder with the dreamy children than almost anything else. Naughty children needed boundaries and direction; that was easy. Motivated children of course easier still. But it was the ones with their heads in the air, miles away, who were the hardest to get through to. You never knew what was going on with them.

Claire had been the best French speaker they'd ever had in the school. But Claire didn't bother doing her homework, skipped class sometimes, and was hardly present even when she did turn up. Mrs. Carr tried to impress on her the importance of the year, but it didn't seem to be doing the least bit of good whatsoever. She might have suspected a boy—so many promising young girls could fall completely apart at this age, look at Lorraine Hennessy—but Claire had always been such a sensible girl, raised in a religious home… Oh, who was she kidding? They were always the worst.

Claire had sixty-two pounds in her post office account, which was enough to get her to France. The problem was how to get it out; she wasn't allowed to withdraw the money on her own until her eighteenth birthday, which was five months away. It might have been five years as far as Claire was concerned; she couldn't imagine it.

But the days went by and the weather turned absolutely vicious, gray and windy and wet, the children wearing hooded parkas that came right up over their faces and completely obscured their vision, so they looked like tiny monsters looming out of the gloom.

Claire knew she was failing at school and couldn't bring herself to care. The Reverend shouted at her, and she stood there, meekly taking it and not really listening. This only annoyed him even more, but she'd been listening to the Reverend rant and rave from the pulpit long enough to take it to heart. When the form came for university, her mother quietly filed it away on the sideboard. Claire didn't even look at it.

The weight she'd gained in Paris fell off her, and the tan faded. The very *experience started to feel like a dream she'd had once, or a story she'd read, or a film. She wasn't that girl who'd skipped down the Bois de Boulogne, who'd scooped fresh avocado and salsa together, its slippery tartness making her eyes pop open, Thierry's generous laugh at her surprise.*

That Claire had gone, and the one who remained looked even younger than before; pale and fragile, trying to keep warm against the darkening evenings, trudging through Kidinsborough like a ghost.

Her friends and contemporaries were living it up: sneaking into bars, drinking cider at parties around each other's houses, snogging and more down by the canal. Claire sat in her room and wrote in her diary. She slipped out one morning and found, right at the back of the tiny tobacconists, the same brand of Gauloises in the bright blue packet that Thierry smoked. Nauseous and faintly horrified, she went into the wood and lit one. The very smell made her burst into tears again, but she found herself coming back again and again to smoke them, in the cold and the wind.

Later Claire thought that, had it not been the seventies, she would probably have been picked up by the school guidance counselor, or indeed at home. It wasn't exactly unusual she learned, after many years as a teacher, to meet a depressed teen. Normally it was just a phase, home problems and the inability to realize that everyone else felt as nervous and awkward in their adolescent skin and sexuality as they did. She was always patient and kind with these kids, their sleeves too long for their hands, clutching at the ends, their infuriatingly mumbled responses. She knew what they were going through and how important it felt to them. She also knew the importance of not letting them pull it down. The biggest failures of her academic career were never kids failing academically, but emotionally.

As it was, everyone just left her to get on with it, and the gray wet world and her sense of being separated from it and every one in it by a piece of gauze began to feel normal. Until she met Richard.

15

For a second the following morning, I awoke without thinking anything, except that I felt refreshed from a good night's sleep. A bright morning light was streaming in through the French window and throwing panes of bright buttercup yellow across my plain white sheets that had come with an old-fashioned blue comforter rather than a duvet.

Then I remembered, and my heart dropped. Oh God. I jumped out of bed and paced about in a rush, not sure what to do first. Well, I had to talk to Laurent—but, I realized stupidly, I didn't have his telephone number. Sami might, but Sami never answered his phone—he thought it was bourgeois—so probably not. Okay, first things first. Get dressed. Coffee. I pulled on my dressing gown and stumbled in, nearly tripping over the most beautiful guest, asleep on the sofa, who appeared to be wearing angel wings. I recovered just in time and fixed myself a tiny cup of espresso, loaded with sugar, and took it to drink on the balcony. I was definitely getting used to it.

I looked out onto the early Paris morning. Far away across the river I saw a group of police horses being led out to exercise. A small group of schoolchildren were already huddled at the stop for the *bateau mouche*. Across the road, a woman was taking in washing that had been hanging outside her window on a pulley. We smiled at each other. It seemed so strange to me that somewhere out there was Thierry, being held together by beeping machines, kept alive by plastic tubes coming in and out of his heart. I wondered if Laurent were still there, holding his hand, his heavy head drooping from exhaustion. I was sure he would be. Alice, on the other hand... I had a feeling I might be seeing Alice today. I groaned and set about the daily lottery of seeing if there was hot water. Then I remembered. I still hadn't called Claire. I could have kicked myself. I glanced at my watch. It was 5:00 a.m. in the UK. She'd still be asleep, hopefully. I couldn't disturb her now. I'd call her from the shop.

I had a lukewarm shower, glanced once again at Cupid asleep—Sami often provided random sofas to various young artists—and let myself out quietly. My toes—no, not my toes. I always forgot. The hospital psychologist had said I had to say "the place my toes had been." Otherwise, I would psychologically not manage to get rid of them—well. That place was aching a little, but it was better than yesterday, which was just as well. I had a feeling I was going to require all my energy today. Nothing could let me down.

• • • •

Claire sat by the window, staring out, then down at the telephone, then out again. She didn't want to do anything else. She had tried to sleep, but it hadn't come. She had wanted to call Anna, but got too nervous when she picked up the phone. If it was bad news... Could it be? What was it? But the tone of Anna's voice had been so panicky. Maybe she'd just been lost, that must have been it. Lost and worried...but why hadn't she called back to say she was all right? Why not? Where was she? Claire truly felt she couldn't bear it if sending Anna to Paris turned out to be the second great mistake of her life. She breathed heavily and looked around for her oxygen cylinder. She could hear Patsy, her daughter-in-law, marching smartly up the path with the wheelie bin. She was a trouper, Patsy, a real life-saver. She couldn't bear being a drain on her children and their families—or at least, had hoped she wouldn't be for a good many years yet—but what else could she do? Most of all she couldn't bear the look on the faces of her grandchildren—Patsy and Ricky had two daughters, Cadence and Codie, and she felt, at fifty-eight, she should be down on her knees playing with them, cutting out paper dollies and dressing up, passing on funny stories and songs, and telling them about their daddy when he was a little boy.

Instead they gazed at her horribly old, gray face and the oxygen machine in utter horror. She didn't blame them. Then Patsy would crossly nudge them and they would come bearing the drawings they had done for her and a new scarf for her head, but truly they were too young ever to remember her as anything other than old and sick and witchlike, and it broke Claire's heart.

"Hello, Claire!" said Patsy, opening the door with her own key. "I'll just put the kettle on. Montserrat's coming around to give you a bath, isn't she? Great. Can I do anything for you?"

Claire stared at the phone in her lap. Was there anything to be done now, she wondered.

* * * *

Frédéric and Benoît were looking positively mutinous and not even smoking. I raised my eyebrows, then I understood, as I saw the long thin figure of Alice opening the shutters. The boys raised their hands to me and I waved back, shyly. I wasn't sure if they saw me as the enemy or not.

"How is he?" I said quickly in English to Alice.

She favored me with a sideways glance.

"The same," she said. "Stable."

"Oh," I said. "Oh. Well, it's not worse," I added lamely.

Stable was, hmm. I didn't really like the sound of it. I'd learned that in the hospital. Critical was the worst. Critical was not good criticism. It was very bad indeed. Recovering was the ideal state of affairs, really. Stable just meant the same as yesterday. Which, in Thierry's case, meant life hanging in the balance. I didn't like it at all.

"Hmm" was all Alice said. Then she handed me her phone. "Take this," she said. "It's ringing off the hook and I don't want to deal with it right now."

I had no idea what she expected me to do with it. I was tempted to throw it in the Seine, but instead I set it to vibrate and put it in my apron pocket, where it started vibrating absolutely nonstop. I ignored it.

Alice pulled up the last shutter and turned to face us.

"Now. The shop will continue as before."

Frédéric raised up his hands.

"Madame, it is just not possible. An orchestra cannot play without its conductor. A kitchen cannot function without its chef. We will be selling substandard goods."

Alice went pale.

"It is his wish," she said. Frédéric and Benoît exchanged a disbelieving look so obvious she couldn't possibly have missed it. She bit her lip furiously.

"Anna, can you conch chocolate?"

Frédéric and Benoît glared at me, but I was too scared of Alice not to answer her. It was a mistake that was to prove fatal.

"Um, well, yes, I can have a shot, but…"

"Fine. You shall do it."

Benoît made a sharp intake of breath. "But I think we should wait until…"

"Rubbish. Anyone who doesn't want to work here can go home right away. If you think this isn't want Thierry would want, you can take it up with him, but there may not be a job waiting for you at the end of it. I am the co-owner of this establishment. Don't think I am soft like Thierry."

None of us thought that.

"I would get rid of the lot of you at a moment's notice if I thought it would keep the shop open and our business alive. In a second. So don't push me."

We all stared at the ground.

"In you go. Open up. Behave as normal. Anna will flavor. *Don't* mess it up. I am now going to be extraordinarily busy, and I do not want to have to worry about you on top of everything else."

And with that, she tossed the keys to Benoît, turned on her heels, and clipped off down the alleyway before I had the chance to remind her that I still had her mobile phone.

• • • •

Not a word was spoken as we entered the dimly lit shop and passed through to the back. The dim lighting flickered then came on. Benoît set the coffee machine, but only made two cups, one for him and one for Frédéric. I cleared my throat.

"I'm sorry," I said quietly.

Frédéric looked at me. "If we don't stand together, we are nothing," he said crossly.

"I know, I know," I said. "But I think…I think she might be right. I think Thierry would want the shop to continue rather than us all just going off on holiday or something."

Benoît muttered something totally unfathomable.

"I mean, we can have a shot," I added.

"And lose our reputation forever? This is what you British do not understand about the French. You think you must work, work, work, work, and open on Sundays and make mothers and fathers with families work in supermarkets at three o'clock in the morning and make people leave their homes and their churches and their families and go shop on Sundays."

"Their shops are open on Sundays?" said Benoît in surprise.

"Yes! They make people work on Sundays! And through lunchtimes! But for what? For rubbish from China? For cheap clothes sewed by poor women in Malaysia? For why? So you can go more often to KFC and get full of fried chicken? You would rather have six bars of bad, bad chocolate than one bar of good chocolate. Why? Why are six bad things better than one good thing? I don't understand. We are not the same, you and I."

"I know that," I said, feeling suddenly near to tears. "I know all that. But I still think we should at least try. Try to make something good, with as much love and care as Thierry would do."

Frédéric and Benoît stared at me.

"Plus," I said. "I don't think we have much choice."

• • • •

In the end I decided on mint, surely the simplest of flavors. Frédéric and Benoît drank their coffee and watched me blankly as I scrubbed and cleaned all the vats, got my hammer, swept the floor, then started gathering ingredients.

"I'm going to do everything myself?" I asked at one point, red-faced and sweating from the effort, getting crosser and hotter and more resentful with every minute that passed.

"It's your choice," said Frédéric, which made me very cross. Benoît, however, surprised me; he stood up, went outside, and had a cigarette. When he came back, he was carrying all the butter and fresh cream. I nearly burst into tears. After that, Frédéric did bits and pieces too, but very off-handedly, as if he needed to keep reminding us that he was only here under duress. There wouldn't be as much time to spare because we couldn't leave the chocolate to set; it would need to be flash-cooled. This was chocolate-making on the hoof. I smashed and crashed things about, sweated and cried a bit at one stage, when I couldn't get the conch.

It was lumpy and bumpy and messy, but it was in the fridge.

Finally, at about eleven o'clock, half an hour after the shop had been due to open, the first piece of chocolate emerged from its molds.

The three of us regarded it carefully. I cut it gently with a knife. The consistency seemed all right—not perfect, a little fudgy maybe.

"Well, here goes nothing," I said in English to the men, who were pretending not to be that interested. I closed my eyes and ate it.

● ● ● ●

Well. Nobody threw up. I've had worse. Once, for example, some off milk powder got into the mix at Kidinsborough and we had to throw away forty thousand pounds. We were all made to taste it as a way of quality control to try to ensure it never happened again. It wasn't as bad as that.

But here was what it wasn't: it wasn't heaven. It wasn't the lightly whipped, melting, astonishing delight that Thierry's chocolate was.

What had I done? We'd churned it the right way, conched it, used all the same fresh, fresh ingredients. But watching someone create and actually doing it yourself are two very different things. Something was missing. It was the difference between an Old Master and a painting by numbers kit.

I made a face. The boys jumped up. Those bastards, they were pleased! I think they'd been terrified this entire time that I turned out to have been good at it.

"This is despicable," said Frédéric.

"It's not that bad," I said.

Benoît simply spat his piece out into a large and grimy cloth handkerchief.

I rolled my eyes. "Come on, you guys. It's my first time!"

"We can't sell this," said Frédéric.

"It's not that bad!" I said again. He shrugged, as if to say there were so many levels on which I couldn't understand how bad it was that there was no point trying to explain it to me.

The bell tinged in the front and our heads shot up. Oh lord, it was Alice.

She clacked back in. To my total and utter astonishment, she'd been away having her hair done. She held out her hand for the phone, and I felt in my apron pocket. The last number, I saw, was Laurent's. My heart started to beat faster. Did he have news? Was he at the hospital? What was it?

Alice nibbled a tiny corner of the chocolate.

"It's fine," she said.

"It's *not*," said Frédéric, but she shot him a warning look.

"Go out and sell," she said warningly. "Or I'm canceling lunch."

This seemed to strike scandalized horror into both of them.

"Right. I'm ready for the hospital," said Alice.

"Um, I think Laurent rang."

Alice looked annoyed, scrolling through her calls. "But not the hospital. So it can't be that serious."

"Aren't you going to call him?" I said as she slipped the phone back in her bag. She stared at me blankly.

"Chop chop, open up," she said in English.

• • • •

There was even more of a crowd in the shop than usual when we finally opened the doors; Thierry's illness had been mentioned in the press and there were lots of people there who knew his reputation for only the freshest of chocolate, anxious to see what was going on and suspicious, I was guessing, about quality control. I sighed, full of nerves. They were about to find out.

• • • •

Nobody said anything, of course, except Frédéric who kept giving me meaningful looks across the counter. They would go outside, nibble a bit, try a piece, then look at each other. If it was their first time to the shop, they seemed to be saying to each other, wow, I wonder what all the fuss was about for this stuff that tastes like any mass-produced supermarket brand.

If they were regulars, it was much, much worse. They would taste a little, like policemen on television testing cocaine, then they would nod at each other as if confirming their worst fears, discard the rest, and leave quickly. It was awful. And at the back all the time was Frédéric, smug and making his *I told you so* face. During my lunch break, I went to seek out a quiet spot—always near impossible on the Île de la Cité—and sobbed my heart out. Then I remembered someone I hadn't called.

"Claire?"

"Oh, thank goodness."

Her voice was frail, but the relief was unmistakable, and I could have kicked myself for not calling her earlier.

"I'm so sorry," I said. "My battery died, and then it was late."

"But you're all right?"

"Ye-es," I said reluctantly.

"What is it?"

"It's Thierry."

• • • •

Claire knew it then. She knew against all the certainties that life should grow over old wounds, that people grew up and moved on with their lives, all the truisms she'd been told and learned from other people and taken to heart and pretended to herself for years and years and years that they were true, even as she had raised another man's children and been another man's wife, and another man's divorcee whose body showed up its own pain…even through all of that, the way the electricity shot through her heart meant it could have been yesterday; the years just fell off her. Nothing had changed, not a tiny thing.

"What about him?" she asked, grasping anxiously at the oxygen cylinder.

"Is everything all right, Mum?" Patsy called cheerfully from the kitchen. Claire didn't like her daughters-in-law calling her Mum; it made her feel about a million years old, but she wouldn't dream of mentioning it.

"Fine, thank you."

"Would you like a cup of tea?"

Claire shook her head in vexation.

"So," she said, "what? What is it?"

A painful lump formed in her throat. He couldn't be… He couldn't be dead. He couldn't be. Mind you, she nearly was, she thought to herself bitterly. But not Thierry, with so much life bursting from him.

• • • •

"He had a heart attack," I said, as plainly as I could. "He's in the hospital."

"A heart attack? A serious one?"

"Yes."

Claire found herself giggling with nerves and hysteria. "Oh, all that chocolate, all that butter," she said. "Is he… Is he… Oh Lord."

"I don't know," I said. "He's in the hospital. He's had an operation to put in a stent. They don't know if he's going to be all right."

"But if he's had the operation?"

"Yes, but it's difficult…" I wasn't quite sure how to say it. "He is terribly fat."

"Oh!" Claire looked down at her pin-thin wrists and shook her head. Her voice quavered; she was still giggling in confusion. The difference between them would be greater than ever. "Oh," she said again. "But he's still alive?"

I didn't understand why she was laughing. This wasn't good news.

"Well, yes, but he's very seriously ill."

"Ha, well, that's… Well, that's…"

Claire was nearly breathless now with her giggling fit. Patsy came rushing through from the kitchen.

"Mum! What's the matter?"

"I'm all right, I'm all right," said Claire, wheezing and waving her away.

"Claire? Mrs. Shawcourt?" I said on my end of the phone. Gradually she managed to control herself.

"Yes," she said finally. "Yes. Thank you. Sorry. Thank you for letting me know."

"That's all right," I said, still amazed about her reaction. There was a pause.

"He's alive?"

"Yes, he's alive."

"But he's not very well?"

"I think that's about it."

Her voice quieted.

"Oh," she said. "Oh, I would like to see him so."

I didn't know what to say to that. How could she get on a plane to Paris? She couldn't walk three steps without running out of breath. She couldn't even change trains. It was impossible. I felt so sorry.

"Maybe when he's better, he can come and see you?" I said. "I'll make him."

Claire looked again at the old, collapsing purple veins in her left hand. Her right hand was getting sore just from holding up the phone. She could see her reflection in the window. He wouldn't know it was her. He wouldn't recognize her.

"No, don't," she said. "Don't. But let me know, won't you? Let me know how he's getting on."

"Of course," I said. "I'll call you."

"And what about you?" she said suddenly. "How are you? How are you enjoying Paris?"

I half-smiled to myself as I wiped away a black glob of mascara from underneath my eye. I wasn't going to be the bearer of any more bad news.

"It's…it's eventful," I said.

"*Tout va bien à part ça?*"

"*Oui, à part ça.*"

• • • •

I realized as I hung up that I had been hoping that Claire could have been my savior, that I could have poured my woes out to her—she would understand, surely. She had been a young girl in Paris once. I wasn't much of a young girl, but she'd sent me here.

I hadn't expected her to be quite so enervated by the news. She was so tired, mostly, so weary; everything took her so long. But when she had giggled, nervously, jumpily, I'd caught a glimpse of another Claire, a younger one. I had thought she would be concerned—but from a difference. When I was recuperating, other people's bad news slightly washed over me; I was too selfish and wrapped up in myself to pay it that much attention. But Claire had responded completely differently, as if Thierry was someone she still knew terribly well, intimately, that this news about someone she hadn't clapped eyes on for forty years was somehow of intense importance to her.

• • • •

1973

Claire had seen Richard Shawcourt around. He went to the same school as her, but he was in a higher year. He wore brown horn-rimmed glasses that made him look too serious to be a schoolboy, and sometimes he'd carry a music case. He was carrying it that day as he swung through the woods.

Claire was skipping school. Some days she felt sad, some days dreamy. Today, she felt mutinous. She'd snapped repeatedly at her mother over the breakfast table (there was no point in cheeking the Reverend if she ever wanted to leave the house again) and stormed out nastily, barely even bothering to check the post. She'd started out in the direction of school— she had French oral practice that morning, which she was good at—but had gotten halfway there and seen a huge gaggle of girls, including Rainie Callendar, all giggling and screaming at each other and laughing at Looby Mary, a big lummox of a girl in their year who always walked alone and never spoke. They were obviously being viciously mean about her, even though Mary was clearly educationally subnormal and barely clean, asking her questions about whether she had a lad and which discotheque she would take him to, and it turned Claire's stomach all of a sudden, the stupid, pointless cruelties of school life. She wondered what Thierry would do. He wouldn't stand for it, she was sure; his benevolent attitude toward the world wouldn't allow it.

She marched up to them.

"What are you guys, eleven?" she said, her voice not even wavering. "For God's sake, you're practically school leavers and you're running around being bullies."

"Get over yourself," said Rainie Callendar, who dyed her hair already.

"Oh, it's the French madame's pet, oh je t'aime," said Minnie Hutchison, who was her evil sidekick. Everyone started laughing, but Claire just turned around to Looby Mary and said, "Are you all right?" and Looby Mary just looked really confused, like she hadn't properly understood what was happening in the first place, and scuttled off. The group of girls had reconfigured and were now talking loudly in shocked tones along the lines of, "Well, I don't know who she thinks she is," and "I suppose she thinks she's better than everyone," and Claire sighed, rolled her eyes, and marched off to the woods.

"Aw, too scared to come to school?" shouted Rainie, and Claire ignored her.

• • • •

She sat in the bough of her favorite tree in the copse behind the school, lighting one of her precious Gauloises—barely inhaling, just letting the smell of the smoke calm her down to stop her kicking a tree.

The sound of someone coming made her scuttle down and put it out, trying not to be seen.

"Sorry," said Richard Shawcourt, looking awkward and a bit embarrassed, his trousers already getting too short even this early in the school year. "I didn't mean to startle you. I just wanted to say well done and make sure you were all right. I never dare stand up to bullies; they break my glasses."

She stared at him up and down.

"What's in that music case then?" she said.

• • • •

It was worse than I had thought. When I got back, Frédéric and Alice were having a full-blown stand-up row in front of the shutters. They were screaming at each other too quickly for me to properly follow them, but it seemed reasonably obvious from the way they looked at me with furious eyes that it had a lot to do with me and my perceived weaknesses. Frédéric was obviously continuing to insist on the closure of the shop. This solution didn't appear to be cutting any ice with Alice at all. They both gazed at me expectantly.

The good thing about our corner of the Île de la Cité is it contains lots of tiny alleyways that are good for ducking down. I ducked down one now. Then I took out the telephone number that I had purloined from Alice's phone.

The voice answering spoke low and quickly.

"Allo?"

"Laurent?" I said. "It's me. It's Anna."

He exhaled slowly. "Anna, I'm at the hospital. I can't really talk. This isn't a good time."

"I know, I know. I'm sorry… How is he doing?"

Laurent sighed. "Still no change. These bloody machines are making my ears hurt. And I have to get back to work. I mean, I really have to. They can't run service without me."

This was the worst news I could hear. I needed him, really badly. I told him so.

"Please," I said. "I need you. To help me out with the shop. I can't do it by myself."

"But I thought you worked in chocolate?"

"Well, I do, but I'm hardly going to be as good as your father, am I?"

"No," he said, a little quickly for my liking.

"I need help. It's all going wrong. Frédéric and Alice are fighting."

"Alice would fight with a dead dog in a town hall," said Laurent. I presumed this was some unusual French saying I wasn't familiar with. He sighed and sat quietly for a long time. I could hear the *beep beep* and the *swishy-swashy* sound of the respirator behind him.

"Okay," he said finally. "I'm going to leave and do my shift, then come back to the hospital. Can you meet me at work? A few pointers, that's all, okay?"

I nodded. "Where do you work?"

"The Pritzer," he said. I'd never heard of it, but he said it like I ought to.

"Come in the back entrance. I'll see you at three."

"What will I tell Alice?"

"Tell Alice you're going to save the shop, and also that she can go pee on scissors."

My French had a long way to go.

• • • •

Alice looked down her long nose at me.

"Well, Thierry won't hear of it. He would never let Laurent's concoctions"—she pronounced the word *concoctions* as if it were poisonous—"near his customers."

"I realize that," I said. "But I think it might be better…"

"What we are making here is *chalk*," burst out Frédéric provocatively. He'd stopped shouting, briefly, when I made my way over to them, but his ears were bright red. Benoît was nowhere to be found. "It is a travesty! It is a sin!"

"Um, can we not go quite that far," I said. "It's not that bad."

"Not that bad is as good as terrible," he said. "In this shop."

Alice bit her lip and thought about it for a moment.

"The shop must go on," she said. "It must. We have bills and commitments. It is impossible that we close now; it is our busiest season… Can you sell the rest of this morning's stock?" she asked Frédéric.

He drew himself up to his full height—about five foot six—and said, "I can, but I will not, madame."

Alice rolled her eyes.

"All right," she said to me. "Go. And when you come back, do it right or you'll find French laws protecting jobs don't cover yours."

16

The Pritzer, I found out, was a very, very posh hotel, on the Place de la Concorde, near the Crillon. It was a beautiful yellow stone and looked like a castle, with small balconies and canopies over every window. Outside were two porters dressed in livery with top hats on, each standing next to a large topiary cock. A spotless red carpet descended the steps onto the pavement. Outside, a large man wearing sunglasses and a very tiny woman who looked like she was made out of icing sugar were descending from a huge black car. They were completely ignoring each other. The woman was holding a tiny dog like a baby. The porters leaped to help them.

"Excuse me," I said when they'd finished. "Where's the kitchen entrance?"

Around the back of the hotel, all was very different. The back entrance was off an alleyway filled with dustbins. The other side of the hotel was old white brick, not sandstone, and a grubby fire door was propped open at the bottom with several staff in white aprons and tall hats crowded around it, smoking furiously. I felt nervous but walked up. Just inside the entrance was an old man wearing a peaked hat and a green blazer, sitting at a desk next to a huge row of time stamp cards. That made me feel a bit more at home; it reminded me of the factory. I told him who I was looking for and he made a call.

A long hall stretched out in front of me, on one side lined with huge carts of linen and women in black dresses with white pinafores. On the other were great swinging doors with round panes of glass set in them, obviously leading to the kitchens, and it was from here that Laurent emerged. In his whites, he looked commanding and rather impressive, firing a list of instructions behind me as he came, looking none too pleased to see me, for which I couldn't really blame him. I'd caused him nothing but trouble since I'd arrived.

"Hello," I said in a small voice.

"Yes, follow me," he said. "Can't you tie your hair back?"

I retightened the loop of my ponytail, hoping that would be enough. He grunted, thanked the commissionaire, and pointed me in the direction of the hand sanitizer mounted on the wall outside the large swinging doors.

I'd never been in such a huge kitchen before. I stopped to goggle for a second; I couldn't help it. It was an utter hive of activity, men (and they were nearly all men) marching everywhere to and fro; not running, but marching very, very quickly. Everyone was wearing white with blue checked trousers and clogs, except some of the men wore white trousers and had their names embroidered on their jackets, including Laurent. I assumed this meant something important.

The noise levels were unbelievable; people were shouting in a variety of different languages; pots and pans were clanked and hurled across the room. In the corner, four younger men in T-shirts were frantically packing and unpacking industrial-sized dishwashers and two had their hands deep inside pots. On my right, a boy who looked to be around sixteen was furiously chopping vegetables. I had never seen anyone chop anything so quickly; his hand was a blur.

To my right was a long line of perfect salads laid out, onto which a man was slicing pieces of perfectly cooked pink duck, all exactly the same, at absolutely precise thicknesses. Another, older man came up to him at one point and told him off furiously for not making them all thin enough and the man, instead of arguing back, stood with his head down until the rant was over and then recommenced, apologizing.

Laurent caught me staring and gave me a half-smile. "Have you never seen a working kitchen before?" but I shook my head; I hadn't. My Saturday job in the Honey Pot didn't even compare; I'd never seen anything remotely like this. It was like a huge airfield, but once you got used to the size and the noise and the number of people bustling about and occasional bouts of steam, it seemed to make a lot of sense; it was organized, like ants, not the chaos it first appeared.

Laurent led me down to the far end of the room. Next to him, two men were kneading bread. They had huge muscular forearms and looked like miners or sailors, not bakers. An almost comically large man was opposite them, icing tiny pastries. The size of the man was completely at odds with the task he was undertaking.

Laurent's station was by the window, which looked out onto the Seine. He had a huge copper pot bubbling on the stove on a very low flame, the chocolate melting very much like his father's. But instead of oranges and mint, there was every manner of flavoring around his work bench. Tiny chilies were lined up in bright green and red; yellow marjoram and little pumpkin flowers jostled next to pine needles and sea salt.

"This looks like a mad person's laboratory," I said.

"I'm going to take that as a compliment," he said gruffly. "Is there any more news? You seem to be the first to know about anything."

"That's not true," I said quietly. "But I do need to ask you this favor."

He checked on one of the smaller pots he was stirring. "Try this," he said. I opened my mouth eagerly, and he smiled. "You are a proper chocolate girl. Okay, hang on."

He blew on it to cool it down.

"What is it?"

He shook his head, then popped it in my mouth.

My first instinct was to spit it out. It was horrible, not sweet at all. It was sharp, bitter, and with an odd warm flavor that I couldn't identify. Laurent was holding up his finger strongly, warning me not to spit it out.

"It's new," he said. "You have to give it some time."

"It tastes like cat food," I said, but then stopped talking as the warmth of the melting sweet gradually hit my tongue. It spread all around my mouth as the chocolate melted and was the most extraordinary, rich sensation on my tongue and around my mouth. It tasted like nothing I'd ever had before. It was also slightly horrible, but as soon as I'd finished it, I immediately wanted another one.

"Wow, what *was* that?" I said eventually, looking hopefully at his pot.

"Slow-roasted tomato chili chocolate," Laurent announced proudly. "If you don't use the very bitterest of beans, it makes you throw up. It's a hard one to get right."

"It's not really a sweet at all," I said.

"It's not," agreed Laurent. "Wait until you see what I do with it and the duck."

I boggled to think.

"And your dad didn't think this was cool?"

"He just wanted to do things his way."

"And you don't?"

He shrugged.

"Well, maybe it's better for fathers and sons not to work with each other."

A small man, quite young, had appeared before him and was now removing trays of quickly hardening chocolate to the enormous fridges. Laurent grimaced at him quickly and checked his watch.

"*Alors*, I need to get to the hospital. What do you need from me, exactly?"

I gave him a piece of the chocolate I'd made. He maneuvered it around his mouth exactly how his father did it. His face fell.

"Oh," he said.

"The shop needs you to help me," I said. "I can't do it."

"I have been thinking about this," he said. "I don't think it's possible.

I've changed my mind. No offense, but you worked in a mass-market factory. You don't have the right genes, the right experience."

"That's nonsense," I said crossly. "It's just that I've only been here five minutes."

"It's pointless," he said.

He started washing his hands, handing over the stove to another man—didn't they have any women working here at all?—who carried on stirring.

"Yes. Yes, we need you," I said. "I can't. I can't do it, not yet. I didn't get to watch him do it often enough. But I'm a quick learner, I promise."

He looked at me, then waved his hand around the room. "Do you know how long it's taken me to work up to this?" he said. "How many kitchens I've worked in, how many people have shouted at me, how much crap I've taken off everyone, how much bullying I've gotten for who my father is? How much I've looked and concentrated and learned and observed? And you want me to, what, just give it all up and come back and put mint in milk chocolate? Is that what you want me to do?"

"It's not what I want you to do," I said. "It's for the shop. It's for your dad."

Laurent blew his thick fringe out of his eyes. "Well, that's interesting, because the last time we discussed it, he said he didn't want me to cross the threshold anymore and that I was a total failure who'd never learned a thing."

I put my arm out, but didn't touch him. "That was before."

"But if I come up, will you let me do my own styles, my own designs? No, of course not. Alice will insist on doing things the old way and I'll be completely trapped again, acting as a slave to my dad, just like he's always wanted his entire life. I will not cook there!"

It was only the general noise and clanging of the kitchen that stopped people turning to look at Laurent shouting. I was still pink anyway; I couldn't bear it. I stared at the ground so he couldn't see how furious I was. But he noticed anyway and didn't give a toss.

"I have to go to the hospital," he said. "And I can't lose this job. Not at the moment. There are...there are no jobs like this. I've worked so long for this, and I'm already taking more time off than anyone else does, just out of kitchen respect for my father..."

I nodded. "I understand," I said in a flat voice. He was walking me out now, grabbing his scooter helmet from the wall.

"He doesn't want what I have to offer," said Laurent. "He's made that totally clear... I'll be back for evening service," he told the man at the door, clocking out.

He saw my unhappy face as we entered back into the bright hazy afternoon.

"Look," he said, "just...try a few more times. It's not difficult what my father does, believe me. It just takes a bit of practice."

"Except I don't have the genes."

"You don't have the genes to invent it," he said. "But a monkey can copy a recipe eventually."

I gave him a look.

"I think that just came out ruder than I meant it to," he said, a look of apology in his features.

"Well, wouldn't be the first time," I said.

"Do you need a lift?"

"No, thank you," I said stiffly.

We stood looking at each other, both cross.

"Send my love to your dad," I said. "Let us know how he is. Frédéric is climbing the walls."

Laurent half-smiled. "Yes, he would be. But Benoît's the one you have to watch for."

I nodded. "Yeah, well, thanks for all the advice," I said sarcastically.

And he got on his scooter and sped away.

17

The next few nights, as the shop closed over what happily turned out to be a bank holiday weekend, I stopped going home at all. I stayed. And I cooked and I stirred and I experimented and I added and took away and did the bloody conching, over and over and over again. I tried the pistachio—a disaster—-and the violet, and the hazelnut. In fact, anything including nuts was a consummate failure.

Eventually, after working until I fell asleep in the workroom, on the fourth night I finally got it figured out. If I stuck to just a couple of things—no nougatine, no caramel, no sculpture, no drinking chocolate, or experimenting with dark chocolate, which I simply didn't have the palate for—I realized that if I stayed simple—very, very simple—and with the right ingredients, which Benoît had already sorted out, I could do it. Well, I couldn't do it; that wasn't the case at all. But I could produce the two simplest chocolates we did—an orange and a dark mint—that tasted almost, but not quite, as good as the real thing. Good enough, at any rate, to pass most of the tourist palates who were looking for a souvenir rather than a gourmet item.

I melted and mixed and poured, over and over again, leaving the radio on and downing endless amounts of espresso to keep me awake. By Monday night, I was as exhausted as I had ever been in my life. My phone rang, unexpectedly, at three o'clock in the morning.

"Allo?"

"You live! You are alive! I can call off the fire brigade and Interpol."

"Sami?" I said, realizing I hadn't spoken to anyone all weekend. "Is that you? You haven't really called Interpol, have you?"

He chuckled on the phone.

"No. I assumed you were off discovering Paris and your first taste of erotic adventure."

"Ahem," I said. "You're very rude." Then I looked around at the workroom. "What are you doing?"

"We're at the Cirque du Soleil after-party. The gymnasts tend to get a little wild."

"Oh," I said. "You could stop by here if you're hungry. I have a lot of taster chocolate left over."

"*Vraiment?*"

And that is how, half an hour later, I found myself drinking something entirely suspicious out of a bottle that Sami told me was pastis. It reminded me of Laurent's chocolate in that at first it was horrible, then almost immediately delicious. It also, given my exhausted and underfed state, got me incredibly drunk very quickly, as I watched beautiful young people whose genders I couldn't exactly ascertain descend on the chocolate with the enthusiasm only people who hang upside down from a roof for four hours a night can gather. It was nearly all gone and the room clean and tidy as the sun started to come up from outside and I realized there was no point trying to get any sleep today either.

● ● ● ●

The scent of Frédéric's cigarette coming up the rue Chanoinesse scattered the beautiful golden circus creatures like some kind of dream, and he sniffed suspiciously as he entered.

"How long have you been here?" he asked suspiciously.

I shrugged. "I wanted to practice over the weekend," I said.

He glanced around.

"I'll clean it all up," I said defensively and he raised an eyebrow. Then he advanced on the latest tray in the cooling rack. I stared at him anxiously. Of course the dancers had loved it, but they would love any chocolate at that time of day. Frédéric was the one who really knew.

He took a long pull of water from an Evian bottle to clear his palate, then took a small piece from the baking sheet on the tray. He held it up to the light, then crumbled a little between his fingers to check the consistency. Finally, he popped the whole piece inside his mouth. I held my breath. I had tried everything I could and this was… Well, if I was totally honest, this was as good as I could do. I waited as he waited, for the chocolate to melt and the full richness of the underlying taste to come through. As he did so, Benoît startled me by turning up silently beside him and watching the process.

Gradually Frédéric turned to me. He wasn't over the moon. I wasn't a hitherto undiscovered genius. But he gave me a tight, trim little nod.

"We can…we can manage that," he said in a quiet voice.

Exhausted as I was, a huge smile spread across my face.

"*Merci*," I said, delighted. And, completely out of the blue, Benoît grabbed a piece, swallowed it quickly, then came up and, without saying a word, kissed me on both cheeks.

• • • •

"This is all you have?" said Frédéric.

"Yes," I said. "I figured I'd just try to get one or two right."

"Good idea," he said. He checked his phone.

"Alice hasn't called you?"

I shook my head.

"Or Laurent?"

"I don't think Laurent wants anything to do with me," I said ruefully.

"Well, we're only keeping their businesses alive," said Frédéric. "Why would they want to tell us anything?"

I thought, though, if Thierry had deteriorated, we would definitely know about it. Which was something, I suppose. I went through to the front of the shop to get some fresh morning air and wash my face in the bathroom and to check if Alice was coming. There was no sign of her.

"Well," said Frédéric. "We shall worry about that as it happens. All that matters is that today we have a shop we can open."

And when I came back from the bathroom, Benoît had made me a cup of coffee.

•   •   •   •

Claire looked up at Patsy.

"Patsy, I've decided, I want to take a trip."

Patsy's face immediately got panicky, as if she'd suddenly gone mad. Claire wondered if she thought she meant trip like a long journey into the night, or suicide or something. Or just a trip, she also considered. Something very different.

"I would."

Ian had gotten her a film out called *The Bucket List*. It looked absolutely terrible—old men on a cancer ward having a hilarious time—but the concept stuck with her.

"There is something I want to do. Before…before it's too late."

"Don't talk like that," Patsy had said hastily.

•   •   •   •

Of course, she had met Richard Shawcourt before. But their school lives were very different. He lived in a bought house, for starters, not something tied to the church; just a bought house, but a nice house, a detached. Although now that didn't intimidate her anymore. She knew a little bit about nice houses. Before, she'd barely have given him a second glance, she was so sure of their differences. She'd have laughed at him, in fact. Very few kids like him even went to Kidinsborough Academy, never mind wielding a clarinet. He'd started off very small, she remembered now, just punchbag material even from her year group, but now, she saw, he'd grown into himself, in the upper sixth, ready to leave for somewhere better, and behind the brown horn-rimmed spectacles, he was actually rather handsome, with his wavy dark hair and strong eyebrows. Not that she was interested, of course. He walked her home from the forest that day, asking her about herself, to which she replied in the most vague of terms; and after that he'd seemed to pop up everywhere. She barely noticed until Christmas came and went, and a card arrived from Mme. LeGuarde, full of family news about the children that didn't even touch on Thierry, but added a fulsome footnote as to how much they missed Claire and hoped she was (Claire thought, correctly, that this was deliberately pointed) concentrating very hard on her education.

And that was it. Nothing more. Nothing from Thierry or Paris; nothing except the faint tinge of lavender that seemed to scent Madame's Christmas card, although that may have just been her imagination.

So when Richard brought her a large bunch of blood-red roses and a small brooch in the shape of a frog at the Christmas dance, she let him kiss her up against the back wall of the gym, in amid all the other snogging, writhing couples, to show the world, and Thierry, and Mme. LeGuarde, and Rainie Callendar how very much she didn't care.

● ● ● ●

It was Richard who, when she failed all her A-levels except for French, comforted her and assured her she could still go into teacher training, and it was Richard—nice, steady Richard, who was going to study engineering science in Leicester—who brought the Reverend around to agreeing to let her leave home. It was Richard with whom she slept in the small modern bedroom in the halls of residence that smelled of pot noodle and incense and hash, shocking and exciting him with her prowess, confirming for her that Thierry was a one-off, not like other men. And gone. And after dating a few of the long-haired young men on campus, self-conscious in their new flares, talking endlessly about Herman Hesse and Nixon in overponderous tones, she gradually realized that Richard was as nice as any man she'd ever met; kind, and sensible, and steady and well-off, and there was no more point in loving your first love than in thinking you were still going to marry Davy Jones.

Much, much later, when they were divorcing—they'd kept it as civilized as possible, waiting for both of the boys to have left home and be nicely settled, very little rancor on either side—Richard, in a rare moment of not being businesslike and distant and organized, had said, "You never really loved me, did you? It was never really me. I thought you were amazing and different and mysterious, but now it seems to me you were just thinking about someone else the entire time."

He'd shaken his head in wonderment. "The thing is, for me, Claire, I got to spend twenty-five years with someone I loved. With someone I really and truly loved. But you... I don't know what on earth you've wasted your life doing."

And Claire had smiled stiffly and signed the papers his lawyer had sent over and waited until she heard the familiar sound of his Rover turn the corner before she'd sunk to her knees and simply disintegrated, becoming unbodied; she degenerated into a wavering mass of tears and snot and pouring emotion, dribbling beyond the bounds of the self, soaking the good John Lewis carpet they'd invested in together.

Although she didn't believe, as some did, that cancer was some kind of malignant force or punishment that snuck into you if you were unhappy or upset, she couldn't help believe that if it was a dark spirit, it would have seen that day—and the nights, the many nights that followed it—as an ideal opportunity to infect a soul that saw nothing but deepest black.

● ● ● ●

"What do you mean, a trip?" Patsy repeated when she saw the tight set of Claire's mouth and realized she wasn't in the mood to be dissuaded and that she wasn't joking either.

Claire stared down at her Hickman line and sighed. This was going to be really complicated and annoying and hard work and dangerous. It was going to upset her children, and quite possibly Anna, who, she now realized, she'd sent on this mission in a selfish way to work out what had happened anyway. It would cause expense and trouble and would perhaps be all for nothing, and she was nothing but what she had always been, according to the Reverend and Richard and everyone, it somehow seemed, who'd known her well: a selfish, hard person, with unseemly desires.

She set her mouth. There was more of the Reverend in her, she thought sometimes, than anyone would ever have suspected.

"I want to see Paris one last time," she said.

Patsy frowned.

"Are you sure?" she said.

Patsy didn't know anything about Claire's past, because not even Richard knew more than a hint or two. She'd been very careful that they never went to France, even on holiday. She actually made her French accent worse than it was and never joined in a conversation about Paris, even though she was asked about it often. She knew he would guess something in an instant; in fact, the very reason he was first so attracted to her was the air of difference she had given off after that summer. So Patsy treated her patronizingly, like it was some kind of whim.

"I am sure," said Claire. "I will sort everything out. And I can pay for it."

She could. Richard had been utterly fair, and her teacher's pension was good, and she had an annuity she'd had absolutely no ability to spend which, she realized dryly, was a great thing for the insurance company and the country as a whole.

"Well, you can take the train now," said Patsy. "Ricky and I did it when we were dating. Mind you, I didn't like Paris at all. So rude, everyone always pushing past you and everything so expensive, and I didn't even think the food was that good. You couldn't get a decent curry, I'll tell you that. Or a cab."

Claire suddenly felt exhausted. She loved Patsy, but couldn't possibly explain to her why getting a cab in Paris could only ever defeat the point. Or maybe it did. Maybe they'd completely built over it, like the new shopping center in Kidinsborough that had turned into a kind of derelict drug run within five years. Or the pedestrian plaza, which was mostly used now as somewhere for people to be sick on a weekend. It was where the ambulances parked up.

Under the Eiffel Tower, there was an old-fashioned carousel. It didn't move very fast, it creaked a lot, and it made its own music. The children had adored it—they had their favorite horses and animals and loved the second story, reachable through a child-sized curved wrought iron staircase, even though it rotated even more slowly than the one underneath it. She wondered if that were still there.

"Well, nonetheless, I want to go."

"Well, let me talk to the Eurostar people. They must have some way of taking sick people."

"I don't want to take the train," said Claire, in a moment of sudden realization. "I have to take the ferry."

"But that will take much longer and be much more dangerous," said Patsy. "I mean, if you can afford it, you should go first class."

Claire saw her favorite nurse, Montserrat, come up the path and attempted a wave. Somehow just having made the plan was already making her feel better about things.

"No," she said. "I shall take the boat. I have friends in Paris. I think they can help."

18

So fortunately, Alice was incredibly grateful for everything. Ha, was she a bugger. Honestly, getting a smile out of her would be like getting her to eat something; her entire mouth was a no-fly zone.

"Is it better?" she asked carelessly.

"Is *he* better?" demanded Frédéric, as if he was going to hold all of the chocolate hostage until he knew.

Under Alice's enormous sunglasses, she looked very drawn.

"He is…he is a little better," she admitted. "Well, he is no worse. And the stents appear to have taken and, well…" Her lip curled slightly. "Every day he loses a little weight. But I wish…" She looked away. "I wish he would wake up and say something, dammit."

This sounded not ideal. I knew a little bit myself about waking up in the hospital, and I knew, courtesy of Dr. Ed, that the quicker you managed to do so, the better it was all around. I was suddenly tempted to ring Dr. Ed, find out if that friendly manner was all it was supposed to be. But I didn't, of course; he wouldn't have remembered my name.

"What does his doctor say?" I said.

"Why, are you a professional?" snapped Alice. Every time I gave her a bit of credit for being under stress, she managed to use up every bit of it and eat into my meager reserves of respect even more.

"No," I said. "But I've spent a lot of time in the hospital."

"What's wrong with you?" she asked bluntly. Everyone was staring at me.

"Nothing, it doesn't matter," I said quickly. I didn't like people bringing up my hilarious comedy injury. It hadn't been the least bit funny to me.

Alice sighed. "She says, 'Wait and see, Madame, wait and see,' as if I have the least option to do anything else. Then she goes off to lunch." She glanced around. "Anyway. As long as you are managing not to make a complete disaster going on here, I suppose this is a relief."

She stalked off.

Frédéric, whose jolly manner was nearly restored and who was almost making up in flirting with female clients what Thierry used to do in charming them, said, "That was the nicest she's ever been to us."

• • • •

I, on the other hand, was utterly at the end of my tether, exhausted by the end of the day. News of Thierry's illness had made the papers, which just made us busier than ever, which struck me as counterintuitive, but nonetheless, there were a lot of happy-looking tourist children standing outside, and even when Frédéric abruptly told people that today they had a choice of orange or orange, everyone seemed to take that as an acceptably French thing to say.

I scrubbed and cleaned and cooked and mixed—although Benoît too helped me immeasurably and silently in the back of the greenhouse—and by 7:00 p.m. felt ready to collapse into bed. If Sami was holding an impromptu masked ball or something, I was going to kill him.

I was last to leave, locking up with the heavy metal key in the large bolt grille—it looked rather like the front cover of a huge old-fashioned lift—when I heard the scooter roar up right behind me. I didn't pay it any attention at first—they were ten a penny around here—but it came to a stop right behind me.

"*Merde*," came a gravelly voice.

I turned around. Laurent was standing there, looking wild-eyed. I turned back again. I was sick of him and his stupid feud with a man lying unconscious in a hospital bed.

"Has everyone gone?"

"Yes," I said, as sarcastically as possible. "Everyone has gone. Everyone important has gone."

He blinked a couple of times as I turned back around to finish closing up.

"Oh," he said. "Only…only…he's woken up."

I turned around. Even though I was utterly exhausted, and filthy, and cross to see Laurent, I couldn't help it; a huge grin split my face.

"Truly!"

"Truly. He's not saying much, but he's swearing and demanding beignets."

"Oh! Well. That is brilliant!"

"We're not out of the woods," he said gravely. "Well, that's what M. le Médecin keeps saying. But he looks…he looks a lot less gray, like a dead elephant."

"Does he know you called him a dead elephant?"

He frowned. "I don't know. I slipped out before he saw me."

I threw my hands up in anger. "Are you *kidding*?"

"No," he said. "Alice was giving me the feud eyes, and he was telling her he was hungry and she was telling him he was going to have to start getting a whole lot more hungry, and it seemed to be turning into a massive family fallout within about two minutes of him regaining consciousness, and I realized why I kept out of their way in the first place."

He paused. "I'll see him tomorrow, I promise. Stop looking at me like I'm the big bad wolf."

He did look a bit like the big bad wolf when I thought about it, with his dark hair and thick brows and bright white teeth.

"You promise," I said gravely.

He nodded and looked around.

"Also," he said. "I wanted to come down here before everyone had left… I felt bad about the other day."

"Good," I said, then, using a word I really enjoyed using in French, "you were unconscionable."

"I know, I know. That's why I'm here. I just…everything was just getting on top of me, you know? I'd been spending all my nights there… I was tired."

"So you came down to apologize?"

"God, no. I came down to show you how to make something."

"Well, maybe I can already make something," I said.

He grimaced. "Alice brought some of that mint stuff you did the other day into the hospital. She thought it was all right, foreigner. It was filthy. None of the staff could believe it."

That was my first day's efforts.

"You are *so* rude," I said.

"No," said Laurent. "I just don't think you realize how bad it was. So, now I am here."

"Well, you're too late," I said.

He waggled his eyebrows at me. "I doubt it."

I sighed. Even though I was exhausted and had spent the last nineteen hours dreaming of a bath and what I'd do to Sami if he'd used all the hot water again to take his makeup off, I took the keys out of my apron pocket.

"Come on then," I said wearily.

Inside, everything was gloomy in the dusk. Laurent looked around with a practiced eye as I fumbled my way through to the greenhouse to switch the lights on there. We couldn't put the lights on at the front of the shop; everyone would think we were open and start hammering on the shutters like chocolate-starved zombies.

Laurent wasn't following me. I turned back to look at him. He was running one of his hands through his thick curly hair.

"I haven't… I haven't been in here for…"

I raised my eyebrows.

"Well. A long time," he said. "Years. Maybe ten."

Even I was shocked at that. "You haven't spoken to your dad in ten years?"

Laurent suddenly looked very unhappy. "The smell in here," he said. "It hasn't changed a bit." He ran his hand along the long wooden countertop, worn smooth over the years. "It hasn't changed a bit," he repeated wonderingly, shaking his head.

"You know, sometimes down the street, I pass someone eating some. I can smell it a mile off. It doesn't smell like the chocolate you get everywhere else. Every time I smell it, or see the bag…it's like being punched in the gut."

I shook my head and put the coffee machine on. "You know," I said, "I know families fall out for all sorts of reasons. Cath's mother didn't speak to her sister for sixteen years over a purloined silver jubilee scarf. But fighting over whether or not you can add spice to chocolate?"

I thought about it. "Maybe all family feuds are totally stupid," I said, thinking of when James and Joe wouldn't speak to each other while sharing a bedroom for two years, on account of some unauthorized hogging of the top bunk.

Laurent looked as if he was going to disagree again, but instead followed me through to the back. He made an involuntary "oh" of nostalgia; it was easy to see that the greenhouse hadn't changed in decades, even to me.

"I used to come here sometimes when I was a little boy," he said, breathing in that wonderful warm scent of plants and cocoa, like a deep chocolate rainforest. "Benoît used to chase me around the vats."

"He's still here."

"No, not him, his dad. My dad is very loyal to employees who never answer him back."

He came over to one of the work benches and easily swung himself up on it.

"Come on then," he said in a challenging way and I was so tired, so sleepy and woozy with everything that had gone on that I thought, just for a tiny instant, that it was me he was asking to go over there. He looked so comfortable and at ease now, his long legs splayed as he surveyed the place he'd once called home that, to my surprise, I nearly found myself walking across the room, letting him haul me up onto his lap. And after that...

Then I realized he was asking me to bring him some of the chocolate I'd made. I flushed bright red immediately, flustered, sure my face immediately betrayed me, but he wasn't paying attention. I found some squares that had been badly wrapped earlier and put to one side. Laurent looked at me and smiled.

"Come on, don't look so nervous. Where's your new stuff? You tried your best, and then I'll give you a helping hand, okay?"

He thought I was nervous about the chocolate. I'd almost forgotten about it.

I extended some on a plate. He started to chew. I'd gotten past Frédéric but there was no way Laurent was going to be satisfied. Still, I was having a shot.

Laurent closed his eyes. There was total silence in the room, with only the tick of the wall clock and the faint rumble of the Metro far below the cobbled streets. After what seemed like an age (that I used to study him—his long eyelashes casting a shadow on his cheek, his unruly curls, the five o'clock shadow climbing up his long jaw line, his lips unusually pronounced for a man), he finally opened his eyes again and looked straight at me. There was something different there from his usual mix of annoyance or amusement. It looked perilously close to respect.

"You did this?"

I nodded.

"Alone?"

I nodded again.

He looked to the side. "You know it's not... I mean, it's not Girard."

I nodded.

"But...I've tasted worse."

"'I've tasted worse'? That's not actually a compliment."

"Oh, it is. It is. You've definitely got...you've definitely got something." He ate another piece. "Okay, well, here you're missing the black pepper. You need it to bring up the base notes. And a touch less butter, okay? This isn't for children, or Americans. And stir a little less, you've overchurned. It messes up the components."

I looked around for a piece of paper to write all this down on. He stopped chewing for a second.

"But really," he said, "compared to last week's...fiasco...I mean, you've done really well."

I didn't want to say that I'd been up for three nights, but he must have seen my eyelids drooping.

"Look, do that, then I'll come and talk mint with you another time, all right? Do you want to go and get something to eat? I am absolutely super-fatigued, and I think you might be too."

I nodded gratefully—another four-hour session in the greenhouse at this point might just have totally wiped me out—and followed him out of the front door, locking up again, then following him down a tiny maze of alleys I still hadn't worked out. Three turns around though, and we were at yet another one of those dark doors that seemed to appear out of the middle of nowhere. I felt for the tourists at the great huge outdoor restaurants that lined the Seine or the Bois de Boulogne; they had no idea, could never know about these places. The locals were jealous and selfish with them, had no interest in sharing them. Paris could be pretty tough on the newcomer. This one had nothing but a tiny mushroom over its door to let you know it was even there.

Laurent knocked and was answered by a stooped man with a napkin thrown over his shoulder. For a second, he paused and stared. Then he took a step back.

"S...Laurent?" he said incredulously.

"Salvatore, yes, it's me," said Laurent.

The old man looked nearly tearful, then threw his arms around Laurent's neck, kissing him three times on each cheek.

"I thought... God help me, I thought it was your father's ghost standing there. You look so like him."

"So they say."

I looked at Laurent again. I couldn't see the connection at all between huge, wheezing Thierry with his skin like uncooked dough and this tall, olive-skinned, flashing-eyed man, his black curls bouncing, so full of vigor and life, even if his passion sometimes overtook him. Surely he wouldn't end up like his father.

"We haven't seen you in..." The man shook his head. "It has been so long. So long."

"I know," said Laurent.

"And now. Finally. You are here to run the shop. Your father?"

"He's recovering," said Laurent firmly. "I'm just helping out."

The old man looked closely at me.

"And this is your wife? Your girlfriend?"

Laurent waved his hand. "Oh, no, nothing like that. She works for my father. Hey, Señor, can you get us something to eat?"

"Of course, of course," said Salvatore, throwing open the old wooden door into a passageway from which emerged the most amazing smells of mushrooms sizzling in garlic and butter, with white pepper and all sorts of other things I couldn't identify.

But I barely noticed the stunning aromas; I was so tired and shaky that suddenly I was furious that Laurent had referred to me in such a dismissive way. I mean, I know that's all we'd been doing and all we were, technically, to one another, but...after everything we'd bloody been through. Couldn't he at least have said we were friends?

I realized as he ushered me through into a tiny restaurant not much larger than somebody's front room—decorated like someone's front room too, with family photographs and knickknacks, nearly every table filled with people concentrating furiously on the process of eating as a tiny little old woman ducked and bobbed between the tables carrying piled-high plates as if she was dancing—that actually, if I was being completely honest with myself, I had perhaps seen us as something more than friends. That if I was being completely honest with myself, I did actually fancy him a bit. I suppose it was the high emotional pitch with which we'd been thrown together, I suppose because I'd been alone for so long—I started to feel very foolish—that I'd just fixated on the first available male. Maybe I was ovulating?

But also something about Paris had reawoken me. After the accident, after my illness, everything in Kidinsborough had seemed so very cold and gray and lifeless. I'd seen Claire and myself as the same, even though she was twice my age. She had noticed it and realized it, and sent me here to bring me back to life. The problem with life was that it had sent a bit of human blood shooting around my veins for once. But I'd forgotten how to do it. I'd forgotten how people fancy each other and how people get together. It's very rarely because one person thinks the other person sent his father to hospital and is a really terrible cook. I bit my lip thinking of how earlier tonight, I'd even thought about going over to him… Oh god. I was such an idiot. I felt so stupid.

"Anna?"

He was asking, not what I wanted to drink, but whether I wanted the red wine Salvatore had already brought over. I shrugged and let him pour me a tiny glass.

"We shall have the risotto of course," he said. "Marina, has it changed at all?"

The tiny old woman had much the same reaction as Salvatore, except her kisses were even more effusive. She spoke in a rat-tat-tat Italian-influenced French accent that I could barely follow, but I did catch her saying,

"No, of course it is exactly the same. We wouldn't change a single tiny thing. If you change a single tiny thing when you have something perfect, it is all wrong! Wrong, wrong and terrible and a disaster."

Laurent cocked an eyebrow at me, but I was too unhappy to flirt back with him. I just nodded, suddenly feeling so terribly, terribly weary. He attempted to make conversation, but I felt so unsure of myself that I could barely mutter responses. Eventually he too lapsed into silence until the food arrived. Then he closed his eyes and inhaled the steam. It smelled almost impossibly rich and flavorsome, full of onions and cream and stock and good things.

"I ate this…as a child. When I came here, I would insist on eating this all the time," he said. "When there was a good day at the shop. Or a bad day. Or an average day. My dad would just say, 'Everyone to Salvatore's,' and we would take the table there"—he pointed to the largest table, which was by the fireplace and had mismatched rickety chairs—"or if it was hot, on the terrace…" He broke off. "Hey, Salvatore. Do you still have the terrace?"

"Would you like to move?"

"Of course, it's terribly hot in here, isn't it?"

Salvatore shrugged—he had obviously lived in this environment all his life—but he lifted the plates and Marina grabbed the glasses before we had a chance to help her, and they disappeared through a tiny door at the side I hadn't noticed before. We followed. I could feel the pain in my toes as we ascended a tiny spiraling staircase three levels above the restaurant, past what was clearly their private apartment. Eventually we came to another door and popped out of the old building like corks.

It was bigger than my little sliver of balcony and completely different. Here, the buildings, so old, bulged over the side of the island and over the water, so it felt as though we were curving over. Marina had brought a candle, which she put in the middle of the solitary table, and fairy lights decorated the balcony edge, but there was no other light, just the swiftly flowing darkness of the river and the blaze of brightness from the Left Bank that felt completely disconnected from us, far away, a different world from the ancient rocks of our old walls. Ivy had been roughly trimmed from the side, which gave the building an added feeling of being a fairy tale. And it would, I thought grimly, have been a fairy tale, if I wasn't feeling so absolutely rotten about everything.

Salvatore and Marina, with some giggling, left us the bottle of wine and vanished. It was oddly quiet up there, away from the everyday noises of Paris enjoying itself in the summertime. Laurent ignored me for at least five minutes as he plunged his face into his meal, eating at a startling rate, with a huge appetite and evident pleasure. I waited a moment, then, seeing as he was never going to notice me, started in.

I wouldn't have admitted it under torture, but I'd never eaten risotto before. I'd had a Pot Rice, but clearly that wasn't the same thing at all. I think if I'd mentioned it at home, my mum and dad would have stared at me, and Dad would have said, "Aye, maybe we should try that," and Mum would have said, "Oh, no, it will be too difficult, I'd get it wrong, it's a bit foreign for me, love," and put on a fish finger sandwich quickly before I asked again. And I could cook a little bit—I could make a roast, and a pie, but this would never have occurred to me. And I knew, the second I had had my first bite, that I would never learn to make risotto; that it would be completely and utterly pointless because it would really require being born into a family who did little else; to spend years learning every fine detail between the different subtle balances of wine and aged parmesan and melting translucent onions and mushrooms precooked in a huge furnace with stone floors and walls so they came out perfectly sealed and slightly crisp and absolutely the most meltingly flavorsome mushrooms I'd ever had, and in fact, as I would learn later, they would be picked fresh and wild in the fields around Versailles by your own extended family every week near fine grass grazed by the finest of organic cows and an original medieval forest, so in fact you didn't have the faintest chance of even getting your hands on them.

Tasting that exquisite, extraordinary risotto made me understand, understand properly for the first time what Frédéric and Laurent and Thierry felt about their chocolate. That there was a right way and a wrong way and that was that. As the first risotto I had ever tasted, it seemed very unlikely that I would ever taste another that could approach its perfection; that I could work half the rest of my life simply trying to approach it. As someone who had worked for eleven years at Braders Family Chocolates, my palate had gotten used to the substandard. But now, at last, I understood.

"Oh," I said, after a few mouthfuls. Laurent's plate was already clear. "How can you eat it like that?" I said crossly. "It's all gone!"

"I know," said Laurent, looking regretfully at his empty plate. "I just couldn't help myself. God, I missed it." He glanced at mine.

"Don't think it," I ordered. "I am going to eat every bite and savor every bite and then I am going to lick the plate. And then I am going to lick the plate again."

He grinned suddenly, wolfishly, and topped up our glasses.

"You like it?"

"I think it's the nicest thing I've ever put in my mouth."

His eyebrows went up at that, but I didn't care. I knew what I was to him, so I could ignore him. I could concentrate, from now on, on enjoying what coming back to life had also bought me. Recovering in Kidinsborough, I had eaten my food spicier and spicier, desperately trying to awaken my taste buds into caring about something— anything. There was no new flavor of chips so stupid that I wouldn't give them a whirl. As a strategy, I now realized, it had been a real failure, adding only inches to my waistline and a sense of slight stupefaction.

I mopped up the juice with some of the wonderful bread set in a tiny basket in front of us. I could barely see what I was eating in the candlelight. A *bateau mouche* passed below us, and I saw the flashes from cameras going off, taking pictures of the cathedral that would come out, I suspected, a bit blurry and disappointing.

I looked up to see him staring at me.

"What?"

"Nothing," he said.

"You're not having any."

"It's not that… It's just… It's nice to see a girl eat. I don't know any girls who eat."

I chose not to answer that with "because I bet you go out with really scrawny French girls who are all bendy and in the circus and stuff," but instead wiped my face with a napkin. I'd obviously missed a bit; he took the napkin from my hand and rubbed away on the other side of my mouth, looking at me intently.

"I like girls who are hungry," he said.

I looked out over the water. In any other circumstances, I thought, this would be so sexy. And in fact, there was a bit of me thought he probably would. He looked tired, and I knew he was sad over his father; he probably would have let me take him home.

But if Paris was bringing my soul back to life, it was also bringing my instincts back to life too. I wasn't some popsy who worked for his father. Well, I was. But I was more than that too.

"That," I said, "is the corniest line I have ever heard in my entire life. I bet it works all the time too." I shook my head.

Laurent raised his hands. "It wasn't a line!" he protested.

"Oh, I'm sure it would work on those other girls," I said airily. "But now I have to go."

It felt good, doing this. Not risking my ego for a little bit of comfort, not lending myself to someone whose embarrassed face I could already imagine in the morning, as he headed back to his world of dainty skinny models who didn't unbalance the back of his scooter.

Suddenly he looked at me as if seeing me for the first time, and

I knew I'd been right. He really had been after some quick sex. I remembered how I'd never seen him around with the same girl twice.

"It's early," I said, glancing at my watch. "Do you want me to text you where Sami is?"

He shook his head. "No," he said. "No, I'm really tired."

"Me too," I said, standing up.

• • • •

As we left, Laurent was doused in kisses for the last time as they waived the bill "as long as you bring your father back next time and come together." I stopped to talk to Marina on the way out.

"That was…that was beautiful," I said. "It was one of the loveliest meals I've ever had. Thank you so much."

Her face smiled politely; of course she must hear this on a nightly basis. "Will you look after Laurent?" she asked me, in halting English.

"Oh, he's not mine to look after," I said, trying not to betray the wobble in my voice. She looked at me, shaking her head.

"You know," she said, "he's never brought a girl here before. Not ever."

19

The email arrived the next morning, as I stumbled from bed. I'd slept ten hours, thankfully, but it either still wasn't enough or it was far too much, as I felt wobbly and bleary. Sami was capering about the kitchen.

"Ooh," he said. "The phone rang for you."

"Sami, what are you wearing?"

He glanced down. "Oh, this?"

"*Yes*, this! I don't want to see it this early!"

Sami was wearing a pair of tiny, tight, bright turquoise Speedos. They were unutterably hideous.

"That," he said severely, posing his lean body in his trunks, "is because you're not getting enough. I'm off to the lido."

He had an enormous tattoo of an eagle spreading its wings taking off from his groin. I assumed when he was naked, it would look like a nest and a worm.

"I've had my offers," I said, only slightly lying because I hadn't really had any offers, at least not in the style I really liked before I felt confident enough to go forward, i.e., very clearly stated, ideally in writing, and undertaken at a time of some intoxication.

"I'll do you if you like," said Sami perkily. "I'm not very fussy."

"Someone not very fussy is exactly the top of my wish list, thank you, Sami. Consider me utterly entranced."

He shrugged. "But you are French now, *chérie*. Don't you want to live in Paris as the French do?"

"By having sex with an omnisexual giant wearing tiny pants?"

"By enjoying yourself. By enjoying sex and not worrying about whether your body is less than perfect."

"Uh, thanks," I said, wondering if it were ever possible for an eight-toed person to have sex without worrying about being less than perfect. I still wasn't entirely sure someone wouldn't just throw up all over me.

"You have to get over your British hang-ups, you know? I slept with a British girl last month. Or was it a boy?"

I rolled my eyes. "Sami, put on some *clothes*. You have enough of them."

"Cost me a fortune in fizz just to get him—yes, it was a him, definitely—in the mood. Then he'd had too much and passed out in the cab."

"See, where I come from, you call that a jolly good night," I murmured, briefly checking the clock. I needed to get a shimmy on. I quickly glanced at my old wind-up laptop on the corner from which occasionally, if you were lucky, you could occasionally steal Wi-Fi from someone in the building who called themselves "Francoisguitare." And there it was, sitting there, from Claire. I didn't even know she could write email. Personal letter seemed more her style.

Dear Anna,

I hope this finds you well.

I liked the fact that she was keeping to the general style of a formal letter.

I have made a decision; I would like very much to visit Paris one more time. I hope very much as I write that Thierry is recovering. I have no wish to see him, but I would like, while I am able, to visit my beloved Île de la Cité. I am sure it is much changed, but then so am I, so is everything. *Alors*, perhaps I shall even eat some chocolate. If you could help me organize this, I would be most grateful. Please don't trouble Thierry with this news; I'm sure he wouldn't be terribly interested.

Sending my warmest wishes to you. Your parents came to visit me by the way. It was very kind of them. Your mother told me not to tell you, but she worries about you a lot and how you might be coping. I told her in my experience, you coped with things very well.

With very warmest wishes,

Claire xxxxxx

I stared at the screen.

"Good news?" said Sami. "Boyfriend coming over to shag you sideways?"

I cut him a look.

Good news or bad news, I had a funny feeling this was going to mean an enormous amount of work for me. And why had she told me not to tell Thierry? Surely she would only tell me not to tell Thierry if it actually meant something. I should probably tell Thierry. I wanted to visit him anyway.

And all this time I'd thought she was just my boring old married French teacher.

· · · ·

Nelson Eddy the dog had a cocky look to him as he marched down the rue Chanoinesse that morning. It was another stunning, heart-melting day, the sky a shady pink and blue in the cracks between the houses high overhead. I'd thrown on the lightest sundress I had and noticed right away that it was fitting more easily. Apart from the risotto, it occurred to me, I'd hardly eaten a meal in weeks. Maybe I should invent a diet that involved tasting tiny bits of chocolate all day long and nothing else at all. It would probably do quite well, now I thought about it. Cath had done that one with the pepper and the maple syrup, up until happy hour cocktailarama at Wenderspoons, where she'd fainted and knocked herself out on the bar rail. I had a sudden guilty attack at the amount of fruit and vegetables I wasn't eating and resolved to go down to the market—it was Wednesday—and buy some of the melons they had, the ripe honeydews. They would put down fresh, ice-cold strips for tasting, and they were heaven. I wondered if there was some kind of a way of getting them into the chocolate. Laurent would know, I thought. Then I grimaced again, thinking of our awkward supper the night before. Well, I wasn't some kind of handy comfort object to him during his dad being sick. That wasn't it.

Although I thought of what Sami had said too; that here, pleasure was for the taking. Would it have been so bad, I found myself wondering, finishing the rough red wine, letting him lick the last juices of the risotto from my fingers, clutching him to me on the bike as we came home and…

My reverie was broken, as ever, by the idea of him suddenly shouting "Oh God, what the *hell* is that?" when confronted with my distorted foot.

"*Bonjour, bonjour.*" The boys were both very friendly this morning. "Do you think you can do it?" said Frédéric.

"I want to stick to the orange," I said, then recited what Laurent had told me to do the night before. He nodded gravely. "You know, they will get sick of the orange," he added. He didn't have to tell me; I would be quite happy if I never went near the stuff again.

But I set it up to churn more gently and added the ingredients more sparingly and topped down the butter and sure enough, while to a purist it would never be mistaken for the real thing, it was once again notably better enough than the day before for me not to have to face up to everyone's rancor.

There was, though, no Alice. I wondered what this meant; news, I supposed. Good or bad, I couldn't tell.

At lunchtime, I announced I was heading up to the hospital. Frédéric looked at me. "Are you taking some of your chocolate?"

I shrugged. I had, in fact, thought I would do that.

Frédéric put his hand on my hand.

"I'm not saying you haven't come a long way," he said. "But we don't want to shock him back into returning too soon."

"You actually think he would leap out of his bed in horror and charge back to the shop as soon as he smelled it?" I said, injured.

"Let's just keep on the safe side," said Frédéric. "Let me know if he's woken up. I can't... After I lost my father, I have had some trouble sitting in hospitals."

"I will," I said.

• • • •

In an ideal world, I would have avoided running into either Laurent or Alice. And for once, this morning, I was in luck. The great white hospital building behind the Place Jean-Paul-II was gleaming and silent as I quietly gave the name to the registrar, who directed me to a small room about a million miles away along endless passageways and differently colored lifts, until I finally found myself outside a door with "Girard" scribbled on a white board in marker pen. Glancing around, I couldn't see anyone else there, so I knocked. Hearing no answer, I pushed open the door slowly.

This wasn't intensive care anymore; it was obviously still a high dependency unit, but nothing like as scary. The heart monitor still bleeped, but the form on the bed was no longer connected to the oxygen mask. He seemed to be sleeping, and there was no one else in the room. The blinds were open and I realized, from the eighth floor, that the view to the south was beautiful in the sunlight, almost dazzling even though the room was air-conditioned and cool. I turned around with the sun behind me, half-blinded. The shape on the bed moved.

"Claire?"

I jumped out of my skin.

"Hey," I said quietly in English, feeling embarrassed about my pounding heart. Blinking to get the sun out of my eyes, I moved forward.

"Thierry?"

He was looking at me, confused. "Claire? You have come."

"I'm not Claire, Thierry. It's Anna, remember? I'm Anna."

I moved closer. His face still looked confused—and slacker. Even in the five days he'd been in the hospital, he seemed to have lost an awful lot of weight.

I patted his hand.

"Anna."

He indicated the water on the table next to him. I poured him a glass and sat down, helping him drink it.

"You've woken up," I said, after he'd finished. He blinked heavily and seemed to come back to himself.

"Yes," he said. "Yes."

"How do you feel? Do you want me to get anyone?"

He looked at me. "I thought you were Claire."

"So I see."

"You're Anna," he said eventually. "You're working in the shop."

I felt a huge sense of relief that he was making sense. I'd suddenly gotten very worried he'd had a stroke or something.

"Yes!" I said. "Yes! That's me."

He frowned. "How is the shop?"

"Don't worry about that just now," I said politically. "Listen. I spoke to Claire."

His big, dark eyes—now he was a little thinner, I could see the resemblance between him and Laurent much more. His long lashes gave him the look of a slightly helpless, very large puppy.

"Oh yes?" he said.

"She wants…she wants to come to Paris."

His lips suddenly stretched into a wide smile. They were cracked and I passed him some more water.

"She is coming?"

"What on *earth* happened between you two?" I burst out suddenly, thinking of Laurent's anger, and Alice's insistence on being French, and Claire's funny turn. "How can two pen pals that met like a hundred years ago… I mean, I had to write to a guy in Poland, but I couldn't tell you his name. It started with a zed though, that was cool. But anyway, I mean. What *was* it?"

With no small difficulty, Thierry shunted himself up a little on the plump white pillows.

"Careful," I said.

"I know," he said. "But I think I am going to get better. Do you know what my doctor said? She said she wants me walking up and down today. Walking up and down!"

"You like walking up and down."

"I like walking to a café and walking toward an aperitif," said Thierry. "I like walking and disputing and setting the world to rights. I like walking over bridges and through parks and along the Champs-Élysées on a Saturday morning to see the pretty ladies and the small dogs. I do not want to walk up and down the corridors of a hospital in a dress where everyone can see my pee pee."

I nodded sympathetically. "I know. I've been there."

"You have?" He looked at me.

I nodded. Then, even though the situation was distinctly peculiar, I slipped off my sandal. That was another thing I missed—flip-flops and open-toed pretty sandals and high-heeled shoes and nice pedicures. Thierry squinted at first. Then he did a double take. "You only have…*un, deux, trois*…"

"Yup," I said. "Then it finishes. They made me walk a lot as well."

"What happened?" said Thierry.

"Same as what happened to you," I said. "Just a thing."

He liked this and nodded his head. "Just a thing."

"Yes."

"And then you got over it."

I considered it. "Mostly," I said. "You're not quite the same afterward. But mostly."

He nodded at this. "If I do the walking."

"Yes. If you do the walking."

He sighed. "But, you know," he said, "I have already lost fifteen pounds."

"Good," I said.

He nodded. "Well," he said, smiling, "I want to look good when I see Claire."

"Tell me about Claire," I said. But at that moment, the door burst open and Alice marched in, holding a very small coffee and a copy of *Paris Match*. She was wearing an immaculate navy jacket, teamed with a red printed scarf and very skinny white trousers. She looked like she was entering a "Who's the Frenchiest" competition.

When she saw me sitting on the bed, she pulled up short. Oh, for Christ's sake, I wanted to say (in English). No, I am not trying to get off with your morbidly obese sixty-year-old husband who's in the hospital after suffering a severe heart attack, okay?

"Oh, Anna," she said in a way in which one might (and indeed, in Paris, often did) say "Oh, dog poo on the streets."

"Hi, Alice," I said. "I just came up to see how Thierry was doing."

"Why?" she said.

I didn't know the answer to that without betraying Claire.

"Frédéric and Benoît want to know," I said. "Frédéric's scared of hospitals."

She sneered at this. "Well, tell them he's on the mend. How are sales? I hope you're not hanging back."

"Let me try what you're doing," said Thierry.

"Best not," I said. "Plus, you're on a no-chocolate diet."

I still wasn't entirely sure he wouldn't throw back the blankets and march down to the shop in horror once he tasted what was up.

They both looked at me.

"I'd better get back," I said, feeling awkward.

"Yes, do," said Alice, fussing around Thierry's bed. Thierry looked at me with a comical look of mute understanding, and I realized that saying the Claire word in front of Alice was as much of a *non-non* as I'd expected it to be.

I picked up my bag and headed for the door. Just as I did so, I heard Thierry say, "No news from Laurent?"

"Oh, no," said Alice.

I stopped short. Did Thierry not know that Laurent had been by his bedside night after night? That he hadn't slept in days? That he'd left his job to come down to the shop to help me out? He must do.

"Of course he's been here," I said before I left the room. Alice turned on me, her eyes blazing as Thierry sat bolt upright.

"*Oui?*"

"Anna, a word," said Alice in English. She followed me outside.

"Have you no compassion?" she said. "How dare you interfere in my family? Laurent hasn't been back since Thierry regained consciousness, and God knows when we'll see him. Don't be so cruel as to tell a sick man that he can't see his son. Much better if it's just done and dusted and they're kept apart."

This seemed to me that it was becoming a bit of a thing, Thierry not seeing the people that he loved.

"I'll tell Laurent to come back," I said boldly.

"You can tell him what you like, it won't work," said Alice. "I think, personally, if you want to hang on to this job, that you keep your nose out of our business. I mean that in a friendly way."

Alice didn't mean anything in a friendly way.

"I'll go," I said.

"Thank you," she said. "I'll tell Thierry you made a mistake. Thank you for coming to the hospital; I doubt it will be necessary again."

She turned and closed the door on me. I looked down the endless corridor and wondered, not for the first time, if perhaps, at thirty, I just hadn't actually grown up yet, that there was a whole adult world out there I just couldn't make heads nor tails of and that was that. Damn confusing to me though.

• • • •

Wednesday was early closing and I got a chance to go home. For once, amazingly, the flat was empty. Sami had a big opening night of *La Bohème* coming up, and I'd promised to go, although I wasn't sure I'd get on with opera. It was a bit highfalutin for me. I liked Coldplay.

I made my way up the stairwell, humming. Perhaps a little nap, then I would log on and see if I could trace a route for Claire. She had asked me outright in the last conversation and I'd agreed. I would go home, see everyone, and fetch her back. This bit about her wanting to come by ferry didn't help; going from London by train would be about a million times more convenient than getting her to Dover, but we'd work something out.

• • • •

"Mum, you have to see it just isn't fair. It's just not right."

Claire looked out of her window again. The nurse had just changed her dressing and given her a mild sedative while she did it, so everything kind of gently washed over her head. Ricky Jr. was talking to her—he was so handsome, she thought. It was amazing she and Richard had turned out such nice children after all.

"We can't take the time off—Ian either, but it's not even that. We wouldn't. It's not right. A journey like this—next year, maybe. Eighteen months. When you're strong enough and well enough. Sitting on a cross-channel ferry in your condition, it's just ridiculous. We couldn't insure you to go, for starters."

Ricky worked in insurance, which Richard had thought was a brilliant thing, and even though he'd gotten wonderful exam results and gone to a good university and married a lovely girl and been, his entire life, nothing but a credit to them, Claire had privately occasionally found a bit of a shame. She adored her sons completely, but they were so very like their father. She would have perhaps enjoyed a mercurial, ambitious, annoying daughter to fight and spar and bond with, or an odd, intense, clever son who ended up at CERN or designing bizarre things for the internet or joined a band and disappeared for months at a time. Ian was a solicitor, and a good one. They were such good men, pillars of their community. In a way, it was a shame when they were born that the Reverend had taken relatively little interest in them; he would have been proud of them. They were both very, very sensible.

She looked at him, feeling a little hazy.

"And you're right in the middle of treatment... It's not fair on any of us. You're just not strong enough. You have to realize that."

"I'm not strong enough for any of it," she said.

"Mum, don't talk like that. You're only fifty-eight."

"I'm fifty-eight with cancer in three different bits of me. That's not like those hill-climbing, marathon-running fifty-eight-year-olds you see on television, all right?"

She hadn't meant to be snappy—detested it, in fact—but she had spent a year now—no, when she thought about it, most of a lifetime—allowing herself to do what other people wanted her to do, gently following their paths, being a good girl, doing what she was told. And where had that gotten her? Stuck in a chair by a window, with her children annoyed at her, even after she'd broken the heart of a perfectly decent man.

"This is what I want to do," she said again carefully, so she didn't sound drugged. She was aware that she sounded like someone trying to pretend they weren't drugged. "My friend Anna is going to help you."

"The one with the chopped-off toes? She was in the paper," said Ricky. "She didn't get anything like the payout she should have done; she was crazy. She should have gone for them."

"I think she just wanted to forget all about it," said Claire. "Anyway, that's not important. I shan't disturb you. You don't need to do anything; we'll arrange it all."

"It's not about the arranging," said Ricky, his face suddenly white. "It's not about that, Mum. It's about whether it makes you sicker."

They didn't know, thought Claire. They couldn't, with their young fit bodies and young families and all their lives spent thinking about the new car and the mortgage and where they'd go on holiday next year and the year after that. Even though every single person on Earth was living under a death sentence, to actually have one written down on paper... However much they tried to pretend there'd be new treatments, new ways of fixing her, more chemo, always more chemo. But she knew. That there wasn't a lot of sand left in the hourglass, that the time was coming. That if there was anything she wanted to do, she had to do it quickly. They were scared they might lose her—well, they were losing her. They just hadn't faced up to it yet. She had.

And there was only one thing she wanted to do. And this was it.

Ricky looked at her mutinous face. "I'm telling Dad," he said, as if he was talking to Ian and they were nine and seven again.

Claire shrugged. "There's not much he can do now, I would say."

She and Richard were always courteous, although she was aware she found it easier to be so than he did. She liked Richard's new wife, Anne-Marie, too, liked her a lot, and her daughter. Anne-Marie in her turn was so relieved that Claire wasn't a terrifying nightmare who would still be phoning Richard every five minutes and turning the boys against her, and had been very kind to Claire, sending her magazines during her illness about soap stars that didn't make a lot of sense to Claire, but in her darker moments she enjoyed looking at the colorful pictures of peacock dresses and losing herself in a world where losing or gaining weight meant love break-ups and romance, not chemo and steroids.

"Well then, I'll call that girl."

Claire raised her eyebrows. Trying to get Anna to do anything she didn't want to do was an interesting challenge at the best of times.

"If you like."

● ● ● ●

I figured I'd phone first. They must have someone who could help out. I took the phone onto the balcony. Hearing the blank computer voice explain that my call to DownSouthNet Rail was important, please could I continue waiting—while I explained back that clearly it wasn't, otherwise they would hire someone to actually answer the telephones, then remembered that I was speaking to a machine and wondered if anyone listened in on these bits, then assumed that they didn't, then started to get impatient and cross and wonder if I could do this later.

Then I thought about Claire, how thin and weak she had looked the last time I saw her, and Thierry, his big face suddenly transformed by the huge grin on his face the moment I had said her name. It was so strange to me. I'd never had anyone to feel that way about—I mean, Darr was all right, but, you know. I don't think seeing Darr would be the last thing on anybody's list, unless you needed some really average rendering done. So I sighed and held on.

"Your call is important to us."

It was strange, what was important, I thought, looking down on the street where already people were gathering for early aperitifs in the sunshine. Tiny glasses of Pernod were brought to the small rackety tables at the bar opposite, along with a jar of olives and a plate of cooked meat; good customers then. It was a man and a woman, in middle age, engaged in an intense and lively conversation. I wondered what about. How nice, I thought. How nice it would be to get to that age and still be together and still have so much to talk about, so much to think of. Mind you, anyone looking at my mum and dad would think the same thing, except that in actual fact, they would be in the middle of a fight to the death as to whether my father should take his extra raincoat to fishing club. When it was abroad, it just seemed so much more exotic and interesting to me. Presumably if you were in the conversation, it might not seem like that at all.

"Please continue to hold."

The great bells of Notre Dame chimed the hour—three o'clock. I thought of Laurent at work, delicately spraying the chocolate with sealant so it wouldn't whiten up if it were to last right to the very final cafés of the evening in the Pritzer's winter garden, each perfect square imprinted with the hotel's signature. Did people even know, I wondered. Did people even know how much care and attention went into the chocolate on their pillow? Maybe in France they did.

I felt anxious and antsy, restless. I know what Sami would have said: get laid. But I didn't want to "get laid." In this big and lovely and scary city, I wanted to do what Thierry wanted to do and Alice, presumably, and Claire, and everybody else; I wanted to fall in love.

"Hello, love? Sorry for keeping you waiting."

The voice was a woman's, reassuringly northern and normal; she sounded motherly and actually, genuinely sorry for a system that I supposed, when you got down to it, wasn't her fault.

"Hello," I said. "I wonder if you can help me."

I explained the situation and she hummed and hawed on the end.

"Well," she said finally. "She'll have to change at Crewe. Or at London."

"Crewe's probably better, wouldn't you think?"

"But I don't think… I mean, we don't accept responsibility for sick people on the train."

"There'll be somebody with her," I said, a little testily. "All I'm asking is can a guard meet the train and make sure we're comfortable in the second train? It's going to be a big stress for her."

"Wouldn't she be better flying?" asked the woman tentatively. "They do lots with wheelchairs and so on."

"You're a train company!" I said, exasperated. "Do you tell everyone to get a plane?"

"You don't need to shout," said the woman. "I'm just saying we don't normally do this. Health and Safety won't allow it."

I snorted, in a proper French way. "You can't do anything? Look," I said, "what's your name?"

"Aurelienne."

It was an incredibly unlikely name to belong to such a normal, comfy-sounding woman. "Really?"

"Yes," she said, her voice softening a little. "My father was French."

"It's beautiful," I said.

"Thank you."

"Well, then, you will understand."

And I told her the whole story, about Claire and Thierry being in love, and how they'd waited their whole lives and now they were both sick and it was their only wish to meet, one more time, in Paris—I laid it on a bit, I will say. At the end, she was silent.

"Well, that's nice," she said.

"It will be," I said, "with your help."

I was all fired up now, sure I could convince her to see the romantic side of it, sure I could stir her latent French heart.

"It'll be in the papers," I lied.

"I just don't…" she started. Then she added, "You know, I've never even been to Paris."

"You haven't?" I said, shocked. "You're half-French."

"Oh, my name is all I have really. He left my mother," she said. "She hates the French."

"Oh," I said.

"Probably just the same in this case."

"No," I said. "They just got separated."

"Hmm," said Aurelienne.

"And now they want to get back together."

"Hmm."

"And you're going to help make it happen."

There was a long pause.

"You know, I don't know why she doesn't just fly."

• • • •

In the end, using Claire's credit card, I booked us both first-class train tickets, thinking at least the seat would be more comfortable for her, and it might predispose one of the Health and Safety guards to give us a hand going over the bridge at Crewe. For the price of them, they really ought to let us drive the damn thing. The lady was probably right about flying. Maybe Claire would let us fly back. I didn't even know if she'd thought that far ahead. I wondered if she had medical insurance. Of course she wouldn't. Life seemed to get more complicated all the time. Maybe Sami was right. Maybe I did need something a bit simpler.

As if on cue, my phone rang. I picked it up.

"Allo?"

"Where were you? You have been on the phone for four hours!"

"Why, what's happened? Is something wrong?"

"No," said Laurent.

My heart skipped a beat anyway.

• • • •

Laurent inwardly cursed himself. He had barely noticed the new little shopgirl—well, obviously he'd noticed her when she'd come at him in the street, but not properly—before. She had just arrived, then it was irritating she seemed to be so close to his father so quickly, and then she'd been all around the place, but that was all she was, a mere disturbance on his itinerary of work and the hotel and nightclubs and generally having a good time.

Then yesterday. He couldn't help it: he was impressed. Genuinely, truly impressed. First, by her dedication to the shop. He knew that a life in gourmet food had to start very young, but she had tried so hard to help out, and help his dad.

Then at dinner last night. Going back there had been a spur of the moment idea, but once they'd gotten ensconced, he'd looked at her properly in the candlelight and realized how pretty her face was, how soft and kind her features: her round blue eyes, with their strong eyebrows, and her very plump, pink lips that made her look younger than she was. And the generous bosom spilling over the top of her pretty floral dress. She was completely unlike the skinny, high-breasted

231

French girls he usually went for, not, he realized, because she was any less attractive, but because she didn't carry herself as if she innately was. She didn't strut, and she didn't look down her nose. She didn't give off a vibe of being untouchably beautiful and effortlessly chic, as even the plainer girls of Paris did—and she certainly wasn't chic; that much was clear. But she was luscious and sexy precisely because, he realized, she didn't know just how sexy she was.

Just at the moment as he'd been coming to those conclusions, she'd eyed him up very clearly and stated how much she didn't fancy him, and he needn't think he was getting his own way with her.

If anything could make Laurent Girard very, very interested indeed, that was it.

•　•　•　•

I looked at the phone, surprised. I hadn't thought I'd hear from him again.

"Well, I've been busy," I said. "What is it?"

Laurent had to think on his feet. He really had no idea why he was ringing.

"Have you seen my dad?" he asked quickly.

"Um, yeah," I said, before working out whether it was politic to answer this or not. Alice had already warned me off of the family once before. Mind you, was I really scared of Alice? I thought about it and remembered that yes, yes I was. But it was too late.

"Did you?"

"Yes."

"How was he?"

"Sitting up. Talking. Smiling."

"Eating?"

"Ha, not yet," I said. "But I'm sure it will occur to him sooner or later."

"It better not," said Laurent fiercely. "I'll kill Alice if she lets this happen again."

There was a pause.

"Aren't you going to go and see him?"

I was expecting Laurent to do his usual furious denial, but instead he went quiet for a little while.

"I should, shouldn't I?" he said.

"*Yes!*" I said.

"What if he gives me a load of grief?"

"Well, you sit there and take it like a good boy, then you thank him once again for giving you the tools to go out and make your own life."

"Which he doesn't respect."

"I know," I said. "The difference between making artisan world-class handmade chocolates in a shop and making them in a hotel is unbelievably huge. I can't imagine how either of you can bear it."

"Are all English girls as sarcastic as you?"

"Are all French men as silly as you?"

Suddenly, his voice changed and deepened.

"Do you think I'm silly?"

In the distance, a fire alarm sounded. It chimed so closely with what was going on in my heart, I almost laughed. The sky was changing now, shades of pink and purple stranding in through the blue, and the streets were filling up with excited young people, mopeds, bikes, everyone out for the evening, meeting their friends, chatting and laughing, up for adventure. It was like a river of brightly colored life below me and here I was, up in my eyrie, watching other people's lives pass by below me like a bird.

"No," I said quietly.

His voice was now totally and completely straight.

"I could come and show you how serious I am."

There was no flirting, no messing around. I had never heard a man be so direct in my life.

I glanced around at the tiny flat—just waiting for Sami to burst in, dressed as whatever bird of prey he was going out as that night, full of light and music. He was living his life. Claire was living her life with this ridiculous train scheme. I was thirty-one years old, in the heart of Paris, and an incredibly attractive man had just made me an incredibly attractive offer.

Could I hold out, coquette with him, buy time, flirt? I could. I expect he would lose interest pretty fast. But, really, was that so important? Did my little life code matter, when every second since I'd arrived had filled my life with more new experiences and expectations than I had ever imagined? I bit my lip. Then I thought, sod it.

"When?" I said, and there was no trace of a joke in my tone either.

20

L aurent had to finish his shift, which gave me several hours to pace about, panicking and changing my mind every two seconds. Perhaps I should just go out. This was crazy. Maybe just pop out and turn off my phone and go for a walk or something and hide for a few hours.

But then he'd just think me an idiot, a child. And anyway, what did I want to happen?

I phoned Cath, even though Cath would probably have recommended I sleep with a tramp on the Bois de Boulogne if she thought it would get me laid. She screamed with excitement.

"He makes chocolate! Oh *God*. So you're going to spend the rest of your life eating chocolate and having sex. In Paris. I *hate* my life. An old woman came in today and asked for a purple perm, Ans. A *purple perm*."

"Well, it's not quite that simple," I said.

"You're telling me! The purple reacts with the perming lotion! Half of it fell out and she wasn't exactly Beyoncé to start off with."

"So…" I tried to trace back the situation. I was marching up and down the tiny apartment, feeling incredibly anxious.

"Are you saying yes, I should?"

Her voice took on a more considerate tone.

"Is he an arsehole?"

"I don't think so," I said. "He's a bit…troubled."

"Oh," she said. "Because, you know, arseholes can be totally amazing in bed, whereas troubled might mean he'll start crying all over you."

"I'm sure he won't do that," I said.

"Is he hot?" she said.

"Yes," I said, without hesitation. "Very French looking. But bigger."

"Hmm," she said. "Does he have, like, a really big nose?"

"Yes!"

"Excellent. I like those."

Her voice turned serious.

"The thing is, Ans, you have to get back on the horse some time, don't you?"

"Yes," I said grudgingly.

"I mean, you're not going to go without forever, are you?"

"I suppose not," I said.

"Give him a go then. Plus, Darr was sniffing around, asking when you were back."

"You are kidding," I said. "What, sick of 'all the single ladies' already?"

"Looks like it."

Suddenly, compared to Darr, Laurent became even more attractive.

"Okay," I said, "I'm doing it."

"Atta girl," said Cath. "Save some French totty for me, by the way. I've had every decent-looking man here, and they're all rubbish."

● ● ● ●

Sami was even more to the point when he returned with a trunk stacked high with night work. He really was working hard for a change.

"Well," he said, sighing. "*That's* not going to work."

"What?" I said. I had changed into a black top and a black skirt, which wasn't very sexy really but was just about the best I could do from my small suitcase. I was too nervous to go shopping; I would probably buy the first thing I saw, even if it was a rubber miniskirt and thigh-high boots.

"You look like you are going to work on the Bourse," he said. "Not like a seductress."

"I'm not a seductress," I said. Sami arched a carefully plucked eyebrow.

"Well, you're something," he said. "I haven't seen Laurent down the Buddha Bar in weeks."

"Perhaps because his *dad's in the hospital*?"

"Perhaps," said Sami. He looked me up and down then dived into his room.

"I'm not wearing the Speedos!" I yelled.

"Be quiet," he said, muffled. After five minutes, he reappeared. As well as an armful of clothes, he was carrying hair curlers and straighteners.

"Now," he said, "let *ton-ton* Sami work."

"Oh no," I said. "Do not make me look like a dog's dinner. The fact that I'm letting him come pick me up is the worst. If I'm all painted up like a trollop…"

"Oh, scared little English girl," said Sami, "I am doing none of these things. I am simply ensuring that you feel and look your best. I just want you to enjoy yourself."

"Everyone does," I said gloomily. "It makes it very difficult."

He pulled out a beautiful red gypsy blouse.

"From the attic scene," he said. "Do you have a red bra?"

I did, but I hadn't brought it. Or worn it in months, I realized. It was a good one too.

"Well, pink will do," he said. "Better, in fact. More sluttish. Now, have you got *hair*?"

I had shaved my legs in the bathroom and wished Cath was there—she'd wax me on the cheap at home. Also once I'd shaved them, I'd realized how hideously pale they were. In Kidinsborough, I'd have gone and had a fake tan, but they didn't seem to do that here; I hadn't seen anywhere advertising it. All the French girls had this perfect olive skin anyway that didn't need anything. Another wave of fear gripped me. Oh God. What if he recoiled in horror at my patchy white bits?

"I think I need a drink," I said to Sami.

"*Non*," he said, to my surprise. "Do not. You will not enjoy so much."

"Well, I won't enjoy it at all if I can't buck up the courage."

His huge black eyes softened.

"Darling," he said. "Darling. It is only pleasure. Happiness. Like with chocolate, yes? It is not there to make you feel guilty, or sad, or ashamed. It is there to enjoy. Think of me. The whole world tried to make me ashamed. It could not."

I looked at him. He was wearing a bright purple boa around his neck and his familiar bright blue eye shadow. It had never occurred to me before to think that Sami might be brave. I'd only ever thought he was off his head. But now I saw it.

"Okay," I said.

"Okay," he said. I put on the red blouse. It was lovely. Matched with cropped jeans, so I didn't look too overdone (and could get on the back of the scooter), it looked pretty and fresh and unworried.

"I would add a scarf, but…" His mouth made a *moue*.

"Scarves make me feel like a politician," I said.

"It's true," he said. "English girls cannot wear a scarf. Except for your queen. She is *magnifique*."

He took out a large, slightly grubby-looking makeup box, sat me down, and went to work, putting on my makeup with one hand and jumping up every second to finish the cigarette he'd left smoldering on the balcony.

"You're going to make me smell all smoky," I complained.

"Little is more sexy to a French man," he grinned at me.

Finally I was ready, and he let me have a look in the mirror. I smiled, happily, in surprise. He'd swept my untidy hair to the side and fastened it with a large old-fashioned silver clip so that instead of being its usual cloudy mess, it looked like a chic '20s style. He'd kept my face very simple, except for my lips, which he'd filled in the exact same red as the blouse.

"Cor," I said, "that's a bit full-on."

"It's gorge," said Sami absentmindedly. "He'll want to kiss it all off immediately."

I stood up.

"Now," said Sami. "Shoes. I don't know why you wear those sandals all the time anyway."

I didn't say anything.

"What have you got?"

"Converse, heels."

"Hmm. Go on."

"I've got ballet slippers."

"Let's see."

I brought them out for inspection.

They were some of the prettiest things I'd ever bought. I'd found them just before the accident. They were navy blue and flat with a little bow in a paler blue ribbon and a striped inner lining and weren't at all the kind of thing you ever saw in Kidinsborough, where everyone wore heels out at all hours, or trainers. I didn't even know what I would wear them for; they'd be useless for clubbing or the pub— they'd get ruined and everyone else would be talking four inches above me. And they weren't a lot of use for walking in, and one splash of rain and they'd be totally done for. And I couldn't wear them to work or to a music festival.

But they were so pretty and so precious, and the woman who sold them to me had put them in a cloth bag before she put them in a box, and wrapped them up in striped tissue paper and stuck it down with a lovely vintage sticker, and I'd taken them home and put them in my old MFI cupboard and thought about the imaginary garden party I'd be invited to one day.

Then I'd had my accident and that was that; I'd never worn

them—they didn't give my foot enough protection and could even slip off.

Sami glanced over them.

"Yes. Them," he said. "They're cute. We'll roll up the bottom of your jeans a bit, make you look like a 1950s starlet on the Croisette."

I rolled my eyes.

"I'll just go put them on," I said.

"Can't you put them on here?" said Sami.

It occurred to me that getting in some practice at showing a man my foot—as I had with Thierry—might not be the worst thing ever. So I sighed, then sat down and took off my slipper.

Sami didn't notice at first. Then his eyes went wide.

"Wow," he said.

"I know," I said. Would I ever get used to it, the precise diagonal line cutting across where two of my toes used to be, the livid red stubs. "I know, it's hideous."

"Darling," said Sami, patting me on the shoulder. "My girl."

"He's going to throw up," I said.

"Nonsense, he'll barely notice," said Sami, casting another worried glance at my foot. "As long as he's not one of those fetishists. Well, as long as he's not a foot fetishist. If he's an amputee fetishist, you're in luck… Oh, darling, don't cry."

I couldn't help it. I was feeling so wound up and emotional, and this was all I needed to set me off.

"Stop it! All your invisible makeup will run and suddenly you'll be a lot more visible!" said Sami as the tears dropped down my cheeks.

I'm not what you would call a pretty crier.

"Okay," said Sami. "Okay. I shall make you a martini. A very small one."

His idea of a very small martini was my idea of a swimming pool, but I was grateful. We sat out on the balcony looking at the darkening sky—me with acute trepidation—and he listened very sweetly to the whole story, shaking his head at the right moments.

"Well, you see," he said eventually, "it was a good thing, because it got you to Paris."

I shook my head. "You're telling me it was worth losing two toes to get here?"

Sami looked thoughtful.

"I lost my entire family," he said.

"They'd be so proud of you," I said, meaning it.

He laughed. "They'd be so proud of a successful accountant in Tangiers with wives and many, many children and a courtyard of his own, eh? Not this."

"Well, I'm proud of you," I said, clinking my glass to his.

"You don't even have the balls to have sex," he said, but he was joking, and he clinked back, just as the heavy old doorbell rang.

"Oh *God*!" I shouted, leaping up and spilling the rest of my drink so some of it went on me. Great, I would smell like I'd been in the bar all afternoon.

"Put your shoes on!" shouted Sami.

"Yes, yes," I said, grabbing my bag. I couldn't figure out if it was practical or slutty to pack a fresh pair of underpants and a toothbrush, so I'd zipped them away in the bottom compartment.

"*J'arrive*," I called into the intercom, then went to the door. I turned back just as I was leaving. Sami was standing, silhouetted on the balcony, finishing up his drink, surveying his Parisian domain as if deciding which arrondissement he would terrorize that evening.

"Thank you," I said to him.

"*De rien*," he said, flashing me his bright grin. "Now, enjoy yourself or I really will introduce you to an amputee fetishist."

"I'm gone, I'm gone," I said.

• • • •

I felt rather than saw the door on the first landing open, just for a second. It was the old woman who'd gotten so annoyed when I'd rung her bell by mistake. Didn't she ever go out?

"*Bonsoir*," I said boldly, trying to give myself a confidence I didn't feel, but there was no reply and the door closed on me in the dark, leaving me feeling unnerved. I threw off the feeling and headed out onto the street.

Laurent was standing there in a casual but expensive-looking soft worn-in yellow shirt and jeans. He didn't smile when he saw me, but instead looked at me rather appraisingly, as if noticing me for the first time. I tried not to blush under his gaze.

"You look nice," he said.

"Thank you," I said, wishing he was as nervous as I was. But he didn't seem to be at all.

"Are you hungry?"

I was not hungry. I would have quite liked to get very quickly pissed, but I knew, I knew that wouldn't help. This wasn't giving Dave Hempson a blowie in his mum's Vauxhall sierra.

I shook my head.

"Then do you fancy a walk? I've been hunched over a stove all day."

• • • •

I needn't have worried about the ballerina shoes. They were light, but they fitted me beautifully, even on the toe end of my right foot, and were like walking on air. We crossed the Pont Neuf and headed down to the Louvre. As we did, old, wrought iron lampposts came on, *pop pop pop*, over our heads, and the long chains of fairy lights that lined the Seine sprang into life, glowing in the dusk.

"I love this time of night," said Laurent. "All the commuters have gone, all the day-trippers have vanished back toward…well, wherever day-trippers go. I have no idea."

It was true. Above the scent of exhaust pipes and hanging baskets and garlic sizzling in the pans of a thousand restaurant kitchens was the sense of excitement, of the night beginning. Chatting about food, and restaurants, and bits and pieces, we turned into the grand place, and I nearly stumbled. Laurent proffered me his elbow without even thinking about it, and I took it. We walked under a huge stone arch, and I couldn't help but gasp; even though I knew about it and had seen it in films of course, I'd never seen it before: we were in Place du Louvre. The huge glass pyramid—with another, slightly farther away—was lit up in glittering white and silver, as if it had drifted into the eighteenth century from outer space.

"Isn't it beautiful?" said Laurent. At this time of the evening, the museum was long shut, and there were only a few people dotted here and there, taking pictures of the fountains and the amazing building of the Louvre itself. The rest of the huge space felt like ours. Above us, the stars were popping out.

"It makes me so proud, all of this."

"You're a proud kind of person though, aren't you?" I said, teasing him.

He shrugged. "No."

"Well, what kind of a person are you?"

"Well, I am dedicated, you know. I care about my work very much. Yes, I am proud of it. I want it to be the best, the best it can possibly be. Otherwise, what's the point, you understand?"

I nodded.

"You feel this too?"

I thought about it. I did see—or felt—since I'd arrived here that I did understand the desire for excellence, for living in a way that didn't settle for good enough. But I'd also seen what it cost—father and son not talking, Thierry ill, Alice.

"I only ever wanted to be happy," I said quietly. It sounded like a low aspiration sometimes. Laurent shot me a sideways glance.

"Are you?"

I looked at him, wondering. Then I turned around and looked at the glorious vista spread out in front of us. I advanced toward the pyramid, my arms outstretched.

"I think you can be happy in Paris," I said.

"Be careful!" shouted Laurent suddenly. "You'll set off the alarms! They'll think you're here to steal the Mona Lisa."

"Really?" I said, jumping back, slightly panicked.

"Um, no," he said. "But I like seeing you startled."

I turned toward him.

"Your mouth goes open like this—'o'—and your eyes pop open," he said. "I like it. I…"

Then, as if losing his drift, he covered the few steps toward me, grabbed me in his arms, and kissed me fiercely under the floodlights. I felt the torch of a passing security guard quickly pass over us before I gave myself up entirely to his hard, hungry mouth, his hand on the back of my neck forcing me to him, and I stopped thinking about anything at all.

• • • •

Claire wondered about packing. It was summertime, of course, but she felt cold these days, always so cold. Like a child who needed her blanket wherever she went. Ricky and Ian wouldn't help her to pack— they were sulking with her—and Montserrat was none too keen on the plan either. Anna had sent her some times of trains but hadn't indicated when she'd come back to pick her up—she was working too, of course. It was a lot to ask.

It was a lot to ask, yes. And she was a stubborn selfish old woman. But even so.

She carefully got herself up the stairs and opened her cupboard door. It was late, and she couldn't sleep. She could never seem to sleep at the right times. During the day, she would doze all over the place, but the nights were very long. She'd taken her painkillers, which normally knocked her out, but tonight she felt slightly excited, more mobile than she'd felt in quite a while. Privately she thought it might be the excitement of the journey that was giving her extra energy, extra strength. This feeling motivated her onward. There was no one sleeping in tonight as people did closer to the chemo. Tonight it was just her. She was supposed to be recuperating, getting ready for a new surgery. Instead, she was packing for a holiday. The thought made her heart tremble in anticipation.

Illness made you so old. She knew Patsy's mother, who was a bouncy sixty-two, older than her, who had Botox and teeth whitening and went to aqua-aerobics and looked after the children two days a week when Patsy went to work as an HR manager for the prison service. She was, in fact, exactly the kind of granny Claire would have liked to have been, except instead of the soft play and cinema and sweets kind of granny, she'd have been an art galleries and culture and stories and libraries and restaurants kind of grandmother, she liked to think. She would have talked to them about politics and their place in the world and never ever let them think that Kidinsborough was the limit of their horizons. Patsy's mother thought she was the most terrific snob. Claire supposed she was.

There they were, lined up. The green dress and the yellow floral, both of them faded and zipped into plastic bags. Claire wondered, if she'd had a daughter, would she have enjoyed these clothes? So exquisitely made—and vintage was so in again these days. Although, it suddenly occurred to her, she'd lost so much weight with her illness she could probably fit them again. The very idea made her want to laugh with the blackness of it. Her, bent over, bowed down, in the clothes of a young girl… She blinked, less sure now she did want to pack.

And next to them, her wedding dress. She'd never been able to throw it away.

It made her feel dreadfully guilty now to look at it, remembering how impatient she had gotten with the little Kidinsborough seamstress, who had fussed around her and stuck her with pins and was nothing like the efficient ladies of the rue du Faubourg.

● ● ● ●

Claire had let her mother choose the dress. It was ludicrously fussy, with a nylon train and long sleeves and a high ruffled neck, so as not to offend some of the Reverend's older parishioners.

She liked Richard, she really did. He was kind and he drove down on a Friday night from university in his car and impressed her mother and was polite to her father and called him sir, and they would go out to dinner and he'd tell her about his plans for setting up a business and push her to work harder, and she had. She was going to just about scrape through teacher training college, and he was so touchingly pleased and interested in her. After three years, he asked her, nervously, if she would like to get married, and she was so busy making everything normal around her and forgetting about Paris that she woke up one day and found that it had worked, that the great crevasse had finally healed over and that marrying Richard and having a nice house and a life and maybe moving out of Kidinsborough would actually be rather fun.

And the weird thing was, to begin with, it was. It was fun. When the boys were small, they would load them up into their Austin Mini Metro and drive down to Cornwall and Devon and spend holidays sheltering from the rain and eating chips on the sea front. They'd moved into a nice detached house—Richard had set up his business in town, so her leaving Kidinsborough dream had not come true—and the boys had had music lessons and football clubs and school friends and birthday parties, and everything was as nice as it could be. If Claire ever felt a sense of "Is this it? Is this really it?" well, a lot of people felt that way, especially women with children in the late '70s and teachers in the early '80s, and she put it down to normal ennui.

And then the boys had gone to college and Richard had had an affair with a girl in his office that wracked him so solidly with guilt she couldn't even believe for a second that he'd gotten enough enjoyment out of it to be worth the bother. She would probably have quite happily let him over that too, until her unruffled reaction to his tortured revelation quite suddenly derailed them both.

He had been shaking and drenched with sweat the night he'd come home. She was making corned beef salad with salad cream. She hated corned beef, it had occurred to her. The boys liked it so she'd served it every third Thursday for about twenty years. Her overwhelming memory of the evening, during which Richard sobbed and begged forgiveness, was a curious sense of relief that she'd never have to eat corned beef again.

It was when he had looked up at her, desperate for her to forgive him, to make it all right, or even to start tearing at his clothes in a fit of deadly jealousy, attacking him with the shearing scissors, that he'd realized. That it gradually dawned on his face that his affair didn't really, at the end of the day, matter to her that much because she wasn't in love with him, not really, hadn't ever been. And that's when he'd gotten really angry.

● ● ● ●

Claire fingered the dress. She had loved him, in her way, as much as she could. Which just wasn't enough, not in a marriage. And she'd felt so lucky too; he had been scrupulously fair in her settlement, always kept the love and attention of his boys. A lot of her friends had not been that lucky. A lot of her friends who had married in the full heat of desperate, undying love, pure soul mates, who had then come to hate their partners and turned bitter, living in much worse unhappiness than she and Richard ever had. There was nothing to say that she and Thierry too, with all their class and cultural differences, wouldn't also have ended up tearing each other apart in despair, ruining their children in the process, whereas Ricky and Ian were as well-adjusted as it was possible to be. The way the world was now, who was to say that level-headed, compatible companionship wasn't the way to run marriage anyway?

Still, she fingered the dress sadly. Oh, there was never any accounting for the human heart. And no one looking at her now, she thought, would ever see anything other than the wispy bald head, the lack of eyebrows, the weight loss. No one would ever see the tentative bride, or the joyously happy teenage lover, or the unfulfilled housewife, or the middle-aged woman who had rather enjoyed living on her own again with no boxer shorts to wash and no huge dinners to make.

It was a terrible dress. A daughter would never have wished to wear it. She sighed. She should probably go to her scarf drawers. Her friends had presented her with a succession of jaunty scarves to wear over her head. She hated them all. She hated having to pretend to be jaunty when all she wanted to do was throw up. But it was so kind of them. It showed that they were thinking of her. And people liked sick people to be jaunty; it made them feel less scared and awkward. So she had better pack a few.

She felt, for the last time, the hem of the floral yellow dress with its tiny picked-out daisies. *Alors*, she thought. Whenever she thought about Thierry, she always thought about him in French, as if she was adding a layer of code to her most innermost secrets. It was absurd to think on some level she was trying to hide her thoughts—from who? From God? If God still sounded like the Reverend, he didn't speak any other languages.

Alors. Thierry would get a shock when he saw her. Mind you, from the sound of things, he'd changed a bit too. And did it matter, in the end?

● ● ● ●

We pulled ourselves away. He smiled at me, completely unselfconsciously. I couldn't help it, there was something very attractive about the fact that he absolutely didn't give a damn about what we were doing or whether anybody saw us. It also made him look a bit wolfish.

"Come with me," he said.

I smiled. It felt a little late to play the coquette now, given that I had the pink bra on and everything. But my heart was beating painfully, partly from the excitement, partly from the nerves.

"I shouldn't," I said. "It's turning me into a double agent."

He laughed. "I need a double agent," he said. "No. Forget that. I need you."

He took my hand in his great big one. It was hard to believe that his thick fingers could make such delicacies out of sugar and cocoa and butter.

"Race you back to the bike," he said.

It had gotten later, and the streets around the Île de la Cité were nearly deserted as the crowds went to eat in the Marais or further north.

"I can't run," I said. Truthfully, I hadn't tried.

"Of course you can," he said, looking at me severely. "You might jiggle a bit, but I like that."

I stuck my tongue out at him.

"On your mark…get set…"

"No!"

"Go!"

We burst off across the great Place du Louvre, my thin soles crunching against the gravel. It had been so long. The soft evening wind blew in my face, my hair out behind me. Laurent was very fast and looked very young, funneling along, occasionally turning his head to laugh at me, the wind whipping his curls in his eyes.

"*J'arrive!*" I yelled, redoubling my efforts. Although I was out of breath, running, properly running at the very limits of my capacity suddenly felt so freeing. I hadn't realized I missed it, didn't even realize I'd ever done it. I had filed running away with summer sandals and my youth. Now, though, I raised my hands in the air with the sheer exhilaration.

Just as we got to the side of the bridge, I tried to jump a tricky step. As I launched into the air, it flashed through my mind in a heartbeat that I wasn't going to make it. My toes couldn't flex properly and I had no stability on that side. I came down on the stairs heavily, right side first, my legs folding up underneath me, knocking the side of my right foot and the tips of where my toes used to be very hard against the harsh stone.

I crumpled, tears springing to my eyes even though I didn't want them to. It hurt like absolute buggery.

Instantly Laurent turned around, his face full of concern. He leaped to my aid, even as another passerby stopped to see if I was all right.

I blinked, trying to breathe properly and not burst into sobs like a baby.

"*Merde*," I said, "That really, really hurts."

He crouched down by my foot, and just at that precise moment, I realized that of course the force of the impact had knocked off my beautiful shoe, which was lying about a foot away, spattered with blood.

"*Mon Dieu!*" he shouted. My hand shot to my mouth as I realized what he'd done; he thought my fall had somehow knocked off my toes. I glanced down; they were not a pretty sight, all grazed from the cobbles.

"No, no, it's okay," I muttered, feeling like the world's biggest freak. I had to get up on my own; he was struck slightly dumb. Then he remembered his manners and darted forward, but he felt tentative as he proffered me his arm.

"It's…it's just…I had an accident," I muttered, my face bright red. I wanted the ground to swallow me up. Everything I had ever feared, everything I had worried about me being a big weirdo, impossible to fancy, seemed to be coming true.

"Of course," he said, and before he could help himself, his eyes flickered up and down my body, as if calculating which other parts of me might be missing. It felt like a slap in the face.

"I…I lost my toes," I added.

The color came back into his cheeks a little bit. "Sorry, I just got a bit of a shock."

"Yes, I know. It's weird," I muttered. This was every bit as bad as I had thought it would be.

"No, no, it's…it's fine."

But it wasn't. Suddenly I felt very strongly that it wasn't fine. That I wasn't comfortable, that I couldn't be the kind of carefree European girl I always wanted to be. Traffic honked and signed on the bridge and I had come down to earth with a literal bump.

He smiled at me finally, nervous. "Uh, do you want to come over and tell me all about it?"

But the extraordinary, breathtaking kiss of just a few minutes ago had evaporated; now we looked awkward, and I was covered in blood and needed cleaning up. I was a bit wobbly and he noticed.

"Are you all right? Can I help you?" He put his arm around me.

I shook my head. "Can you just help me home?" I said, leaning into his reassuringly broad chest. "I'll be fine. I just… Another time maybe," I said. "It's getting late. I have to work tomorrow."

"Come on then," he said, propping me up. "You can't hop the entire way."

Part of me was absolutely terrified he was going to offer to carry me, but we leaned together like two old drunks and made silly small talk of the kind you do when you've just kissed someone and then kissing has, for whatever reason (like blood), suddenly fallen off the agenda. He didn't ask me where I'd gotten the injury, for which I was grateful.

At my door, I tried to get away as quickly as I could. He noticed it and seemed slightly hurt. I covered it up by being as brisk and breezy as I could.

"Lovely to see you," I said, suddenly sounding like I came from *Downton Abbey*.

He blinked. Then he looked as if he'd just made up his mind about something, leaned forward, and kissed me very, very gently on the lips.

"Perhaps one time you can tell me about it," he said. Then without another word, he raised his arms and walked away, disappearing into the night. I listened until I heard the scooter fire up with its usual roar, then turned into the house, finally letting the tears flow.

I didn't even bother putting the lights on as I marched up to the sixth floor, sobbing loudly, uncaring of who heard me. At one point I thought I heard a door open again, but I didn't even bother turning around.

Sami was in the middle of looking at himself in the mirror and putting on a gigantic earring made of peacock feathers. I suspected he'd done nothing else since I'd left.

"*Chérie!*" he cried out, jumping up. "*Chérie…*"

He saw my stricken face, the tears messing up the beautifully applied makeup he'd done just hours before.

"What happened?"

"He saw my foot and completely freaked out," I said. "Can't say I blame him."

"Didn't you warn him?"

"What, that I'm hideously deformed?"

"Yes!"

"No, I didn't get the chance. I fell over and my shoe came off."

Sami hit his forehead with the flat of his palm. "My love."

He jumped up and disappeared into the tiny kitchenette, reappearing shortly with a tub of warmish water, a soft cloth to bathe my foot, and a cocktail glass full of clear liquid with three olives in it.

"Dirty martini," he said. "It's the only way."

He then gently lowered my foot into the bath.

I looked at the glass, took a gulp, then nearly choked. It took about five seconds to hit my bloodstream.

"God, that is helpful," I said, feeling its warmth spreading about my body. "It's like medicine."

"It is," said Sami. "I'm a doctor."

I managed a grin then burst into tears again. "No one will ever want me again," I said.

"Don't be stupid," said Sami. "You almost scored a really hot bloke. All the girls love Laurent. He has an air of mystery."

I snorted. "There's nothing mysterious about him. He's just a bit grumpy. Well, sometimes. Then he lightens up and, well, he's really interesting."

Sami sighed. "Yes. Maybe you being unimpressed is why he likes you?"

"No. It's because he's unimpressed by me," I said sorrowfully. "Why can't everyone just fancy me and then I could choose the ones I wanted?"

"Ah yes," said Sami. "The great beauties, they have such happy lives. Anyway, you are dressed. Come with me."

"Where are you going?"

"You will like it. It is a rehearsal."

"That's what I needed. A rehearsal. No, hang on," I said, the cocktail getting to me. "Laurent was meant to be my rehearsal, so I could go off and find the real thing. And I stuffed it up."

"No matter," said Sami, glancing at himself once more in the mirror to his satisfaction, then putting on a silver waistcoat, a pink scarf, and some incredibly tight trousers.

"Oh Lord," I said.

"Darling," he retorted, "as if anyone's going to think you were with me."

• • • •

I followed Sami down to the street and he disappeared. Did anyone in Paris actually walk down the roads? It was as if there were streets for the tourists and shortcuts for everyone else. I wouldn't be in the least surprised to hear about him climbing over the rooftops. He had gone around the back of our house, which I saw to my surprise contained an old, overgrown garden into which someone had placed some sheds of gardening tools and assorted odds and ends, then cut over a major thoroughfare to the Pont Saint-Michel. We went into a huge building that appeared from the top to be some kind of radio station, but down some steps by a side door, with a commissionaire lazily peering over his copy of *Paris Soir* to nod us through, was what was clearly a recording and theater space. It had red velvet seating, thick walls, plush carpets, and a huge stage that was dimly lit. There were about six or seven other people there down the front, two of them smoking. One raised his arm to Sami, who waved back madly as I followed him.

"Anna is unlucky in love," he announced to the throng, who all made sympathetic noises and budged up to let us sit in the middle.

At the front of the stage, an anxious-looking man with long gray hair and a walking stick was talking quickly into a walkie-talkie. Then he hit the stick on the ground quickly, twice, twisted around, and shouted to someone in a dimly lit box over our heads. Instantly, lush waltz music started up from a huge sound system. Startled, I jumped. The lights changed on stage, and suddenly it was as if it were lit by millions of flickering candles from behind the screens. Figures started to emerge from the wings; men from the left, women from the right. The men were wearing buttoned jackets, and the women were in wide crinolines, their faces pale. They looked like they had come from a different age. To my eyes, the two groups came together absolutely seamlessly, the women slid into the men's arms, and they began to dance. It was sublimely beautiful to be so close to them, as they spun and floated across the dance floor with the music, the skirts rustling as the men picked up the tiny women and spun them as if they were feathers. The music changed and slowed down, but the dancers, instead, sped up, now beating double-time and pirouetting faster and faster. It seemed incredible that none of the couples would hit each other moving across the floor, and I was riveted.

"*Non non non non non!*"

The gray-haired man was beating his stick on the floor again.

"That is insupportable! Do it again but correct."

The dancers stood in a row, the music stopped, but they still looked ethereal to me, like something from a dream.

"It's disgusting, do you hear? Like sixteen cows stamping in a meadow."

"They're amazing," I whispered to Sami, who shook his head.

"They're from the Ballet de l'Opéra de Paris, so they've been rehearsing for something else all day. Now they're tired. But, you know. They must eat. This will be our ball scene in *La Bohème*."

"Don't ballet dancers get paid well?" I said, truly surprised. As the music started again and they glided back onto the stage, I couldn't help appreciate every perfect arm extension, every perfectly turned-out leg. I had seen dancers at the pantomime, but never anything like this, so exquisite. The girls were unutterably tiny, like little fragile birds, their delicate bones visible through the skin until I almost felt worried for them. I wondered, as they leaped up on their toes, if having flat toes might not give me some kind of an advantage.

As I watched them dance again and again, totally hypnotized, I gradually started to see the tiny incremental difference in rhythm that might make them less than perfect and made the choreographer burst into apoplectic shouting, but like cowed army recruits they never talked back or did anything other than meekly follow orders. Until finally the music swelled one last time, getting on for midnight, and even the porter, who had let us in and was now sweeping up the back of the room, paused to watch them twist, float, and fly in circles in the air in a movement that was glorious together, as if they weren't sixteen separate people, but one spinning circle, with component parts. It struck me that it would also look perfect if seen from above.

Everyone felt it; there was harmony and joy in the room as, finally, they stepped and twirled faster and faster as the music got slower and slower, until the great wide skirts were almost a blur and the men were lifting the women in the air, then swapping them one after another until you couldn't see who was who. It was ravishing. The gray-haired man let them play all the way through to the end, whereupon they finished, perfectly, almost silently, and in the next second, disappeared off the stage so quickly, it looked like a trick.

Although there were only six of us there, we clapped our hands off. The dancers appeared back onstage, pink, pleased, and clapped for each other too. Sami had been right; it was exactly what I needed to take my mind off it.

"Okay! Dinner!" shouted Sami, starting to round everyone up. "We shall go to the Criterion. They won't mind."

I glanced at my watch. It was nearly midnight, and I had a busy day ahead.

"I shan't join you," I said, suddenly distracted by the sight of one of the dancers taking off her shoes and revealing blood on her toes. She was so exceptionally beautiful, but her foot was disgusting; covered in weird lumps and bumps and bunions. The toes were in fact all mis-shapen and bunched together. I couldn't take my eyes off them, until I realized she was aware of me staring at her and wrenched my face away.

"I know," she said, smiling. "They are disgusting, *non*?"

"Mine too," I said, suddenly feeling slightly excited to be in any way included in this otherworldly gang. "Look."

I showed her. There was still blood on my ballet slippers.

"My God," said the girl. "Ah well. Who wants to wear heels anyway, right?"

I smiled at her and she smiled back. She must have been about five foot one.

"Right," I said.

I went up to Sami and kissed him.

"Good night," I said. "Thank you."

Sami kissed me back on the cheek. "Don't worry, *chérie*. It will be all right."

"Thank you," I said.

21

The next few weeks, the queues for the shop definitely fell off a bit. I panicked. It was full August now, and Frédéric did try to persuade me that this was normal, that most of Paris emptied out and most of the businesses shut down—in fact, we would be closing ourselves for a fortnight at the end of the month. I had no idea what to do with myself. I supposed I should go home, see Mum and Dad. Or maybe invite them over, although they'd have to get a hotel, and the whole process would worry my mother to bits. If I could get to Thierry, who was being kept in the hospital for what seemed to me a very long time—the French, it seemed, did things very differently—then I could nail down the exact date for Claire to come over. It seemed to me, the sooner the better, although I know her periods of feeling better and worse ebbed and flowed. It was difficult to time them, exactly.

I called her late one night. "Hello?"

"Anna!"

I tried to gauge the tone of her voice. It sounded a little breathier, but not much.

"Have you been running?"

"Ha, yes, very amusing. How's your accent coming along?"

I smiled secretly to myself. In fact, people had almost stopped addressing me in English, as they usually did—Parisians all seemed to speak wonderful English and take great delight in showing it off to you, thereby thoroughly dissing your French in the process. But the last couple of weeks, as I'd spent more and more time out the front of the shop, that had really started to calm down. I would never be an Alice, almost pass for French. Everything from my hair to my shoes screamed "*rosbif*." But no longer did everyone scramble into English at the first sight of me; people now even forgot to slow down when they were talking to me. I took it as the greatest of compliments (even though it meant I had to ask people to repeat themselves all the time).

"Super *bien*, *merci*, madame," I said cheekily. I could almost hear her smile down the telephone.

"I have written to Thierry," she announced out of the blue. "He never gets my letters, but I have told him I am coming. With you of course. On the twentieth of August."

"Perfect," I said. He must be up and about by then.

"Can he... Well, I would like him to meet me at Calais."

I thought privately that Alice would rather let him climb Mount Everest without oxygen, but I didn't say it.

"Okay," I said guardedly. "I mean, he's had a major operation. Um...I'm just a bit worried about you and the bags and everything... I mean, I'm confident I can help you, but I'm not sure he could get to Calais."

Claire bit her lip. "Ha! No one wants me to go. Not one other person. Everyone thinks you're trying to kill me."

"I do want you to go! I'm coming to fetch you! I booked the tickets! But I'm not sure I can perform miracles."

I wondered briefly if they were right, then put the thought out of my mind. If I got really, really ill—well, I suppose we all do one day, there's no way around that. But if I got really, really sick, and there was something I really, really wanted to do, I'd have liked very much for someone to help me, even if everybody did think it was a stupid idea. If you asked me, the stupid idea was cancer. It was a bloody stupid idea, but hardly my fault.

Claire calmed down instantly.

"I'm sorry," she said. "I'm just getting agitated. Don't worry. I've left…well, if anything happens. You'll be totally exonerated."

"Um, okay," I said, not entirely sure how I felt about that.

Laurent hadn't been in touch at all, which made me slightly annoyed, then slightly pleased that I hadn't slept with him, as presumably that would have come to the same end, and regardless of Sami's libertarian spirit, that would have made me slightly unhappy.

Given, though, that Alice had also told me to back out, it made it very hard to find out how Thierry was doing and how much he knew about Claire's plan. Alice popped down to the shop every couple of days and hummed crossly when she looked at the cashing up, but was frustratingly tight-lipped on Thierry's progress. All I knew was that he had to still be at the hospital because, as Frédéric said, if they'd let him out even for a second, he would have been back in the shop before they'd taken out the drip.

22

Claire was ready. So ready. Everything in the house was immaculately tidy. Her oncologist had been cross at first—like all doctors, Claire surmised, he liked mindless gratitude and obedience. Well, like all people, she supposed. But then he'd gradually gotten used to the idea, postponed her next round of chemo, and prescribed her several very strong emergency painkillers just in case. He'd warned her repeatedly that she wouldn't be insured in France and that her health insurance card wouldn't help her out with her preexisting condition and that she could get in serious trouble, but she clearly wasn't listening, so in the end he had smiled and wished her all the best and reminisced about a time as a young medical student when he'd snuck into the Folies Bergère and it had been the best night of his life, and she had smiled back. Paris touched so many people.

Her suitcase was packed. Her sons had both come around and sighed heavily and complained and begged her to change her mind but of course to no avail. She had more color in her cheeks than she had for over a year.

• • • •

Taking the train back to the UK was a revelation. I couldn't believe how nervous and anxious I'd been on my way here, how sick I still felt, in body and in spirit, really. How I was convinced it would be such a disaster and I'd be thrown out for being a fraud, or that I would sit in a rented room for three months not talking to anyone because everyone would be so rude to me and I wouldn't be able to speak the language.

And before I got on the train even, I would probably have said, on balance, that more bad things than good had happened. Thierry's illness, my nonstarter flirtation with Laurent, my very slow learning to make one or two types of chocolate that even now I was only beginning to truly appreciate.

But on the train, as I smelled the awful fake scent of the hot chocolate dispenser—which had never bothered me before—and watched the brightly dressed, blond-headed British girls get on, with their big bosoms and ready smiles and little gin and tonics in their hands, I realized I had changed. That I was more comfortable, more confident—not just than I'd been before the accident, but maybe than ever before. Okay, so I had hardly taken Paris by storm, but I had made friends and kept my job and eaten some unbelievable food. I stroked my plain pale gray Galeries Lafayette dress, which I wouldn't have looked at three months ago but now I felt suited me very well, listened to the safety announcements, feeling quite at home in either language, took out my magazine, and settled my head back and realized how happy I was to be going home, but how happy I would be to come back too.

● ● ● ●

I hadn't rung Laurent, for lots of reasons, the main one being I was a big fat crazy coward who hated dealing with things straight on, but I had emailed him, telling him when we'd be arriving in Paris, with all the dates, and hoping that Claire would be able to see Thierry. What I meant by this, clearly, is that I hoped Laurent would smooth everything over with Alice, but I didn't put it like that.

Anyway, I was putting stupid thoughts of stupid Laurent out of my head completely. As if in strict defiance of what he or any other French person might think, I marched straight up to the buffet and ordered a large packet of Walker's chips—cheese and onion—and ate them, straight from the packet, in public, something no French person I had yet met would ever have done. So there, I thought to myself.

• • • •

Mum burst into tears when she saw me. Which I know, I know, should have made me happy. Obviously, it's nice to be loved, of course, I know I'm lucky but, you know, *Mu-um*. Also I hate the implication: that she was totally sure that I couldn't leave the house on my own without being eaten by crocodiles or kidnapped by white slave traders. It was a bit insulting to be honest, that she was crying tears of full relief that her useless daughter who couldn't be trusted in the real world hadn't actually died when traveling to the nearest possible foreign country to Kidinsborough. (Unless you counted Liverpool. Hahaha, only joking.)

I didn't say any of this, of course, just buried my head in her shoulder, so pleased to be home. Dad patted me lightly on the back in his jolly way.

"Hello, girl," he said.

"Hi, Dad."

I found myself choking up a bit, which was ridiculous as I'd only been away for two months, but I hadn't been like that girl Jules in my class who'd gone away to university miles away, then worked in America and traveled all over the place. That wasn't me at all, never had been.

I looked at Kidinsborough with a funny air through the car windows. Another pawn shop had opened. Another little café had closed down. The people seemed to walk so slowly. I wondered, almost abstractly, if I was turning into a snob, but it wasn't that. If you believed the papers (which I didn't really understand anyway), the UK was doing well, while France was pretty much running on fumes, but you really wouldn't see it to set up a street in Kidinsborough against the rue de Rivoli.

On the other hand, that was hardly fair. I was sure there were plenty of grim former industrial towns in France, cluttering up the border with rusting railway tracks and thundering lorries. I watched a woman shouting at her pram. She was wearing two tank tops, both grubby, neither of which reached all the way over the rolls of fat down to her leggings. She was pushing a buggy loaded with huge thin plastic bags through which the family bags of chips were clearly visible.

I winced. I was turning into a snob.

• • • •

"*Anna!* Have you turned into a total and utter snob?"

It was Cath on the phone. I was so pleased to hear from her.

"*Yes!*" I screamed back. "I can't help it! I don't know what to do. I'm kind of horrible now."

"Everyone in France is horrible," she said with all the authority of someone who'd been told off by a ferry operative on a school trip to France in 1995.

"Everyone knows that. They eat dogs and stuff."

"They don't eat *dogs*," I said crossly. "Where did you even hear that?"

"Well, dogs, or horses or something."

"Mmm," I said.

"Oh. My. God. It's true. Do they eat horses?"

"Well, if you eat cows, I don't really see the difference…"

"Oh my utter God, that is total rank. Did you eat a horse? Oh man, that mings the mong."

I started to feel less snobby.

"Get ready," said Cath. "We're going out."

It was good to be home.

• • • •

Cath let herself into my room, armed with blow-dryers and curling tongs. She stopped short when she saw me.

"What?" I said.

"Dunno," she said, but she didn't look pleased. She had a bright blood-red streak through the top of her hair that made her look like a particularly cheerful vampire. "You look...different."

"That's because I'm not in bed vomiting up blood and crying," I pointed out.

"No, even after you got sick."

"Well, I'm not out of work and crying in the morning."

She shook her head. "Neh. It's more than that."

She opened up her hairdressing bag and pulled out two clanking bottles of WKD.

"Um, Cath, we're thirty," I reminded her. "You don't need to smuggle drink into the house. Dad would make us a martini bianco if we asked him nicely."

"It tastes better like this," she said. "Can I smoke out the window?"

I rolled my eyes. "Yes."

She lit up and climbed on my bed, regarding me closely.

"You've lost weight," she said accusingly.

Actually I'd lost a lot of weight in the hospital, then regained it all again by staying indoors being depressed and eating extra-spicy KFC. Then the last few weeks had been so busy I hadn't even really noticed, which was, I will say, not at all like me. But my jeans had certainly felt looser. But I still considered myself fatter than every other person in Paris. The women were so tiny. Maybe I was just falling into line.

"You've gone Frenchy-thin," she said. "Hmm. Do you smoke now and eat nothing all day except frogs' legs and dog?"

"It's horse," I said.

"I knew it!" yelled Cath.

Her eyebrows would have arched if she hadn't had that dodgy cheap Botox that she didn't even need. It had given her a look that screamed Botox. She adored it, all the sheen without the need for repeated injections. Everyone assumed she had it about once a week.

"What's this man like?" she asked.

"There's no man," I said. "Well…I mean… No, no man."

"Oh my God, what's he like? Is he tiny and without an arse? French men never have arses."

"How come you're so well-informed?"

"Everyone knows that," she said dismissively. "I've met a few men in my time."

This was undeniably true. I drank the blue drink. Had it always been this revolting? I wasn't sure.

"Well, I kind of nearly met someone, then he saw my foot and had a serious freak out."

Cath put her glass down. Her voice was quieter. "Seriously?"

"It's all right," I said, taking a swig. It wasn't much better than the first one, but I persevered. "It doesn't matter."

"What a twat," she said.

"Oh no, it wasn't really his fault… My shoe fell off and he thought my toes fell off too."

She paused for a second, then, suddenly, we both burst out laughing.

"What an idiot!" she said when she paused for breath. "Thank God you didn't brush your hair. He'd have thought your head was falling off."

The blue drinks must have been getting to us, because we found this very, very funny too, and suddenly I realized that while I might have been learning lots of new things and experiences, I hadn't had a bloody good laugh for ages.

We headed out to Faces, and there were loads of people there I hadn't seen for absolutely ages and everyone was dead nice and bought us drinks and congratulated Cath on beating that shoplifting charge, to which Cath assumed a heavenly look and pretended she wasn't in the least bit surprised, and a bunch of lads we went to school with were there and that was so funny, the married ones all fat and tired-looking, the unmarried ones all flash-looking and bragging about their cars. A few more blue drinks and everything seemed hilarious again and I even ended up giving Darr a bit of a snog for old times' sake—well, he was right there, and I felt like I needed the practice, but he was absolutely, I realized, rubbish compared to Laurent, so I quickly knocked that on the head. Then me and Cath marched home arm in arm, singing a Robbie Williams song, and it was exactly what I needed.

Even with it though, I still felt different. Like I was an outsider, looking in. That I was playing at being a Kidinsborough girl rather than actually being one. Even though I was, wasn't I? Of course I was.

It was very kind of Claire not to ring until the afternoon the next day.

● ● ● ●

Actually, it was better than kind; it was bliss. I sat in front of the gas fire, watching TV—my mum had taped loads of reality shows; she likes anything where people come to a sticky end—and we ate toast (no one could believe it when I told them the French had never really heard of toast and ate this indigestible crunchy preburned stuff) with Marmite. The boys let me eat some of their massive supplies of chips, which was their way of saying they were pleased to see me, and my dad didn't really say anything much, just popped his head around the door every now and again, smiled, then popped out again. I'd forgotten how nice it was at home. I'd also forgotten that by the next day, Mum and I would probably be driving each other up the wall and I'd be down at the discount store begging for a job and tripping over the boys' sneakers...

And I had promises to keep. The second I saw the wheelchair, I knew this was going to be a bigger task than I'd counted on. It was… Well, it was huge.

"I know," Claire said. "I hate it too."

"It's just so…"

Claire was sitting on the sofa and we were both staring at the ugly, hideous big National Health Service wheelchair that we both knew so well from trips through hospital corridors, to operating rooms and blood-testing departments, with jaunty porters who always had a cheery word. But now it was just us.

"Well, I'm sure I can fold it up," I said, not sure at all. I'm only five foot three and a bit wobbly on the one side.

"And people will be kind," said Claire firmly.

I looked at her. She'd lost even more weight; the bones on her face made her look like one of those ballet dancers from the opera. Blue veins were visible underneath her skin, except on her arms, where repeated stabbings had caused them all to retreat and hide. The story was that she was off the chemo so she could get well enough to operate on. She insisted this was the case, but she didn't look better to me. Not at all.

She didn't wear a scarf or a turban in the house, and I inspected her head. It was covered in a tiny fuzz, like a duckling's.

"I reckon Cath could do something with that," I said, but she didn't smile. I noticed she didn't like to get too far away from her drip, which usually indicated, psychologically, that she was in pain.

"How are you feeling?" I asked softly, even though I knew it was a question she got asked ninety times every day.

"Well, I'd be a bit better if everyone didn't keep telling me not to go," she said, almost snappily for Claire, who never snapped, not even when I burst into tears over my inability to grasp the subjunctive (a really stupid tense they have in French solely for shouting at people).

"We'll be fine," I said with renewed vigor. "We shall charm every porter from here to the Gare du Nord."

She gave me a slight smile and her hand fluttered a little to her neck.

"He…he knows I'm coming."

"He does," I said. "It's the first time he's smiled since his heart attack."

I didn't tell her about Alice and Laurent. I would deal with all that later.

I looked at the large suitcase Patsy had packed, under duress. It contained an oxygen cylinder we would have to declare at customs. I was terrified of it and the situation in which I might have to use it. I was terrified, full stop. What if they didn't let us go? That might even be better, part of me thought. Then we could say we'd tried our best and that was that, and now they could talk like sensible people, on Skype, and I could go back and work the shop back up for Thierry and after that…well, come home, I suppose. Go flatting with Cath again, figure something out. I'd worry about that when it happened. But for now…one thing at a time.

"I only have a small bag," I said, although my mum had loaded me up with bacon and cheddar cheese and anything else she heard I couldn't get ahold of easily. She felt I was fading away. The idea of changing in London scared the crap out of me. I didn't know London at all, and it didn't open itself up to walking in it the same way Paris did, but I'd worry about that later too.

We were leaving Tuesday morning. I had Sunday lunch at Mum and Dad's, made conversation with my brothers, saw a lot of Cath and tried to persuade her to come and visit me—I reckoned her and Sami would get on, even if they didn't speak the same language, but she'd gotten unusually sheepish.

"Neh," she'd said. "I don't think it's for me."

We were walking down by the canal on Monday night, looking for something to do. It was warm out still.

"You'd love it," I said. "There's a party every night and champagne everywhere and it's really beautiful and I live right at the top of this spooky old house."

She turned to me sadly.

"You're dead brave, you are," she said. "Everyone thinks you're the quiet one, but it's not like that really."

"Don't be daft," I said. "You're the one who jumped into the canal fully clothed that New Year's. I thought you'd kill yourself."

Cath shook her head.

"Oh, it's one thing hanging around here," she said. "Out there…neh. You might as well take me to the Amazon jungle. This is where I belong, Anna. Along with the shitty shopping trolley in the canal, and Gav, and me mam and everything really. You're not like that."

"Course I am," I said.

"Neh," she said. "You are the brave one."

And we linked arms and walked back home together.

· · · ·

Seven a.m. and my dad was running the car outside. It had suddenly turned cold and he was sounding very cross. Our train wasn't until twenty past eight, but I had decided better to be safe than sorry, which was just as well, as we were having a heck of a job trying to fold the wheelchair into the trunk of the car, and I was starting to wish I hadn't bothered and wondering whether the very first half hour was an acceptable time to give up the trip altogether.

Dad got out and helped me, while Claire sat in the front seat, the seat belt almost flat against her, so thin was she now. I'd locked up the house—it was immaculate, the fridge empty, which I found slightly off-putting. She'd be back in three days. This felt like an empty house. But I wasn't going to argue with Patsy (again).

Claire watched us in the rearview mirror swearing and sweating as we tried to maneuver the wheelchair in by taking down the back seats, but we still weren't having much luck. We were going to be very tight for the train as it was. And the London train went from the opposite platform. I could feel myself starting to panic.

"Are you sure you know what you're doing, love?" said my dad quietly, to which I could only reply, "I haven't got a clue, Dad."

Being my dad, he just patted me on the shoulder, and that was the best thing to do. Even so, it wasn't boding well.

Suddenly up the quiet street glided a very large, very quiet car. You didn't see one of those often around Kidinsborough; it looked to be one of those enormous Range Rover things, all shiny black. It slowed down next to us and a distinguished-looking man stepped out beside us on the pavement, dressed in a smart tweed jacket.

Claire gasped in the mirror, then opened the front door of the car and, holding herself carefully, got up and out of the car on her own.

"Richard?" she said.

• • • •

She wouldn't have guessed it in a million years. She stared at him, completely dumbfounded.

"Richard," she said again.

It sometimes felt to her like he had hardly changed a bit, was still the awkward boy with the clarinet case and the brown horn-rimmed glasses. His glasses were still horn-rimmed, but she'd always liked the style, so he'd never changed it. He'd kept his hair, and having a new wife and a stepdaughter had kept him trimmer than he might have been otherwise. She could still remember his admiring tone from so long ago. He'd never taken her off that pedestal. That had been the problem, really. No, she chided herself. She had been the problem. She had always been the problem.

"What are you doing here? I am going, you know. It's kind of the boys to worry but I truly feel this is something I have to…"

"No," said Richard simply, raising his hand. "I'm here to help."

• • • •

I had no idea who this geezer was—he was pretty handsome for an old bloke, that was for sure—but it became clear pretty quickly. I looked at his huge Range Rover.

"Yes," he said. "Why don't I drive you in that? Then you won't have to get on and off the train."

I thought about all the money Claire had spent on first-class rail tickets but didn't mention it. I was enough in her debt already.

"Great," I said, with massive relief, and I meant it. The folded-up wheelchair fit into the back of the car with ease, and I helped Claire up the high step—I'd never been in such a fancy car before.

Dad looked on, a bit crestfallen. I felt bad about that.

"Look, it's good Richard's helping us," I said.

Dad looked at his old Peugeot.

"I like your car," I said. "This is a stupid car. It's going to destroy the planet and kill us all. Oh look, it has a TV in the back seat!"

Dad smiled ruefully. "You're off again then," he said.

"Not for long," I said. After living in pajamas and one slightly ill-advised neon miniskirt for two days, I'd put my Paris uniform back on.

Dad shook his head.

"Your mother thinks it is for long. She thinks you've left."

"Don't be daft," I said, my voice cracking a bit. "This will always be my home."

Dad gave me a hug.

"There's always a home for you here," he said. "That's not quite the same thing, mind. Anyway, you're thirty, love. About time you got your life started, don't you think?"

• • • •

I felt like a kid sitting in the back seat, but I didn't mind. There was a stack of DVDs carefully put on a little shelf, obviously for the grandchildren, and Richard offered to put one on for me.

Claire hadn't spoken much about her ex in the hospital, although the boys were very good at coming to see her, and it was clear they must have resembled him. I understood that it had ended and that they weren't in touch, but what had ended it and why I had no idea. So I figured it was best to slip the headphones on and let them get on with it.

• • • •

Claire glanced briefly at Anna in the back seat, completely engrossed in the film like a child, and smiled to herself. She was in a little pain—her joints felt sore, as if she had a strong flu, and a headache was circling and threatening to descend from any quarter, but thankfully she wasn't vomiting. For that, small mercies.

Richard had asked her why on earth she wouldn't just take the train, but she was adamant. She wanted to take that boat again. She didn't like words like closure, but yes, it was important to her.

She and Richard chatted here and there—mostly of the boys. It was funny how quickly they fell back into their own ways together. She glanced at his hand on the gearshift. He had always been a good driver, took it seriously, got upset if she had a dent or scratched the side. It used to matter a lot.

Once they hit the great long stretches of the M6, empty in between the rush hour and the holiday traffic, he put the cruise control on and sat back in his seat a little. She heard his knees crack. She wasn't the only one getting on a bit.

"So," he said quietly. "It was him all along then. I mean, this is a very, very long time to keep a flame burning, Claire."

Claire shrugged. "I think… I mean, it's too late now. I know that."

She stared at her lap. It always seemed easier to talk in cars, when you could stare out of the window, she supposed. And you weren't staring face to face.

Richard shook his head.

"Do you know what I wish?" he said, his hands steady on the steering wheel. "I wish just after we'd met and you were all dreamy and distant that I'd called you on it. That I hadn't pretended that it was just because you were some mystical fairy, or been so terrified of losing you. I wish I'd just said 'Who is it?' and then let you go. I bet by the following year, the glow would have come off it anyway."

"Maybe," said Claire.

"And you could have come back to the UK and then you'd have been pleased to have me."

"I was always pleased to have you," said Claire.

He glanced at her, as if he thought she was being sarcastic. A light squall of rain had gotten up.

"Well," he grumbled. "Too late for that now."

"I know you want me to apologize," said Claire. "But I can't. We raised two lovely boys. We spent twenty-five years together. That's more than a lot of people do. I didn't mean to make you unhappy."

"I know," said Richard. "And I shouldn't have done what I did."

She shrugged. It was water under the bridge now.

"The boys don't tell me much… Well, I'm not sure how much you tell the boys. You're so damned closed, Claire…"

His irritation threatened to spill over, but he managed to temper out, swinging out to overtake a lorry that was wobbling precariously in the middle lane, water sluicing from its chains.

"I mean…I mean…"

"How bad is it?"

Richard nodded, as if he couldn't say the words out loud.

Claire turned to him. She had spent some time living with this, which was why she had spent so much time living in the past.

"Um, it's spread again," she said quietly, the only sound in the car a slight buzz from Anna's headphones and the swish-swish of the windscreen wipers.

"It's the reason my hair's growing back. I told the boys I'm resting up, but no. There are no plans to continue the chemo."

Richard took a sharp intake of breath.

"Jesus."

"I know. You wouldn't believe the fight I had on my hands to get these."

She opened her palm to reveal a tiny bottle of diamorphine.

"Shh," she said, almost smiling.

"But you seem so… I mean, you're just yourself, except thinner."

"I would say my days are better and worse," said Claire. "At the moment, a little better. I think my body is just so pleased not to have any more chemo. But I don't know how many good days there will be."

"How long?"

Claire took on her oncologist's ponderous tones.

"Well, Mrs. Shawcourt, I wouldn't say months."

Richard let a hiss of breath escape through his mouth. Then he said the one word Claire had never heard him say in his entire life.

"Fuck," he said.

23

Laurent looked at Anna's email and ran through it again. This was ridiculous; it didn't make sense. His dad was only just home, he'd heard through the grapevine, but under strict diet and movement controls for at least another three months. Alice would have absolutely nothing to do with it, that much was sure. And he could hardly do it; even if his father would consent to look at him, he still had work to do, and the logistics were horrible. All for that woman.

Though she was old now, he knew, old and sick. Well, maybe when Anna and that woman got to Paris, he'd try to arrange something. Yes, that would be better.

He thought about Anna. It struck him suddenly as a very "her" thing to do, to go straightaway on this wild goose chase to help out an old lady. She wouldn't even think twice, the same way she didn't think twice about staying with his father or trying to make things right in the shop or…

He cursed himself again for freaking about her foot. He'd hurt her feelings, for something she obviously couldn't help, and he hated doing that. She wasn't like the tough, hard-edged Parisienne girls he knew—not at all. She wasn't chic and tough; she didn't know the right places to go or the right things to wear. She was soft and a bit squishy and…

It came to him in a blinding flash. She knew the right things to do. She just did. And that was what made her different. He didn't; he was a stupid coward who walked away from things the second they got difficult. He needed her.

Suddenly he wanted Anna back in Paris as much as he had ever wanted anything. He stared at her email again. Tomorrow. She would be here tomorrow. He hit respond then realized that he didn't know how to say what he wanted to say. He didn't know what he wanted to say or what he was going to do. He stared at the blank page, then shut down the internet window and did what he always did when things got on top of him and he started to worry. He went to work.

* * * *

I woke up without the faintest idea where I was. It was raining outside. I was stretched out on a back seat so comfortable it felt like a huge leather sofa. I jerked my head up. We were at a gas station. Claire was asleep in the front seat.

Richard came back to the car. His eyes were red and he was rubbing his nose a little and I didn't want to bother him. Plus, of course, I didn't know him at all. I shushed him as he glanced at Claire, and he went around to the trunk, pulled out a picnic blanket—of course they were the kind of people who would have picnic blankets—and very, very gently put it around her.

I wondered. I mean, Thierry was great and funny and fun and life-enhancing, but I couldn't imagine him for a second putting a blanket around Claire like she was made of porcelain. I could imagine him talking about it, and asking someone else to do it, and suggesting it, and making a joke of it. But not calmly and precisely tucking it in, with the utmost respect for her.

Not wanting to make any noise, I smiled at him and he smiled back.

"I got you a sandwich," he whispered. "I don't know what you like so I got one of each."

277

I grinned. "Lovely! Can I have the ham and tomato?"

He passed it over with a bottle of fizzy water and a bar of Braders chocolate.

"Sorry," he said. "I didn't know if you ate absolutely loads of the stuff or if you were practically allergic."

He got in and started the car, again very gently.

"I can probably eat both if you don't want it."

"No," I said, looking carefully at the familiar midbrown wrapper.

The factory had sent me (along with numerous official-looking letters absolving themselves from responsibility) a huge basket full of Braders products while I was in the hospital. I couldn't even look at them now without remembering the fever, the throbbing pain. I hadn't been able to so much as glance at them in a newsagents ever since.

I picked it up. "I think it's time," I said, but Richard was already signaling his way out onto the motorway.

I peeled away a corner and inhaled the smell, carefully and fully, just as Thierry had shown me. Suddenly I was back in the factory with Kyle and Shaz, and punching in, and Easter overtime, and the visit from the Duchess of Cambridge that time everyone else had gotten wildly excited over and had made me feel like an underachieving troll.

But, I suddenly realized with excitement, I could smell more than that. I could take it apart in my head. I could smell the vegetable oil, the tiny note of additives that we covered up with more sugar, the grade of the sugar, the weakness of the cocoa beans. It was rather thrilling to realize that if I wanted, I could probably cook up a batch of this at home. I blinked several times. Frédéric would have hurled it from himself in utter horror like it was a live snake, of that I had no doubt. Instead, I closed my eyes and took a bite.

Here was the weird thing: even though I knew that it was made as cheaply as possible to serve in large quantities, that it wasn't anything

THE LOVELIEST CHOCOLATE SHOP IN PARIS

like the high-end, pure product we did at Le Chapeau Chocolat, that it was meant for bland generic tastes, designed to be unchallenging, rather than delicious…it WAS delicious. It melted at exactly the right moment on the tongue; it filled my mouth; it tasted sweet and creamy, even though I knew exactly how much cream was in there (none at all), and it broke off in soft crumbly chunks. It was completely gorgeous. I didn't know what it would taste like if you hadn't been born and raised with it, but to me it was good and British and comforting and reassuring, and I wished Richard had brought loads of it to stash under my bed in Paris for when the tasting all got too much.

"Mmm," I said quietly.

Richard grinned at the wheel.

"It's like having the kids back again," he said, but not in a mean way.

A road sign showed we were less than one hundred miles from Dover.

• • • •

I looked at the sky dubiously. How bad did it have to be before they stopped the ferries running? Our tickets were for tonight, and I had been planning on finding a cheap hotel by the terminal, then doing the final leg tomorrow when we were all better rested. I had pointed out that we could fly in an hour from Newcastle, but of course this had cut no ice at all.

Anyway, my plan had all changed now. We had train tickets, but I had no idea what Richard was intending to do. Was he going to drive us all the way to Paris? I didn't want to ask him in case he then felt obliged to take us all the way—I could already tell he had impeccable manners. He might not even have his passport. I decided just to sit tight and see what happened.

Claire didn't wake up all the way through passport control. I thought customs officials might get suspicious and make us wake her up, but they didn't seem too fussed and waved us on through. Richard had hopped out and bought a ferry ticket for the car so quickly and unfussily I had hardly noticed him doing it, and when I tried to thank him and offer him money, he waved me away.

"If Claire pays you back, it will be my money anyway," he pointed out, but not unkindly. We were both getting worried about how soundly she was sleeping. She had absolutely assured me that her doctor was happy for her to control her own medication for three days, but now I wasn't so sure.

"Claire," said Richard lightly as we drove on to the great clanking ship. It was full of cheerful-looking holidaymakers, their cars piled high with sunhats and inflatable chairs and tents and bicycles and excited children, desperate to start racing all over the boat. The train may be more convenient, I thought, but I doubted it was quite as much fun for the little ones.

Claire nodded a little in and out, and Richard prodded her again, after we'd been led into position in the lower deck and stopped the engine.

"Claire?"

• • • •

She had bugged him for ages and he had said, "Don't be ridiculous, only tourists ever want to go up the Tour Eiffel," and she had said, "Well, I'm a tourist," and he had said, "You are not a tourist, you are a muse," and that was undoubtedly the most thrilling thing anyone had ever said to her in her entire life. She had jumped on him and locked her legs around his waist until he had laughed his huge booming laugh and agreed, so one very warm lunchtime, when everybody else was off eating properly, like normal people did, he said—he was absolutely rigid about his mealtimes, as was nearly everyone she met there—he had led her threading through the new Metro line and up right at the very base of the huge metal structure, queuing in the heat, Thierry mopping his forehead with a large handkerchief.

"I love it," she said.

"It is for chocolate boxes," scoffed Thierry.

"It is," said Claire. "You should put it on chocolate boxes."

Thierry had frowned at her as they'd waited for the lift, then it shot them up, at an angle of course, like a rocket, and she had trembled in excitement as they went up, the première, deuxième, troisième *stage. She would not be happy until they had reached the very top, he noticed, and smiled at her enthusiasm.*

Although Paris below was warm and still, up here the wind blew back and forth and there was a chill to it. Thierry immediately took off his jacket and put it on her shoulders, but she didn't want it there; she wanted to feel the breeze after the heat of the city. Her pale hair streamed back against her shoulders, and she turned and smiled at him, and he managed, with rare presence of mind, to pull out his Leica and take a quick shot of her, her dark red lips—it was the same color Mme. LeGuarde used, and she had taken it onboard—pulled back in a huge, laughing smile, the freckles popped up on her nose, as she tried to hold her large straw hat on her head. As they had gone around the other side, looking out over the river and the flat lands beyond, the wind had finally gotten the better of them and it had gone, blown off, dancing on the thermals just out of reach.

"Noooo!" Claire had yelled, reaching for it, then had turned to him, once more buckling with laughter.

"Little hat! Little hat! I will save you!" Thierry had shouted, pretending to climb up the iron balustrades until a guard came along and shortly told him to stop what he was doing immediately.

"I shall buy you hats," Thierry boasted, as they finally made their way back down, having exhausted every view and examined the instruments of M. Eiffel himself. "I shall buy you every single hat in Galeries Lafayette, and you shall keep the ones you like, and as for the others, we

shall return here and let them fly away. And I hope that whoever finds your hat shall be as happy as you and I."

And she had kissed him all the way down in the elevator, as the lift operator averted his eyes. Le Tour Eiffel *often did that to people.*

Gift boxes from Le Chapeau Chocolat had carried a tiny, discreet hat mark in the corner ever since.

• • • •

"Claire!" Claire felt the hand on her shoulder and looked up to see Richard and Anna looking at her anxiously.

"Phew," said Richard.

"It's all right," said Claire. Her mouth was very dry; a side effect of the drugs, she knew. Fortunately Anna was already holding out the bottle. What a dear girl she was. She took it and tried to smile, but her lips cracked painfully.

"Just napping."

She tried to swallow. Some of the water ran down her neck. She realized sleeping in the car had made her terribly stiff. She didn't know whether she could actually move at all. Everything hurt. Anna wiped away the water and helped tilt the bottle. It was one of those "sports" ones with the teats like a baby's bottle. Claire wondered dimly why it was called sport, when it was clearly for the opposite of sports people—babies and invalids.

Suddenly the great engine of the ferry sprang to life. The deck, which had already been swaying, started to move and tremble. Claire glanced around. She remembered the *Herald of Free Enterprise* suddenly and how frightening it had been. A voice came over the loudspeaker announcing in English and French that conditions weren't ideal and advising passengers to leave the car decks but to stay inside the boat, as some choppy waters had been forecast. Claire suddenly realized where she was.

"I want to go up on top," she announced.

"There's a lounge," Richard said, looking worried. There was a wheelchair lift, but the boat was moving so much he wasn't even sure about getting the chair out of the back of the car without it swinging about wildly. All the other passengers had left, climbing up the colored stairwells into the body of the ship.

Claire shook her head. "No. Up. I want to get up."

She saw Richard and Anna share a look and nearly cried with frustration. Her stupid, stupid wretched body that wouldn't do a single thing she wanted it to.

• • • •

Claire looked awful; she could hardly drink out of a bottle. We had to get upstairs, but I didn't have a clue how we were going to manage it. I went around to the back of the gigantic Range Rover—I could hardly reach up to open it, swaying with the boat as it seemed to reverse itself. I hadn't been on a ferry since I was fourteen with Cath, but we'd been too busy singing Oasis songs to notice.

Just as I was trying to figure out the lock, I felt Richard's eyes on me. As I glanced back at him, he looked at me, shrugged, then reached into Claire's side of the car, undid her seat belt, and gently, as if she was a child—she was as light as a child, I could see—lifted her up in his arms. I grabbed the blanket.

"Richard!" Claire protested, and I could hear the pain in her voice, but I think we all knew there wasn't a better way. Carefully, Richard mounted the narrow stairwell. "All right there, sir?" we heard a cheery sailor say, and Richard muttered something about not wanting to bring the wheelchair out, and the sailor said, "Let me know if you need a hand then," in a way that made me want to swear blind to travel with that ferry company and no one else for the rest of my life.

The top of the ferry was bright and bustling, like an old airport terminal. There were shops and bars and duty free and an amusement arcade already full of children screaming and stabbing at the flashing lights and bells. I could smell fries cooking and glanced into the large lounge, full of seats, the reclining ones already taken by the frequent travelers who clearly knew what they were doing. We attracted a few curious glances, but we simply ignored them and forced our way through to as quiet a corner of the lounge as we could find, where Richard settled Claire as gently as he could, then pretended not to be out of breath.

"Why don't I get us all a hot cup of coffee?" I said.

• • • •

Alice was standing in the doorway when Laurent arrived at the large wooden door, her arms folded. Behind her he could see expensive-looking private nurses moving silently over the highly polished parquet. Fresh orchids sat in the corner.

"He's not here," she said.

"Don't be ridiculous," said Laurent. "Look. He doesn't need to talk to me. But he needs to have the choice."

"No," said Alice. "And he doesn't want to talk to you."

"Fine," said Laurent. "I'll drive and not talk."

"No," said Alice.

"Yes," said Thierry, stepping out from the anteroom, where a fire was blazing despite the warmth of the afternoon. He was wearing an enormous smoking jacket. If Laurent hadn't been so wound up, he might have smiled.

Alice looked at them both, her fingers tightening and her high cheekbones stretching taut and pink.

"*Non!*" she insisted again, but Thierry was already beckoning someone to pack a bag, and Laurent had grabbed the keys to the company van and stood there. The two men wore a very similar expression and walked together to the van in an injured silence.

Alice could do nothing but stand and watch the van drive away. She swore under her breath. In English.

• • • •

When I got back with the coffees, I could see they were in the middle of an argument. Claire, I noticed, still hadn't moved. I rummaged in her medical bag for the Tiger Balm—I remembered how much she'd enjoyed it in the hospital—and quietly started to rub it in to her shoulders. There was nothing to her, I felt. Just knotted bits of muscle, struggling on when there was almost nothing left in her. Her tufts of bird hair—the scarf had slipped off again—made me want to cry.

"I'm not taking you up there," said Richard. We could see out of the porthole windows the waves bouncing up and down; there was a slight tang of vomit in the air, as if it had already affected some of the passengers. The sea looked an odd mixture of green and black, and a mixture of spray and rain bounced against the windows. Even though this was only a tiny section of water to cross—people swam it, for goodness' sake—it didn't feel like that. It felt like we were out in the middle of the ocean.

"I need the fresh air," pleaded Claire, her voice quiet now. I glanced at her medicine. She had taken a little more, but she seemed to be entirely compos mentis. I wondered how powerfully it could fight the hideous viper, the tumor growing inside her, spreading, filling her with blackness, hollowing her out. Her face was still composed, still beautiful even.

"It's not right," said Richard. "Don't you want to see the boys again? And Cadence and Codie?"

Claire looked away. "Of course I do," she said. "There are…there are a few things I want to see again, yes." Her jaw looked stern.

"You'll catch pneumonia."

"I've had worse," she said. "I have worse."

Richard put his fingers on the bridge of his nose and rubbed, fiercely.

"You didn't have to come," she added, pressing home her advantage. "I didn't ask you too. Me and Anna would have been all right on our own."

I tried to appear inconspicuous and not point out the obvious, that is that Richard had made it all about a million zillion times easier than he might have done, and if it hadn't been for him, we'd still have been at Crewe station probably or, more likely, back at home.

Richard glanced at his watch. "Okay," he said. "When we're coming in to shore. And not before. Okay?"

Claire nodded weakly, and Richard pulled out his phone and stormed off before we could badger him anymore.

I carefully did Claire's elbows and wrist joints. "Is it very bad?" I asked quietly, feeling her wince.

"It isn't important," she said back, and I wondered if she felt as I did, fearful, regretful that we'd undertaken this at all.

Three-quarters of an hour later, after I'd taken Claire to the bathroom and we'd done what we could in the swaying room, Richard reappeared, again with food, which none of us felt like. The storm hadn't abated, and even the happy screaming holiday children had quieted down.

"Are you still set on doing this then?" he said gruffly.

"Yes," said Claire with dignity. "And I think I can walk now."

Her muscles had slackened up with the drugs and the massage; very carefully and precariously, she made her way up out of her chair, and Richard and I took an arm each and we started to move, very slowly, out of the salon and toward the steps at the back of the boat.

There was a man standing there too, but we explained that we really wanted to go up top, and he looked at us and told us to be careful but wasn't stopping anyone, just kids, he explained.

Through the swing doors at the top, the wind caught us straight-away and nearly sent us staggering right to the side. It was extremely strong, the clouds above us black. Seagulls screamed through the air, desperately searching the boat's wake for discarded chips and other excellent human morsels. The wake churned up the already foamy waves behind us in a long line.

Then we turned around to face the front, and Richard let out a low whistle.

Straight ahead of us where the beaches and cliffs of Calais spread out in front of us, the little old section of the town on top of the hill, the weather had cleared. It was as if someone had drawn a line down the middle of the sky between the UK and France. Calais had hardly any cloud and the late afternoon sun was piercing down to illuminate it.

"You did this on purpose," muttered Richard, but Claire wasn't listening. She was walking forward, on her own, hand on the railing but otherwise steadily. The deck was deserted. She skirted around the lifeboats and buoys until she was right up at the prow.

"Ma belle France," she muttered under her breath as I ran to keep up with her.

And we both stood as far front as we could, as the wind gradually slowed and the rain died off, and gradually things came into focus and we saw the ferry port closer and closer, and, right at the very tip of the farthest dock, we saw two figures, one standing, one slouched in his own wheelchair. My better eyesight caught them first.

"Look," I said to Claire, taking her hand to point in the same direc-tion as if she were a child. "Look over there."

24

Richard stayed at the entrance to the basement, and as the loud-speaker came alive again, instructing everyone to return to their cars and buses, he held the door open for us.

"You go this way," he said, indicating a line of foot passengers lining up with bicycles and rucksacks.

"What do you mean?" I said.

He shook his head. "I've come…I've come as far as I possibly can."

I realized then he'd seen the figures on the dock.

"I booked this when I got the tickets," he said, seeing my face. "It's all right, they know I'm coming straight back."

The boat was sloshing about, maneuvering itself up to the jetty.

"What do you mean?"

In such a short space of time, I realized, I'd come to rely on him as being the grown-up.

"I'll get the chair and your bags," he said. "You're going to be fine."

His face was grave and full of sadness as he disappeared down the stairs. I watched as a long ramp, to let pedestrian passengers off, extended to the quay side. There was a passport box with a hot, grumpy-looking man in it—I still couldn't believe the change in the weather. It was like a great dotted line, like on a map, had separated the UK from the rest of the continent. People were blinking in the sunlight. The smell of fried breakfasts and sprayed perfume and damp carpet from the ferry receded as we breathed in the fresh air.

"Oh," said Claire. "I think I need to sit down."

• • • •

Claire still couldn't believe Richard had done all this for her, even when he set the chair down, as if he'd been handling wheelchairs all his life instead of filing actuarial tables.

"Thank you," she said, feeling both weak and terribly nervous. She hadn't been able to eat a thing, which she knew wasn't good for her, but she dreaded vomiting and being unable to clean herself up; she couldn't face it. Cancer was such a disgusting disease on top of everything else. Sometimes she wished she had something at least a bit romantic, like typhus, maybe, like in *La Bohème*, where she could lie on a sofa, cough into a handkerchief for a bit, then die in an elegant fashion, without the vomit and the diarrhea and the baldness and the bollocks of it all.

Her heart, she thought, fluttered. Her eyesight wasn't what it once was, and she hadn't recognized the figures on the pier at all, even though Anna had jumped and shouted and clapped her hands in excitement. She would just have to take her word for it. Maybe Thierry was half-blind too. That might be useful. She tried to stare out of the ferry, now rapidly emptying, but it was hard to focus in the bright sunshine.

Richard was crouching next to her suddenly. He made a slight noise getting down there.

Richard was face to face with her now. That was one good thing about her eyesight, she thought. He didn't look massively different to her now than he had at school, his tufty hair, his thick glasses. She smiled. He didn't smile back. He took her hand.

"This is as far as I go," he said quietly.

She nodded her head. She understood. "Thank you," she said from the bottom of her heart.

He shook his head. "Oh, it was nothing."

She was cross he didn't understand what she was saying.

"No," she said. "Thank you. Thank you for everything. Thank you for making me go to teacher's college, and for taking me away from the Reverend, and for marrying me even though you knew I didn't really... And for the wonderful boys, and for making me secure."

"I'd rather have made you happy," said Richard, tears glistening in his eyes suddenly. She hadn't seen him cry since that awful night so long ago when he'd confessed his affair.

She shook her head.

"I don't... I think I was too stupid to realize it. But I think I was happy. Silly, daft, head full of nonsense..."

They both looked out on the French shoreline and smiled quickly at each other, a smile of long understanding. Seeing the beach, she had a sudden memory... The boys must have been very little and they were on a huge beach, first thing, almost no one else around except some dog-walkers, but Ian had always been up at the crack of dawn, even on holiday. The boys had been in their bathing costumes already and they had charged headlong into the water, then squealed like tiny baby pigs when they realized how freezing the surf was. And instead of laughing at them or ignoring them, Richard had seen their predicament and gone tearing in too, straight into the perishing ocean waters, picking up a boy under each arm and throwing them all around until they'd gotten used to the water and could splash at each other and laugh and laugh and laugh, until they came out, blue and chattering, and she had wrapped them all in towels and poured Richard hot coffee out of their Thermos, and he had declared it the best drink of his life.

How could she have forgotten all of that?

"But it has been a happy life. Full of happy things. It has. I just wish I had appreciated it more at the time..."

Richard pulled her tufted head into his shoulder, and she smelled a scent she hadn't smelled in years.

"Shh, my love. Shh," he said, stroking her scalp, and she real-ized then what he was really saying, and that it was good-bye, and she pressed her cheek against his, already marked with five o'clock shadow, and they stayed that way until the crewmen started to come up with apologetic looks on their faces. Anna was staring at them, she realized, with a worried look on her face too, but that didn't really matter now, and she clasped Richard's hand very tightly and said she would see him soon, and he grimaced and didn't reply. And one of the nice young sailors helped push out the chair down the ramp, and Anna pulled the wheely suitcase behind them. She tried to turn her head but her neck was so stiff, and the sun was so bright she didn't think she could have looked into the dark of the great ship at any rate, and she knew Richard. He wouldn't have waited; he wasn't that kind of man. And then they were being whisked through passport control, and Anna had taken control of the wheelchair, and there were two fig-ures waiting, right at the edge of the dock house, and her heart started to pound faster than she knew her oncologist would have liked.

• • • •

Claire was quite wrong about Richard. He stayed watching until they were two invisible dots disappearing behind the barbed wire gates of the ferry terminal. He watched as all the happy, burned holidaymak-ers filed back onto the ferry. He watched as they cast the lines and the great ship revved itself up again, and he stayed watching up on deck as the coast of France retreated farther and farther behind him into the darkness of the oncoming night.

Then he drove home through the rainy night, arrived in at two o'clock in the morning, smiled when he saw the roast beef and mustard sandwiches Anne-Marie had made and left out for him, then sat in his front room and got drunk for one of the very few times in his life.

25

At first, Claire thought with a terrible start that Thierry was standing right in front of her. He was exactly the same; the thick curly hair, the twinkling eyes. No mustache though, but...

Then she realized that this must be Laurent, whom Anna had told her about. He was incredibly attractive. She wanted to look at Anna and see her face, but she knew, she knew...she must look at the person sitting straight opposite her. She focused.

She tried not to wince. It was Thierry, of course it was, but he looked...he looked so unwell. She knew this was ironic under the circumstances, but even so. His face was gray. He had an oxygen cylinder set up nearby. His skin looked rumpled and ill-fitting, a result of massive recent weight loss.

But the mustache was still there, and under the heavy brows, his black eyes were the same...

He gazed and gazed at her for a long time, equally, Claire realized with a sinking heart, horrified at what they had both become. Was forty years really so much? Reaching out, she clasped Anna's hand, hard.

All of a sudden, Thierry burst out laughing. In that instant, Claire saw immediately the flashing eyes, the infectious noise of it, and smiled too. It was impossible not to.

"Look at us!" he shouted. "Look at us! We are the very last donkeys in the knacker yard, Claire! The worst!"

With great difficulty, and his son giving him his arm with a dubious-looking expression, he stood up on slightly wobbly legs. He was wearing, Claire noticed, smart pale linen trousers and a light pink shirt. Always stylish.

Not to be outdone, she gave Anna her arm and wobbled to her feet. She went to him, and he took her in his arms.

"My little bird," he exclaimed, "you are even smaller than you were!"

"You aren't," said Claire, her voice muffled in his shirt. He started to feel a bit wobbly so they drew back a little. Suddenly Claire felt the pressure on her arm relieved a little. She turned to see Anna rush toward Laurent, throw her arms around his neck, and kiss him.

Thierry looked at her, raising the eyebrow she knew so well.

"Aha, life goes on," he said in his booming voice, and Claire was so startled and pleased she laughed and sat down in her chair with a thump.

●　●　●　●

I couldn't help it. Not when I saw him. I thought he was being petulant with his father, difficult. I had underestimated him, not understanding that of course he would do it, could change and shift all his plans, deal with Alice—God, Alice, I would worry about her later—and the fearsome French doctors. And his father. It was basically a kidnap. I was truly overwhelmed. And emotional too, I told myself afterward. I couldn't even believe Richard and Claire had bothered getting divorced. If I had a nice-looking decent man who looked after me like that... Well, I didn't, so there was no point in thinking like that.

Apart from that, Laurent's handsome face, that full, biteable mouth, that mop of curly hair; I had to own up to myself. He wasn't Sami's little concept of a fling. He wasn't a holiday romance, a story to laugh about with Cath down at Faces. He gave me a look, a half-smile that said, as clear as a letter would have done, that he was sorry, and that this was his make-up offering…and in that instant, in the sunshine, I forgot all about Claire and Thierry, forgot all about anything except how much I wanted to kiss him.

When I finally came to my senses and stood back, pink and a little breathless, he gave me that broad smile.

"Well," he said, "I am pleased to see you too."

Then I cuddled Thierry and told him to cover his neck in the sun and asked him how it was to see Claire again, and he beamed and said she is still beautiful. Claire blushed like a girl and said no, she wasn't, and Thierry said well, she was doing better than him, and Claire laughed and said, yes, yes she was. I asked Thierry if Laurent had kidnapped him, and he sniffed and said yes and that we must stay out of the way of the police, and Laurent looked a bit awkward.

Then I suggested if we were going to get back to Paris tonight, we would probably have to get a move on—the sun was setting—but Thierry pshawed that idea and said, well of course, we had to eat first, and he knew just the place, and I laughed that both Thierry and Laurent were utterly horrified at the idea of missing dinner.

Calais wasn't very glamorous, full of hypermarkets selling cheap cigarettes and booze and travelers' hotels that offered cheap weekly rates, but Laurent took over the wheel of the white Le Chapeau Chocolat van and put Thierry and Claire carefully on the front bench seat (I rode perched in the back) and spun us off the autoroute and into a network of country roads and flat green fields until we arrived at a tiny farmhouse that barely seemed to be a restaurant at all.

Laurent marched in confidently and a fat man came out, muttering, with a harsh northern accent I found difficult to understand, but I quickly realized that Laurent had basically pulled a "don't you know who I am" on him and was insisting that they feed the famous chocolatier, the way they might have behaved for a footballer or a rock star in England. When Laurent lifted Claire down, she made a little "oh" sound, as if she recognized it.

The man fussed and worried around his elderly visitors. I was worried about Claire; she seemed so frail and she'd hardly eaten all day. But in the tiny restaurant, which was absolutely full—the waiter had pulled up and washed down fresh tables and chairs himself and put us outside under a shady chestnut tree—I ordered her a beautiful lobster bisque and took off her shoes so she could let her bare feet touch the grass. The meadow nearest us had cows wandering back from pasture, the grass full of the poppies unavoidable in northern France and Belgium, bees humming wistfully around us, reminding us that autumn was just around the corner. Thierry ordered snails and seemed on the point of ordering a second starter, but Laurent gave him a very sharp look, and he didn't and had the fish instead. Everyone had one small medicinal glass of red wine, and at first conversation was difficult... Where did you begin after forty years? But Claire did her best with her soup—I had it too, utterly sensational, followed by a side of bream I would never have dared order just a few months ago, with locally harvested mushrooms. I wasn't surprised this place was so busy.

"So," said Claire, finally putting down her spoon. "Where did you go? You must have realized I wasn't getting your letters."

Thierry stopped mopping up the garlicky butter of his snails. Alice was going to have her work cut out with this one.

"*Algerie*," he said, as if it was the most obvious thing in the world.

"Algeria? What happened? Did you get called up?"

"Of course I got called up," said Thierry crossly. "Everyone got called up."

Claire's hand went to her mouth. "Military service?"

"But of course."

"But I thought military service was just marching up and down and having fun."

"There was an insurgency," said Thierry. "Didn't they report it in your papers?"

Claire had spent that entire year mooning about and focusing entirely on herself. Of course she hadn't read the papers. "I didn't realize," she said.

"I had the papers in my pocket when I waved you off," said Thierry.

"We came here on the way," said Claire faintly, playing with the grass with her toes.

"Yes, we did."

"You made me try the hake."

"I'll make you try it again in a minute."

She smiled, weakly. "But…letters…"

"Mme. LeGuarde took in my post. She did not forward me to you?"

Claire's hand flew to her mouth. She remembered the elegant woman again. *"I hope you will take your good memories, Claire."*

"I thought it was my *dad*," she said.

"I thought you had gone back to England…got married…had children."

Suddenly everyone looked at Laurent, furiously doing arithmetic. Laurent muttered under his breath and excused himself from the table.

I was worried about Claire getting overtired and agitated. I'd much rather she was asleep in bed right now, but she was a determined so-and-so.

"Oh," said Claire quietly.

"*Oui*," said Thierry.

I nearly swore out loud. No wonder Laurent was so cross with his father…and his skin so olive.

"I did… I could not stay," said Thierry. "I was a soldier. Then I was not a soldier. And I was so young, and I had a business to run."

We were both looking at him. I felt for both of them, so young, and a local girl, pregnant and shamed…

"But I sent for him," said Thierry quickly.

"You did not send for me," said Claire, softly and sadly, nodding to herself.

"Has he forgiven you for that?" I added.

"I don't think so," said Thierry.

Thierry was suddenly interrupted. The proprietor had come over. The second course plates had been cleared away and coffee and eau de vie had appeared from nowhere. I tried to explain that we hadn't ordered them when the little man put down a plate, full of Chapeau chocolates.

We all gasped, amazed.

"Where did you get these?" said Thierry. The cost of sending away for them was astronomical, Alice saw to that, and Thierry hated fulfilling private orders. He preferred everything to get chomped on the day. To keep longer, they needed less cream and a touch of preservative, which he hated using.

"I keep them," said the man, "for my most special customers. Which you undoubtedly are."

And then he insisted on getting his photograph taken with Thierry, and then some other customers came to have a look at what was going on and, when they realized who it was, were also effusive in his compliments until the proprietor had to open the entire box and Thierry had to promise to send him another one and sign the photograph.

When the hubbub finally died down, Thierry turned his kind, ruined face to Claire.

"*Chocolat*," he said. "It's all I'm good for, really. You see what I am saying?"

Claire nodded and moved a hand to his arm.

"You," she said softly. "It's you I was only ever good for. It didn't do me a lot of favors either."

Thierry put his huge hand on her tiny bruised one and held it there, as the crickets started to make noise into the night and the huge bright stars overhead popped out, one by one.

• • • •

I crept off to find Laurent. He was finishing up a slim black cigarillo by the trees. They were loud with insects.

"Sorry," he said when he saw me. "Filthy habit. Very rare."

"I don't mind," I said, and I didn't really. The smoke smelled exotic on the warm summer evening. "I quite like it."

There was a silence.

"So now you know," he said.

"He was very young," I said.

"So was my mother," said Laurent. He glanced back toward the table. "Claire," he said. "She is very, very sick."

I jumped, guilty at being away.

"She is," I said. "I'd better go check on her."

Gently Laurent ran his hand down my face. "You like to fix things?" he said softly. "Can you fix me, AnNA Tron?"

26

I would have put us up for the night, but Thierry had promised to come home, and Laurent was anxious to be off. I was more concerned about Claire. Her breath sounded thready and ragged, and she had had a very long day. Thierry was exhausted too. Laurent and I exchanged worried glances as we got into the van, propping them up as best we could against each other. Claire helped herself to another dose of the morphine, which I watched surreptitiously, trying to figure out how much was too much, before shaking my head at the craziness of it all. As Laurent barreled down the road at top speed, Thierry and Claire leaned against one another, lolling against their seat belts, her head nestling under his arm as if they'd slept that way every night for forty years.

We didn't speak. I felt as if anything I might say would be wrong. Laurent drove furiously fast, all his concentration on the road. I looked at him, wondering why he still couldn't talk to his father. But I put that out of my head.

Instead, I would just try to enjoy the very fact that they came for us; Claire's look on the dockside; the kiss we had shared once more. I touched my mouth briefly. He was a very good kisser. Those lips. But why hadn't I noticed… He probably, I realized, had a strange accent I simply hadn't picked up on because my French wasn't good enough, like Americans being completely unable to distinguish between Scottish people and Irish people. Sami, now I came to think of it, probably spoke very differently too. How odd I had simply never noticed, lumping everything I had come across in Paris as simply terribly foreign, without considering how foreign, exactly.

I watched his head of shining black curls in the dim light from the dashboard as we sped along the dark motorway, incredibly fast. He was focusing entirely on driving and I felt myself in such safe hands that I, too, must have drifted off to sleep.

The suburban lights of Paris woke me up as they flitted against the windscreen and I stretched uncomfortably. I had put Claire up in a very nice hotel not far from the apartment, and we practically lifted her into it. I made sure she was settled and breathing but she barely stirred. I would have to stay. The room was small, and I sat down on a chair by her side. She tilted her head.

"It's all right," she breathed.

I patted her hand. "It is," I said. "Everything's going to be all right."

With difficulty, she shook her head. "No," she said, "you don't have to stay. You've done enough. Go get some sleep."

"No chance," I said.

She smiled. "Oh, for goodness' sake, Anna. I promise not to die tonight. Is that enough? Now do what your teacher says and go and get some rest. I have a lot I want to do in the next few days, and it won't help if you're buzzing over me like an annoying bee."

"I'm not an annoying bee," I said.

"Shoo!"

I stood, hovering, not quite sure what to do, until I heard her breathing slow into sleep, and it sounded better, like normal sleep. I looked at her for a while until I heard the faintest of voices say, "Stop staring at me," and then I backed out of the room. I'd come back first thing.

● ● ● ●

Outside the shop, in the middle of the road, Alice was waiting, look-ing absolutely and completely furious, and Laurent and I hopped out of the van, both bone-tired, and she strode in without a word to either of us, fired up the engine, and disappeared.

"She'll get over it," muttered Laurent.

"Did you *steal* the van?"

"I sent her a text."

"Hmm."

I wandered over the deserted cobbles around the corner. Up in our tiny apartment, I could see lights flashing. Oh God, Sami must be having a party. Of all the things I didn't feel like, that was definitely right at the top of my list. My face fell.

"Well, good night then," I said to Laurent, wondering if I might manage to sleep through it anyway.

"Good night," he said, made to walk away, then suddenly stopped himself. The street was in total silence, apart from some calypso music I guessed was coming from the flat.

"No," he said, almost to himself, then strode back toward me. "No, no, no, no, no." He took me in his arms and kissed me again, deeply and thoroughly, until I felt, like magic, my tiredness evaporate and a heady, sensual longing overtake my limbs.

"Come back with me," he said. "Please. I don't want to be alone tonight. Come with me."

"I have to be back," I said, half laughing. It was stupidly late. "I have to check on Claire, and I have to open up tomorrow."

"Well, there's no point sleeping now," he teased in a challenging tone. This was more like the Laurent I knew. I found myself blushing.

• • • •

I couldn't help thinking the last people to see me naked had been about one hundred and fifty student doctors, a score of agency nurses, my mum and, on one awkward occasion during my convalescence, my dad. But it had been a long time for me.

"Hop on," said Laurent, firing up the scooter.

● ● ● ●

This journey felt different from the first time he had taken me home, when I had been so lost and confused. It went quickly, as we flashed past the holidaymakers drinking in the Place des Vosges, the lights of the great hotels on the Place de la Concorde making them as brilliant as ocean liners in the night, snatches of orchestral music issuing from their windows open against the warmth of an evening. I snuggled in close to him and smelled him through his heavy shirt, the warm heavy scent of him. It was better than any perfume I'd ever known. We headed north, once more, back to Montmartre where we'd first met, the great thoroughfares thinning out as the road became quieter and narrower until finally the scooter was bumping over cobbles and I had to hold on just to avoid losing my balance on the corners I now knew to lean over for.

My heart now was thumping hard, and the feel of him filled all my senses as we charged on through the night. Occasionally he would take his hands off the handlebars to caress my knee in a reassuring way, and each time he did so, I felt a thrill go through me. I tried not to panic. It was only sex. I used to do it all the time. Okay, I used to do it after I'd drunk a few shandies and pulled Darr again, but that was different. Now, although we'd had a couple of glasses of wine, I was stone-cold sober, certainly more sober than I'd ever wanted to be before I slept with someone for the first time, especially someone I fancied as much as Laurent. My brain was in a turmoil; I barely saw the fun fair we passed, lit up still, and the rows of hanging lights between the old-fashioned lampposts.

If Laurent knew what was going through my mind, he didn't mention it. We drew up in a tiny little back street that wasn't a thoroughfare at all, but rather a little three-sided place situated around a little bench. The buildings weren't the traditionally grand arrondissement apartments; they were older and made of gray stones, which matched the color of the cobbles beneath them. They looked like they had been transplanted from some other part of France altogether. Many of the buildings had ivy growing up them, with balconies only on the top floor. He led me to one of these, a large door, painted bright red, slap bang in the middle of it.

"This isn't an apartment," I said, suspicious. "Where are we?"

He looked a bit awkward and pulled out a large set of old keys.

"I never have anyone here," he said. "Well, welcome, I suppose, my shy English *mademoiselle*."

Then he winked at me to show me he wasn't really that nervous, turned the old-fashioned door handle, and waved me inside.

• • • •

I gasped when I stepped inside, into a formal hallway opening into a huge reception room with paneling that wouldn't have looked out of place at Hampton Court. A large, abstract candelabra with random candles dotted in it added to the illusion. The room was at the back of the house, away from the little square, and the entire back of the wall was glass. Outside was a spot-lit garden on several different levels, immaculately raked in squares and rows of herbs and vegetables, with gravel paths running between them. Looking through the glass, I could see to the right another glass wall which obviously housed the kitchen, a shining stainless steel affair, very professional-looking.

"*Wow!*" I said, unable to say anything else. From the hallway back, there were floating steps leading upstairs, presumably to the other levels. Bookshelves lined one side of the huge paneled room, and on another was an enormous fireplace, currently with a large glass bowl of limes sitting in the unused hearth.

"Why do you never come here?" I said, my voice echoing in the room. "If I lived here, I would never ever leave it, ever."

Laurent looked a bit shame-faced. "Mm-hmm," he said. "It's...it's my thing."

"What do you mean? You drive a really rackety old scooter."

"I know... I don't spend much money really. So it all goes on the house."

I glanced at him, a half-smile playing on my lips. "Your dad didn't buy it for you?"

He looked fierce. "As if I'd take a penny."

"Well, it's lovely."

"Would you take a house from your parents?"

I thought about it. "I can't imagine anything making my dad happier than being able to buy me a house."

Laurent winced. "He did offer..."

"Aha!" I said in triumph. "So he's not totally evil?"

"I was so proud," he said, miles away, staring out at the little garden. "I wanted to show him I could do it as well...do it better."

I patted him on the shoulder. "You're going to hate me for saying this," I said. "Are you quite alike?"

Laurent half-smiled and shook off my hand as we headed into the kitchen. Unusually in my experience for a man's fridge, it was full of butter and cheese and eggs and vegetables. I was impressed and made a mental note never to invite him around to dinner at Sami's. He pulled out a bottle of champagne. I perked up immediately. I *knew* we hadn't had enough to drink to do any shagging yet.

"When my dad moved to Paris from Lot-et-Garonne, he lived in a single room in an attic with no hot water or heating," said Laurent. "He slept in every item of clothing he had in the wintertime. And he worked his way up. I've heard the story a million times...normally from Alice." He snorted.

"So of course, you had to do the same?"

He nodded. Then he grinned. "Do I sound like an idiot?"

I shrugged. "It is," I said, "a very nice house."

His face lit up. "Thank you!"

Standing there, lit by the fridge, which was still open, and the spot-lights in the garden highlighting the curls in his hair and the shadow of his long eyelashes against his cheeks, I thought he was the most gorgeous thing I'd ever seen in my life.

I moved forward and kissed him, and he kissed me back, with none of the amused nonchalance he'd shown before, but with a total, committed fervor. It was fierce and it was fantastic.

"Now can we stop talking about your dad?" I said, when we finally came up for air.

He put the champagne bottle down on the side of the counter. "I will sweep you upstairs," he said, grabbing me under the arms.

My eyes strayed to the bottle he'd put down.

"Oh, my little English girl," he laughed. "Do you think you need to get drunk to enjoy yourself with me?"

I wriggled, red in the face. "Not drunk exactly," I muttered. "But a bit of Dutch courage wouldn't go amiss."

Laurent took my hands in his strong grip and stared into my eyes intently.

"You, my gorgeous Anna, are going to come upstairs with me. And we are going to make love, if that is what you want, and you will be perfectly sober, and you will enjoy every second. *Oui ou non?*"

Oh Lord.

● ● ● ●

The sun was coming up. It shone through the pale gauzy curtains where I lay trapped in Laurent's arms. He was asleep, but I was not and felt that light, dreamy way when you're not sure what is real and what's a dream. I turned and kissed his hair. He had, in the end, lightly caressed my toes. He had lightly caressed every bit of me. Then we had become less gentle. A lot less gentle.

"Oh, Anna," he said from his snoozing form.

"I have to go," I whispered.

"Don't." A huge hairy arm came and trapped me.

"I have to," I said. "I have to work."

"Oh Christ," he said, shooting bolt upright and searching for his watch. "So do I. I said I'd take the early shift."

"Surely not this early?"

"You've never worked in a hotel, have you?"

"No," I admitted. He smiled at me and kissed me.

"You are even more luscious in the morning," he said. "Oh, my love. Stay a while."

"I thought you were going to work?" I said. "Anyway, no. I'm worried about Claire. I shouldn't even have left last night."

"She was happy and sleeping," argued Laurent. "Anyway," he smiled, "didn't you enjoy what we did instead?"

I smiled back, feeling myself flush again. He cupped his hand to my cheek. "I like it when you turn red," he said.

"Shut up," I said.

I grabbed my clothes—it felt odd to think I had put them on in Kidinsborough; I desperately needed a bath—and went to leave. I didn't want to. I felt like I was coasting along on a sea of happiness.

"Oh God, I don't know how I'm going to open the shop today," I giggled. "It'll be worse than normal."

"Just concentrate. You'll be fine."

"Okay," I said. I looked at him. "One thing you haven't told me about," I said.

"There are a million things I haven't told you about," he said, smiling. "Now I think we will have the time to get to know each other."

I smiled. "Yes, please. But, Laurent, what about your mum? Wouldn't she like to know about Thierry? Wouldn't she like to see him?"

I knew the second it came out of my mouth what a dreadful mistake I had made; the shutters dropped down almost immediately.

"I'm sorry," I whispered. "Another time?"

"This is…"

I thought of the Laurent I'd seen around town, handsome, charming, keeping everything light.

"Am I moving too fast?" I said. He said immediately *non, non, non*, but I left anyway. After I let myself out, when I passed his scooter, I wanted to kick it.

27

Claire was dreaming. She was dreaming she was in Paris and the light reflecting off the rocks onto her face was the one that only came when she was there. She felt lighter than air; in her dreams, she could move as freely as she liked. Why had she thought she was sick? She wasn't sick at all, she was fine; the doctors had gotten it all wrong. Silly doctors, she was so fine she could fly, look.

Suddenly, even in her dream, she realized that of course, she couldn't fly, and little by little she started to float, her disappointment as bitter as ashes in her mouth, to the surface, still caught, still trapped in her body riddled with blackness, useless and shaming. All her mornings felt like this; beached from morning dreams into the harshness of another daily struggle through reality.

She blinked twice. One thing was different though. It was that rock. It was that light. With a burst of pure happiness, she remembered. She was in Paris. They had made it. She was here.

There was a knock at the door, and Anna entered, carrying two small cups of coffee she'd brought up from the lobby and a bag of fresh, flaky, still-warm croissants between her teeth. She did a smiling grimace—she looked exhausted, Claire noted, but rather well—and went over to the window where she pulled open the thick curtain to reveal a window box filled with white roses and a view all the way to the Eiffel Tower. It was enchanting.

"Not bad, eh?" said Anna, putting the coffee down and kissing her on the cheek. "Good morning. How are you feeling?"

Claire shrugged.

"Actually," she said, sounding surprised, "I didn't have a bad night."

Normally she woke three or four times, often feeling as if she would choke.

Anna helped her to the toilet and to get dressed, then apologized for the hour and disappeared to open up the shop. Claire watched her go with a smile on her face. She was dedicated that girl. She'd been right about her. She'd do well.

Then she sat back with the complimentary copy of *Paris Match* by the window Anna had opened and listened, for the first time in forty years, to the noises of Paris waking itself up, as she sipped the strong sweet coffee and nibbled at the croissant and felt the sun warm her aching bones.

● ● ● ●

I was earlier than Frédéric or Benoît this morning, which was a first. Mind you, they'd probably gotten some sleep, which was better going than me. I hovered around on my own—Frédéric had the keys—wishing I had something to do with my hands, like smoke.

The van pulled up first. My heart sank and I cursed. Now I was going to have to deal with Alice all by myself.

She was alone and almost fell out of the driver's seat. For once, her face wasn't immaculately painted. She was wearing yesterday's clothes, and her hair was scraped back in a ponytail. She looked nothing like herself at all. I barely recognized her.

"Alice?" I said.

She looked up at me. Yesterday's mascara was running down her face. She was in a terrible state.

"Are you all right?" I asked in alarm.

"No-o-o," she said in a long shudder, launching herself across the cobbles and sitting down on the step. Then she burst into huge sobs.

"What's the matter?" I said, fear gripping me. "Is Thierry all right? Was the trip too much for him?"

Unable to speak, she shook her head.

"No, it's not that... He's better," she said bitterly, almost spitting the words out. She looked up at me in undisguised hatred.

"How can you...how can you take him away from me?" she said, then burst into fresh floods of tears.

"What do you mean?" I said, genuinely confused. She couldn't be talking about Laurent, could she? No, surely not. No, that would be absurd. Nonetheless, I found a blush covering my face. My face. Oh God, that stupid arsehole. I hated the effect he had on me.

"My Thierry," she said, as if I was a total idiot. "You take *my* man, *my* partner, and you behave as if I don't even bloody exist, and you set him up with some fantasy from his past... I mean, how the *fuck* am I supposed to compete with that?"

She sounded funny in English, not nearly so posh, more Essex if anything. She rubbed fiercely at her eyes.

"Well, thanks very fucking much. I'm only the one that's kept everything going, kept the books, kept the suppliers happy, kept everyone away from him so he could concentrate on doing what he does best...and this is the thanks I get."

I blinked several times. It was true; she was completely right. I hadn't given her feelings a second thought, except to try to stay out of her way. But of course I wasn't trying to usurp her. I was trying to help someone else. I didn't know how to explain it.

"I'm sorry," I said, unsure whether this would work or not. "That's not what I meant..." I knelt down. "You know how ill she is?"

She glanced up. "Thierry said she was sick, but he's so happy to see her, he's like a little boy. He's spent the last week doing his physiotherapy exercises, after he'd told his doctor he absolutely wouldn't do them. He's been eating veg and making plans and...I haven't seen him so alive in a long time." She looked up at me. "He's going to leave me."

"Of course he's not going to leave you," I said, thinking privately that if he ever was, her genuine bad temper would have driven him away a long time ago.

"Listen to me," I said, sitting down next to her on the curb. "You know and I know that Thierry is an optimist, yes?"

She laughed a tiny bit. "You could say that."

"Doesn't really like facing life's difficulties."

"He does not," she said. "Like his own blasted belly."

I smiled at that too. "You have to know," I said, "Claire is really sick. Really, really sick. She shouldn't be here. She should be in a hospital."

The reality hit me.

"No," I said slowly. Claire hadn't said anything; the true state of her health was between her and her doctor. But gradually I realized what I was saying was true, took in the full enormity of it.

"No," I repeated. "She shouldn't be in a hospital. She should be in a hospice."

I looked at Alice to make sure she realized the importance of what I was saying, although it was for myself as much as her. "Alice, coming here…this is the last thing Claire is ever going to do. Do you realize that? She's going to go back to the UK, and then…"

I hated to say it and bit my lip.

"And then she is going to die," I said.

Alice's eyes went wide.

"Really?"

"Yes," I said.

"Oh God," said Alice. "Oh God."

She fell silent, obviously thinking about how recently she had nearly lost Thierry.

"He never told me," she said.

"He may not know. She's keeping it quiet," I said.

"Even if he did, he would pretend it wasn't happening," said Alice and we both smiled.

We sat a while longer, watching Benoît lump up over the arch of the street.

"So," I said eventually.

"So just let them get on with it," she said ungracefully. "Is that what you want me to say? Butt out, Alice?"

I thought about it. "Yes," I said. "But not for long. He is yours, I think. Don't you?"

She half-smiled. "I doubt anyone else would put up with him."

I smiled at that as she headed back to the van.

"That goes double for his son by the way," she shouted, but I pretended not to hear her.

Frédéric arrived too, kicking away his cigarette and petting Nelson Eddy the dog.

"Good day," he said. "Ready for a full day's work?"

I watched as the grille rattled up. "Sure," I said.

28

By 8:00 a.m., I was completely hazy with tiredness, and we'd already had to throw away two full trays of milk chocolate oranges because I'd overcreamed them and they tasted like chocolate yogurt. Benoît was muttering, and Frédéric was looking very agitated and asking me what Alice had said, which of course I didn't repeat. For some reason, I had promised to gen up on hazelnuts over the holiday. Of course I'd done nothing of the sort, but with *le tout Paris* aware that we were reopening today, it was a bit too late to start. I halfheartedly started roasting the nuts, Frédéric coming fussily over my shoulder to pull out the green ones. Then I turned around too quickly when he startled me and knocked the second copper vat so it sputtered and started spitting out chocolate all over the floor, which I then skidded in and got a flashback so quickly I burst into tears. Frédéric did his best to be sympathetic, but I could tell it was only making him more agitated, and Benoît muttered something to himself along the lines of how he'd never had a woman in the kitchen before and this was absolutely why, when suddenly I heard a noise on the roof of the greenhouse.

Nobody could get back there without going through the shop. All three of us jumped. Someone was crouching on the roof! The shadow was plain above us, an ominous mass above our heads.

"*Merde*," said Frédéric, jumping back to the sink and grabbing the huge knife we used to chop melon and pineapple.

"Who's there?" I shouted, my voice quivering. There was no

response. I was glad the boys were there. We moved toward the window. A large dark shape hung there, ominously, then it moved. Suddenly, with a slump and an enormous noise, it jumped down into the courtyard beyond. In a second, Benoît had opened the back door and we'd all piled out on top of the crouching figure.

"AARGH! ARGH! STOP IT! GERROF!" it shouted, and I realized it was Laurent.

"Stop it, stop it, everyone," I said, standing back.

"I can't believe you're attacking me again," said Laurent, shaking himself off.

"Try not breaking and entering into our workshop then," I said, breathless and annoyed. "What the hell were you doing up there?"

"Nobody would answer the front door. What the hell were you doing in here?"

Nobody grassed me up for my noisy boo-hooing, fortunately. Laurent looked at me, then glanced at the floor.

"Um," he said, "I'm sorry. I'm sorry, after last night. I clammed up. It was rude."

"I'm used to you being weird," I said unhappily.

"I know," he said. He sighed, then suddenly switched to English. "This is hard… I am trying, Anna."

"I'm trying to get done for assault and battery," I said, but the joke was lost on him.

"Frédéric, can you get us two coffees?" he said. Frédéric, amazingly, went and did it without complaining. Benoît, muttering, went back to mop up the workshop. I shivered a little; it was chilly out here in the little courtyard that got no sun. We accepted Frédéric's coffee with thanks. I glanced at the clock, a little worried.

"I grew up in Beirut," Laurent said slowly.

"Ooh no," I said sympathetically.

"Actually," he said, rather snippily, "Beirut is a beautiful place. Beaches, skiing, the food…oh, the food."

I stared ahead and decided to let him do all the talking.

"Dad was stationed there during the conflict. It… Life there was very hard." He lost his thread.

"Your mother?"

He shook his head. "Can you imagine how she was treated when her family found out she was pregnant by a French soldier?"

I shook my head. "No," I said.

"My grandmother used to steal around. In the middle of the night, you understand? In case anyone saw her? To bring us food."

"So they didn't…"

"Did he offer to marry her, you mean?" He shook his head. "Oh no, he had different ideas about this. He even told her about Claire."

I bit my lip. That seemed so thoughtless, even for him.

"What about when you came along?"

"He sent money," allowed Laurent. "And when I was seven, he brought us over. He'd met Alice by then."

"Was she kind to you?"

He snorted. "My mother was far more beautiful than she was. She was insecure from the get-go. Pretended I was some little slum boy who didn't exist."

"Why didn't they have children?" I wondered.

Laurent shrugged. "Because she's a witch?"

"She's all right," I said. I was learning more and more about how difficult it must have been to hold on to this strong-willed, selfish man.

"What was it like?" I asked.

"Paris? Amazing," said Laurent. "Oh my goodness, it was so clean and airy and cool! The huge houses and the streets…and no one looked twice at my mother, once she took her headscarf off! It was like she was free again, not like Dahiyeh, when everyone knew about her shame."

"She sounds amazing," I said.

He nodded sharply. "She was. She did a fucking good job on her own."

"Did you want to stay?"

"Mum couldn't. They weren't married. She couldn't just settle here. Anyway, even though being at home was pretty horrible, it was still home. Her mum was there."

"What did you think of Thierry?"

"When he was interested in me, it was great. To be the focus of his attention, you just felt you lit up his world. And he showed me all about his work and I was interested…very interested, you know."

I nodded.

"So he liked that, so I was his little funny dolly for a while. Then, you know, we'd go back and it was as if he'd forgotten all about us again."

"He's not a great letter writer," I said.

"Men like Thierry…" Laurent said. "They are the sun, yes? Everyone else just has to orbit behind. It is the same with any great chef, with conductors, with great tennis players. They are the light."

There wasn't, I thought, any bitterness in his voice. I looked up at him. It was as if he'd seen his father for what he was and accepted it. He caught sight of me.

"Have you been crying?"

I nodded.

"Did I make you cry?"

I nodded again, not trusting myself to speak.

"Oh *God*," he said. "I am the worst, most selfish man in the world. I don't want to be like him, Anna."

He grabbed me onto his lap and held me, close and tight, my head burrowed in his shoulder.

"I never want to make you cry again," he whispered in my ear. "Never again."

"Too late," I said, making a funny snortling noise and holding on to him like I would never let him go until he was kissing me again.

316

There was a stern knock on the window. Frédéric was looking anxious. Benoît, I was amazed to notice, appeared to be smiling.

"CUSTOMERS!" Frédéric was saying.

"YES!" said Laurent, leaping to his feet. "Let us cook!"

"Hang on," I said. "Just…your mum."

"Brain tumor," said Laurent shortly. "When I was fifteen. Dad paid all the hospital bills. Wanted her to come to Paris, but she didn't want to intrude. Then he brought me here, got me into an apprenticeship, set me cooking. It's been all I wanted to do ever since."

"But not in the way he wanted?"

"No," said Laurent. "He felt guilty, and I was fifteen and needed someone to blame. He offered to set me up in a house; he never did for Mum. She lived in that crappy apartment block all her life."

"That's why you wouldn't take his money?"

There was a long pause.

"You know," I said, "I bet you didn't ruin her life. I bet you made her very happy."

"That's what she said," said Laurent. "Doesn't stop me hating fucking hospitals though. But I think I've just about forgiven Dad."

He held me by my hips and looked straight at me.

"I don't know what it is about you, Anna Tron," he said. "You seem to make me calm and happy when you're about and miserable when you're not. I don't know what that is."

I fumbled. I was thirty years old and I had said the words, but never in a way that I meant as truly and as sincerely as I did now; not to Darr, God bless his spotty soul.

"It's because I love you," I said. I wouldn't have, normally, said it first, but oh, I was so exhausted, punch-drunk, emotional. And, I realized, I loved him so very terribly much, even when he was petulant, even when he was grumpy, even when he was teasing me. I thought I might very much have been in love with him from the second he'd given me a lift on his scooter.

"Oh," said Laurent, his mouth opening. "Yes. Yes, that must be it. I must love you. We must be in love. Of course. Of COURSE!" He comically banged his hand on his head. "I can't believe I didn't think of it."

And he gathered me up into himself as Frédéric banged "CUSTOMERS!!!" repeatedly on the windows of the greenhouse, and Laurent only stopped kissing me for long enough to shout "But we are IN LOVE!" back at him.

And then I realized something else. It was like someone turning off a radio I hadn't even realized was still playing. Suddenly, the itching, the fuss, the pain, the twinges, all the sense in my missing toes that weren't really there simply vanished. And I felt completely whole.

• • • •

Thierry was fastening his tie in the mirror. For the first time in a very long time, he seemed to have space in the collar. Alice came up behind him and smoothed down the shoulders.

"Ah, don't fuss me."

"No," she said and looked away. "I shan't fuss you."

He looked at her. He had slept so well and woken up feeling better than he had in years. He found it annoying on a very deep level that less wine and pastis was making him feel this much better.

"Alice," he said, his voice softening. "You know in my life I have loved three women. One of them is dead, one of them is dying, and one of them is you. So please, do not be cross with me today."

Alice came back up behind him and ran her hands through his still thick hair. She burrowed her face in it.

"I can't lose you," she said.

"You won't," said Thierry. "You won't. I promise."

He twisted himself around, carefully, to face her. She could see the scar, still angry-looking, through his unbuttoned shirt.

"I have done so many… Well, no. I have not done many things in my life. I have made chocolate and thought that that was enough."

Alice blinked hard.

"I have not looked after my toys like a good boy," he said, smiling ruefully. "Can I make it up to you now?"

Alice thought of the years she had spent loving him, even when he was old and fat, even when she had shelved her plans for children, knowing they were too busy, seeing how he was with his own little boy, who hero-worshipped him so painfully. Some people always sacrificed more, she knew.

"Yes," she said, kissing his head.

"But I must also…"

"Do this. Yes. I know."

She drove him to the hotel as he requested, to see the woman he had never forgotten, the slender Englishwoman who had shaped his taste so very much…but she did not stay.

● ● ● ●

I had seen him in the kitchens at his hotel, but not here. I knew my place; I sat at the back out of the way, my arms around myself, as if I was hugging a secret too good to hold. He knew his way around it, though; of course he did, probably better than anywhere—he'd played beneath it as a boy. He looked at the plants along the back walls as he set the vats churning in motion, husked faster than anyone I'd ever seen, doing the conch like an artist, his arms moving with the same graceful flow as his father's, taking yesterday's batch, adding cream and testing, taking it away. Then he went up to a high store cupboard and found what he was looking for: a large pepper grinder Benoît used sometimes to season his lunch when he brought it in. He seized it in triumph and bounded back down the stepladder, winking at me as he did so. Then he went to the lemon tree and stripped it completely of all its lemons. We'd never used them; Frédéric said they were only for nougatine. Laurent chopped them roughly, then stood over the churn, squeezing and tasting again.

"This is the only way," he said to me. Well, I suppose it was for him. I wouldn't know what I was tasting for. Until I learned, I supposed. He added more, then lifted the pepper grinder.

"M'sieur!" protested Benoît, but it was too late. He unleashed the ground black pepper directly into the chocolate mix.

"That," I stated, "looks like it's going to be disgusting."

"We will make a gourmet of you yet," said Laurent, grinning. He tasted a little more and made a face.

"Yes, you're right. It is disgusting. You have to balance. Without balance, it is just horrible. With balance, you can do anything."

He looked at me.

"When you lost your toes, could you balance?"

"No," I said.

"But now you can do anything, right? You compensated and made it better?"

I shrugged. "Yes, I suppose so."

"Well. Just like that. And I will hold up this chocolate just like I will hold you up."

"I'm not sure this metaphor is really hanging together," I said, smiling, but he hushed me and kept on working feverishly.

Finally, he tried one last time, then immediately stopped the paddles from turning.

I opened my mouth obediently.

"That's what I like to see," said Laurent, then let a drop cool and rest on my tongue.

I'd expected it to be awful, just weird, but it wasn't. The depths of the chocolate base were deepened by the pepper, giving it a dark edge, but then shot through with a sublime light sharpness. It was clean, delicious, and utterly moreish.

"Oh my God," I said. "I have to eat more of that."

"Yes!" said Laurent. "That's right." He tried some himself. "Yes, exactly. Perfect. I am a genius."

"Can you teach me how to make it?"

He looked me up and down. "Two months ago, I would have said no. Now, I think you can do anything."

Frédéric interrupted us kissing to say that there was going to be a riot in the queue lining up outside and did we want him just to call the Bastille now? Everyone left in Paris knew that we reopened today and there was a rumor that Thierry was on the mend and would be here too—I knew the hotel was going to call a taxi for Claire and Thierry, but I wasn't sure when. I felt a momentary stab of concern, before remembering Claire chiding me to get on with things. They would be all right.

Frédéric set the chocolate in the freezer double quick and started slicing, as Laurent twirled off to start another batch of mint and bitterest aniseed. I started to clean up, then out of interest, went to see what happened when the lemon went on sale.

The first person to try some was M. Beausier, one of our regulars. He was small and slight, considering the amount of our chocolate he put away. Perhaps it was his staple diet. He took one bite and his eyes popped open.

"*Mon Dieu*," he said. "Is Thierry back in the kitchen?"

Excitedly he turned around to the queue and started handing out little squares for people to taste.

"Try this, try this," he was saying excitedly. "I must have some more!" he called over to Frédéric, who raised his eyebrows and sighed in a dramatic way. The people in the crowd who'd tried it started muttering excitedly and placing large orders.

"I think you'd better make some more," I said, coming back to Laurent. "They're going to start a stampede out there."

He straightened up. His face looked nervous and exhilarated at once.

"What do you mean? They're hating it?"

"Nooo," I said. "They're loving it."

"Really?"

"Of course really! Come on, my love, you know you can cook."

"But in my father's kitchen…" he muttered, pushing his hair out of his eyes.

"Yes," I said. "In your father's kitchen. You are also wonderful."

He smiled, and I felt in that instant both immense love for him and a sudden immense rush of love for my own lovely father, who would love me no matter what, whatever I did and how. He wasn't famous or a brilliant genius or world-renowned. Except to me.

"Now, get on with it," I said, but Laurent couldn't; he had to come and see for himself. The crowd was standing around in the shop, unable to disperse, telling each other how amazing it was. And of course because there were lots of people, other people had come up behind to see what was going on and were watching and adding themselves to the queue, and the entire stock had nearly sold out.

M. Beausier, who had known Thierry a long time, gasped when he saw Laurent. But everyone else's attention was diverted by a long car pulling up outside.

• • • •

Thierry seemed stronger already than when she saw him yesterday, Claire thought, as she said "come in" to the soft knock at the door. He was very smartly dressed and carrying a large bunch of flowers. This would be how it would be, she supposed. He would get better and better and recover as she got worse and worse. She had had a very bad coughing fit in the bathroom that morning that, she knew, would have made her oncologist order her straight back to the hospital. For a moment, she nearly weakened, thinking suddenly how nice it would be to call an ambulance and let the professionals take over, slip into a drugged sleep, and let them clear her lungs and drain what they needed to drain to make her more comfortable...

But she knew, more than anything, that the next time she went into the hospital, she wasn't sure whether she would be coming out again. She had one chance, only one chance, to do this. Plucking up all her courage, her hand shaking, she managed to insert the tiny chips of emerald in her ears.

She didn't want to take too much morphine either; it helped, but it blurred the edges, made her feel as if she was walking through a cotton-wool dream, where nothing really mattered. This did matter; it mattered to her a lot. And it was only one more day. So she wanted to stay clear for it, even if she felt at any moment that her bones might shatter or her whole body might simply curl up and immolate, like a film she had once seen about nuclear war.

She had drunk some more water and did her best with her face. She could not, she found, walk across the bathroom to get back to the bedroom.

Cursing roundly in a way that would have surprised many of her ex-pupils, Claire crawled, very slowly, across the floor.

"How are you?" Thierry asked emphatically, covering her with kisses. "I have been ordered to walk about and take exercise so I walked to the lift to see you."

Claire smiled.

"Can you take a walk with me?"

"No," said Claire. "Not today."

"Well, that is a shame," said Thierry. "I always enjoyed our walks."

"So did I," said Claire. "But I have ordered tea. Now tell me everything."

"And you too," insisted Thierry. "Then I shall take you to the shop."

"I would like that," said Claire. "I would like that very much."

•　•　•　•

323

I realized later that the taxi hadn't had space for a wheelchair, and the hotel had had to order a bigger car. But it did look a bit like a limo had drawn up, as Thierry stepped out of the big black car.

The crowd instantly burst into applause. Thierry looked incredibly jolly and better already than he had the day before, never mind those awful days in the hospital, and acknowledged their applause with his hand. Someone started taking photographs.

Then father and son saw each other. Thierry stood stock-still for an instant. I saw a look of fear and nerves and defiant pride pass over Laurent's features as clear as day; I could already read him so well. Someone handed Thierry a piece of the chocolate. Slowly, very slowly, Thierry placed it on his tongue and held it there, closing his mouth. There was absolute silence on the rue Chanoinesse. All the other shopkeepers had come out to see what was going on.

Thierry chewed, meditatively and carefully. Then he stopped and gave a short sharp nod.

"*Mon fils*," said Thierry simply, and he opened his arms. Laurent ran into them like a little boy.

● ● ● ●

I helped Claire out of the car and into the chair, which barely fit in the narrow shop, and through into the greenhouse beyond. Laurent went back to making his new chocolate and another batch of the lemon. Thierry kept a beady eye on him and remarked, as Laurent wielded the pepper grinder, that he was going to give him another heart attack, but mostly stayed out of the way. Claire sat comfortably by the plants and I took a couple of photos. It was funny to think she'd been here before. Had it changed?

"Not at all," she said. "Benoît, I knew you here as a boy."

Benoît merely grunted.

"That's what he was like as a boy," she confided. Thierry went over to the sink and washed his hands.

"I am going to make you some medicine," he said to Claire, who smiled.

"I would like that very much."

I watched, fascinated, as he picked up a tiny whisk, which looked absurdly small in his huge hands, and a little metal pole and started working in his own way over a low heat, adding brandy and vanilla in tiny drops, tasting too as he went. I spotted Laurent watching him while pretending not to.

Eventually it was made and warmed and poured into a huge clay cup, slightly chipped. Thierry took a tiny knife and carved tiny, perfect scrolls of chocolate from a large plain bar to decorate the froth at the top. Then it was taken over to be presented to Claire as if it was on a silver salver.

"It's the same cup," she exclaimed with pleasure.

"I kept everything that reminded me of you," said Thierry simply. "When I returned from the fighting...ah, I had changed. Life had changed. It made everything more complicated and less free and... well. I liked to keep some things to remember."

I watched as Claire drank. She closed her eyes briefly. We didn't serve hot chocolate in the summertime, but I knew how legendary it was because people kept telling me about it.

"Oh," she said, and this will sound fanciful, but she really did look slightly restored after she drank it; more color in her cheeks and a sparkle in her eyes. And she drank the whole cup with obvious pleasure, the first time I had seen her eat or drink with real appetite in nearly a year.

"Did you come all this way for a cup of hot chocolate?" I asked, and she smiled slightly.

"Well, mostly."

Thierry followed the exchange and burst into a huge grin.

"I still have it."

"Of course."

He poured the last dregs in her cup and she finished them regretfully.

"I shall make you another."

"You can make me one tomorrow, before I go," she said.

I looked at Thierry, who had nodded without trying to insist that she stay longer. She had obviously told him everything then.

"Now, Anna," said Claire, turning her attention to me. "I want to see where you live."

"Do you?" I said. I wondered who Sami would have staying over today from the *demimonde*. "No, don't. It's up loads of steps, and it's just a tiny apartment, just a box room really."

"I've come here to see you and I'd like to see it," said Claire in a "do your homework" voice, so I wheeled her around the corner over the cobbles, leaving the boys behind to work and deal with the lengthening line of excited customers.

● ● ● ●

It didn't take long, even though maneuvering the wheelchair on and off curbs was a tedious business. Paris is not a city built for wheelchairs. As usual, the hallway was in total darkness. Claire scanned the faded list of bells.

"I haven't put my name on it," I said. "I'm only here temporarily."

Claire looked at me with that penetrating gaze of hers.

"Are you?" she said. I squirmed and looked down.

"Um, I'm not sure."

"Well, be careful of those Girard boys," she said.

I pushed open the heavy door. She could walk if she held my arm.

"I wish...I wish I'd held on to mine," she added. "I left."

"I know."

I found the light and squeezed it hard, then we progressed, very slowly. Upstairs I heard the mysterious door on the first landing open again. My heart sank. Oh no. That scary old woman. The last thing I needed now was for her to march out on the landing and start having a go at me because Sami's chums kept leaving the door on the latch and played music at unlikely times of day.

We ascended the stairs at a glacial pace, as the door creaked itself wide apart. Claire stopped still on the landing. I blinked. Just before the light went out, I saw the other woman standing there too. She was incredibly old, her hair white, her figure bent over.

"Claire?" she breathed.

•　•　•　•

Madame LeGuarde's apartment still contained much of the old furniture from the days when her family had owned the entire house. It was grand and baroque, but a little much for the space. It was, however, impeccably tidy and luxurious, a thick Persian rug in the spacious front room. There was even a maid, who sat us down and went off and brought back cups of lemon tea in bone china cups.

The two women were gazing at each other.

"I didn't know," said the older woman.

Claire shook her head. "Why would you?"

She finally turned around to introduce me.

"Anna, this is Marie-Noelle LeGuarde. I lived here too when I first came to Paris."

"Upstairs?"

"Yes, upstairs, but it was all one house then."

"Before the socialists," grimaced Mme. LeGuarde. "And of course, we all divorced. It was quite fashionable back then."

"What about Arnaud and Claudette?"

"Both well. Claudette lives near here and comes around often; her children are wonderfully good to me. Arnaud is in Perpignan, getting a suntan."

Claire smiled. "They were dear children."

"They are," said Mme. LeGuarde. "And they were very fond of you."

A silence fell between them.

"With…with Thierry…"

Mme. LeGuarde lowered her head.

"I apologize. I am sorry. I thought it was a summer fling that would fizzle out and you would both be better for it. So did your mother."

"My *mother*?"

Mme. LeGuarde nodded. "I miss her very much, you know. We were pen pals our whole lives."

"My *mother* said you could take the letters?"

"I was Thierry's *poste restante* when he was at the conflict, yes. We both thought it was the right thing to do. And you know, then the divorce and I will say, I had very little time for romance in my life just then."

"All that time I blamed my dad."

Mme. LeGuarde smiled. "Never underestimate the power of a woman. I am sorry. I thought it was right."

Claire shook her head. "I was so sad."

"He was too," said Mme. LeGuarde. "And when he got back from Beirut… Oh, Claire. You would not have known him. He was not the same man. He saw some things he should not have seen. He put on a happy face once more, but he was not happy, not anymore."

Claire nodded. "I see."

"And then, of course, you got married and your mother was so happy… She liked Richard a lot, you know."

"I do know. He really spoiled her, was always taking her out for tea or buying her presents." She smiled in memory. "I thought he was being a suck-up. Now I think about it, he was being terribly polite and kind. He's a very good man."

"That's what she said."

We finished our tea and the two women embraced.

"You are not well," observed Mme. LeGuarde. She seemed, I thought, a very straightforward kind of a person. I liked her.

"No," said Claire.

"And I am very old."

"Yes."

"When do you leave?"

"Tomorrow."

They paused at the door.

"So," said Mme. LeGuarde. "In another life."

"I hope so," said Claire, and the two women embraced and I stood back a little.

• • • •

Claire wasn't sure she could make it to the top floor. Mme. LeGuarde had invited her to see the hideous garages that had been built when they'd sold off the garden—a heartbreak she clearly wasn't over—and she'd had enough trouble managing that. But she didn't want to let Anna down or to worry her. Tomorrow Thierry wanted to take her back up the Eiffel Tower one last time. She would think about that when she got there. Now all she wanted to do was take enough morphine in the bathroom to get her through the next half hour. Then the next. Then the next.

• • • •

"GREETINGS!"

The entire apartment was covered in draped material, and Sami had a manic look in his eye and a mouthful of pins. A grumpy, short, fat man was standing with a large cummerbund swathed around his middle.

"It'll be ready! It'll be ready!"

The man looked at his watch.

"Five hours until the dress."

"Oh *shit*!" said Sami. "Darling, have you got any Dexedrine?"

"Yes, Sami," I said. "Of course I have Dexedrine."

He was so caught up he missed my being sarcastic for a couple of seconds, then remembered his manners and apologized to Claire.

"Forgive me, we are on tonight. The grand dress rehearsal. It will all be *fine*."

"Ow," said the man, as Sami pricked him with a pin.

"And you are all coming?"

"Um," I said.

"You are coming! Of course! To the opera house!"

"Oh, I'm not sure…"

"You are not sure?" said Sami. "These performances have been sold out for months. They will be attended by the president, by the Prince of Monaco, by everyone who is anyone in *le tout Paris*, and you get offered a sneak preview for free?"

Claire spoke up. "Which opera is it?"

"*La Bohème*," said the young man. "And I am Rodrigo, and I should be warming up my voice right now."

"Oh!" said Claire, then glanced at me. "I love that opera."

I'd never been to an opera in my life; all I knew was that song from the football. Suddenly the man, who was the most unprepossessing young gentleman I'd ever seen, opened his mouth.

Even Sami stopped moving. The sound that came from him was as thick and rich as Thierry's chocolate. It was melting and dreamy. He sang just a fragment—I couldn't even understand the words, but the swoop of his voice filled the house to the rafters. An expression of calm began to spread over Claire's features.

"Okay," I said quickly. "We'll come." I turned to Claire. "If you're up to it?"

"If you could take me back to the hotel now for a little nap," said Claire, "I can't think of anything I'd like more."

29

Thierry and Laurent met us in the lobby, both wearing dinner jackets and bow ties, Thierry's looking rather baggy around the neck, Laurent's looking very hired and utterly gorgeous. "It's only a rehearsal," I said, but I was delighted nonetheless. Claire was wearing a very simple gray wrap that did its best to make her terrible weight loss look chic. I was wearing a present from Claire; it had been a total surprise. She'd looked a bit nervous back in the hotel room but said she thought it might fit me now (I must have lost weight, I could tell by the way she said it). It was old, but it might pass for vintage, and if I didn't like it not to worry, she didn't know much about style these days.

But when I saw the dress, I did love it straight away; it had little daisies around the hem and though I had thought it might be a bit young for me—I was no spring chicken after all—in fact, the cut and the shape of it were so sophisticated it worked perfectly and showed off my light summer tan. It was the nicest dress I'd ever worn, and I could tell by Claire's face when I put it on that she thought it suited me too.

• • • •

Claire hadn't even understood why she'd brought the dress in the end, until she saw Anna's eager face, flushed and clearly in love and so happy. If she had been prone to thinking a lot of herself, Claire would have been proud that she'd sent her here.

The nap had helped a little, but nothing much. She could no longer hold down food; she'd pretended to eat lunch while Anna was out of the room. She hadn't needed to go to the bathroom all day either. "If you can't go," her doctor had said, "that's a sign. Hospital, double quick. No messing."

"Yes, Doctor," she said.

And now she was running on fumes, she knew. It was odd, as if her body was giving up like an old boiler, or a car, one bit at a time, just gently shutting down.

She turned her face to Anna, who suited the dress well, but whose face was so brimming with happiness and excitement she would have looked lovely in a sack. She was lovely.

• • • •

"Lovely," she said briskly, and nothing more, and I made up her face for her and put some mascara on the two baby lashes she had growing and some pale pink lipstick, and we looked at each other in the mirror and she said, "Well, I guess this is as good as it's going to get," and we quickly hugged each other.

Laurent's face lit up when he saw me, and Thierry made a sharp intake of breath and glanced at Claire in a way that made me think he might have seen the dress before. Then I got one of the hotel staff to take a picture on my phone, and Laurent was holding Claire up out of her wheelchair and tickling me, and he held us and we burst out giggling at the exact same moment as the flash went off.

• • • •

There were absolutely loads of people there for the dress rehearsal and all of them were studiously dressed down in a way that said, "We are totally music professionals who only care about the art of it and not the silly fripperies," but we didn't care. Sami had arranged good seats for us in the middle of the stalls by dint of putting a huge turquoise roll of cloth over the top, and Thierry insisted on bringing a box with sandwiches and a bottle of champagne in a cool flask. I tutted at him and said Alice would kill him, and he smiled and said it was a very special one off and popped the cork as the tuning up finished and the lights started to fade.

I thought, *I will be totally bored at this.* I won't get it and it will be obvious to everyone that I'm just dumb Anna Trent from Kidinsborough, average student, speaks French like a Spanish cow, likes Coldplay.

But then the conductor marched on, without ceremony—nobody clapped; this was a rehearsal after all—and raised his hands, and all these musicians I could see, hardly any distance away from me...they just started to play these strings, running up and down their violins, and it was just totally amazing. It wasn't weird or boring at all; it was beautiful. Then the curtain went up and I gasped. Two men—including the little short arse I'd met at the flat—were in a bare, cold-looking garret just like mine. It too had a window, with a view over Paris full of twinkling lights and smoking chimneys, and through the window, although I had absolutely no idea how they did it, snow was falling. It was exquisite. Then the men began to sing and I was transported. Sami had told me the story before one night when he was hemming, and it didn't seem necessary to watch the cold, starving men burn their books. Then the other man—who was taller and more handsome—met the beautiful Mimi, who wore a dress that was patched and faded, but still fit her absolutely perfectly, as she showed how poor and helpless she was in a voice that reached the very heights of the rafters.

Laurent didn't take his hand off my leg the entire time, as I leaned forward, more and more transfixed. I glanced at Claire. Her eyes were half-open, her head leaning against Thierry's shoulder. He had his arm around her. She looked awful. I felt a sudden lump in my throat.

"Are you all right?" I whispered.

She nodded. "Yes, my love."

"And I'll take you home tomorrow," I said. "Richard will meet you and take you back to the boys."

She nodded. "Yes," she said. "I am so lucky," she said and squeezed my hand. Thierry whispered something in her ear.

• • • •

Claire could barely make out the figures on the stage. The two boys… Her boys… Oh, where were her boys now? She wanted to see them so much. She missed them so much: the fresh smell of their hair, the way they slept, arms thrown out, spread-eagled on their bunk beds, their little arms around her neck…

Thierry whispered in her ear, "Don't go."

And she smiled. "I must," she said. "I must go home to my boys… and to someone I should have loved better."

Thierry kissed her bald head gently. "You couldn't have loved me any better."

"No, I couldn't," she said.

• • • •

There was no interval, no pause, as the singers carried on with their scenes. But I preferred that; I didn't want anything to break the spell, that even though these people were singing, I was with them, at the dance, which was perfect, with the sellers, and finally, as Rodolfo laid her down gently on the poor couch, kissing her repeatedly, the tears slipped steadily from my eyes. Laurent gently whispered the name of the aria they were singing, "Your Tiny Hand Is Frozen," and my heart jumped and stuttered with panic. I turned, and straightaway, even before the orchestra fell apart and fell silent and the cast stared at us openmouthed, and the shouting, before Sami came charging full-pelt right from backstage across the footlights toward us, his long turquoise scarf fluttering behind him, and the ambulance and the lights and the noise—I knew, I just knew. We all knew.

epilogue

The elderly gentleman, clearly once very handsome, now slightly heavier, but with his bushy mustache as luxuriant as ever, pushed his way to the front of the queue with his cane. He was tall and beautifully dressed and as most of the visitors were foreigners, not French, they let him march through with his air of authority as he bought his ticket to the top.

In the lift, he stood with his hands clasped behind him. It had been a beautiful autumn. The leaves after the hot summer had burnished bright red and gold, and everyone had returned to the city rejuvenated after their summer breaks and wildly excited to hear that the great Thierry Girard had gone into partnership—with his son, no less—and was no longer relying on past glories and turning out old classics, but was turning out cutting-edge work and taste surprises. Laurent's oyster chocolate had been talked about for weeks. And working shoulder to shoulder with Anna, who had turned out to be such a find… They looked so happy together, bickering affectionately over flavorings, forcing each other to taste some new concoction—he didn't feel the need to go in nearly as much. He had much more time to walk, to spend time with Alice, who was less frenetic now the financial future seemed secure but still watched his diet like a hawk, to reflect on how close he came to losing everything, everything good about his life. Well, he had years now, barring accidents, years Claire had never had. He owed it to her to enjoy them, he felt. Make it up to her now.

Up at the very top, he turned left out of the lift—most people would turn right, he knew—and went right around to the east side, from where you could see the towers of Notre Dame, their little island, their little haven in the center of the world. From up here, the movements and traffic and noise felt like nothing, all the tiny business of the human world, scattering around, each carrying inside them a multitude of happiness and sorrow, all those loves lost and found.

The wind was blowing, an autumnal chill in it. He was glad he was wearing the pink scarf Alice had bought him.

He opened up the box. He had wanted so much to give it to her, had meant to, up here. But they had not had time. They hadn't had time to...well. He was not going to dwell on it now.

Thierry took the brand-new straw hat out of its white box, lifted it high in the air over the fencing, and—*pouf!*—let the wind carry it away, watching it dance and fly in the air, high above the chimney pots and cathedral bells and steeples, watching it twist, its ribbon flapping, until it flew up and up, into the blue sky and out of sight.

THE END

chocolate recipes

Here are some of my very favorite chocolate recipes. They start from very, very simple and go up to a big impressive birthday cake. I will say that although one is meant to use a double boiler to melt chocolate, that is a bit technical for me, and I normally do it extremely slowly in the microwave, ten seconds at a time, stirring all along.

chocolate krispie cake

• • • •

Seriously, we all have to start somewhere, and this is perfect for kids and as yummy as you remember them.

Ingredients:
* 3½ ounces melted chocolate—dark or light, depending on preference
* 4 tablespoons butter
* 3 teaspoons corn syrup
* ¼ cup Rice Krispies
* marshmallows or raisins (optional)

To make:
Melt the chocolate slowly, then add the butter and make sure that is all melted in too. Then add the syrup and the Rice Krispies to the mix. You can also add tiny marshmallows and, if you're weird, raisins. (Seriously, there is a time and a place for raisins, but I feel very strongly that this is not it.)

Spoon into paper cases, allow to cool.

never fail chocolate cake

• • • •

This is absolutely the easiest chocolate cake in the world. You will look at it and sniff and think, *Hmm, vegetable oil*, but I promise, it makes it all moist and delicious, and you can decide to make it at very short notice, always very useful, and the ingredients don't even need to be exact.

Anyway, preheat the oven to 350° and line the baking pan. I used a loaf pan for this, which makes it nice and tidy.

Ingredients:

* 4 eggs
* 1 cup sugar
* ½ cup cocoa powder
* ½ cup vegetable oil
* 2 cups flour
* 4 teaspoons baking powder
* ½ teaspoon salt
* zest from 1 or 2 oranges
* 1 teaspoon vanilla
* Nutella (for icing)

To make:

Beat eggs, sugar, and cocoa powder, and add the oil gradually. Stir in the flour, baking powder, and salt, then add the zest and vanilla at the end. Pour, then 40 minutes in the oven, but do check it—it can be very runny. Mine had to go back in for a bit longer. Ice with Nutella. Delish!

chocolate cookie cake

• • • •

My friend Jim first made this, and I got totally addicted to it. I really, really love this cake. Thanks, Jim. N.B.: He says Shamrock fruit and nuts because he's an Irishman. We just mean mixed, really. And please invoice him for the slimming classes afterward, not me. ☺

Ingredients:

* 14 tablespoons unsalted butter
* 2 (very generous) tablespoons corn syrup
* 8 ounces good quality chocolate
* ½ x 14 ounces packet of chocolate cookies (roughly crushed)
* ½ x 14 ounces packet of rich tea biscuits (roughly crushed)
* ¾ cup shamrock fruit (sultanas, apricots, cherries), optional
* ¾ cup shamrock nuts (walnuts, brazils, almonds), optional
* 1 Cadbury's Crunchie honeycomb toffee

To make:

Line a 6-inch, round cake pan or a 2-pound loaf pan with a double layer of greaseproof paper. I used a silicone loaf mold. There is no need to line the silicone mold.

Melt the butter, syrup, and chocolate in a pan over low heat. This took some time, as I used the lowest setting on the stove. Make sure the pot is large enough to take all the crushed cookies, etc. Stir to make sure all the ingredients are well mixed together.

Add the cookies, fruit, and nuts. Stir well. Make sure to break the cookies relatively small, as they will not fit in the mold/tin otherwise.

Transfer to prepared pan. Level it on top and press down well to avoid "air gaps." Allow to get cold and hard. It needs about two hours in the fridge or about 45 minutes in the freezer. The longer, the better. It tastes even better the next day. Wrap completely in greaseproof paper and store in a fridge.

brownies with coffee
and chocolate chips

● ● ● ●

Of course we have to have a brownie recipe, and this one is just
the ticket:

Ingredients:
* 4¾ cups flour
* 1 teaspoon salt
* 1 teaspoon baking powder
* ¼ teaspoon baking soda
* 2 ounces ground coffee
* 16 tablespoons of butter
* 2½ cups packed dark brown sugar
* 2½ cups chocolate chips
* 3 eggs, lightly beaten

To make:
Set the oven rack in the middle of the oven and preheat to 350°F.
In a medium bowl, mix together the flour, salt, baking powder,
baking soda, and coffee.

In a double boiler or carefully in a microwave, melt the butter,
brown sugar, and half of the chocolate chips, stirring to combine
well. Let cool slightly, then stir the dry mixture into it. Stir in the
eggs. Pour into an ungreased pan. Sprinkle the remaining half of
the chocolate chips on top.

Bake until the cake has shrunk from the sides of the pan, 25
to 30 minutes. Let cool, then refrigerate until completely chilled.
Remove and cut into squares. Eat cold or at room temperature.
Makes 24 brownies.

best ever hot chocolate

• • • •

This works well on freezing days for tired children. I don't think I can specify how many marshmallows you may need. Just assume two times as many as you think you'll need.

Ingredients:
* ½ cup double cream
* ½ cup milk
* 3½ ounces excellent quality dark chocolate
* pinch cinnamon
* marshmallows

To make:
Gently heat the cream and milk mixture—do not allow to boil! Or get a skin! So very, very, very gently! Melt the dark chocolate carefully, and mix slowly together. Serve with a pinch of cinnamon on the top and marshmallows. If you're a grown-up and were visiting us, you'd get a slug of either Drambuie or Lagavulin in yours too.

mum's cheesecake

• • • •

Here is my friend Lauren's mum's amazing chocolate cheesecake.

Ingredients:

Crust:
* ✳ 4 tablespoons butter
* ✳ 10–12 chocolate cookies
* ✳ 1 tablespoon honey or corn syrup

Filling:
* ✳ 5–6 eggs at room temperature
* ✳ 2 cups sugar
* ✳ 1 pound Philadelphia chocolate cream cheese
* ✳ 2 tablespoons flour
* ✳ 1–2 teaspoons vanilla

Glaze:
* ✳ 1 pound cherries in syrup
* ✳ ½ cup sugar, optional
* ✳ 2 tablespoons corn starch

To make:

Preheat the oven to 300°F.

Crust: Melt the butter in a medium saucepan. Whiz the cookies in a food processor to fine crumbs. Stir into the butter with the honey. Grease a pan with high sides and press in the crust evenly over the bottom. Bake 10 minutes, then cool.

Filling: Separate eggs and whisk yolks until thick and pale.

Gradually beat in the sugar, then the chocolate cream cheese, flour, and vanilla, until smooth. Whisk the whites until stiff but not dry and fold into the yolk mixture with a metal spoon. Pour over the crust and bake for 70 minutes. Turn off the oven and leave it in for another hour. Chill.

Glaze: Drain the cherries, reserving the juice. Add water to the juice to make one cup. Combine with the sugar and starch in a pan and cook, whisking constantly, until thickened. Boil for 1 minute. Remove, add the cherries, and cool. Spoon on top of the cheesecake and chill.

chocolate meringue cake

• • • •

OOH, I do love this. And it is flour-free, which is good for people with intolerances. It's lovely and crunchy on the top/bottom, depending on how you like to turn it out, and gooey in the middle.

Ingredients:

* ✳ 1 shot espresso/strong coffee
* ✳ 2–3 tablespoons brandy/liquor of your choice (gin is amazing with chocolate)
* ✳ 12½ ounces good dark chocolate
* ✳ 7 tablespoons unsalted butter, at room temperature, broken up into small cubes
* ✳ 4 large eggs, separated
* ✳ pinch salt (chocolate always benefits from salt)
* ✳ ⅞ cup superfine sugar
* ✳ More chocolate for grating over the top, if you like that sort of thing

To make:

Preheat the oven to 350°F.

Grease an 8-inch springform pan and line the bottom with baking parchment.

Make your espresso/strong coffee and add it to the brandy. Pour it over the top of your chocolate, broken up in a heatproof bowl, and melt together, either in the microwave or over a pan of simmering water, until it's smooth and glossy. Set aside to cool.

Beat the butter and egg yolks together until they're creamy, then add the cooled chocolate mix and beat again.

In another *very clean* bowl, whisk the egg whites and salt to soft peaks, then add the sugar, bit by bit, beating with each addition until it makes a lovely glossy meringue.

Fold the meringue, about a third at a time, into the chocolate mix, then spoon it all into the springform tin and level it out.

Bake for about 40 minutes. What you want is a crispy, slightly cracked top and a middle that's still soft but not actually liquid.

Turn the oven off and leave the cake inside to finish cooking in the diminishing heat. It should be done in about an hour. Take it out and leave it to cool completely, then turn it out by running a knife around the side in the tin, taking off the walls, then either turning upside down onto a plate if you like a crunchy bottom or sliding it onto one if you like a crunchy top. Grate chocolate over the top if you think it needs more decoration, but I never bother.

chocolate chip cookies!

• • • •

So easy, so delish.

Ingredients:
* 2¼ cups unsifted flour
* 1 teaspoon baking soda
* pinch salt
* 9 tablespoons softened butter
* ⅜ cup granulated sugar
* 4½ cups firmly packed brown sugar
* 1 teaspoon vanilla extract
* 2 eggs
* 5-ounce package semisweet chocolate chips
* ¾ cup chopped nuts

To make:
Preheat the oven to 375°F. In a small bowl, combine the flour, baking soda, and salt; set aside. In a large bowl, combine butter, sugar, brown sugar, and vanilla; beat until creamy. Beat in eggs. Gradually add flour mixture; mix well. Stir in chocolate chips and nuts. Chill the mix for an hour or so, if you have the time, then make little cookies on the baking sheet. Bake for 8 to 10 minutes.

chocolate mousse

• • • •

I am unashamed to relate that the first time I made this and it came out perfectly, I was INCREDIBLY excited. I had a guest over who's a wonderful cook, so I had to pretend I totally knew it was going to be fine all along. Anyway, I have made it a few times since, and it seems pretty fail-safe and impressive; you just need a little time. You can also add flavoring to it, if you like—Grand Marnier is delicious in it.

Ingredients:

* 1¾ tablespoons butter
* 7 ounces chocolate, half light half dark
* 1 cup water
* 3 egg yolks
* ¾ cup sugar
* 1 cup whipped cream

To make:

Melt the butter and chocolate with ¼ cup of the water. (I do this very slowly and carefully in the microwave, checking every ten seconds, but you can use a double boiler, if you'd rather.)

Whisk the egg yolks, the sugar, and the rest of the water over low heat, and whip the cream if it isn't already.

Combine all the ingredients and chill 3 to 4 hours in the fridge.

cherry ripe

• • • •

My husband is from New Zealand, where this is a national treasure of a chocolate bar, so I re-created it for Anzac Day and it worked very well. Well, I think it worked well; the entire tray was gone by the time I turned around… This kind of treat that chops up into a bar is great for parties, school fetes, etc.

Ingredients:

Base:
* 7 tablespoons butter
* 1½ cups self-rising flour
* 2 teaspoons cocoa
* ⅞ cup sugar
* ½ teaspoon baking powder
* ¼ cup milk

Filling:
* 1⅓ pounds glacé cherries
* ½ cup condensed milk
* 5 ounces desiccated coconut
* vanilla extract

To make:
Preheat the oven to 350°F. Butter and line a square pan.

Mix the base's ingredients and bake for 15 to 20 minutes.

Whiz the filling ingredients together and spread on the cooled base.

Top with melted dark chocolate and leave to set, if possible.

malteser (malt ball) cake

• • • •

The great thing about this really simple cake is that it looks much more beautiful and finished than it actually is. It is a **big cake**, I shall tell you now, for big occasions and works very well for birthdays.

Ingredients:

Cake:
* 1¼ cup sifted cake flour
* ⅔ cup sifted superfine sugar
* 10½ tablespoons softened butter
* 4 eggs
* 3½ tablespoons cocoa powder
* 8½ tablespoons sour cream
* 1 teaspoon baking powder
* pinch salt
* ½ teaspoon vanilla essence

Icing:
* 2¼ cups superfine sugar
* 7 tablespoons cocoa powder
* 17½ tablespoons butter
* ½ teaspoon vanilla essence
* milk if the mixture gets too stiff, to water it down

To make:
Preheat the oven to 350°F and grease and line two (same-size) cake pans.

Mix the ingredients until nice and smooth, bake 20 to 30 minutes or until a toothpick comes out dry.

Ice the cooled cake between the sandwich layers and all over the top.

Then, take four bags of malt balls (actually, scratch that, buy five, just in case you eat one) and start decorating. Even a total klutz like me can make lovely straight lines from malt balls, and once it's done, it looks like something out of a fancy patisserie shop window. Hurrah!

heaven and hell cake

• • • •

I am including this cake not because I have ever made it—I am *terrified*, quite frankly—but because I thought it was so beautiful and amazing. It's the winning Heaven and Hell Cake from John Whaite, which won the *2012 Great British Bake-Off*. This is a show I love dearly and watch religiously. I do bake some things from it and, like any right-thinking person, worship Mary Berry as the queen she so clearly is, but this was just so full of chutzpah and imagination and amazing baking, I could only applaud its skill and ambition, and it made John a worthy winner. Thanks to the BBC for letting us reproduce it here, and if anyone has a good go at it, *please* let me see it! I might just make the "hell" half…

Hell: dark chocolate and orange cake. **Heaven:** lemon and coconut meringue cakelets. A stunning cake worthy of a Bake-Off final.

Equipment and preparation:

You will need an 11-inch cake tin, 16 2-inch cake tins, a chef's blow torch, a 6-inch cake board, half a dozen straws, and a piping bag with a small nozzle.

Ingredients:

For the hell cake:

* 9 free-range eggs, separated
* 5 tablespoons cocoa powder
* 1 cup hot water
* 1⅓ cups plain flour
* 1 pound golden superfine sugar
* 1½ teaspoons baking soda

* 1½ teaspoons salt
* ¾ cup sunflower oil
* 2½ teaspoons vanilla extract
* 2 oranges, zest only

For the heaven cake:
* 1¼ cups plain flour
* ¾ cup water
* 1 teaspoon baking powder
* 1½ teaspoons salt
* 1 cup golden superfine sugar
* 4 fluid ounces sunflower oil
* 2 unwaxed lemons, zest only
* 6 free-range eggs, separated
* 1 teaspoon vanilla extract

For the hell filling:
* 21 ounces dark chocolate
* 1⅓ cups double cream
* 1 cup good quality cherry jam

For the hell mirror glaze:
* 2 leaves gelatin
* 1 cup sugar
* ½ cup water
* 2 tablespoons golden syrup
* 11 tablespoons cocoa powder
* ½ cup double cream

For the heaven meringue and filling:
* 3 free-range eggs, whites only
* ¾ cup superfine sugar

* 1 teaspoon corn syrup
* 2 tablespoons water
* ½ teaspoon vanilla extract
* 7 ounces best quality lemon curd
* 1¼ cups desiccated coconut
* 1 booklet (5 sheets) gold leaf, to decorate

For the hell piping and chocolate shards:
* 7 ounces dark chocolate

To make:

Preheat the oven to 300°F. Grease and line an 11-inch cake pan.

For the "tartarus" hell cake: Beat the separated egg whites in a bowl until stiff.

In a large mixing bowl, mix the remaining ingredients for the hell cake together. When well combined, fold in the egg whites.

Pour the mixture into the prepared cake pan and bake for 75 minutes.

Remove the cake from the oven, and once hot enough to handle, turn out, upside down, on a cake rack to cool.

For the "caeli" heaven cake: Grease and line 16 2-inch-diameter cake pans.

Repeat the process for making the hell cake with the heaven cake ingredients, but pour the cake mixture evenly into the 16 molds rather than one cake mold.

Bake for 17 minutes. Remove from the oven, trim the cakes to make them exactly the same size, then turn them out upside down onto a cake rack to cool.

For the hell cake filling: Make a ganache by placing the dark chocolate and cream into a bowl and heating in the microwave for 30 seconds at a time, until the chocolate has melted. Mix the cream well into the chocolate. Set aside in a bowl.

For the hell cake mirror glaze: Soak the gelatin in cold water for five minutes until it softens.

Heat the sugar and ½ cup water in a pan until boiling. Add the corn syrup, cocoa, and cream. Heat through, then strain the glaze through a sieve into a jug. Add the soaked gelatin to the strained glaze, stirring to make sure it's evenly dissolved. Set aside until needed.

For the meringue coating for the heaven cakes: Place the egg whites, sugar, corn syrup, and two tablespoons water in a bowl set over a pan of simmering water. Whisk the mixture for 7 to 8 minutes, or until stiff and glossy. Add the vanilla extract and mix well. Set aside.

Cut the cooled hell cake horizontally to make two disks. Wrap each disk in cling film and place in the freezer for 10 minutes to firm up and cool further.

Place the lemon curd in a piping bag with a small nozzle. With a small knife, cut a hole into the heaven cakes, to create space to pipe the curd into. Pipe the curd into the cakes.

Cover the filled heaven cakes with the meringue (reserving a little of the meringue to hold the heaven cakes in place) and roll in the coconut.

Stack the heaven cakes on a 6-inch cake board using straws to hold it in place.

Remove the two hell cake disks from the freezer and spread one with one-third of the ganache and another with the cherry jam. Sandwich the cakes together. Using a palette knife, cover the outside of the cake with another third of the ganache.

Carefully place the coated hell cake in the freezer for 10 minutes to firm up.

Meanwhile, temper the chocolate for the chocolate shards. Chop the chocolate into equal pieces, and place half in a bowl set over a pan of simmering water. Allow to slowly melt. Once melted, take the bowl off the heat and add the remaining half of chopped chocolate. Mix into the melted chocolate until everything has melted and allow to cool to 86°F. (Use a thermometer to measure this.) Once it reaches temperature, it's ready to use. Spread most of the tempered chocolate onto silicon paper and leave to cool completely—once cooled, it should snap into shards. Pour a few tablespoons of the chocolate mixture in a piping bag with a small nozzle and pipe "tartarus" on the silicon paper—leave this to cool too.

Add another coating of ganache (using it all up) to the hell cake to get very straight sides, and return to the freezer for 15 minutes.

Remove the cake from the freezer, warm the glaze in a small pan, and carefully pour the glaze over the hell cake and smooth.

Heat the glaze with a blow-dryer so it is very shiny and even.

Place the "tartarus" piped chocolate nameplate on the cake.

Insert straws into the hell cake, to hold the heaven cakes in place. Cut the straws off to a suitable height. Place the stack of heaven cakes onto the hell cake, secured with the straws.

Pipe swirls of meringue over the gap between the heaven and hell cakes, then toast the meringue with a chef's blow torch.

Finish the cake with shards of tempered chocolate around the edges.

Finally, add gold leaf to the heaven cakes to decorate.

about the author

Jenny Colgan is the bestselling author of more than eleven novels, including *Rosie Hopkins' Sweetshop of Dreams* and *Meet Me at the Cupcake Café*. She also writes regularly for the *Guardian* and the *Times*, as well as the BBC's *Doctor Who*. She is married with three children and lives in London and Cannes, where she bakes, drinks pink wine, and plays the piano to an extremely disappointing standard.

MEET ME AT THE CUPCAKE CAFÉ

A NOVEL WITH RECIPES

Jenny Colgan

International Bestseller

A sweet and satisfying novel of how delicious it is to discover your dreams.

Issy Randall can bake. No, Issy can create stunning, mouthwateringly divine cakes. After a childhood spent in her beloved Grampa Joe's bakery, she has undoubtedly inherited his talent. She's much better at baking than she is at filing, so when she's laid off from her desk job, Issy decides to open her own little café. But she soon learns that her piece-of-cake plan will take all of her courage and confectionary talent to avert disaster.

Funny and sharp, *Meet Me at the Cupcake Café* is about how life might not always taste like what you expect, but there's always room for dessert!

Praise for *Meet Me at the Cupcake Café*:

"Sheer indulgence from start to finish." —Sophie Kinsella

For more Jenny Colgan books, visit:

sourcebooks.com

SWEETSHOP OF DREAMS

A NOVEL WITH RECIPES

Jenny Colgan

International Bestseller

Rosie is about to get a taste of the sweet life.

Rosie Hopkins's life is…comfortable. She has a steady nursing job, a nice apartment in London, and Gerard, her loyal (if a bit boring) boyfriend. And even though she might like to pursue a more rewarding career, and Gerard doesn't seem to have any plans to propose, Rosie's not complaining. After all, things could be worse. Right?

It certainly seems that way when Rosie's mother sends her out to the country to care for her ailing great aunt Lilian. Rosie is shocked to find that the elderly woman, who lives alone, is barely mobile and eats only sweets from her shuttered candy shop. But as Rosie gets Lilian back on her feet, explores the wonders of the old-fashioned sweetshop, and gets to know the mysterious and solitary Stephen, she starts to think that settling for what's comfortable might not be so great after all.

Praise for *Meet Me at the Cupcake Café*:

"Colgan folds in a colorful cast of characters and whips up an easy, sweet read." —*USA Today*

"A satisfying read." —*Publishers Weekly*

For more Jenny Colgan books, visit:

sourcebooks.com